Thomas Mullen

Thomas Mullen is the author of *The Last Town on Earth,* which was named Best Debut Novel of 2006 by *USA Today* and was awarded the James Fenimore Cooper Prize for historical fiction, and *The Many Deaths of the Firefly Brothers.* His books have been named Best of the Year by such publications as the *Chicago Tribune, USA Today,* and Amazon.com. He lives in Atlanta with his wife and sons.

Visit his website at www.thomasmullen.net or follow him on Twitter @Mullenwrites.

THOMAS MULLEN

THE REVISIONISTS

MULHOLLAND
BOOKS

HODDER

First published in Great Britain in 2011 by Mulholland Books
An imprint of Hodder & Stoughton
An Hachette UK company

First published in paperback in 2012

1

A CIP catalogue record for this title is available from the British Library

Paperback ISBN 978 1 444 72767 8
eBook ISBN 978 1 444 72766 1

Printed and bound by CPI Group (UK) Ltd, Croydon, CR0 4YY

Hodder & Stoughton policy is to use papers that are natural, renewable
and recyclable products and made from wood grown in sustainable forests.
The logging and manufacturing processes are expected to conform to the
environmental regulations of the country of origin.

Hodder & Stoughton Ltd
338 Euston Road
London NW1 3BH

www.hodder.co.uk

For my sons

When we act, we create our own reality. And while you're studying that reality—judiciously, as you will—we'll act again, creating other new realities, which you can study too, and that's how things will sort out. We're history's actors . . . and you, all of you, will be left to just study what we do.

—unnamed aide to President George W. Bush, as told to
Ron Suskind in The New York Times Magazine

Mailer was haunted by the nightmare that the evils of the present not only exploited the present, but consumed the past, and gave every promise of demolishing whole territories of the future.

—Norman Mailer, The Armies of the Night: History As a Novel,
The Novel As History

History has taught us that often lies serve her better than the truth.

—Arthur Koestler, Darkness At Noon

PART ONE

PRESENT SHOCK

Z.

A trio of bulbous black SUVs passes sleekly by, gliding through their world like seals. The city shines liquidly off their tinted windows, the yellow lights from the towers and the white lights from the street and the red lights they ignore as they cruise through the intersection with a *honk* and a flash of their own beams. People on the sidewalk barely give them a glance.

I cross the street, which is empty in their wake. Most of the National Press Building's lights are still on, as reporters for outlets across the globe type away to beat their deadlines. Editors are waiting in Tokyo, the masses are curious in Mumbai, the public has a right to know in London. The sheer volume of information being churned out of that building is unfathomable to me, the weight of it, and also the waste. As if people needed it.

It's just past ten and my mark is on the move. He has an important date—a date with history, in fact, though he isn't thinking of it that way. He's meeting his source, the mysterious individual who has provided him with glimpses of a golden but dangerous truth, a mythic grail whose existence he was beginning to doubt. The source has promised him the grail, tonight. But only if they meet in person.

My mark is thin, harried. He doesn't look like he's slept much lately. Even my rough understanding of contemp style tells me he has little: his white shirt is stained with coffee and is untucked in the back; his jeans seem tighter than he's comfortable with; he's had to adjust himself in the glass elevator that isn't as private as he believes it to be. He is thirty and aging too quickly, his thin hair graying along the temples (but then, my judgment of age in this beat isn't good either; the legacy of their insufficient medicine, diet, and hygiene is difficult for me to puzzle out). He lives with the realization that his life's work, his reason for being, is overlooked by this world he thinks he is serving. He is unimportant. He doesn't say this to the people he works with, but he blathers about it on his pseudonymous blog, and in the constantly revised, unpublished memoir hiding in his computer, both of which he turns to late at night after filing a story few people will read.

Oh, but you *are* important, Mr. Karthik M. Chaudhry! You have no idea how much value is placed on what you do, and how terrible is that value.

I've been watching him for days. He talks on his phone and attends press conferences at which he is relegated to the back rows, then he sits in libraries or cafés with his laptop and reads and writes, reads and writes. So much information here, they spend the majority of their lives losing themselves in it. As far as I can tell, he doesn't have any friends. His apartment is devoid of women's clothes or toiletries, not even a secret photograph of an idolized, untouchable someone in his top drawer. It's because of his dedication to work, or that's what he tells himself. He is, after all, very good at what he does, and it's getting him into trouble.

We crossed paths in the hallway of his building earlier today and I slipped a Tracker onto him, so I know when he leaves his office and enters the elevator. That's why I've left the bar across the street, the Anonymous Source, where I've been staking him out, nursing a couple of drinks against Department regulations.

I walk into the lobby, past the elderly Chinese man selling his magazines and newspapers and brightly colored candy bars, past the tie boutique and the shop of tourist paraphernalia: framed photographs of the White House, coffee mugs and pencils emblazoned with U.S. flags. My mark is descending in the glass elevator.

Seeing him is all the confirmation I need, so I walk back out and get into my car. I know where he's going and when he'll be there. I also know that he doesn't own a car and will take the Metro, which, due to a disabled train on the Blue Line, will make his ride a good ten minutes longer than my drive. I'm in a rented tan Corolla, which the people in Logistics had recommended based on its not being conspicuous. Before they sent me here, I trained on a replica they created for me, but I find the real thing awkward to handle, and I have to hope I don't break some obscure traffic rule and get pulled over. The vodkas I drank make this even more surreal, the vehicle large and bulky, this sprawling extension of myself, numb and careening into a world I barely understand.

And what a city! The perfect geometric layout, the wide avenues and clean sidewalks, all the monuments bathed in celestial light. The contemps around me have no idea how long it will take to rebuild something like this. Do they see the beauty around them? Are they dizzy from the heights of this pinnacle their civilization is teetering upon? No—they troop along, necks crooked into their ancient phones like bent marionettes'. Their right cheeks glow.

The night is cool and I drive with the windows down. I love the air here, the crispness—I forget how bad our air is, despite the recent improvements, until I come back to a time like this, before all the burning.

At a traffic light I check my internal GeneScan and see that the hags too are in motion. The GeneScan tells me when someone of a non-contemporary genetic makeup is in the vicinity, allows me to track him down. Right now the hags are doing some tracking of their own. One of them, I think, but possibly more; despite the best efforts of the people in Engineering, my GeneScan detects hags accurately only within a mile, and anything much beyond that comes across as just a faint shimmer, a certain foreboding.

Yes, Mr. Chaudhry, you are important indeed. You have no friends and no lover, but you have me, your guardian angel. Well, not really that—indeed, the furthest thing from it. But you do have me, as well as a few others—we're all intertwined like strands of DNA, like subject and verb and object, unspooling into the future, the generations and sentences extending endlessly.

Again, not really. The end for you, I'm afraid, is quite near.

I protect the Events.

That's the most succinct way of putting it, and that's how my superiors at the Department first explained it to me. I used to know as little about these particular Events as anyone else did, but now I'm an expert on this era. I know why these people are fighting each other, why they hate those they hate, what they most fear. At least, that's what they told me in Training. *Don't be intimidated,* they said. *You will know these people better than they know themselves.* After all, how well do we truly understand what we're doing, and why, as we're actually doing it? It's only later, as we're looking back, that events fall into easily definable categories. Motive, desire, bias. Happenstance, randomness, intent. Cause and effect, ends and means. One thing this job has taught me is that when people are caught in the maddening swirl of time, they do what they need to do and invent their reasoning afterward. They exculpate themselves, claim they had no choice. They throw their hands up to the heavens or shrug that Events simply were what they were. They used to call it fate, or God, or Allah, though of course such talk is illegal now.

Now. I barely know what the word means anymore.

This is my tenth day in Washington, just before the start of the Events that culminated in the Great Conflagration. On each mission, the Department sends the Protector back a bit earlier than the hags— the historical agitators—are expected to show up, so he can muddle through the initial disorientation and establish his position. Every advantage is vital. But ten days is more than double the usual prep time, and it has me wondering if this was all a colossal mistake, if I should begin the complicated procedures for being sent back.

The contemp patrons at the Anonymous Source were ignorant of the coming calamity, but they were hardly carefree. They had their complaints, they had their crystalline views of the chasms between their desires and their actualities. I almost wanted to clap their shoulders, tell them to enjoy what time they had left.

A few tables away, four young women finished a round of something orange and umbrella-adorned and were moving on to something aquamarine. Along the bar, the backs of navy suit jackets were strained by abdominal fat. A man sat alone at one table, anxiously wiping the spilled drink from a computer in his lap. A young couple sat on the same side of their booth so they could both see a basketball game on TV. The music was low and deep, all bass and thrumming.

I was in a corner booth, safely layered by darkness. People could see me, and if I'd been following Department protocol I'd have learned their names or surreptitiously taken genetic samples or at least burned their images into my drive so I could enter them into my Report of Historical Contacts. The Department wants to know everyone with whom I interact, as the whole point is to *leave no trace*. But I saw how drunk and preoccupied they all were, how circumscribed their little worlds. The quiet man in the corner booth did not exist to them. Which was fine with me. I'm used to not existing.

Six men and women at a sprawling table to my left were celebrating something with gallows humor. "Print is dead!" one of them called out to jeers and boos from his companions. I caught words like *restructuring* and *buyouts,* odd contemp phrases like *do more with less* and *new business paradigms.* They seemed to feel they had reached the end of something.

A waiter took my plate; I had ordered a salad and some risotto, the only things on the menu that didn't include dead, burned animal flesh. I've gradually grown used to the sight of people gorging themselves on "meat"—this is my fourth assignment now—but still, the immorality is stunning, the blitheness of it. Geneticized foods are in their infancy during this period; it's always a struggle to figure out how to eat enough to maintain energy without succumbing to their carnivorous ways.

My insides have mostly recovered from the illness that hit me my second day here. An unfortunate and inevitable part of the process, as my body is feasted upon by all these bacteria and microbes to which it has no resistance. I still feel a bit weak, having eaten little more than rice and bananas the past three days. I love bananas. For the taste as well as the novelty—they don't exist in my time. It's like eating a dinosaur, forbidden and impossible. But as I chew, it becomes a part of me.

In the bar, I periodically checked my GeneScan while I flipped through the issue of the *Post* that someone had left on the table. I was struck by the amount of information contained in these old, baked slips of hammered pulp, as well as by the unfiltered nature of it all, the varying viewpoints and opinions. But once I got past that initial unfamiliarity, what I truly found amazing was all the intergroup hatred. The smallness of it, the predictability. The Russians hated the Chechens. The Sunnis hated the Shiites. The whites hated the blacks, who hated the Latinos. The English hated the Irish. The Hutu hated the Tutsi. The Bosnians hated the Serbs, and I lost track of all the people who hated the Muslims or the Jews or both. The Japanese hated the Chinese, who hated the Taiwanese and the Tibetans. The Salvadorans hated the Nicaraguans. The Saudis hated the Yemenis. And I was only on page A-9.

Some of these stories I already read as part of my training. Studying up on the beat, immersing myself in their ugly mind-set. It almost attains a certain logic, the more time I spend here. Which is why I need to get out. I worry that if I'm here too long, I'll learn to enjoy it, like some deranged visitor to the zoo suddenly climbing the fence to commune with the beautiful tigers, running to his doom.

The road slices between museums and monuments, then merges with a highway to rise above a river that glimmers coldly in the moonlight. I turn south, skirting the river, toward the launching point of the jets that scream above me.

I park in the airport deck and walk not toward the terminal but to a narrow asphalt path flanking the road. The trail is used by cyclists and joggers during the day, but no one walks it at night. Once I put the airport behind me, I leave the path and cut around a fenced-off lot of tankers and luggage trucks. Soon I reach the small park, now empty, where families bring lunches so their kids can marvel at the size and sound of the outgoing planes whose tailfins nearly scrape their picnic blankets. By the water are a few trees; I walk to the one closest to the water and position myself behind it, the river at my back.

The sky is so much clearer than I'm used to, a black sheet punctured with a few holes for the stars to stare through. We don't see the stars anymore—our atmosphere too opaque—though we're working on it. Some people don't believe stars were ever visible, think it's a folktale, some slice of fabricated history that's managed to circulate through the collective subconscious. But I stare up at them and wonder, like these ancestors of mine must, at the vastness of things, and the smallness.

The empty lot tells me that Mr. Chaudhry's source has not yet arrived. My GeneScan tells me the hags are close, though I still can't tell quite how many there are. I also don't know how exactly they plan to disrupt the Event, but they tend not to be terribly imaginative. I picture a lone gunman crouching in the weeds, his heart pounding as he struggles to claim his space on history's as-yet-unwritten page. Lone gunmen are always the easiest.

The data pertaining to this Event is somewhat fuzzy, as it usually is. The people in Veracity do their best with the limited information they cull from the old files, the burned paper, the half-deleted records. I know that Mr. Chaudhry is on his way to this lot, but the exact time of his source's arrival is wrapped in mystery.

Mr. Chaudhry's meeting with the source will boost his career beyond his wildest imaginings, but not in the way he'd like.

Each plane roars like some massive beast exhaling. Amazing that Mr. Chaudhry thinks he can have a conversation with someone out here. But that's part of what intrigues him. The odd locale, the darkness, the paths crossing in the heavens above him and along the highway to his side. Even I'm excited. I love these moments, these tiny fulcrums of history, the gears turning before my eyes.

And there are the two hags, crossing the highway on foot. They're so stupid, it's a wonder they even get this far. They're nearly run over and someone honks at them—I hear tires squeal—but they make it to the other side. They must have parked in another lot, not wanting their car to reveal their presence. One of them is carrying a large duffel bag.

They hurry to a thick tree twenty yards in front of me. One opens the bag, the zipper shivering, and pulls out a rifle. The other leans against the tree, watching the parking lot. I cautiously advance toward them, keeping low, the sound of my approach lost in the next jet's sonic boom. I watch the parking lot too, and there we all see Mr. Chaudhry, hands in his pockets, bag slung over his shoulder, strolling down that lonely bike path, making his soon-to-be-famed appearance.

After nine days of waiting for the hags to show up, of sitting in my terrible motel room and venturing out only at night to learn the city, watch Chaudhry, and scout the locales without leaving a trace, I finally allowed myself to roam about by day that afternoon. The Department would not have condoned it, as I was supposed to limit my appearances to errands of strict necessity, but I was bored, and I figured that by wandering the National Mall I could be just another tourist cloaked in anonymity.

During my first gig, the details were what had stunned me, the tangibility. I had expected it to feel like being inside a video, like walking upon a two-dimensional image—had expected to look at people who would not look back at me, to touch objects that would not tease my fingertips with their warmth. The sounds and smells, too, the three-dimensionality, took me aback; the irrefutable fact that this place existed, that I was here. But at the same time, the insanity of it all, the wrongness. It was like waking to find myself in a different hemisphere: a sudden shifting of the seasons, the air all wrong,

the constant surprise from seeing the skewed angle of the light playing tricks with how ordinary objects appeared. A shine to everything.
I was in a new, old world, and it was real and it had weight.

At the Mall this afternoon, the tourists around me snapped pic-
tures and struck poses in front of their inflated tributes to former presidents and judges and warriors. I tried to enjoy this unprecedented
ability to tour an ancient time, to take in wonders that would soon
cease to exist. The white limestone gleaming in the afternoon sun, the
awestruck comments in countless languages, the yawning buses and
bored taxis, the sweaty office workers squeezing in lunch-break jogs.
Silver jets seemed to hang in the blue sky as they dipped their wings
seconds after lifting off from across the river. Government-crested he-
licopters passed at low altitudes, buzzing our chests.

Walking along a reflecting pool at the base of the Capitol building, I saw a young woman carrying her toddler, a little black girl in
a pink sweater, her hair braided with white beads. Residue from cotton candy encrusted the girl's lips, and I thought to myself, *She's two,
maybe three.* I wanted to know her name, look her up in my databases,
see if by any chance she would be one of the survivors. It was in-
credibly important to me. I followed them for a block, then another,
trying to concoct an excuse to start a conversation with the mother
or at least get close enough to take a sample or a savable image. The
girl smiled at me and waved. Her mother never noticed, never turned
around, and after they reached an intersection I made myself stop. *It
doesn't make any difference,* I told myself. *She'll likely die, or, if she's lucky,
she won't*—yes, if she's "lucky" she'll get to grow up in one of the most
violent periods the world has ever known.

I waved back, as helpless as she was.

Fifty yards away from me, a Metro train worms itself from the earth,
emerging from its tunnel and heading toward the airport. The hags
are still crouched at the tree, the only true cover to hide behind while
staking out Chaudhry. Beyond them the ground slopes downward,
slowly, toward the river, and I'm about twenty yards back. The Po-

tomac at low ebb smells of fuel and the rotten dankness of things that should have stayed buried. I can see Chaudhry in the distance, standing forlorn in the parking lot, lit up by the one streetlight, an actor alone onstage. He's looking around nervously, afraid some Homeland Security agent is going to ask him why he's loitering outside an airport at night. Don't worry, Mr. Chaudhry, I know the schedule of the DHS agents' routes; they won't be here until later.

In my right hand I hold the pistol that the Engineers designed to look, sound, and function like an early-21st-century nine-millimeter automatic. Attached to it is a silencer, though the thing is still too loud. We have more efficient methods in my time, but the Department limits the amount of technological advances I'm allowed to bring back, in case they're discovered by a contemp. At least I was granted a Stunner, which I clutch with my left hand.

Each time a plane takes off, the ground vibrates and I inch closer. I keep low so Chaudhry can't see my outline against the bright backdrop of the city, though I'm probably too far away for him to see me, as he has bad eyesight and is always squinting through his thick glasses. (It's embarrassing how much I know about him.)

One of the hags checks the rifle's stock; the other peers through binoculars. The low rumble of a plane accelerating on the tarmac is my cue. I aim my pistol at the hag with the rifle. He's still fiddling with it; they probably don't quite understand how the antique device works, though I'm impressed they found a way to procure one. They're getting better at this.

A black car loops off the exit ramp to the parking lot, slowing as it approaches Chaudhry. Then I see the plane, and I almost cower instinctively as it rises up like some predator, shiny steel breast exposed. Chaudhry has turned away from us to face the car, so he won't see the flash from my gun.

The jet's roar is at its peak when I pull the trigger. The hag was facing away from me and I get him in the back of the head—it looks like he simply nods, agreeing with something unspoken, and then he drops.

I shoot his partner low in the back. That may give me a chance to ask him a few questions afterward. I scramble toward him and tag him with the Stunner, mainly to keep him from screaming. His body is leaning into the tree and I pull him to the ground.

I lie beside the bodies and watch Chaudhry, now standing in the lot with two other men. One is bald; the other has dark hair with a streak of white above each ear, like he made a wig from a skunk's pelt. A third is behind the wheel of the black car, whose lights are off. These men are good at what they do—they stand at either side of the shorter, thinner reporter, boxing him in against the car. I'm only surprised they didn't find some way to break the streetlight before they did this. (The bubble of a security camera is perched beneath that light, but later reports will reveal that the camera malfunctioned on this night.) I hear a raised voice, two disjointed syllables, and then there's a quick motion and Chaudhry doubles over. One of the men opens the back door, and they push him inside. Again he is surrounded; the doors are closed. They hit him a few more times as the car drives toward the on-ramp.

Chaudhry's appearance at this parking lot will not be known for a few days, not until a concerned coworker taps into his e-mail account and finds a message sent from someone—exactly who, no one will know, as the mystery person's account traversed many complicated networks and domains and secret portals—asking that Chaudhry meet him here tonight. Despite much investigative effort by police, his outraged employer, his stunned colleagues, and his grieving family, this is the farthest Chaudhry's path in life will ever be traced.

The car drives onto the highway—heading south, in case any students of history are curious—although even I don't know where they're taking him from there.

I reverse the Stunner on the hag who isn't quite dead yet. What an awakening, to be revived to this state, a bullet in one of his kidneys. I hate myself for doing this; I should have just shot him in the head, like I did his partner. He gasps, confused, possibly numb from the waist down, and starts to cough blood.

"Where are the others?" I ask him.

Cough, cackle, spit.

"How many did you take with you? Tell me. This is your one chance to make right—you probably have about ten seconds."

He bashes me in the side of the head with something that can't possibly be a fist. My stomach turns and I go dizzy, catching myself with my hands before I hit the ground. He's about to hit me again— he's holding a rock—but I manage to block his arm, then roll onto him. I wrestle him for a moment; he has much more life in him than I thought, though he's losing it fast. Then I hold him down and hit him once, square in the face. I stand up, and as I hover over him, his eyes go wide, and then he's gone.

I stare at the mess I've made. *No, it's their mess—they're the ones causing the problems that I need to fix.* As if rationalizations can make shooting two people any easier.

I breathe deeply and try to get my stomach under control. The dizziness is gone already—it was a short, sudden burst—but it's being replaced by a worse pain, just behind my left ear and radiating out.

I have about ten minutes before a DHS agent or Coast Guard boat or some other security personnel patrols the area. I reach into the hags' pockets and remove their wallets, complete with fake IDs—again, I'm impressed. They're learning. They don't have any other weapons or hotel keys, nothing that tells me where they're based. I scrape them for genetic samples so I can record exactly whom I've dispatched. The Department prefers it if we dispose of the bodies, and I do have a few Flashers with me. They'd eliminate the corpses, as well as everything else within a radius of a few feet, but they're too bright and would attract attention. So I grab the hags' legs and drag them to the river-bank. As the planes continue to scream overhead I toss a body into the river, then another, then their rifle. The confluence of the Potomac and the Anacostia should get the bodies far enough from the airport that the police won't connect them with Mr. Chaudhry, but I'm not really worried about it. Their fingerprints will turn up no matches, their dental health will be meaningless, and their DNA will be rather puzzling to whoever analyzes it. The corpses will constitute quite a mystery, but this is Washington, and the assassination of two nameless men will likely be assumed to be the tip of some iceberg best given a wide berth. Local cops will quietly ask the federal police, who might ask the creepy and suspicious denizens of the clandestine forces' many branches, none of whom will betray any interest whatsoever with their glazed and nocturnal eyes and all of whom will assume one of the others is to blame. The discovery of the bodies will be shielded from the newspapers and TV reporters, the citizenry will not be alarmed, and my superiors will be impressed once again by my ability to perform complex duties while leaving no trace.

I try to run another check on the GeneScan, in case more hags are coming late—such incompetence is hardly beyond them. But nothing happens. The GeneScan is supposed to look like a series of dots and images superimposed on what my eyes perceive in front of me or spread out radar-like over my internal GPS. But the GeneScan isn't working. Hopefully it's just the headache from that blow with the rock interfering, and this is only temporary.

I use a towel to clean up the last of the blood from the base of the tree. The towel too I toss in the river, which darkly glitters at me like tinfoil. I must seem like some odd throwback, not to this time but an even earlier one, what they once called prehistory, when strange little cringers offered sacrifices to sea gods they themselves had invented, throwing possessions of varying import into the murky waters. Praying for a calm and fecund world without flood, a land of everlasting peace.

There are so many questions I didn't think to ask when I was offered this job. They knew I was interested from the start, even though their recruitment was so heavy on flattery that I figured there was something they weren't telling me. It's hard to pay attention to what isn't being said, however, when what *is* being said is so mind-altering. It was an honor, something that could not be refused.

I've been thinking about that lately, about whether I could indeed have refused. About how much free choice there had been, whether my hand had been forced or had moved of its own accord. What is predetermined, what spontaneous? You get to thinking about such things after this long on the job. You start pondering options that most people don't even realize are there, seeing secret paths and hidden escapes. Or the opposite happens: you see the larger forces that guide you against your will or without your knowledge. If you are what you do, then what does it mean if others make the decisions for you?

My previous three gigs were in a different beat, back in the 1940s. One of the things I never thought to ask was how long the average Protector stays on the job. Given the amount of training and expertise necessary for a person to navigate a beat, transfers must be rare. But my current assignment wasn't so much a transfer, they told me, as a response to an unexpected development. The Department of Historical Integrity was created when the Government realized that revolutionary factions had access to the technology and could navigate time themselves, and since its inception the Department has done an excellent job of determining which Events the hags would target. First the hags tried to alter World War II, focusing in particular on the Holocaust. That had been my beat. The hags wanted to prevent the genocide—they were a Jewish extremist group, though I suppose that's a redundancy. They wanted to save those millions of innocent lives. An admirable goal. But that would have altered history. Meaning, it would have altered our Perfect Present. The Department's motto, engraved on the crest that every Protector walks across upon admission to headquarters (a headquarters no one else knows exists, for a Department no one else knows exists), is *The integrity of history must be preserved.*

I protect Events that no one in my forward-thinking time knows about. We Protectors are the silent warriors, toiling in a vacuum. We stop the hags from removing the pillars of our Perfect Society and tearing it all down. What would have happened if Napoleon had been killed as a little boy? Or if Mao hadn't unleashed his Cultural Revolution? Or if bin Laden hadn't hurled airplanes like darts at his global targets? The hags' argument is that lives would be saved and tragedies averted, and they're right, in their shortsighted way. They choose to overlook the fact that such changes would destroy our Perfect Present, meaning that the Great Conflagration, or some similar event, would still be happening, and the suffering would never end. All the problems we've solved, all the broken aspects of society we've fixed, all the efforts we've made to eliminate human meanness and frailty—these accomplishments must be protected, no matter the cost.

After watching the dead hags bob along the river, I drive into the city. My mind is wandering across subjects, across time, thinking of my wife and the home that I will never again visit, when I'm startled by the GeneScan. It turns on suddenly, but it's not working as it should. I see dots and blips and streaks everywhere, the world before me fractured into a universe of constellations, as unreadable as the stars above.

I swerve out of my lane, distracted. Some of the dots vanish, but one lingers; the GeneScan seems to be telling me there's a hag close by. That's not in my intel, though. I have a detailed agenda of the hags' targets; I hadn't expected anything else tonight, and nothing in this particular neighborhood. Perhaps I've stumbled upon the hags' hiding spot—a fortuitous occurrence, as it would give me an opportunity to snuff them all out. I was that lucky in Poland once, finding the distant barn from which they were planning their bombings of Nazi rail lines; I eliminated them with a late-night fire and some well-placed rifle shots, my easiest gig ever.

I do my best to follow the GeneScan, trying to link it to my internal GPS. It doesn't work. The geographical info that the Logistics people provided to me was the best they could find, but that doesn't mean much. The Archives themselves are imperfect, full of errors or taken from the wrong year. Excavators and dump trucks are parked all over this neighborhood, sudden detours rendering my maps useless, the trucks tearing down buildings and creating new ones. It's sad to watch people so painstakingly build this world.

Then I see police lights in my rearview. Annoyed at the fried circuits in my brain, I manage to turn off the unhelpful GeneScan as I pull over.

The cops walk toward my car, one on either side. I've been driving with my windows halfway down, and I wonder how badly I smell of alcohol. And gun smoke.

"License and registration," says the cop to my left. He is amazingly white. His skin seems to glow, illuminated by the headlights of passing cars. I've adjusted during my different gigs, grown more accustomed to how pale the "white" people look and how dark the "black" people, but still, the racial markers are so odd here. It's like being asked to describe the taste of something cooked with ingredients one has never heard of; there are no touchstones, no points of reference. Just foreignness and wonder.

I hand him my driver's license and the rental agreement. Identity theft was a big problem in this beat, and the Logistics people make use of such tricks in constructing covers. They peer through old files and computer systems—whatever survived the Great Conflagration and the many wars afterward and then the long decay of time— to find names that can be lifted, data that can be transferred, lives that can be stolen. They choose people we can "replace" by finding those who vanished or disappeared, those who died mysteriously, those whose records outlived them for a few days.

The license says my name is Troy Jones and that I hail from Philadelphia. Within the Department, I go by Zed, and I don't really live anywhere.

He looks over my information, and I realize: *These could be hags.*

Adopting covers as cops would be impressive, something beyond what they've done in the past. I turn the GeneScan back on, but it lights up suddenly and then, as if overwhelmed by the pressure, flickers off. I try again but nothing happens; my trusty sidekick has made an early exit from this adventure.

I notice the cops have unsnapped the holsters on their sidearms. I'm not sure if that's a routine move in traffic stops here. My own gun is in the glove box and might as well be a mile away.

The other cop stands to the right of my car. I can't see his face, only his midsection, a ballooning that suggests the physical requirements for officers in this era aren't as stringent as in my time. He shines a flashlight into the Corolla, the beam lingering on the lightweight jacket that rests on the seat beside me.

"Anything under that jacket, sir?" He sounds older than the first cop, tired.

"No, Officer."

"Lift it real slow and show me."

I obey. Then he beams the backseat. Without the GeneScan to rely on, I feel momentarily adrift, a traveler dazed after losing his translator in a busy market.

"Is there something wrong, Officers?"

"You disobeyed a yield sign, Mr. Jones, and you switched lanes without signaling," says the cop holding my license.

"I'm very sorry. I'm a little lost." I choose a random address a few blocks away and tell him I've been trying to find it. "I'm not from around here."

"I see that. Interesting accent too, you don't mind my saying so." That hurts more than he realizes—I spent days working on the voice, listening to old audio and watching video that the Archives people turned up, studying the contemp cadence and flow.

"You don't really look like a Jones to me," the other one says, leaning down to shine his light in my face.

I look away from the light, back at cop number one. "I have a complicated family tree."

"What brings you to Washington, Mr. Jones?"

"I'm a defense contractor in town for some meetings. I'm trying to find the office of one of my colleagues for a strategy session."

That cover was chosen for its vague air of mystery and severity, I was told. But the cops do not seem impressed. "A defense contractor? Really."

19

"Pretty late for a strategy session, isn't it?" the other one asks.

"Strategy is a twenty-four-hour thing in the defense industry," I say. "Plus I did get a bit delayed on the drive down."

"We take defense strategy awfully seriously here in the District as well."

"Exactly what kind of strategy are you and your colleagues hatching, Mr. Jones?"

I wasn't expecting this reaction. I think for a moment, wondering what I did wrong.

"I can't really go into detail," I say. "I can say that it's intelligence related."

They wait a beat. "So if you're going to a business meeting to discuss your strategy, shouldn't you have some business papers?"

"They're in my trunk."

"Mind if we take a look?"

"You can look there if you'd like, Officer, but the papers themselves are classified."

The fat cop laughs, an odd thing to witness since I still can't see his face. I make a note of the name clipped to his dark blue shirt and do the same for his partner, for my Report of Historical Contacts. He says to his partner, "Can't tell if we've pulled over Zawahiri or Colin Powell."

The names register in my Contemporary Persons, Locations, and Events file, linked to my brain via the implanted chip. It's almost like memory, but not quite. Takes a second. Even if the names hadn't been familiar, I'd still have understood—regardless of era or culture or language, all insults sound the same. The cops are having a hard time figuring out my race, their gut-level mistrust of intelligent-sounding darkies mixing with their fear of Arabic evil. My superiors told me that to the eyes of a white contemp, I might look like a "very light-skinned African American" or a "Pacific Islander" or someone "interestingly multiracial."

The second officer leans down and I can see his face for the first time. Like his partner, he's as white as anything I've ever seen that isn't dead. I glance at his thick cheeks and red, glassy eyes for an instant before he shines his flashlight at me and I look away.

"Sir," he says, "I'm asking you to pop your trunk. We won't go through any papers. We barely even know how to read. We just want to see what else you might have there."

I nod and search for the button that opens the trunk. My inexperience with cars no doubt strikes them as a suspicious reluctance to comply with their orders. Finally I find the button and I hear the gentle pop behind me. The fat cop checks the trunk, and the cop on my left returns to his car to type my information into his computer.

I carefully open the glove box and take out my gun while the trunk lid is blocking their view. I slide it under the jacket, which I nudge closer to myself, hoping they won't notice.

I've read through the papers in my trunk; they're incomprehensible gibberish. If whatever the Logistics people printed out for me is indeed representative of contemp defense contractors' reports, then no wonder everything fell apart so fast.

The fat cop closes the trunk and returns to his previous position on my right. After another minute, the second officer rejoins us, handing me a pink slip of paper and explaining the citation. They're not hags, just bored contemp cops wishing they'd stumbled onto a plot and settling now for their minor roles in this city's busy narrative.

"Be more careful when driving in the city, Mr. Jones. Now, what was that address you were looking for?"

I repeat the address I'd given him before, passing his test, and he gives me directions. They bid me good night and return to their car.

I follow the directions to the meaningless address, well aware that they're following me. After a few turns, there it is, a glass-and-steel apartment tower. I find a spot to park in—parallel parking an automobile is not one of my greatest skills, but performing under pressure is—and the cops wait behind me as I muscle into the space. Then they drive on.

I walk down 16th Street, which was where the GeneScan seemed to be leading me before it flickered off. This is a busier road, cars passing on either side, late-working lawyers and lobbyists and propagandists rushing home to their television and children and insulation.

Before me is a large, redbrick church. This seems a fitting reconnaissance point for hags, many of whom are religious, driven by unyielding devotion to their dangerous creeds. One would think they'd be happy just to be in a time like this, to be surrounded by so many churches and synagogues and mosques, to walk into a bookstore and see their beloved tomes for sale.

A sign in the tiny front lot tells me it's a Catholic church. According to the schedule of services, nothing should be happening this late.

I feel an illicit thrill as I approach the sacred building. A cross hangs over the entrance, and at my side are whitened sculptures already in disrepair—a digit missing here, a streak of dirt there—as if they know their era is on the wane. The heavy door is unlocked. I step inside and gaze at the rows of dark pews, the gray tile floor, the stained-glass windows looming above the bare altar. It's so quiet my breath almost echoes. Toward the front I see the backs of two gray heads, hair pinned up in buns. I try to imagine what these women are thinking as they kneel here, as they make themselves small before some being of their imagination, something that has taken on such power through shared belief.

"Can I help you?"

I turn to see an old man, angel white. He smiles kindly. Above him are depictions of their Messiah being tortured, whipped, murdered.

"I'm sorry, I was just looking..." I'm not sure what to say. It was a mistake to come in here.

The priest is wearing a white dress shirt and black slacks, and the cross around his neck glimmers in the dim light. I burn his image, then thank him and step back. White and yellow pamphlets tacked to a corkboard beside me advertise bake sales, babysitting services, and political rallies in favor of "life."

He steps closer and asks if I'm sure there isn't anything else.

"The country where I'm stationed," I try to explain, "doesn't have any churches. It's ... interesting to be inside one again."

"Sounds like a terrible place. Which country?"

I offer him a short smile. The people in this city are used to being told only the barest snippets of facts. "I should go. Good night."

"Peace be with you."

I don't bother extending the same wish to him.

Outside I run another check on my GPS and realize I'm only a block north of Lafayette Square, essentially the front yard of their president's grand estate, the White House. Could the hags have designs on such a heavily fortified building? Probably not, as such a disruption would have historical echoes even they couldn't predict, but I'd be remiss not to look into it.

I notice a crowd ahead. Soon I hear someone on a loudspeaker reading a procession of names. *Sergeant Wilfredo Dominguez. Private First Class Martin Dithers. Specialist Gloria Wilcox.*

Filling the southern end of the square are approximately two hundred people. Facing away from me, standing still as statues, light emanating from their chests. It's like I've entered some contemp art installation, a maze of motionless human forms and the tiny white candles they hold before them.

I run a check on the names I've heard thus far, searching every database. They belong to servicemen and -women who died in the contemp wars.

It's haunting to stand among the mourners. We don't have protests in my time, or demonstrations (such an odd word choice, because what exactly are they demonstrating, their helplessness?). This is a peaceful one, eerily so. The tears on some of the people's faces are the only things moving.

I look for a sign bearing the group's name but don't see anything. I check the date and time against various databases but find nothing. Whatever this is, it isn't considered important by the Department. So why did the GeneScan lead me here?

During my gigs it's tempting to think of myself as the only living

23

person in a land of ghosts, and the effect is heightened now. The city feels peaceful from inside the park, as if the silent prayers of all these people can blot out the world's noise.

Then the names stop, and, one by one, the people blow out their candles. Little flecks of hope are extinguished all around me. The world grows darker; orange glows scar the inside of my retinas and dance like a busted GeneScan. Some of the people drop their candles, ends still smoking, into a pile. Others hold on to theirs. They stay where they are, alone or huddled in sobbing groups, or they leave the square, slowly. There was no announcement calling this activity to its end; it was as if some telepathic message were sent, or some genetic instinct requiring no conscious thought.

It's amazing how sadness can be so beautiful.

Ghosts are floating past me in every direction, and I slowly walk around, looking for I don't know what. Something. Something of obvious import. As if the job is ever that easy. Again I'm revealing myself to countless contemps, egregiously violating Department norms, but I don't know what else to do.

"You look about as skeptical as I feel," a woman's voice says.

Her skin is very dark to my eyes, her hair tied in thin braids that fall behind her shoulders. She wears glasses with thick purple frames. We'd been standing next to each other, just looking at the square. Some people have relit their candles and are walking around with them, as if needing the light to guide them, or afraid to let go.

What does she mean? Maybe I'm not doing a good enough job blending in—she noticed I'm one of the only people here who haven't been crying, whose eyes aren't red. But neither are hers.

I motion to the extinguished candle resting in her joined hands. "Who are you here for?"

"Lieutenant Marshall Wilson, my brother. He was in the army. Killed last June."

"I'm sorry for your loss." We don't say that in my time, but I learned it in my Customs training.

She looks at my empty hands. "How about you?"

"My brother too." The lie just comes out because I don't want her to realize that I don't belong here. A harmless mistake, perhaps. And I want to keep her talking to me. Her eyes are so wide and somber, and the air feels charged with its candles and prayers and memories of the lost.

I burn her image into my drive, but not for any report I plan on filing. Just a little something to carry inside me after she's gone.

She repeats what I said to her, expressing her sorrow for my "loss," completing the ritual, our little tragic circle.

"So I suppose if it really mattered what people think," she says, "if all this combined yearning could do anything, then they'd all come back somehow. What happened to them would be undone. But that's crazy. So it makes you wonder, doesn't it, what the *point* is."

I don't know what to say.

She continues. "Some socially acceptable way to make us feel better, I guess. And maybe I did feel better, for about two minutes." She shakes her head. "But now I'm only angrier."

I'm not sure if people here always speak so freely with strangers or if she's given herself up to the mood of the event. Or perhaps she assumes from my mere presence that I agree with her on all things, or at least the important ones.

I met my wife at a public gathering—very different from this one, of course, but I can't help thinking of it. It was so very long ago, and so far in the future. I miss her. I wonder if that's why I'm still standing here talking to a woman who desperately needs someone to hear her.

I notice that she wrote words on the circular piece of cardboard that rings her candle. "What did you write?"

She instinctively angles the candle so that I can't see the words. "Oh, just an old saying me and my brother used to have. Inside joke."

"Sorry. I shouldn't pry."

"No, it's okay. I'm the one who started a conversation with a strange man."

I allow myself the faintest grin. "I'm not that strange."

25

She smiles. "No, I meant—"

"I know. A strange man in a park at night. You should know better."

"I guess I figured this was a safe enough environment."

Lady, I just killed two people. And, in a way, millions.

"True," I say. "And there are all those heavily armed police officers in case I was to try anything inappropriate."

She follows my eyes to all the cops and security guards who stand at the gates of the White House and atop nearby buildings, their hands gripping rifles, their chests thick with bulletproof vests. They stand there and pretend not to watch the ghosts floating away from their territory.

"I'd heard about these sorts of things but never wanted to go before," she says. "I was supposed to come with my parents, but my mom caught a cold and they decided to stay in." She shakes her head, as if she's been searching for a way to express her feelings but is finally giving up, accepting that they're inexpressible.

"I've never seen anything like this before," I say.

"Yeah, they don't usually get much press. I don't think anyone really cares."

"No, I mean..." What do I mean? "I'm not from here. I live in Philadelphia, but I'm stationed here for work, for a little while. It's an interesting time—I mean, an interesting place."

We stand there talking for a few minutes. About politics, the wars. I ask about her brother and she doesn't know what to say at first, then she says so much. She didn't support the wars before, and certainly doesn't now, after losing him. She wishes she'd done more when he was alive, when it would have mattered. But now it would matter to all those still fighting, wouldn't it? she asks me, and I nod. I want to tell her that I have no right speaking to someone like her, that she should run screaming from me, from what I've done, for what I'm here to do. But I want to stay here, with the calm park wrapped around me, the night wrapped around me, her words.

She says she's sorry for prattling on, that she doesn't mean to sound so selfish. She asks me about my brother. Perhaps a similarly long and rambling explanation is expected. Instead I shrug and say, "It's still hard to accept that it actually happened."

I leave it at that and she nods. "I know what you mean."

The square is emptying around us. She doesn't seem ready to leave. Perhaps it would mean leaving her brother behind. I wonder about all the old superstitions and beliefs, wonder what mystical power she feels in thrall to. But I'd felt something too when I stood among the candlelit statues, hadn't I? What had it been?

I shouldn't be here. I shouldn't keep talking to her like this.

"Anyway, thanks for the conversation," she says. Then she dares to remove one of her hands from the candle, extends it to me. "I'm Tasha."

"Troy."

I love how real her hand feels. Cold from the night, clammy from clasping the wax.

"You said you don't live here?"

"Well, I do temporarily. I'm a consultant." I make the quick calculation that defense work would not meet with her approval. "Health-care policy."

"While you're in town, would you like to get dinner some time?"

"Sure." No harm in making false promises. And I allow myself to fantasize for a brief moment, to imagine having that freedom. "That would be great."

Tasha says we should exchange phone numbers so we can coordinate, and I confess that I don't have one.

She raises an eyebrow. "No one doesn't have a phone."

"Well, I had a cell, but it died on me just before the company sent me here, and I haven't memorized my hotel phone yet. Why don't you just give me your number?"

She gives me a look. I've trampled on some social code. But she recites her digits, and I record them. Then we say good night and she walks away.

I feel my heart beating faster than usual, as if I've just protected some vital Event. The GeneScan led me astray, and I let pure carnal desire, or maybe heartache, do the rest.

As I walk toward my car I notice a man lying on one of the park benches. He's wrapped in a filthy gray blanket; beside him is a large pile of miscellaneous possessions. I decide that I've already violated so many rules tonight, what's one more?

"Spare change, brother?" he asks. He has a thick beard and skin that doesn't look real. There are layers there. If I could peel them all off, I wonder who I would find beneath them.

"You sleep here? And we're, what, across the street from your president's house?"

"Hell, he don't sleep there, brother. That's just his spectral projection. He's floating above us in his ship, you know, pulling the strings."

I remove a one-hundred-dollar bill from my wallet and hand it to him.

"Bull*shit!*" he shouts, and I step back. "This ain't real!"

I wasn't expecting this anger, like I've pulled a trick on him.

"Maybe none of this is real," I tell him. "But that's legal tender, friend."

I wait another moment as he holds it up to the light of a streetlamp. He doesn't thank me, and hopefully he won't throw away the money, which I withdrew from Troy Jones's account earlier in the week.

I drive off to my terrible motel. Still thinking of Tasha, I check every database they've loaded into me. As I expect, all records of her cease at the start of the Conflagration.

2.

People in D.C. liked to drive in the middle of the road, Leo had noticed. The narrow side streets lacked lane markers, so each car tended to glide down the center, staying clear of the parallel-parked cars on either side, seemingly confident no other traffic would dare come its way. Opposing drivers waited until the last possible moment to pull to their own sides.

It was a warm night and Leo drove with his windows down, the city drolly exhaling in his face. He wound his way through D.C.'s bingo board of alphabetized and numbered streets until he reached the Whole Foods, whose opening here in Logan Circle, when Leo was stationed in Jakarta, had officially jump-started the gentrification process a few years back. He barely recognized the neighborhood.

He entered the store and joined the young women in post-gym outfits—recently showered, hair pulled back, no sweat to be seen—talking on their cell phones; the mothers balancing babies on their hips and gripping their carts with their free hands; and the young men like him, some looking comfortable in their suits and some whose concert tees and tight jeans were wielded in a desperate attempt to define themselves as D.C.'s Other. Leo had been back for a while now, so culture shock was no longer an issue. But still he felt something, a sense that he did not belong here, and it never went away. What do you call that, culture trauma? Present shock?

The grocery carts were half size to allow for some semblance of maneuverability through the cramped urban aisles. Leo tossed in vegetables whose colors and textures shone forth like they were works of art, still lifes waiting to happen. He had become something of a cook during his time in Indonesia. So far, he hadn't been able to find any Indonesian restaurants in D.C.—the outer suburbs were spawning more ethnic restaurants than the city as real estate prices pushed the immigrants out—and since he had few plans for the upcoming weekend, he figured he could spend some quality time in his kitchen. He grabbed some natural peanut butter and extra-firm tofu for *gado-gado,* sifted through shallots and garlic for *nasi goreng,* grabbed a coconut. He realized too late he was planning a veritable feast and found himself wondering, sadly, if there was anyone at all he'd want to share it with.

He stood in the middle of the Asian foods aisle pondering this, and received a new shock. Standing farther down the aisle, frantically comparing the contents of her cart to a crinkled paper in her hands, was a gorgeous young Southeast Asian woman. Everything about her was jarring, and slightly off: She was awkwardly dressed in a yellow sweater, the color of which clashed with the warmer luster of her own skin and which was at least a few sizes too big for her, the sleeves rolled up. Her black sweatpants also were too large, and she seemed to be wearing men's bedroom slippers. She would have looked like a homeless person if not for her perfect face and the fact that she was in the most expensive grocery store in D.C.

But no, not perfect. An indigo crescent moon curved beneath her left eye. He thought it might be a birthmark, because the only alternative was too unfortunate to consider: that it was the fading trace of a shiner. They made eye contact and he looked away, caught leering— was she as beautiful as he thought, or was he just thrown by all the conflicting signals? Her near-black hair was pulled in a loose ponytail, the strands seeming to sigh as they drooped around the elastic. There was a wide space between her eyebrows, a place he imagined a lover kissing.

Her fingers accidentally knocked a can off the shelf. She reached down and picked it up hurriedly. He saw red marks on the side of her neck as she did so. She placed the can back on the shelf and chose a replacement.

She furtively glanced at him, as if expecting to be scolded.

"Don't worry," he said, "I won't tell anyone."

She looked down again and attempted a three-point turn with her heavily laden cart. He saw that her small cloth purse had a patch of brown Javanese batik on it.

"Are you from Indonesia?" he asked her in Bahasa. He hadn't spoken the language in weeks and it felt clunky yet comfortable on his tongue, like putting on clothes that were three fashion cycles too baggy but favorites all the same.

She looked up at him in shock.

"Yes," she said, amazed. She stared at him for a moment before asking, "You speak Bahasa?"

"A little. I lived there for a few years." He was not accustomed to divulging much of himself to strangers, but it spilled out. "Do you speak English?"

"No."

He could tell now that it wasn't a birthmark. The skin below the eyebrow was still the tiniest bit puffy. He ran the possibilities: A young immigrant with an abusive husband and very particular grocery needs? A badly dressed graduate student who'd been in a car accident? Her sleeves were too long for him to see any defensive wounds.

"I haven't heard anyone speak my language in weeks."

"There aren't many Indonesians in D.C."

"You speak very well," she said, and seemed to laugh without smiling.

"Thank you. I haven't spoken it in a while myself. I'm grateful for the opportunity."

She looked down quickly, not to check the contents of her cart but again as if she'd been scolded. He wondered if he'd gotten his words wrong.

He felt a charge coursing through him. The memories streaming back, the collision of worlds to be speaking Bahasa in D.C. And her odd appearance and demeanor, as if life were trying its damnedest to stamp out her beauty, but failing.

"Actually," he said, "could I ask you a cooking question? I didn't bring any recipes with me, and I was trying to remember, do I need Kaffir lime leaves to make *dendeng ragi?*"

Both of her hands were gripping the cart tightly, her knuckles white, the crinkled grocery list gasping out of her left palm as if attempting an escape. He wondered if he had made himself look like a fool in her eyes, a man doing woman's work.

"Yes," she said.

"Do you know where to buy them around here? The only Asian grocery I know is out in Arlington."

"There's a store around the corner, on 14th Street," she said.

"Excuse me," said a shopper trying to get past Leo.

He twitched his head. "Sorry," he said, and slowly propelled his cart forward. The Indonesian woman turned and did the same.

The aisle emptied into the dairy section, where customers inspected the dates on yogurt. Leo maneuvered his cart beside an island of gourmet cheeses and he watched as the woman continued. If he'd kept shopping, he would have remained right behind her, but everything in her body language told him she didn't want him with her.

Except her eyes. And the glassiness he'd seen there when she seemed to revel in the sound of her native tongue, even when spoken badly by this tall white man.

Forget it, he told himself. *She's shy and isn't used to being spoken to by strange men, and you misinterpreted that as interest. Or she's an illegal hoping to avoid attention. And the definite and underlying truth: you're attracted to her and acting out of character.*

The checkout lines were long and he glanced at the strange magazines the upscale grocers sold, as if *Time* and *Newsweek* would ruin their organic vibe. Headlines about new uses for soybeans and the benefits of transcendental meditation. Beside them, a few lefty journals warned that citizens' civil liberties were disappearing in inverse proportion to their fears, that there was a government conspiracy behind the wars, and that the next round of violence would come from places you'd never expect, unless you bought this issue for $5.99. Leo was in more of a *National Enquirer* mood, would have liked to read about imminent alien invasions or the most recent subway attack by tentacled leviathans—an unreal threat for a change, terror you could laugh at.

The conveyor belt whisked his baubles to the scanner, and the freckled Ethiopian clerk greeted him curtly before turning to her mindless task. Halfway through, she needed a moment to look up the UPC for jackfruit, and Leo saw the Indonesian woman, who'd made her way to the front of a new line. How old was she, early twenties, maybe younger? That had been one of the hardest things for him about living there, never being sure of people's ages. The dozens of different ethnicities on that long archipelago, the effects of the sun and the poverty, the litany of life's impacts so much harder to read.

With some disappointment he watched as a multicolored array of baby food jars paraded down her conveyor belt. Her stack of wrapped meats confirmed that she was not in the same income bracket as a typical immigrant.

Leo's order was finished when her items were still being scanned at the other register. To stall, he entered the wrong password after sliding his bank card, twice. The people behind him were sighing, the aggrieved impatience of urbanites. Finally he entered the correct code. She was pushing her cart out the door now, and he did the same, slowly, allowing another shopper to walk between them.

He told himself he wasn't stalking her and was merely practicing surveillance technique. Outside, the beeping of scanners and the printing of receipts were replaced by a distant siren and the incoming sonic boom of a Metrobus racing to catch the yellow on 14th. His path was soon blocked by a series of knee-high metal bollards—rusty iron ones to prevent shopping-cart theft, lesser versions of the steel-and-stone behemoths that had sprouted around federal buildings all over town like some superprotective fungi. And there she was, just a few feet away, loading bags into the trunk of an illegally parked black Lincoln Navigator. Leo saw the reflected neon letters of liquor writ backward across the SUV's glossy windows.

The SUV bore diplomatic plates, and the mystery was partly solved. A diplomat's wife, or an ambassadorial maid, the dissonance between her dress, manner, and language and her expensive purchases finally resolving itself. Still there was the matter of her blue crescent moon. He found himself memorizing her tags—which bore not the Indonesian diplomatic prefix but some other country's—almost despite himself. Funny how the job seeps into your blood, an incurable virus you carry around without realizing it until the sores pop up at inopportune times. Jesus, did he just compare his career to a venereal disease? He needed sleep.

Her clothes were too loose for him to get a sense of her body, but as she leaned into the SUV her sweater pulled up and he could see a strip of skin the color of wet sand. He told himself to leave. He threaded his hands through the plastic hoops of his four bags and turned around, the bags swinging like pendulums as he made his way through the night.

He walked toward his car, checking the storefronts. As she'd said, there it was: a small window cluttered with unfamiliarly labeled canned goods, a hand-lettered sign proclaiming ASIAN GROCER. He'd passed it a hundred times but overlooked it. Funny the things that hide in plain sight.

It was nearly nine o'clock, and the wrought-iron trellis was menacingly poised above the door. He pushed the entrance open with his back and nodded at the old Chinese woman who stood inexpressively at the register. One look at the store told him he'd never find anything himself, so he dispensed with complete sentences and asked, "Kaffir lime leaves?"

Her expression did not change as she turned to walk down the aisle. He left his bags on the floor and followed her, and after she handed him the small plastic package he hit her up for some galanga as well, which she retrieved from a freezer that reeked of fish guts. He was following her to the register when the door opened and in walked the Indonesian woman.

He smiled. "Thank you for telling me about this place."

She nodded slightly, not quite a smile, shoulders hunched. Leo was six two, and during his time in Indonesia he'd grown used to looming above most people, particularly women.

She passed him, the sharp scent of bath soap cutting through the store's aquatic miasma. He followed her into the aisle.

"Have you been working in America for very long?" he asked as he pretended to look for something.

"A few weeks."

"Have you done any sightseeing?"

"I have no time for it." She put a couple of cans in her plastic basket, then looked at him. "Where, ah, where did you live in Indonesia?"

"Jakarta."

Finally, a smile. "I'm from Jakarta."

"Really?" He'd guessed that already—her accent was Javanese, and Jakarta was the biggest city on Java. "I loved it there."

"What brought you there?"

"I was working for a bank," he said, the lies so natural now. "It was an American company that has branches throughout Asia."

She nodded, as if there were so many things to say about her homeland that she didn't know where to begin. But then she said, "I'm sorry, I must go now."

That was quick. She walked deeper into the store, and he figured he'd pushed this as far as he could.

At the register, the proprietress forcefully punched the register's keys as if punishing it for some offense. She looked up at Leo and let the numbers on the display speak for her. This woman would be a beast at diplomatic negotiations, he thought as he paid. She made the change and deigned to give it to him.

He picked up his Whole Foods bags and was about to back his way out when the Indonesian woman, walking to the register, asked him in Bahasa, "Excuse me, could you tell me your name, please?"

Again he wondered if his mental translator was in error. "What?"

"Your name? Please?"

She was facing him, ignoring the stone-faced matron, who had already punched in her order and was waiting silently for her $9.82.

"Leo," he said, putting down his bags.

She took the blue Bic that was anchored to the counter by a thick thread and a tourniquet of black tape and jotted his name down on the back of one of those obnoxiously long coupons that Whole Foods' machines printed out. "And your phone number," she said.

This was without doubt the strangest pickup he'd ever experienced, if that's what this was. His heart was double-timing and he wondered if he was blushing—he was not a blusher—as he felt both the store owner's harsh gaze and his inquisitor's soft breath. He looked at the Indonesian woman, who, finally, was not cowering or moving quickly from one thing to the next but standing at her full height—perhaps a foot shorter than Leo—and looking at him calmly, fully. He had scrutinized her clothing and car and purchases and license plate and ass and visible scars and noted her lack of girlie oils and perfumes, yet he felt that she was focused entirely on his eyes, as if she were gathering all the necessary intelligence from them.

Then she was the hurried foreigner again, stuffing the piece of paper into her pocket and pulling out a change purse.

"Nie o'clock!" the store owner called out suddenly, and Leo jumped. It was like being attacked by a statue. "Nie o'clock!"

Leo picked up his bags and walked to the door. He was leaning against it, the moisture on his back steaming his shirt flat, when he asked, "What's your name?"

A piercing ringtone emanated from her sweatpants, some processed Asian pop song. She seemed afraid of it, dropping her change purse while trying to retrieve the phone, more of her hair coming loose from its band.

"Nie o'clock!" the store owner reminded her distracted customer.

In the midst of this manic activity the young woman stopped to look at Leo, a photograph in a maelstrom. "Sari," she said.

Then the cyclone picked up again and she answered the phone, pocketed her change purse, lifted her bag, and then paid the store manager. She spoke quietly into the phone in what sounded like Korean, nodding furiously as if the phone's camera lens were watching her.

Leo stepped outside and hurried to his car as the bags' plastic handles sank their fangs into his fingers. He unloaded the bags and sat in the driver's seat, keys in his hand. He watched the store—the owner flipped a sign on the door, informing passersby in four languages that it was CLOSED—and the young woman emerged. She was still on the phone. She walked quickly, her eyes drenched in worry.

He looked at himself in the rearview mirror, curious what she could have been staring at so intently. What had she seen in these eyes that gave away so very little?

He pulled out and joined the mania of 14th. Only forty-five minutes before the next meeting of the peaceniks and conspiracy theorists he was keeping tabs on for his mystery client; he'd have to hurry home if he wanted to make it in time.

Driving north, he checked his rearview, hoping for a glimpse of her SUV, but he didn't see it. A crescent moon dangled in the sky before him, just above the scaffolding for a new high-rise condo on U, and he found himself thinking of the crescent on her face. And of how much he hated his new job. He had the uncomfortable feeling he was immersing himself in something trivial and meaningless, and that he'd just let something important slip from his grasp.

At the next red, he popped open his glove box and found a pen and an old oil-change receipt. He jotted down her license-plate number before he could forget it. Hoping.

Z.

I wake up thinking about my wife. Traffic rumbles outside my motel room, the window's thin shade only beginning to lighten from the sunrise. I roll over and reach out with both arms, feeling coarse sheets and loneliness, and wait for the dream to pass.

When I dream of her, sometimes it's a memory and sometimes it's just a fragment. There are times when I'm not sure if it's an actual memory or something my subconscious is stitching out of itself, out of my desires and fears and the myriad colliding impulses of my self. I dreamed we were walking along the coast, wearing heavy jackets, her scarf blowing in the wind and tickling my nose. Did we ever walk on a beach in winter, or did I see that in a video? I try to remember. It seems hugely important to remember this. Was our daughter with us in the dream, or did I forget her? There is a sourness in my gut, made worse by that thought: *Did I forget my daughter?* I wake with this sourness every day. They say it fades, but it's the only thing that hasn't. Everything else—my memories, my sense of my family, my sense of myself and my role in the world—these things are on the verge of erasure.

I get up and wash my face and wait out the daily, awful period in which the dreams or memories are replaced by the latest reality I've surrounded myself with. A forsaken motel room in a forsaken city. Okay, yeah, that's familiar. I open my Personal Info Link and fill out an entry. I note every detail of my successful protection of the Event ending Mr. Chaudhry's life. I leave out my afternoon spent sightseeing and the little black girl with the pink sweater, as well as my drinks at the bar and the vigil with Tasha.

I have a headache, which isn't like me. There's a tender lump behind my ear where the hag got me with the rock, and my GeneScan isn't even pretending to work anymore. I've never had any malfunction like this, and it worries me. It makes me wonder what else inside myself could be broken.

It's not yet nine o'clock when I walk out of the motel on a cool day, light rain falling like tiny miracles. They don't realize how rare this will become, this moisture from the skies. A few umbrellas bob along the sidewalk, and a parade of cars waits at a traffic light, most of them heading into the city but a few trying to escape it, as if they know.

My motel is crouched beside chaotic, shambling New York Avenue, in one of the city's forgotten corners. Across the street, a swarm of yellow school buses are caged in a lot lined with barbed wire. Unlit neon signs stretch into the distance, advertising liquor, check-cashing services, and ethnically acrobatic restaurants specializing in both pizza and Chinese food. Few pedestrians venture here, as if they've been chased away by the desolation of the city's northern pole; those who do walk the streets are clad in overlarge, brightly colored jackets. They stand at intersections, some of them on phones and others slapping hands and laughing.

I wonder if anyone died in this motel during the night. If anyone overdosed; if anyone threatened to kill his or her lover or whore or dealer. It seems that kind of place. There are stories here, buried in grit, walled off from the rest of society. I hate the Department for making me stay in places like this, even if I see the logic.

I drive with the traffic and as I crest the hill suddenly there in the distance is the Capitol dome, so large and unexpected it's like a moon that's veered out of orbit. I cut across a side street, and the moon is eclipsed by a corner row house with a chunk of bricks missing from it, as if a truck drove into it, or something exploded.

My mind wants to revisit my wife, but I direct myself to pay closer attention to my surroundings. *Live in the present,* the Department tells us, not realizing the irony. I turn onto another of Washington's wide avenues, the painted brick row houses gleefully flashing their different colors as I pass. The trees are losing their leaves, and I tell myself I'm lucky to have been sent back to autumn in a beat when foliage still changed colors like this (I'd read about the phenomenon but hadn't entirely believed it). *Try to concentrate on the beauty of things,* I tell myself. *Try to wrap your arms around what's actually here.*

Between assignments, we Protectors are kept on the Department's sprawling campus, as if we're under quarantine. We are plagued by something that can't be released into the public bloodstream.

They say this is better for us, that it helps us stay in character. Our ability to blend in with our beats would be compromised if we were allowed to circulate in our own time between assignments. We'd start using slang terms from the wrong beat; we'd act according to the social mores of some other age; we'd let slip historical facts that our conversational partners weren't supposed to know. Better for all involved, then, for us to stay tucked away.

After we finish missions and are recalled to our own time, after the meetings and near-endless reports and the temporal decompressions, we're shuffled to our dormitories and briefed on our new assignments. There's always new assignments. Then, more files and videos, more facts to be absorbed as we prepare ourselves to reenter that fractured cosmos. Given the length of my last few gigs, I've barely been outside the Department campus for the last few months—or maybe even years?—of my own life. To the outside world, however, only a couple of weeks have passed. I wonder if I'm aging quickly in my superiors' eyes, as the arc of my life span curves in an ever-taller parabola over their short linear paths. I mentioned this once, but they told me I was thinking too much.

One day, after my previous mission but before this one, two other Protectors and I broke protocol. Between meetings, we hatched a simple escape plan, and later we met at a restaurant a couple of blocks away. The Department is at the edge of downtown, in nondescript buildings that most citizens tried to ignore. Derringer, Wills, and I had been in Training together but had met only a few times since. We were eager to swap stories. And to drink, quickly. It was like a race to purge the memories from our minds.

When was this? A few weeks ago, I think. A few weeks ago or hundreds of years later, depending on one's perspective.

"How did yours go, Zed?" Derringer asked after the first round had loosened us. He was tall and athletic, as all the Protectors are, and completely bald. I was the one whose mission had ended most recently—I'd been back only a day, still felt bleary-eyed and nauseated from the Recall.

"The integrity of history was preserved."

They laughed ruefully.

Leaving campus had been less difficult than I'd expected. Most of the guards were low-level grunts who all but genuflected in our presence; few had the clearance to know what it was we did. Some of them hadn't even looked us in the eye, just nodded when we told them we'd be back in a couple hours.

"It was fine," I continued. "The same. They're not getting any better at it."

"The ones in my beat are," Wills said. He had thin, intense eyes the color of gold. When he focused on you, you had the uncomfortable sense he was determining your character flaws, or plotting the quickest way to knock you unconscious. "They came close this time, very close. I neutralized the last of them just a few minutes before the plane took off."

Within the Department, we were the unlucky souls assigned to the Disasters Division. We were sent to ensure that awful events unfolded as originally dictated by history, that the hags did not rewrite the final acts of tragedies to make them comedies. Protectors in other divisions had the decidedly less troubling task of stopping the hags from wreaking unexpected havoc during otherwise calm events— they prevented benevolent, two-term presidents from being assassinated during their first months in office; or ensured that the hags didn't detonate nuclear bombs on one of history's originally meaningless days. At least each of those Protectors could look himself in the eye and know that he'd performed an inarguably good deed. Wills, Derringer, and I weren't so fortunate. Derringer had recently elimi- nated a group of hags who were trying to prevent the terrorist strikes of September 11, 2001. He strangled the final hag in a bathroom be- fore the troublemaker could board one of those fated flights out of Boston, and then he sat at a bar in Logan airport and started drinking martinis minutes before TV journalists interrupted their telecasts to show images of the burning towers. He'd gotten so drunk he laughed at the news coverage, he told us, until an off-duty cop took a swing at him. And Wills had just neutralized a group of hags trying to in- filtrate the U.S. military days before its planes were to drop nuclear bombs on Hiroshima and Nagasaki.

Wherever we went, countless people died in our wake.

"I stayed a couple days more," Wills said. "I just wanted to see it, you know? I boarded one of the planes, conned the pilots into think- ing I was military intelligence and needed to be on the flight."

"Are you serious?" Derringer raised his eyebrows. It was dangerous for Wills to admit this. Any deviation from a mission could lead to severe reprimands, if not outright expulsion.

"I *had* to see it. We flew lower over the city than I had expected. And then, the flash." He shook his head. "One hundred thousand dead, in a second. *One hundred thousand*. Try to imagine it. All that heat. All those lives. And then the thousands who went afterward, who took a few days or even weeks to go. *Imagine* that."

"They came up with worse," I said, "less than a century later."

We drank in silence for a bit.

"The looks on people's faces in that airport, when they saw their towers fall," Derringer said. "You should have seen them."

"I cheated too," I confessed. The drink was getting to me, along with everything else. "After I'd finished off the hags in Poland, before I started the Recall, I made my way into one of the camps. Had a uni- form and everything; they let me in."

"Glad you did it?" Wills asked.

"No. I wish to hell I hadn't." I'd never realized a human being could get so thin and not die. They were dying, of course; plenty of them. But the ones still alive were the worst.

More silence, more drinks.

"What I console myself with," Wills said, "is that they're all dead anyway. Really. So long ago, and so long dead. Nothing we can do about it."

"I'd thought it would feel like that," I said, "but it doesn't. They're in front of you. They're real, they breathe. The pain doesn't seem very *historical* when you're steeping in it."

The screams I'd heard in that camp. The vacant expressions I'd seen. And my job was to ensure that it happened, that the hags didn't save them.

"It makes you hate all these people, doesn't it?" Derringer asked later, after the third or fourth round.

"Which people?" I asked.

"*All* of these people." Derringer glared at the diners in the restaurant. It was a glitzy place, only blocks from the Capitol—not the Washington I'm currently assigned to, of course, but the new Capitol. Most of them were upper-level officials with their supplicants and tempters. "The more I do the job, the more I hate how *stupid* people today are."

"They're not stupid," Wills said. "We're very...privileged to know what we know."

"They're gerbils. *Rats*. It's our job to keep their cage nice and secure."

"Maybe you should request some time off before your next gig," I said.

"*Time.*" Derringer practically snarled that. "What a hilarious concept."

We all pondered that one for a while.

"Imagine being able to kill a hundred thousand people in one instant," Wills said. "Imagine that power, and that hatred."

"They all hated each other then," I said.

"I know. They made up some military excuse, but they really only dropped the bomb because they thought the people in Hiroshima were subhuman. They wouldn't have done it to people like themselves. They didn't think of it as murder, exactly. It was more like . . . wiping a slate clean."

In my time, the different races and ethnicities have been blended together for generations. The survivors of the Conflagration had better things to do than cling to biases against rival groups—they were just desperate to find mates and rebuild their lives. People eventually forgot what *race* even was, and the Government closely guards all records of past internecine conflict due to the dangers they could inspire. The Perfect Present lacks the blood feuds that are so rife in my current beat.

"But isn't it sad," Derringer asked, "how no one else knows about this?"

"Are you kidding?" Wills looked shocked. "I'm practically suicidal having all this history in me. You think other people should know about it too?"

"*Yes*. Absolutely. So they won't be ignorant and—"

"It isn't ignorance," Wills said. "Why is knowing about some ancient grievance between one group of people and another important? Why should that matter to who people are today? The people in my beat"—he shook his head in pity—"are *consumed* by that nonsense. Hating another group because of something that group did years ago, which had only been in response to what *their* group had done decades earlier, et cetera, et cetera. Spiraling back in time, endlessly, and they're trapped in the vortex. Today, we're *free* of that."

Derringer stared at Wills. "You call that *freedom?*"

"Freedom. Joy. Innocence."

Derringer looked at his glass. Wills and I exchanged glances. "Guess you're right," Derringer finally said. "Maybe I'm just tired."

We all were. We finished our round and decided we'd sufficiently bleached our brains and should return to campus.

We started to walk back. I was disturbed by what Derringer had said but more disturbed to realize that I agreed with him. The people of our modern world *were* strange. I had never thought of them that way before—I was part of them—but this was one of the first glimpses of the present I'd had in a while, not counting my time on campus. This was my city, what I'd been born into, where I'd fallen in love and worked and toiled and suffered, but it seemed so different. Colder than I remembered it. Fewer people on the street, the air fouler. I barely recognized certain blocks. It made me worry about what the job was doing to me.

We'd been walking for a few minutes when Derringer turned around and faced a wide intersection, a few pods lined up patiently. "Lemmings!" he shouted at no one in particular. "You're all lemmings!"

Wills clamped a hand on Derringer's forearm. Derringer shook him off, and both backs straightened as the space between them narrowed.

Before a word could be spoken or fist thrown, a Security pod pulled to the sidewalk and out leaped four officers. The synthetic material of their black uniforms reflected the streetlights. Their visors were down but I could read their alarm from the tension in their jaws, the thinness of their lips. They encircled us, visors twitching back and forth between our drunken trio and the outside world, in search of some nonexistent enemy.

"Are you all right?" one of them asked.

"We're fine," Wills said, taking a step away from Derringer. "Lovely evening for a stroll."

"You aren't supposed to be off campus."

"You telling us what to do, Officer?"

"I have my orders, sir."

"We were heading there anyway," Wills said. Derringer seemed too angry to speak. I was holding back to see what would happen next. I'd gotten so used to working my beats, to knowing all the plays in advance; I was thrown by this sudden spontaneity. "Care to walk with us," Wills asked, "or were you going to try to stuff us all in your little pod?"

The officers eyelessly looked at each other. "We can walk," one of them said, as if doing us a favor. "I'll radio the SAC and let him know what's happened, but I'd appreciate your explaining what it is you're—"

"Give it a rest, buddy," Derringer said, "or next time they send me back I'll kill your great-grandfather before he hits puberty."

"Shut up, Derringer," Wills scolded before I could.

It was unclear if the officers understood the remark, but hopefully they didn't. The three near androids pointed their mirrorlike visors at each other again, dark reflections of reflections of reflections.

We walked back in silence. A siren occasionally rang out, but not nearly as often as they do in my current beat. A heart attack maybe, or a pod accident. We heard laughter and saw smiling faces through the ground-floor windows of new towers, more people in bars and restaurants, some of which I'd visited with my wife so many, many lifetimes ago. And at the same time, only yesterday. Grief is funny that way. Time stretches and stretches and you think you've eased into it, but then it snaps back at you and you feel you haven't moved an inch from the moment you first heard the awful news.

A few days later, as I was preparing for this assignment, one of my superiors mentioned that Derringer "had been removed from the Department." No one ever said what exactly became of him, but we could guess. It was a warning to the rest of us.

During Training, they crammed various theories into my uncomprehending brain, ideas on how time travel works, theoretical frameworks I supposedly needed to bear in mind as I muddled through my beat. The one I understood best was the Great Man theory. There are so many minor players scurrying about, and we all like to kid ourselves about how important we are, about our own impacts on the lives of others. We like to think we can change the world. But we can't. A few can, the great men and women of history, and if a hag was to disrupt those life paths—if he was to prevent George Washington or Joseph Stalin or the first grand magistrate from being born—

then history would tail off in an entirely new direction, not just an alternate path but a previously unimaginable one, foreign to what we see in our Perfect Present. This is precisely what the hags want. So they attempt to assassinate historic leaders, or they send themselves to major historic Events, turning points at which the very axis of humankind seemed to shift. Which is why a group of hags is running around in pre-destruction Washington, D.C., the very epicenter of the tectonic rifts that set off the Great Conflagration.

I think about this as I sit here in a neighborhood park named after a great man, President Lincoln. I've learned that he set this nation's slaves free during a vicious war that pitted brother against brother. In the center of the park is a statue of Lincoln pointing forward, standing above a depiction of a cowering unshackled slave. What strange images these people celebrate.

I'm sitting on a wooden bench before a brightly colored playground of slides and ladders and swings and various other structures children could conceivably fall from. Toddlers and their older siblings climb up the steps and slip down the slides; they gleefully push toy trucks into miniature collisions and wreak other disasters, all while pointing excitedly at the life-size recycling trucks and backhoes that amble along the nearby road. Scattered on the benches are pale young mothers and darker-skinned women tending other people's children. They talk to one another in various languages, or chat on their phones, pacing in distracted circles, or walk alongside their little ones, fingers extended to guide them.

So many people outside, reveling in their ability to let the sun shine on their skin, as if they know that their descendants won't be able to do this. It feels funny for me to be outside for so long—I instinctively sit in the shade, afraid of the radiation that their atmosphere still manages to protect them from.

I spent the morning monitoring two of the hags' next targets, but all seems well. Today's Event is still a few hours away, so I decide to wander the neighborhoods.

"Which one is yours?" a young woman asks me. She's pale as soap, wearing a shapeless green shirt over black jeans. Her unwashed blond hair is pulled back, her eyes are puffy with exhaustion, but she looks content. I remember that look.

"None of them."

I'm still watching the kids, this quotidian scene of marvels tiny and huge, and it takes a second for me to realize the mistake I've made. She's staring at me and her body is rigid.

"I used to live here, with my wife and daughter," I lie. But I mix in some truth: "They had an accident."

I'm too consumed by my own past to look back at her. I just stare at a little girl, maybe four years old, who reminds me of my lost jewel. Little pink and white baubles bounce at the ends of her braids as she darts across the playground, an autumn sprite spreading joy without even realizing it. I scan the adult faces, looking for one with a genetic similarity to the child's, wonder whose she is.

"I'm so sorry," the woman says.

I shouldn't be here, revealing myself to so many contemps. And I certainly shouldn't be sharing memorable stories, horrors that will haunt this young mother as she puts her child down for a nap.

So I try to hold the past inside me. I mix in more lies, cushioning my vulnerabilities in them. "I live in Philly now, but my company sends me here a lot. I can't help dropping by the old playground sometimes, watching the memories dance around me for a few minutes."

I look at the kids again, staring at a world that has no place for me. The woman's eyes stay on mine.

"I've made you uncomfortable," I say. "I'll go."

I don't look back at her as I walk away. I bend to unlatch the child-proof fence, swinging it closed behind me to lock the children in and keep them safe.

4.

L eo Hastings's employer, Targeted Executive Solutions, was not terribly executive, and it did not always offer solutions. But the work did involve targets.

TES occupied a building in one of the many nondescript office parks that sprouted from the Northern Virginia asphalt thanks to heavy watering from the government's defense budget. Also in the building were the offices of a dentist, an accountant, and a real estate firm. Across the pedestrian-unfriendly street was a Chick fil-A, and faintly in the background was I-395's constant arterial hum of personnel and dollars into and out of the capital. TES's office had no windows. Anyone curious enough to Google it discovered a slick though merely three-page Web site offering bland assurances about the company's commitment to its clients' success. The listed phone number led to a voice-mail box that an employee checked once a week. Clients used a different number.

This was where Leo had beached himself after being thrown from the Agency's boat, a mere half a mile away. Some of his ex-colleagues had encouraged him to think of it as a sort of promotion. Plenty of people were leaving the Agency, which was still being blamed for 9/11, for failing to predict the future, for not having a crystal ball, for not being perfect. And being blamed for everything it was doing to prevent another one. Talent was leaching from the government side to the contractor side, but it wasn't really going anywhere, his ex-colleagues explained. *Hell, you'll get to do basically the same thing, and for more money.* Spooks and analysts were trading in their blue government ID tags for green contractor ID tags, patrolling the same halls at Langley, only this time as consultants in better suits.

But Leo was hardly doing the same thing for TES that he'd done for the Agency. He wasn't sure if he *wanted* to do the same thing anymore.

How he had become involved in this sort of work was a complicated tale, one he himself didn't always understand. Part of the problem was that he couldn't tell anyone. And isn't that how we learn things, how we commit them to memory and make them a part of ourselves, by telling other people, wrapping our experiences into tidy stories? Sitting at a bar having drinks with old friends: *Hey, let me tell you how I was recruited by the Agency.* Or lying in bed with a woman: *Have I ever told you about the time I helped track a cell of Islamist terrorists in Jakarta?* Or on the phone with his father: *There's this time I fucked up and a bunch of people died. Anything like that ever happen to you?* These were stories and questions he was not allowed to voice. So they silently caromed in his head like echoes of words that hadn't been spoken, soundless reverberations, ghosts of stories. They took on a spectral power, haunting him.

Leo had always been a thinker, a quiet one, studiously independent. He'd grown up in Bethesda, the son of an energy executive and an intellectual property attorney who had heroically managed to have a child despite their hectic schedules and who seemed disappointed that they weren't congratulated for this more. Leo read a lot. He scored a spot at Harvard, majoring in history with a focus on modern Asia; took a semester in Kyoto; and spent his first two years after college teaching English in Indonesia, living in a borderline-prehistoric village three hours from Jakarta. Why there? Mainly because he didn't know what else to do with himself, partly because he wanted something unique, and, yes, partly because he was intrigued by hints from an acquaintance about how even normal-looking white guys could easily score with hot Asian chicks (which turned out to be woefully untrue at the Muslim village where he was stationed). He spent another year backpacking the continent, and then it was back to Harvard for grad work.

He somewhat perplexed his parents by choosing neither law nor business but political history as his field. They reminded him often of how paltry a salary professors earned. The brilliance of their son was never in question, only the best way to make use of that brilliance.

Leo spent years crafting an unwieldy dissertation on Asian dictators, paying particular attention to the Kims in North Korea and Suharto in Indonesia. Despots fascinated him. The cults of personality, the secret police, the godlike ability to not only rule but also define reality for their subjects, the various and unbelievably creative ways to kill dissidents—how could anyone not find this interesting? The thing that uncomprehending citizens of free countries often missed was how charismatic tyrants were, how frighteningly *likable* these guys could be when they weren't torturing you or murdering your family. Kim Jong Il was beloved for the way he'd fought off the Japanese invaders, appreciated for his backslapping bonhomie. Suharto had a magnetic smile, a way with women, and was cheered for cracking down on Communists and convincing the islands' hundreds of ethnic groups to play nice. That sort of charm was a mystery to Leo. He learned to speak Bahasa while in Indonesia, he taught himself rudimentary Korean and Cantonese while studying the Kims and Mao, but that certain *something* that the great leaders possessed, that *it* quality, was utterly beyond him. Which made it all the more fascinating.

Leo was preparing to defend his dissertation when the Twin Towers fell. He was in Logan airport that very morning, awaiting a flight to Washington to visit his parents. Maybe he was even sitting in the same chair one of the hijackers had occupied a few hours earlier. The burning tower had been on the TV for a few minutes before Leo realized it; he only noticed when he found himself staring at a young coed, maybe ten years his junior—God, he was getting old—and finally he heard what the announcer was saying, saw the screen. He stood, walked closer. By the time the second plane hit, there was a crowd. First everyone so quiet, then one by one the gasps, the cell phones materializing in shaky hands, the airport staff running in both directions. People watched the planes on the tarmac with a sort of helplessness, as if those flights too were doomed but the passengers inside them didn't know it yet. Then the planes stopped lifting off, the constant rumbling on the other side of the glass was silenced, and unhelpful announcements droned in the static as lines formed everywhere, as if people still believed that order would be restored if they were patient and found the right person to complain to.

When the second tower fell, he stood motionless, surrounded by an equally frozen group in front of the TV. And then this one man at a nearby bar who had been sitting the whole time, like a sort of sacrilege, like some apostate churchgoer who refused to kneel at the appropriate moments, this man started *laughing*. Again there were gasps. Was the guy crazy? He wore a suit, had short hair, an athletic build. He was ethnically interesting, darker skin without actually being dark-skinned, and he was fucking *laughing*. Finally an equally imposing, Irish-looking guy—a construction worker or off-duty fireman—yelled at the laugher. The laugher took that as his cue to leave; he stood and dropped some bills on the table beside his empty martini glass (who drank martinis at that hour?). The fireman said something. Words were exchanged. Then the fireman punched the guy in the face. There were more gasps and a few claps of applause. Then the laugher, who wasn't laughing anymore and wasn't even smiling but still somehow *seemed to be* smiling, like with his eyes maybe, shook off the blow and walked away. Only later did Leo think to himself, *Jesus, that could have been one of the terrorists, he could have been left behind for some reason. He wasn't really drinking, the martini glass was just a cover. And we let him escape.*

In a weird way, in a way that Leo knew didn't make sense and was due to the shock, he felt that his own proximity to the mysterious laughing man implicated him in the day's horrors. He should have punched the man himself—he'd thought about doing it, he'd wanted to do it, but he'd stayed motionless and impotent until this burly fireman or longshoreman or cop had stepped in to play the hero. Leo never *did* anything; despite all his academic laurels and achievements, when he was honest with himself, he knew he had done nothing. People who did things were guys like that cop or fireman (his brethren who minutes earlier had perished by the dozens in Manhattan) and the young soldiers from rural and ghetto America who would be sent to pay those bastards back. Leo was a lucky representative of the creative class, except he didn't really create anything, and over the following weeks he began to feel like a complete, utter asshole. God or good fortune or luck or the Constitution of the United States or his white skin and Y chromosome had given him so much, and what had he ever given back?

One month later he defended a dissertation that suddenly seemed less relevant to the world. His own words sounded stale—he almost wanted to revise the whole text, but it was too late. Afterward, one of his advisers took him out for celebratory drinks that Leo didn't feel he deserved. Like a confused foreign correspondent, Leo tried to describe the conflict roiling in his mind, tried to analyze the two warring camps and explain their historical grievances to his audience. *Is this what I'm supposed to be doing with my life?* The professor said he understood, that he felt the same way sometimes. And then he told Leo that it was interesting he'd brought this up, as the professor knew of a certain job opportunity. What did Leo think about working for the government? There were people who would like to talk to Leo, who were impressed by the arguments elucidated in his papers, a few of which had landed in policy journals and on the desks of important think tanks. His recent experience living in the world's most populous Muslim nation and his fluency in Bahasa certainly didn't hurt. Leo's adviser gave him a name and a number, which Leo saved into his phone but was afraid to call.

The number stayed unused in his phone for two months.

In December he rode Amtrak to Manhattan to attend the American Historical Association's annual meeting, where all the young PhDs begged and groveled for teaching positions in the safe ivory tower, like escapees of police states pleading for asylum. He had a few interviews the first morning and heard himself trying to convince not only his interlocutors but also himself that this was what he wanted. *Yes, put me somewhere safe. Surrounded by books. Where all I have to do is read and teach and think. And not* do *anything.* He felt the shame burning in his stomach, rising up to consume him. He blew off his afternoon interviews so he could walk to Ground Zero. He stared into the gaping hole, and the gaping hole stared into him.

He walked a few blocks west, found a relatively quiet corner, and called the number his adviser had given him. He was routed from person to person and then had a long conversation with a man who did not introduce himself. When an ambulance drove by in the middle of one of Leo's answers, the man asked Leo where he was.

"Um, honestly, I'm standing in what would have been the shadow of tower number two."

There was a pause, and then the man asked him if he could take a cab to Penn Station and buy a ticket to Washington so they could talk in person.

"Right now?"

"Unless you have something better to do."

Leo caught the train.

A few years later (and a few misadventures later and a few politically motivated, territorial clusterfucks later) here he was, walking the postapocalyptically deserted hallways of TES.

He was still fuzzy on how the company's organizational flow chart was structured. There was no watercooler gossip, as the operatives were discouraged from fraternizing—he'd only met a few of his co-workers, and they were not friendly. The walls were soundproofed, and employees were told to keep their doors shut at all times, so he could never tell if he was the only one at work or if dozens of other drones were typing and collecting within the hive. Leo didn't know if his accomplishments would be noticed by anyone important, or if this sanatorium-like space would be his prison, a solitary confinement lasting the rest of his professional life.

More irritating was the fact that he hadn't yet met his client. All he knew was what was expected of him: he was to keep tabs on various D.C.-based domestic activists, learn what they were planning and when, find out where their funding came from (particularly if any of it was from abroad), and, specifically, determine the sources of some distressingly accurate muckraking stories on new Web sites such as knoweverything.org. It was an extreme Left site, the typical rants and diatribes, but a handful of its articles were unusually sound journalistically, suggesting that these people knew what they were doing. But which people? There were no bylines on the stories, no masthead listed. A search of the ISP had yielded only an obscure holding company in Sweden, which meant that a lot of work had gone into covering the authors' tracks. They had written exposés on military contractors' financial excesses and uncomfortably accurate stories on the activities of government intelligence agencies overseas and at home; they'd reported rumors of illegal wiretapping, and even posted a sensitive (and, actually, pretty funny) transcript of a drunken conversation between an anonymous reporter and a nameless administration official in which the official had spilled some rather delicate secrets. Some of the site's stories were filtering out to the mainstream media, causing problems.

There were various foreign organizations and persons with vested interests in dampening the American public's appetite for the wars, and Leo needed to learn which of them were funding the activists. Some of the stories on the Web site could only have been written by people with access to classified intelligence, meaning that the publishing of those stories was a crime. Also, it was wise to stay informed of such groups' activities and learn their recruiting strategies, study the ways in which they conned impressionable young people into joining in their dissent. It felt light-years away from the counterterrorism work he'd been doing in Jakarta, but his new boss had argued that there were many parallels indeed, and that Leo's experience infiltrating groups of youthful malcontents was invaluable.

Two months earlier, after readjusting to life in America, he'd started the assignment by showing up at a multiorganizational meeting to discuss an upcoming antiwar rally, and he had barely gotten comfortable in the hard plastic chair when an aging hippie with a bad case of the touchy-feelies had started blathering to him about the importance of what they were doing ("I just want to get involved, you know, have an *effect* on something," she'd explained in a quick but monotone voice, a prophet crossed with a zombie). He'd already known what was in store: unbelievably long meetings, torturous portions of which would be dedicated to deciding arcane matters of nomenclature and semantics; motions in favor of or against items whose importance he could not fathom; spirited debates between people whose opinions were so closely aligned that their minute philosophical differences would drive them into apoplexies of conscience. He had been sure to have a strong cup of coffee beforehand. And there he had sat, fidgeting from caffeine and boredom, hoping he might stumble upon some information that could possibly interest his client. He entertained himself by mentally composing sections of his report. How many *d*'s were in *pedantic*? Did *pathetically* have a hidden *a* in the penultimate syllable? If he made the report as boring as possible, would that be a sly way of spurring his boss into granting him a new assignment, or would institutional inertia maroon him on this desert island?

He'd had enough in the bank that he could have taken time off, traveled, maybe tried to write some political essays or even a spy novel. Yet still he felt the calling, so he'd put out feelers for any kind of opening. Which had brought him to Targeted Executive Solutions, but he saw immediately that the job was beneath him: it could have been handled by any rent-a-spook who looked young enough to fit in with a roomful of angry twentysomethings.

He filed his reports with his boss, Mr. Bale, who passed them on to the unknown client. Leo was unclear if this extra layer of insulation was at the client's request or if it was TES's way of controlling how the company's image was presented to its cash-laden government handlers.

He knocked on his boss's door at ten exactly.

"Morning," Bale said as Leo sat down. Bale pretended to smile, and Leo tried too. On the wall behind the desk were four framed nature photographs Bale had supposedly taken while hunting in Michigan, images of a wolverine devouring a deer carcass.

Bale had some follow-up questions from Leo's report from the previous week: what meetings Leo had attended, what Web sites he'd trolled, what contacts he'd made.

"Still no closer to the source of those stories?" Bale asked.

"I get pushback from certain people whenever I try to get too close, which tells me something. But I'm worried I'm making myself *too* present—this overeager guy who shows up at every meeting of every group in the city? I'm making myself too visible."

"I suppose." Bale always spoke in bland tones, whether he was talking about the Hoya game or ethnic cleansing. He was like a minor character actor whose name you never learned even though you'd seen him in twenty films. Bale could be an accountant, a market researcher, a soccer dad, an Internet porn addict, a failed novelist, a quiet neighbor, just another suddenly middle-aged guy who'd been left behind. Which made him good at what he did. Leo feared that in another ten or fifteen years, he'd look just like Bale. At least Leo was taller. "What are you getting at?" Bale asked.

"I wonder if it might be better for me to stand down for a little while, do something else."

"I know you aren't thrilled with the assignment. But we need someone on it, and you seem right for it. Unless you have a way of getting an agent or two to do the work for you—which I'd be okay with depending on the circumstances—we need you out there."

Leo had thought of this too. He'd tried to identify conflicts within or between the various groups, leadership rivalries, unappreciated members whose divided loyalties could be exploited. There were many such rifts, but the right situation had yet to present itself.

The tone of Bale's comments—"you *seem* right for it," the remark about Leo's inability to turn an agent—annoyed him. He was about to be dismissed when he found himself saying, "There's something else, unrelated. Something that could be interesting for the firm."

He kept it short: He had met a young Indonesian maid who was possibly being abused by a South Korean diplomat. He could prove nothing, but he let slip a few of the more telling details.

"What did she say about her situation?" Bale asked.

"Nothing. I think she was just so stunned I spoke Bahasa. But she took my name and number."

Rising eyebrows undid Bale's poker face. "You get hers?"

"No. She had a cell, but when it rang she seemed scared of it. I don't think it was hers."

"Still, a diplomat beating a maid isn't exactly illegal. Neither is keeping her chained in the basement and raping her—nothing they do is."

"But Korean men have their pride. It's all about face with them. If we have something that could embarrass him—he's beating this poor girl, or not paying her—that's leverage."

"And if it turns out he's raping her, that's even more leverage, huh?"

It was one of Washington's dirty little secrets, how diplomats sometimes brought over servants from their home countries, usually immigrants there, whom they paid slave wages or no wages at all. Sometimes the servants were kept locked in the house, or were beaten, or worse. Diplomatic immunity protected their ambassadorial bosses, as did the fact that, usually, no one ever saw the servants or had any idea what was going on inside that charming Tudor in the Palisades. The Americans were hesitant to raise a stink, as their own people working abroad were hardly without fault. Leo knew from experience that American diplomats hired entire crews of locals for pennies a day, and often the young women's services extended to duties more physical than dusting. The moral line was fuzzy when national borders were crossed, and no one wanted to lose his own perks by eliminating someone else's.

Bale leaned back in his seat. "Even if it's really egregious, the worst we could do is pass it on to State, and they can complain and maybe the diplomat gets reassigned."

"I'm not saying we should bust the guy, just scare him. Let him know we know what he's doing, see what we can get out of him if he's afraid he'll be reassigned to Uzbekistan. But even before that—what if I can run the maid, get her to eavesdrop around the house, see if she can copy some documents or clone a laptop? That worth anything to anyone?"

TES, Leo had been told many times, was in the business of collecting information. Usually this was done for a specific client, most often a government one, but that didn't mean the company's employees couldn't snoop for themselves. Sometimes they sought out information simply because it was there and they could get it; they liked to hoard what they learned, as one never knew what someone else might one day find valuable. It was entrepreneurial intelligence—a growing field now that the government espiocracy was drowning in liquid cash but thirsting for information.

Leo hadn't meant to say anything about Sari, had still been weighing the best way to handle it. But Bale's condescending tone had left him needing to prove himself.

"Anything we could use on a Korean is gold these days," Bale mused. "The guys on North Korea? They have nothing. It's like that country doesn't exist. You think we're bad in the Arab states, Jesus, North Korea is the fucking moon."

Leo waited.

"Was she pretty?"

Somehow Leo had known Bale would ask that. "Yes."

Bale smiled. "Why hire ugly domestic help? Gotta admire the balls, you know?" He shook his head. "Grocery stores are fascinating windows. I saw a black guy hit his kid in a Safeway once. Kid was maybe five or six. In the produce section. His kid asked him something I didn't quite hear, and *bam,* dude whales on the kid's shoulder, one blow, knocks him on his ass. Kid just started howling. Crazy things happen in grocery stores." He stared into space for a moment. "How do you know her boss is Korean?"

"Checked her plates."

"She *was* cute, huh? Followed her into the parking lot and everything."

"Just curious."

"I know a lot of guys love doing the Asian thing, but those chicks are too petite for me. Nothing to hold on to while you bang 'em, you know?"

Leo figured he was supposed to nod, so he did.

"What would your next step be if I was to approve this?"

"I think she's going to call me. I think she's thrilled to have discovered someone in this city she can talk to. But she's probably watched, so she'll skulk off to the phone late one night. If she calls me, I can—"

"Their phones might be tapped."

"I'll keep it brief, invite her to meet me again."

"She probably isn't allowed out very much."

"So I meet her on her next grocery run, or at the dry cleaner's, or wherever."

Bale nodded. "Don't tip your hand yet. I want to do some digging on the diplomat first."

Leo recited the tags and Bale said he'd talk to some people. With that, Leo was dismissed, off to another day trolling the paranoid sites of the leftist mind.

The people at the party were talking about reality.

"The wars aren't real to us," one of them said. "I mean, it's something that happens to other people, far away. None of us are in the military or even know anyone who is. We're totally detached. This is the horrible thing about it. It makes it somehow unreal."

They all nodded. Leo had just walked into the kitchen in search of the booze. He reminded himself he was supposed to be having fun.

He'd been back in D.C. for weeks and hadn't done anything more social than see a few movies alone and then loiter in Kramerbooks hoping to bump into a hot-librarian type. Which never happened. Most of his friends from the Agency were stationed abroad, or were too busy to meet up, or were distrustful enough to concoct excuses. This left the old friends from his earlier life, people he had cut off for years. He'd bumped into one of them, a friend from Harvard named John, on the Metro the other day. John knew a bunch of other Harvard pals who lived in D.C.; they were having a party in a few nights, Leo should totally come by.

So here he was, in a cramped Glover Park apartment that struggled to contain all the brilliant theories and witty takes on society that its partyers were offering. There were a few old faces from college and grad school, some of whom Leo remembered fondly and others he remembered less fondly.

Interpol and Bloc Party and Franz Ferdinand and other retro-eighties impostors were jangling on the speakers, and at one point Leo hovered on the periphery of a fierce debate about whether such bands were fabulous reinventors of a once-neglected sound or apologists for a horrible, horrible decade.

All the attractive women wore the same glasses and were attached to boring men.

John was now an associate professor of American Studies at GW. He'd just helped his chances of winning tenure by publishing a novel of which several newspapers' book critics were very fond. The party was a sort of celebration for this. When Leo arrived at the party, he'd asked John what the book was about, and John had answered, "Real life."

He went on, "It's about real people, you know, there's this family, the eldest kid is a graduate student, the younger one wants to be in a band, and the father is a financial analyst having an affair with his secretary. It's kind of about all of them and also about this illegal immigrant one of them hits with their car."

Leo was desperate for a smoke. Smoking had almost been a requirement for every important social interaction in Indonesia; he'd surely erased years of his life standing on street corners and sitting in cafés and restaurants sharing cigarettes with prospective agents. Ever since returning to D.C., he'd been trying to quit, which was yet another reason he felt jittery and uncomfortable at this weirdly smoke-free party.

He attempted to smile when meeting new people and tried to remember the way one was supposed to act at soirees like this. It had been his job to meet people in Jakarta, of course, but the circumstances were quite different. Tonight's crowded bookshelves and philosophical air and loud music and spirit of very safe adventure (*Let's get wasted in the city!*) were familiar. Yet the women's low-rise jeans and the men's snug T-shirts were evidence of the stylistic changes a few years could bring, as were the occasional gray hairs and bald spots. This was the real life Leo could have had. It was as though he'd slipped into a slightly broken time-travel machine and emerged in a new time on an alternate path.

He wondered if there was something wrong with him. If what he had done in Indonesia, and what he had witnessed in his brief trips to the satellite locations, had scarred him somehow. He had chosen his new life and rejected this one. Then the new life had rejected him.

"When people complain about *Washington,*" a young adjunct politics professor at Georgetown was saying, "what are they really complaining about? The people of the District of Columbia? No; we have nothing to do with national politics—we don't even have a vote in Congress, thank you very much. No, they're complaining about the congressmen and senators. But guess where those people come from? Not from D.C. No, *they* send those congressmen and senators to *our* town. The politicians they all claim to hate are *their* politicians, not from Washington but from the fifty states, from their own hometowns and districts. So when people bitch about *Washington,* they're really bitching about *themselves.* They're bitching about *democracy.*"

"They don't *want* democracy," someone else said, "they all want a tyranny of their own desires. A despotism of their personal politics."

A few drinks in and Leo was ready to leave. He walked up to John and tried to find a polite way of bowing out.

"What *was* it you were doing in Indonesia, man?" John asked him. They were in a circle with John's friends.

Leo had lied to his school buddies about his job. They were landing fellowships and teaching positions and gigs at research firms, and he'd told them he was taking a job doing risk analysis for some international conglomerate in Asia.

Leo retold the old lies, hoping they were the same lies he'd given them those many years ago.

"Very vague, Mr. Hastings," John said, his cheeks red with drink. "Very suspicious. It's like, the other day, I met a guy at a party, a big guy, and when I asked what he did he said, 'I work with the Justice Department,' and that's it. Like, basically saying, *I do things you aren't allowed to know about, and leave it at that.*"

"It's a weird city," Leo conceded.

John drunkenly put his hand on Leo's shoulder and faced the group, as if forgetting that he'd already introduced Leo to them a couple of hours ago. "This is my pal Leo, and though he says he did some obscure sort of business work in Indonesia, he was most likely a CIA agent."

Leo wondered if John could feel his shoulder muscles tense up.

"So you were a waterboarder!" one of them said with a wasted smile.

"Is it true we were torturing monks in Thailand," another asked, perhaps only half in jest, "pulling out their fingernails?"

"We didn't really waterboard them," Leo said. "We dunked them in vats of our own urine. Sometimes we poured boiling oil down their nostrils. I personally chopped off their ears. Although it's not really chopping; you kind of have to saw them off."

The music was still terse and frenetic but the faces pointed at him were silent.

"Nice meeting you all." He walked toward the door.

Leo was outside wondering how often cabs visited this neighborhood when John hurried after him, jacketless shoulders huddled against the cold.

"Dude, you okay?"

"I'm fine, just tired. Thanks for having me. Your friends are great."

"I'm sorry if what I said was out of line. I just meant it as a joke, you know. You kind of disappeared, for years, and I just thought—"

"Just thought what?"

John seemed to be shrinking. "I just thought I was being funny."

"You were." Leo paused. "Have fun with your real life, John. I hope nothing fake ever intrudes on it."

If he'd seen an old cigarette butt on the ground, he would have picked it up and lit it, but there was none. He'd walked a few blocks toward Wisconsin when his cell started ringing. He didn't want to answer, figuring it was John or someone else calling from the party. On the third ring he took it out and checked the number, which he didn't recognize. He answered it anyway.

"Hello, is this Leo?" she asked in Bahasa, and he stopped walking.

5.

Lately, chains of events had become confusing to Tasha. Everything seemed connected, and twisted; it was hard to discern where one event ended and the ramifications began. But if she had to figure out what had brought her to Troy Jones and Leo Hastings, and to all her subsequent troubles, it was not the vigil by the White House but an event a few weeks earlier than that, the day she'd taken both a physical and figurative walk away from her job and discovered the forgotten memorial.

Walking was what she'd been doing with whatever free time she'd had since Marshall died. Walking along the buckling brick sidewalks of Capitol Hill, where she'd bought a row house a year ago; strolling north of the Mall through the cold shadows of the office buildings, where she worked; trudging up Meridian Hill and into the gentrifying frenzy of Columbia Heights, where she'd been born. Her parents lived out in P.G. County now, had moved there in the eighties after fifteen years of fallout from the riots had finally turned them against their once-beloved city. She walked the old neighborhoods, seeing some familiar faces and many new ones; the racial makeup was changing, the former homes of African Americans now welcoming the whites and the Latinos, the multicolored row houses themselves not seeming to care but the old-timers on the stoops looking skeptical. She spent hours walking, hours she should have been billing for the firm, her feet wasting the potential for thousands of dollars, her very self nothing but a financial pedometer in reverse. She would return home after a few hours, her feet sore and her head worse. Sometimes she would cry somewhere, hopefully in an inconspicuous spot, the back of a chain bookstore or on one of the overlooked benches that the District placed beside the third-tier statues—Taft, or maybe Gandhi—that no one ever looked at.

On this particular Sunday, weeks prior to the White House vigil, she had been working at the firm. She and five other young associates were in a conference room exhuming boxes of documents provided by one of their clients, GTK Industries, a sprawling conglomerate that made and built and sold and did more things than even the most anal of accountants could keep track of. Among GTK's many other pursuits, it earned a fortune as a contractor for the wars, building army camps in the desert, shipping food to the soldiers, erecting cellular towers, and setting up satellite TV hookups to provide the overworked troops with some entertainment. Tasha had handled various projects for the client, and she'd always felt a strange fondness for the work, a sense that it kept her closer to her brother. It felt different now.

GTK was having a dispute with a subcontractor that provided its ships with oil for their long voyages to the Middle East. Rates were not what had been promised; surcharges had added up mysteriously. Unseemly opportunism and perhaps even foul play hidden in the fog of war were suspected. The lawyers were trying to determine if the subcontractor's fluctuating oil rates were legit—if the contracts had possibly provided the subcontractor with legitimate loopholes—or if GTK should threaten legal action.

Tasha had already spent many hours that week learning about the intricacies of international marine transport laws and treaties, and poring over contracts, e-mails, correspondence, and other files. Her skull felt numb from reading things that weren't relevant or were relevant but really, really boring.

It was past one and she hadn't had lunch yet when she read, and then reread, a certain e-mail exchange.

"Hey, Jill," she said to her coworker, "read through these and tell me what you think."

She and Jill had attended GW Law together, had crammed and quizzed each other and consumed far too much espresso together, had uproariously celebrated each academic and then professional milestone with nights of dancing at Dream and the Eighteenth Street Lounge. They'd interviewed at the firm the same day and for the past two years had served as each other's bodyguards and shrinks as they tried to survive the long hours and intense pace.

Jill read the e-mails, Tasha guiding her through them chronologically.

"I think this isn't material," Jill finally said. "Nothing about the subcontractor or the dispute."

"I know. But, Jesus."

The e-mails were linked to cost-benefit analyses and noted that GTK could save millions of dollars on shipping if it delayed the processing of one of the government's orders by a few weeks. Tasha knew from other research that the shipment in question consisted of bulletproof vests, ammunition, and other matériel. There was even a tidy back-and-forth between two midlevel executives, one of them positing the theory that it might be unethical to delay items deemed essential by the grunts in the desert, the other exec assuring him that this was a simple business decision, and if the dollars made sense, the company should do it.

"We gotta focus, Tash. I want to be home in time for the Skins game." Jill handed back the files.

"You can't tell me you don't think this is wrong. People probably *died* because of this."

She felt her throat tightening, and Jill looked at her. "Sweetie, come on." Jill put a hand on her friend's arm, squeezed it. "I know what it makes you think. But we're stressed as hell and you're connecting dots you shouldn't. You need to put that away now, and keep your mind on this, okay?"

All she could do was nod.

"Maybe you should get lunch, clear your head a minute."

They were surrounded by boxes and stacks of paper, and at the far end of the conference room four other associates were reading and scribbling, oblivious to this drama. Tasha felt herself nodding as she floated toward the elevator, dazed.

She made it only three blocks before she felt her emotions loosening again. She needed to hide, couldn't risk one of her colleagues on lunch break seeing her crying in public. She was near the almost ridiculously fortified White House, at the messily trapezoidal intersection of Penn and 14th and E Streets, when she noticed a set of stairs ascending a gentle slope of landscaped grass, a hilly miniature island in the convergence of all that asphalt. Where had that come from? It seemed a miracle that it existed, that she'd never noticed it before. She walked up the steps, grateful for the hiding place that God seemed to have rearranged earth and stone to create just for her.

The stairs crested the hill and then descended to a long stone walkway. Before her was a wall upon which maps of Germany and France were etched. The lines and arrows represented military fronts, the movements of armies. She stepped back and saw the sign declaring this the World War I Memorial. It was protected from the view of pedestrians and traffic by the slope of the hill and the trees planted around it. A small copper-stained fountain burbled, and strewn on some benches were the homeless men whose collective knowledge of safe places to crash constituted the only human awareness that this spot existed. Tasha thought of all the fanfare and press and Hollywood stars surrounding the dedication of the World War II Memorial, and of its prime location beneath the Washington Monument, and she was struck and saddened by the contrast with this place. A memorial that hardly anyone knew existed, not even a lifelong Washingtonian who had spent countless hours writing legal briefs only three blocks from here. She sank onto a bench that was not currently occupied by a derelict and she cried. She had often wondered what kind of memorial would be built for soldiers like her brother—a trivial and petty concern, but what Washingtonian wouldn't at least wonder this, surrounded by the damn things?—and the sight of this place, its utter forgottenness, the way it existed outside memory, outside anyone's real life, outside any curious tourist's itinerary, broke her heart.

Eventually she wiped at her eyes and tried to read the etchings in the stone, the facts about this war, the staggering number of dead. No bouquets were laid here. These men had all died, and what descendants were left had gone on to fight other wars and forget about this one.

She walked away and reentered the world, running from all that history. Yet she carried it with her, like the photo of Marshall she kept in her wallet. Her memories of the Marine Corps marching band strutting down Eighth Street on the Fourth of July, of the grainy images she'd seen so many nights on CNN, of the fog and wail of Marshall's memorial service. She carried these with her as she walked not back toward the office but south, past clusters of tourists snapping shots framed by the White House's manicured lawn and its rooftop snipers. Soon she could hear the commotion; something was happening on the Mall.

Something was always happening on the Mall. On weekdays, the grass looked sickly and dead from having been trampled by this march or that rally over the previous weekend. Tasha had stumbled on NRA rallies, gun-control rallies, Impeach the President rallies, Support the President rallies, rallies for peace, rallies for war. So much conflict, so much disagreement, so many ways to disrupt traffic. She'd once seen a Recognize Taiwan rally, a group of happy Asian youths waving unfamiliar green-white-and-red flags at the curious onlookers, the passersby smiling at them, and something about the demonstration's complete irrelevance to her own life had made it both comical and wonderful. *Yeah, go, Taiwan!* That had been a few years ago, before everything seemed relevant to her life and nothing seemed comical or wonderful.

She knew what today's rally on the Mall was. She'd seen the articles in the paper warning residents which streets to avoid. She told herself she had not gone on this walk so as to stumble upon it like this, but maybe she had. Her subconscious was doing crazy shit lately. She was confused, not really making decisions for herself. The events of the world were what they were, and she followed.

Followed them here, past Constitution, in front of the Museum of American History, to stare at this, history in the making. Or maybe a refutation of history, an insistence that we stop history, redirect it. The marchers were chanting and singing, waving signs, carrying banners that sagged over their heads. END THE WARS. SUPPORT OUR TROOPS. BRING THEM HOME.

She was against the war and said so when talking with her like-minded friends, but she'd kept silent about her opposition when talking to Marshall and her parents. She knew he had been excited, though nervous. He didn't need to hear her criticism of U.S. foreign policy. She loved her brother, even though they had lived such different lives. She hadn't tried to change his mind about anything. And she would wonder for the rest of her life how things might have turned out if she had.

She was the big sister, for God's sake. She was *supposed* to offer guidance. She was *supposed* to tell her little bro what she thought. But she'd been afraid to. She'd let him down, and he was gone.

Who was she kidding? You couldn't talk Marshall into or out of anything. All she would have done was piss him off. Maybe this was the toughest thing to admit: that she'd had no impact whatsoever on his fate. She was a tiny, insignificant footnote in another person's story. Insignificance felt even worse than guilt.

She didn't trust the official and very abbreviated story the army had provided her family. Things didn't add up, and she couldn't get anyone from his unit to talk to her. Why had a regular e-mailer like Marshall (amazingly regular, considering the responsibilities he had) stopped sending his family messages a week before his KIA date? And why had his blog been taken down six days before his KIA date, as opposed to afterward? She'd heard that soldiers could get in trouble for posting certain things. After the army banned soldier blogs, he'd taken down his old blog, but then he'd launched a new, anonymous one—he'd mentioned the link to Tasha on one of their rare calls, but in an offhand manner, as if he knew people were listening. Had he gotten himself in trouble with the army or with someone else?

Maybe she was just grasping for something to be angry at. Maybe she just needed an enemy. *We all do, don't we?* she thought.

She wished the firm didn't demand all of her waking hours (and more). With what little free time she had—usually at two in the morning, when she couldn't sleep—she had started the project of finding and compiling all of Marshall's old e-mails and blog entries and journals, trying to shape them into some kind of memoir or book in his name. Which meant she needed more detail from the army about what had happened to him. She knew her parents didn't fully believe the official story either, but they were hesitant to push. Well, she would push—that was a big sister's job, even if she wasn't really a big sister anymore. She vowed as she stood there watching the march that she'd find out what exactly had happened, even if she had to call every press office in the armed services, even if she had to track down every soldier in Marshall's platoon.

She needed to have an effect on something. She stood there as the ex-hippies and college kids marched past, some of them chanting as they tried to merge themselves into something greater. Over to her right a smaller group of Support the Troops boosters waved American flags, holding their own signs and mocking the "Commies," telling them to go back to old Europe, decrying their misguided rage and weakness.

She stepped forward and joined the flow of protest, let it carry her. She didn't want to be alone for this anymore. She didn't know if marching did anything at all, but she would try it.

The day had started cloudy and was only getting grayer as it aged; the Capitol dome seemed to glow in contrast. Tasha marched with the crowd to the steps of the Capitol, read the pamphlets that were passed out, and ignored her cell phone as it buzzed and buzzed at her. She listened to the speakers, some of whom were inspiring and some of whom ranted about the environment and racial inequality and every other conceivable grievance of the Left, totally irrelevant to the war except within the tangent-happy interrelatedness of the orators' minds. People were bringing whatever of themselves they could into the cause. The cause was enormous, sprawling; it contained multitudes. It was as ugly and yearning and flawed as human nature, and at times she felt embarrassed to be a part of it. But at least she was a part of something. As her outraged cell phone continued to buzz as if it had its own violent opinion, she stood there, sublimating herself to this unnamed thing, this unified hope or harmonic rage, and tried to stop thinking about those GTK files.

A few nights later she found herself at a meeting of antiwar activists. According to one of the pamphlets at the march, the activist group was hosting a meeting to "channel this weekend's energy toward concrete and comprehensive goals." Tasha was down with concrete goals. Part of her trouble since Marshall had died was the lack of goals, the lack of energy, the plain not knowing what to do with herself.

The name of the group was Peace Now and Forever. That sounded rather utopian to Tasha, but maybe she was wrong to disparage those with lofty aspirations. So many people settled for the easy win these days, you had to tip your hat to those aiming higher, even if you knew they would miss.

The meeting was held at a small, damp Sunday-school room at the Baptist Holiness Church in Shaw. Yellow Rorschach stains from water damage decorated the ceiling, and the windowless white walls were adorned with religious drawings from the local child artists: the sun rising on the empty cave Christ had fled, multiplied fishes and loaves heaped on picnic tables, Saint George decapitating a dragon with one mighty stroke.

The different speakers told the audience about opportunities to volunteer for this letter-writing project or that PR campaign, to sit in on and possibly interfere with congressional hearings on the war, to screen documentaries at local apartments, to organize teach-ins and "spread the truth about the administration's global goals." Then a couple of "visiting economics professors" (likely unemployed) gave a long, meandering lecture about "world capitalism's master plan for the subjugated people of the Middle East." Tasha tried not to fall asleep as she sat there listening to old white men discuss how the free marketeers had deliberately seeded chaos in Baghdad, just like they did in New Orleans after Katrina and in South Asia after the tsunami; even supposedly random events like meteorological disasters were ascribed to a nefarious cabal's master plan. If the making of legislation and sausage were two things you just did not want to witness, Tasha thought, the same seemed to be true of world peace. This was some seriously tedious shit.

After the fortunately not endless (it only seemed that way) lecture, the two profs sat down. Then, to Tasha's surprise, she found herself looking at one of her college boyfriends.

The new speaker was T.J., a veritable supernova from her freshman winter and spring. They'd lasted nearly a semester, hooking up during a snowstorm in February and breaking up on a lily-speckled quad in May. He'd transferred that summer, and she'd never heard from him again. Now here he was, taking the stage like he owned it, telling the audience about his own related group. They were conducting an anti-recruitment project, in which activists would visit high schools and "hit kids with the truth about being a soldier," the things that military recruiters would never tell them. For every recruiter who tempted teens with stories of honor and dignity and getting a good education, T.J. explained, an activist needed to tell America's impressionable youth about the prevalence of PTSD among returning soldiers, about the squalid conditions at VA hospitals and the army's lack of interest in its wounded veterans, about the human cost of militarized murder. And of course they had to tell kids about "the real reasons for the wars," which, he said in such an offhand way as to defy even polite disagreement, were gravely immoral indeed. Tasha tried to imagine what Marshall would have thought about an appeal like this.

T.J. made eye contact with her in the middle of his appeal, and a brief smile graced his lips. How long had it been, nine years? She had to admit: He looked *good*. Boy had great bones, a Hollywood face, plenty of planes for a cinematographer to light up from different angles. His hair was natty, the harbinger of dreadlocks, the tips slightly bleached, as if he'd changed his mind halfway through the process. He had dark skin and green eyes that shone with a certain playfulness, even when he was talking about "the atrocities committed by our military."

She hadn't thought of him in years, but now that she saw him, she realized it wasn't surprising to find him in a place like this. He'd been a constant irritant to their college during his one year there, leading protests at the administration building over the school's paltry financial aid packages, its anti-union policies toward the janitorial staff, and its bloody-fingered investments in crooked multinational corporations.

Her confusion and nervousness about what she was doing here built. Were these people good and well-meaning, sacrificing their time like this, willing to make themselves look like fools? Or *were* they fools, just plain crazy and angry, looking for any excuse to pick a fight with a world they didn't understand? Seeing T.J. made it all the harder to sit there through the whole rigmarole, the reports and the minutes, the grudging way the organizers allowed anyone with a raised hand to speak his or her piece, even if it meant listening to some old lady go on and on and on with no discernible point.

Finally, when the meeting ended and a few people coalesced into "planning groups" for the different events they were orchestrating, Tasha walked up to T.J. and said hi. She was hesitant, but he smiled at her as if the last decade had never been, wrapped her in a hug, and called out, "My girl! What's up?" He immediately asked if she was free for a drink, like, now.

"So," he asked as they sat at the bar of Busboys and Poets, off U, "is that you who writes the Ask Tasha part of the *Word on the Street*? I've read those wondering if it could be the same Tasha I knew back in the day."

A few years ago she'd started writing a very intermittent column for one of D.C.'s arts weeklies. It was political comedy of sorts, modeled on advice columns, and Tasha crafted both the Qs and the As. "Dear Tasha, I just discovered that my husband voted the opposite ticket as I did. Would it be wrong of me to withhold sex for the next four years?" "Dear Tasha, I'm convinced that the cable guy at my house today was actually a CIA spy planting bugs. Should I cancel my anarchist book club this week?" "Dear Tasha, I'm a Dem but the Republican across the street from me is smokin' hot. Can you recommend any GOP pickup lines, or would it be more politically pure for me to masturbate while watching her out the window?" It had started during the slow months of her final year at GW Law, an occasional thing she'd done for an old friend who edited the paper, and it had grown into a needed escape from her humor-impaired job. She hadn't written a column in a few months, though.

"Maybe not the exact same Tasha," she said, "but pretty much. The same DNA, at least."

"I'm happy to see it," he said, and she noticed him giving her a quick once-over, really a twice-over because she'd caught him doing it once already. "I loved the one about the staffer with the unnatural crush on the sidewalk *Politico* dispenser."

"Thanks." She'd wanted to be a writer but had gone to law school instead. Her parents, a high-school history teacher and a manager at the water company, had worked too hard for their daughter to waste their money, or her own fat loans, on an English degree. All through law school she had consoled herself that once she was finished, she could write stories in her free time. But then she'd started at the firm and realized that there was no free time; it all had to be billed.

She and T.J. caught up on the last nine years. He'd taken some time off from college after leaving Oberlin, then enrolled at Reed for a year, or maybe it was two, he couldn't remember anymore— he'd been a bit too into drugs at that point. After detoxing, he'd built houses in various ghettos for Habitat. Next came Peace Corps in Moldova, for only a few months, as local Mafia strongmen extorted protection money from the office and made uncomfortable propositions to the female workers, prompting the organization at home to evacuate the volunteers early. His adventures since then he rendered in careful snapshots: helping a buddy film a documentary on Chiapas (had she seen it?) while crossing the line between video journalist and guerrilla activist; a year in LA spent working in vain against one of those California propositions that basically made it illegal to be Latino; a few months with a traveling impromptu-art group that projected poetry onto skyscrapers and government buildings; rock-throwing protests at WTO meetings in Seattle, D.C., and New York. Currently, he explained with mock humbleness, he was a mild-mannered bike messenger zipping at supersonic speed between foreign embassies, Hill offices, and the evil headquarters of the World Bank and IMF by day and a superhero activist saving the world one good deed at a time by night.

His black T-shirt proclaimed, in alternating red, white, and blue letters, NOT A SHAREHOLDER, and his shoulder bag was armored with political buttons (STOP TORTURE; LOGO-FREE ZONE; END THE CORPORATIST STATE; I'M ALREADY AGAINST THE NEXT WAR). On the right side of T.J.'s neck was the tattoo of what was perhaps an Asian character, or maybe an Egyptian glyph. It hadn't been there in the days when she'd traced her tongue on that skin.

She put the tab on her credit card, violating chivalry partly out of goodwill and partly because his income bracket seemed several rungs below hers. She wasn't sure if this should make her feel beneficent or guilty for being condescending.

"Few years ago," he said, gesturing to the plastic that the bartender had taken from her hand, possibly needing this story as a distraction from any male shame at letting her pay, "I remember reading that the CEO of some credit card company said their goal was to eliminate cash. Completely eliminate it—everyone would use plastic, for even the tiniest purchases. All the while paying those invisible fees and the interest. When I told people about it, they all laughed, *Yeah, right, it'll never happen.* And now, maybe five years later, tell me, how much cash you got in that stylish purse?"

"I think seven bucks."

"See? It worked, faster 'n they thought."

"So next you're gonna tell me you hoard gold? You got three months of canned goods stored in your basement for when the revolution comes?"

He smiled. "Gold's for gangsta rappers. And no on the canned goods, but only because I refuse to follow the Homeland Security advice, the duct tape and all that. Although, honestly, it's probably a good idea, but not for the reasons they're thinking."

It was amazing how it all flooded back. Not just the memories of their brief time together, but the whole collegiate energy, the anger at the rotten world, the desire to remake it. Even the smallest decision—going vegetarian (for one year) to save a few hundred animals or boycotting clothing chains that used sweatshops—seemed to carry enormous moral weight. Years later, she still considered herself a politically engaged citizen, but full-grown adults who even mentioned sweatshops tended to sound like teenagers chanting slogans at a rock concert, and people who didn't eat meat were a bitch to plan around at dinner parties. Bringing up the plight of the oppressed sounded ridiculous when buying five-hundred-thousand-dollar row houses in what had recently been dilapidated neighborhoods.

And here T.J. was, someone who'd made all the opposite choices she had: living off the grid, still dressing like a grungy college student, and crashing at a group house in Columbia Heights (only a few blocks from the very neighborhood she and her family had fled for the safety of the suburbs), while she in her Prada slingbacks and boutique jeans sipped her fifteen-dollar Belgian beer. Modern living made you choose between your morality and your desire to fit in, to not be a freak. But what if the freaks were right?

She just wanted something to believe, or believe in. It seemed such a modest goal, yet was anything but. *What do I really believe? That the government unjustly started these wars for the oil that enables my lifestyle, that they sent my brother to die and covered up various profit-minded plots? Or that our country is a benign force for good, and Marshall died a hero trying to bring peace to an area whose years of wars had sent out long trails of destruction that led to deaths here on September 11 and that will inevitably lead to even more unless we take the fight to them?* Which was the naive view, and which the pragmatic one? She felt like some displaced fairy-tale heroine in search of the one shoe that would fit perfectly and solve all her troubles, or at least make it easier to walk on this constantly shifting terrain.

"So other than those columns, are you doing any writing?" he asked. "I seem to remember you were going to be a famous novelist."

"Nah, that's just *my* superhero thing. My Clark Kent is being a lawyer."

"Knowing a lawyer is always good when you're arrested as much as I am."

"Seriously?"

"What, you thought that was a pickup line?" He laughed. "We were picketing one of Hellwater's training camps in South Carolina, filming a documentary. Cut through some razor wire, got shot at." He pulled his right foot onto the lower rung of his bar stool and rolled up his pants leg. It was dark in the bar but she could make out something gruesome above his ankle. "German shepherd did that."

"Jesus Christ."

"Jail doctor stitched it for me, many hours later. The worst part is they stole our film and cameras, but we're thinking of maybe doing a re-creation instead, like a political version of *Cops*."

"You do walk the walk, don't you?"

"I was limping the limp for a couple weeks."

By her second drink, the music on the house stereo had become indefinably better, the beats echoing those of Tasha's heart. Which only made her wonder: How much fun was she allowed to have anymore? She was tired of wondering that. Everyone else seemed so damn insulated from what was happening. She was raw.

Then T.J. asked after her parents, and Tasha lied, said they were doing fine, thanks.

"That brother of yours still getting into trouble?"

There could have been no starker reminder of how much had

changed in the nine years since she'd seen T.J. When they were fresh-
men, she now remembered, Marshall was a high-school junior at risk
of flunking out. He was hanging with the wrong crowd, enraging his
parents and big sister with each decreasingly minor scrape with the
law. And now: "He's dead."

T.J. looked like he thought he'd misheard her, the music was so
loud, or maybe he thought he was being fucked with. But then his
smile vanished.

"Oh, Jesus. I'm sorry. What happened?"

"Preemptive war happened."

No matter how people reacted to the news, she always hated the
reactions.

"He was in the army?"

She nodded.

"Jesus, Tash, I'm so sorry."

She sipped her drink so she wouldn't have to think up a response
to "I'm so sorry."

"Your parents really okay?"

"What do you think?"

He didn't say anything, belatedly realizing the minefield he'd
walked into, afraid to take another step. She regretted sounding so
harsh.

"My dad hated the idea of Marshall enlisting, tried to talk him
out of it. He didn't realize he was only pushing Marshall toward the
recruitment office. Once he'd enlisted and we all showed up for the
ceremony, we had to accept it. Honestly, it was good for Marshall. I
mean..." What *did* she mean? How could it be good for someone if it
ultimately kills him? Just because it turned his life around, kept him
out of trouble, helped him grow up? Can final moments negate everything that happened beforehand? Or is the life preceding the death
all that matters? "He grew up a lot. I was proud of him. I am proud
of him."

T.J. took the hand that she'd left lying atop the table. She wished
he hadn't.

"Anyway," she said, a word she'd been employing often, a way to end conversations, or re-steer them, or just throw up a roadblock: thou shalt not pass this marker. "Sorry, I didn't mean to bring this all up. I was having a pretty good time."

"Me too."

She squeezed his hand and then took hers back.

"So," he said, hesitantly restarting, "you came to the meeting tonight because of what happened to your brother?"

"I came because I'm trying to figure things out. Life used to make just enough sense for me to get by. But now, just like that, it doesn't." She shook her head. "You and I probably have a lot of different opinions, but... I envy your certainty. You're certain that things are crooked and that we're all pawns and that we need to act now before it's too late. I don't know that I want you to be right, but I do wish I had that kind of certainty. About anything."

"I don't have everything figured out, Tasha."

"Well, you fake it very well."

"I remember once you called me a very skilled actor. At the time I was so full of myself I took it as a compliment."

She smiled. Then suddenly she felt like she was going to cry. She made herself cough, to cover it up.

"I'm just a skeptical bastard," he said, looking at the few remaining people in the bar, and the empty street beyond them. "I don't trust people. I'm always looking for the angle. When *I* see people who seem certain, like fundamentalists who insist that Jesus or Allah will find a way and that we're all a part of a *plan*—fundamentalists in Baghdad or Tulsa, it's all the same thing—I think *they're* crazy. I'm too skeptical of them." He shrugged, looking back at her. "But maybe I need to be more skeptical of people like me too."

"I was trying to compliment you."

"Look, if you do want to help out in the anti-recruitment thing, or anything else, let me know; I'm involved in a lot of different projects. Or if there's anything I can do to help you, really, let me know."

She thanked him. That appeared to be their cue to leave, but she found herself taking another sip of the drink she hadn't planned on finishing.

"Here's something you can do: answer a question. Let's say, totally hypothetically speaking, that you had a job that allowed you to come across very privileged information. Stuff that wouldn't interest most people. And also you've taken a vow never to disclose anything relating to your clients. But one day you read something about one of your clients, something very damning. Something that makes them look very bad—hell, something that *is* very bad. Secrets. You know that if you took it to the press, it would be a major story. That it would get bad people in trouble. But doing that could cost you your job, and maybe worse."

"Secrets that compromise whom? And what kind of secrets? Financial disclosures, marital infidelity, the ingredients of someone's special sauce, murder?"

"Kind of the first thing and maybe kind of the last thing."

"Murder."

"Not really. But decisions that put lives at stake."

"*Put* as in past or *put* as in present? What tense we talking here?"

Hell, that was an excellent question. She hadn't thought of that. She had been so focused on what happened to Marshall, so irate at these middle managers who'd made decisions that put troops' lives—including her brother's life—at risk, that she hadn't even considered the fact that such business dealings were likely ongoing. Which meant that blowing the whistle wouldn't just expose past wrongdoing but also prevent future wrongdoing. It would save lives.

"I guess both."

He held out his two palms as if he were the impartial scales of justice. "So you got other people's lives here, and you've got your own job here." He wobbled the hands up and down for a second. "I think you can guess how I'd judge that one. But it's not my job we're talking about."

She finished her drink. God, she must be drunk to even mention this, however elliptically, to anyone, let alone someone she really didn't know anymore. Yet what he'd said had helped.

He motioned to her empty glass and asked if she wanted another round.

"Love to, but some of us have to work tomorrow."

"I work. I just don't have to think much at my job, other than trying to predict when a car is going to switch lanes without signaling."

Outside, she wondered if T.J. would make a move for a goodnight smooch, and she wasn't sure if she was relieved or disappointed when he didn't. (God, when had she become so uncertain about *everything?* But now there was one thing she was less uncertain about.) They traded phone numbers, shared a quick good-bye hug along with vague plans to reconnect, then she hailed a cab. During the ride home, she plotted her next move. Suddenly, she had a long night ahead of her.

She walked straight upstairs to her second bedroom, opened the file cabinets, and reached for the buried folder she'd randomly labeled ADDTL. INSURANCE. Inside were *the files*—the offending GTK e-mails, which she'd secretly copied and ferried out of the building the Monday after she'd stumbled upon them. Copies of those files had remained in her apartment for days, tempting her with their illicit knowledge. The e-mails that, as Jill had noted, were not relevant to their case. The e-mails that merely revealed their client's decision to put extra profit over its contractual—and could she add patriotic?—obligation to outfit U.S. troops as quickly and fully as possible. Dated six months earlier, when Marshall had been alive. The two issues were not related, Jill had argued, and maybe she was right. Except Marshall had been alive once and things had made a certain sort of sense, and now neither was true.

And maybe, Jill, everything is related.

Still buzzing but hopefully not drunk (sober enough to drive, but perhaps not sober enough to make potentially life-altering decisions), she drove a few blocks to the sketchy copy place on Pennsylvania. Risking suspicion by wearing leather gloves the whole time (not that the dudes at the desk paid any attention to her other than giving her the up-down when she first walked in), Tasha made new copies and bought a package of envelopes. There was a reporter for the *New York Times* whose work she admired. He would find this information interesting.

She heard the law school professors in her head reminding her that this was a clear violation of attorney-client privilege. If caught, she would be fired, and likely disbarred. She tried to imagine disbarment, with all the loans she still needed to pay back for all those law school professors' advice. But this was more important than that.

And, really, she was smart enough to get away with it.

Outside the sketchy copy place was a blue mailbox, sitting there patiently like it had been waiting all its life for this little contribution to justice and democracy. Tasha opened the lid and slid the envelope into its depths.

Z.

After my ill-advised trip to the playground, I still have some time to kill (what a wonderful and terrible phrase! And, for me, so literal) before the next Event, so I drive through the leafy neighborhoods of Capitol Hill. Black men stand on corners, white women push strollers, Latinos paint the row houses or fix their roofs. Amazing how specified the races are to their tasks.

I pull over at the corner of 15th and E Street SE. A few buildings down, on the left, is the house belonging to Tasha Wilson. The street is quiet and residential, just removed enough from the main thoroughfares to be free of pedestrians at this pre–rush hour. I focus my eyes on the second-floor window of her row house, and my internal microphone locks on the spot. At first I hear only silence, which I should have expected, given that it's late afternoon and she's probably at work. But then I hear her muttering to herself. She talks in a sigh, all exhalation, like she's angry at herself for talking, some reflexive inner madness. She's coaching herself, I realize, reciting what she's going to say when making an important call.

I activate my embedded router to tap her phone. I hear the dial tone, the flat music of her touch-tone keys, then the buzzing pulse. A young woman answers the line.

"Hello, may I speak to Aurelio Gomez?" Tasha asks.

"I ask who's calling?"

"My name is Tasha Wilson, and my brother, Marshall, led Private Gomez's unit until a few months ago. I was hoping to talk to him about Marshall's experience if I could."

A pause. Someone exhales, though I can't tell who. "He doesn't need to be talking about that right now."

"Ma'am, please, I'd just—"

"He needs to be left alone for a while, all right? He doesn't need to be bothered by—"

"My brother died over there. I just want to talk to the people who knew him last."

Another pause. "I'm very sorry about your brother."

"Thank you."

"Aurelio's not here. And, honestly, I don't know that he wants to be talking about that sort of thing, at least not right now. But I'll give him the message. Good enough?"

"Yes, thank you." Tasha gives the woman her name, e-mail address, and two phone numbers. "Please tell him he can get in touch with me anytime."

"What did you say your brother's name was?"

"Lieutenant Marshall Wilson. He was killed June eleventh."

The sound of handwriting. "I'm sorry for your loss. I thank God every day that my man's back for good."

"Is he doing all right?"

"Day at a time, you know? But he's gonna be okay."

They chat for another moment, then hang up. Listening in on the microphone, I hear Tasha writing something, I hear her take deep breaths, mutter to herself, place another call. Again it is answered by a woman, this one older; again Tasha asks for a man; again she is asked why and she delivers her speech.

"Ricky's at Walter Reed, miss. He's going to be there for a while."

"Oh, I didn't know. I'm sorry to hear that. How is he?"

"He's going to be fine." Interesting how they respond to present-tense questions with future-tense answers.

"Was he, um, you wouldn't know if June eleventh was the day he was injured?"

"I don't know. Why do you ask?"

85

Tasha explains the date's relevance. I can tell that, for her, every day of her life will be measured by its distance from last June 11.

You are haunted by your past, Tasha. It casts its pall over everything you do. I wish you could see my time, the world I'm from, the advances we've made. I wish I could stop you from wasting more of your life, chasing after a past that cannot be restored. I wish I could see your face right now, wish my technology was that advanced, but all I can do is stare at that brick wall and listen to your voice and try to imagine the rest.

"You're welcome to call Ricky, and he'll try to help you if he can. He's a great kid. But I hope you're really doing the best thing here."

"...I'm not sure I follow."

"I lost a brother once too. In Vietnam. So I know what you're going through. And I still miss him, every day. But nothing I did could bring him back."

"I understand that." Tasha doesn't so much speak those words as bite at them.

"I'm very sorry, miss. I wish these things never happened. I wish God didn't test us with so much evil in the world, but He does. I do hope you find a way to come to some peace."

Tasha's voice sounds different when she says thank you, and then they hang up. This time there's a much longer pause before she's able to make another call.

A few houses down, a man in khaki military regalia opens the front door and comes out. He's holding a briefcase in one hand and in the other a metal rod, at the end of which is a small circular mirror. He walks down the sidewalk and stops at a silver SUV. He crouches down beside it, telescopes the rod out a few feet, and slides it under the car. Checks it, moves it back a few feet, checks it again. He does the same thing on the other side. He stands up, dusts off his knees, and only then does he get in the SUV and drive away. People are so frightened here.

Tasha dials Walter Reed Army Medical Center, a local call that's routed from one corner to the other of the fractured diamond that is

D.C. She's transferred between operators and nurses before an impatient young man answers.

"Yeah?"

"Hello, I'm trying to reach Sergeant Velasquez?"

"Who?"

"I was told Sergeant Ricky Velasquez was in this room."

"Nah, he's been transferred. Yesterday I think."

"Oh. Um, do you know where I can find him?"

"No clue, lady. Look, I don't even know why I answered." Then the line goes dead.

Silence for a while inside her apartment. Then the off-tempo percussion of a keyboard, and I switch to my wireless function, tap into her account. She's online, reading Web sites about the military, blogs run by veterans and their families. So much information here! But why, Tasha? Does this bring you peace? I read along with her for nearly an hour, only an occasional pedestrian walking past my car, and none of them ever look at me. They're used to people loitering in cars here, apparently. They're used to being watched.

I should leave. But first I tap an unused line and call Tasha.

"Hello?"

"Hi, Tasha? This is Troy Jones. We met outside the White House last night?"

"Yeah, hi, how are you?"

"Just bored at work. I thought I should call and see if we could set a date, unless you've decided that having dinner with that strange man is a bad idea after all."

"I have had bad ideas from time to time," she says, and I hear her smile, my little gift to her after the stressful calls, "but dinner would be good."

She names a restaurant downtown, and I say I'll be there. This is very against the rules. Just calling her like this is bad. But I wanted to put a smile on her lips.

I mention an article I just read, something about soldiers and the war, some diatribe from a political journal about veterans' lack of decent benefits. Of course, I just read it because she just read it, and I was there over her shoulder.

"Wait, the one in *Mother Jones?*" she asks. "That's so weird—I read that story a second ago myself."

"Wow, really? I must have been sending telepathic messages."

"I literally was just printing a copy. That's so funny."

I want to ask her, *What is it like? To push, and push, and push, and not feel that wall budging in the slightest?* Maybe she thinks she *is* making the wall move, but really what's happening is her feet are slipping from beneath her. It's been my job, for longer than I care to remember, to keep that wall standing, to bolster it on the other side of people like her. I've never really understood them, but I want to.

We chat about her government for a couple of minutes. I'm probably not following everything, but I do a good enough job.

"Anyway, I should get back to work," I tell her. "Take it easy."

"Yeah, you too." And there's no way to be sure, but I swear she's still smiling.

I sit there for a few more seconds, and Tasha gets another call.

She picks it up on the third ring, even though she's probably sitting next to it. Maybe she has caller ID, doesn't recognize the number. Or perhaps no number shows up on her screen, confusing her.

"Hello?"

"Good afternoon, Ms. Wilson. I didn't expect to find you at home at this hour."

"To whom am I speaking?"

"I'm someone who would very much like to meet with you as soon as your busy schedule allows," he says. The voice sounds middle-aged. It is calm and seems to be faking friendliness. "I'd like to discuss GTK Industries."

Silence for two seconds, three. "All questions about GTK should go through my employer, at their office in Washington," Tasha says. "Their number is—"

"This question does not relate to your firm's official business with GTK. It relates to more ... extracurricular matters."

Again she is slow to respond. When she does, she is professional and polished, but it sounds like an act to me. Surely it sounds that way to him too. "I'm really not sure what you're referring to, but, again, the attorneys handling GTK would be happy to answer—"

"You do not want me calling your firm with this information, Ms. Wilson. That would be very bad for you and your career. Not to mention your ability to walk about as a free woman."

Another pause. I can hear breathing, probably hers.

Her voice is less strong than before, and there's a bit of a tremor that she can't quite contain. "I really don't know what—"

"You *do* know what this is about." Still calm, his voice is ever so slightly louder than before, just to show her he does not have limitless patience. "And if you'd like me to mention it on the phone like this, I'd be happy to. Lord only knows who is listening these days. But I think a face-to-face chat would be more in your interest? You assume I'm your enemy here, which is understandable. But I have a little mercy in me, and if you're smart you can play into that. Understood?"

An even longer silence than before. I wish I could see her, wish I could help her. But that's not my job.

"Sir, though I'm still confused as to the nature of this call, I'd be happy to have a meeting so I can clear up any misunderstandings."

Ever the attorney, doing what she can to cover herself. I want to applaud, even if she's losing badly.

"Excellent. Let's meet tomorrow afternoon. At the Topaz Bar, near Logan Circle. Two o'clock work for you?"

"Sure. Who will I be looking for?"

But he's already hung up. And it's time for me to protect the next Event.

It sounds like the introduction to a bad joke from this century: a Saudi Arabian and a Chinese walk into a coffee shop. But the punch line is still a few weeks away.

They stand in a long queue separated by a half dozen political staffers, lobbyists, and underpaid strivers for nonprofit organizations. It is four o'clock in the afternoon, a time when normal people are not choosing to recharge their systems with steaming cups of Brazilian or Javanese energy. But these aren't normal people; they're all trying to change the world, one way or another. They are idealists and utopians, Machiavellians and madmen. Some of them are working in concert, others in opposition, so many actions and plans and strategies neutralized by the other sides, by their enemies, by a world careening too quickly in one direction to respond well to sudden twists of the steering wheel. Their world-changing is tiring work indeed, and this particular branch of the Starbucks global empire does smashing business.

Across the street from us the ornately carved Library of Congress looms like the fortress of an even earlier time, its thick walls protecting the illuminated manuscripts from the plebeians, who would rather check their e-mail anyway. It seems I am surrounded by text in this city. Even without my seeking it out, it haunts me, hovers in the background, is invisibly sent from one handheld to another. I am a mere punctuation mark—we all are—in stories someone else is writing. Or has already written. Because, once again, I know the lines before they're spoken: The Chinese is in the front, ordering a cappuccino, specifying his preference for soy milk. Perhaps he is more enlightened than his fellow contemps when it comes to consuming animals and their body fluids. In the back of the line is the Saudi, hands fidgeting inside the deep pockets of his finely tailored suit. He pretends not to recognize the bald moon in the middle of that round head at the front of the line; the Chinese now turns in profile to take his beverage to the sweetening kiosk. The Saudi stares straight ahead while the Chinese finds a table in the corner.

The Chinese sips his drink and plays with his PDA. He wears a crisp white shirt with red and blue stripes, and on his cuff links are tiny stars, as if his wardrobe is a deconstructed flag of this country where he lives and works. He operates under cover as the administrator of a group dedicated to "freeing Tibet" and keeping China's influence out of Taiwan, and he diligently reports back to his mother country on the developments within the organization. His watch is very expensive and he never looks at it.

When the Saudi finally reaches a point within earshot of the baristas, an American is added to the joke: a large but not quite fat man with unkempt dark hair and a beard, an ex–football player who isn't as skilled at blending in as these other two. He sits down—sans beverage—and shakes the Chinese's hand, and then the Saudi joins them. The American's back is to me, the Saudi is in profile, and the Chinese would be looking right at me if he could see through the American, which he probably can.

It is amazing how openly such important and secret information is exchanged here. There is no need of darkened hallways, windowless rooms, passwords. Either they know that people are watching and are so used to it that they've developed ways to operate on several levels, or they're confident that they're being protected by people even more powerful than the ones pursuing them. Either way, it's very different from the other beats I've worked, requiring me to come out before the sun has set, revealing myself to the view of countless contemps. The Department won't like it, but without a GeneScan it's the only way I can protect this Event.

The Saudi is the youngest of the three, the scion of a powerful family with varied business interests in America. He lives here on a student visa that has no expiration date, and he hasn't taken a course in years; he has, however, sampled more than a few coeds in that time, and his trimly bearded face is a fixture at parties and bars along M Street.

If the coffee shop were less busy, I would be able to hear them, but if it were less busy they wouldn't have chosen this spot. Instead of hearing what they say, I am treated to alternating snippets of conversation from the closer tables. A young white woman with an electric frizz of hair is impressing upon an older man the importance of investing in Guatemala and El Salvador at this particular moment. Two young men in fashionable suits try not to flirt with each other too obviously as they show each other images on their cell phones. An elderly couple consults the map of D.C. they've laid on their table, debating which sites their sore arches can tolerate getting to.

I'm wearing a blue Nationals hat that I bought from a street vendor pulled just low enough to help me evade detection without drawing suspicion. I stare vacantly at a *Post* that has been left behind by someone unconcerned with the violence and love and despair its reporters are so desperately trying to convey. There's nothing about Mr. Chaudhry's disappearance yet; it will show up in the day after tomorrow's edition.

I aim my internal microphone at the three men's table without looking at them, which is difficult to do. The microphone cuts through the noise around us.

AMERICAN: We see ourselves as being in the predictability business. It's our job to eliminate unpredictability, eliminate spontaneity. Spontaneity is destabilizing; it causes unforeseen problems. With our product, you never have to worry about unforeseen problems, that something will pop up to derail your plans, disrupt your agenda. We create predictability, which means creating a monopoly, which means you, our client, alone on top. Now, as Salem's testimonial shows, our product is the most complete either on or off the market.

CHINESE: Is there some way to test the product against what we currently use, in order to be sure that this really adds value?

AMERICAN: We do have a few demonstrations we could show you, but that would need to occur on-site. We'd need visas to get in.

CHINESE: That wouldn't be a problem.

SAUDI: You should tell him about that new application, you know, the one we started using last month. It's been amazing.

They make it sound so bland. The American hands his current customer and his future one sheets of charts and bars. At least he takes a quick scan of the room before doing so, and he's careful to keep them flat on the table, lest any photographer be hiding across the street.

Because I already know what's happening, I don't need to watch them very closely and can instead focus on the others in the room, the people walking by on the sidewalk. The hags should be here, at least one of them. This meeting is so important, despite the outwardly dull, pinstriped trappings. How could the hags be letting this go so smoothly?

The elderly couple is bickering now: He is tired of museums and wants to pay his respects at Arlington Cemetery tomorrow, but she replies that they spend quite enough time in graveyards as it is, and wouldn't it be better to see the Monets? The stylish young men are slinging their bags over their well-sculpted shoulders, having decided they are sufficiently caffeinated to begin their all-night consumption of more exciting beverages. And at the only table that matters historically, the Chinese spy nods at something the American contractor says, taking out his PDA once again, typing numbers that the Archivists will pore over so many years later.

I look outside and see no suspicious loiterers on the sidewalk. On Third, two young women walking dogs have been chatting—I don't like how stationary they are, but they don't look like they're hags—and finally they break up their conversation and go their separate ways. I can now see, previously concealed behind them, a man in a parked car.

His face is so colorless, almost waxy. I'm tired of being surrounded by corpses. People from my time aren't usually as dark or as white as most of the contemps here, but then again, hags tend to come from those groups that are most resistant to mixing, that have stubbornly clung to their outdated beliefs.

I give the trio of conspirators one final glance as they continue to discuss this excellent business opportunity. Then I walk outside.

A taxi heads toward the Capitol; an announcer on a tour bus regales me with factoids as the bus sits at a red light. An apparently homeless woman offers to sell me a special newspaper about people like her (how varied and bizarre is all this printed matter!), but I shake her off. An athletic-looking man with FEDERAL MARSHAL printed on the back of his navy blue jumpsuit stands at a corner patiently nodding at his phone as he looks up the street, then down it. I watch his reflection in the Starbucks window, and the reflection crosses the street.

If the hag in the car were smarter, he would have done something to disrupt this meeting before it happened, maybe kill one of the three men on his way here. Could he perhaps have grander things in mind, a triple killing? But not out in the open—that would run contrary to their goals. He's probably planning on following one of them, likely the American, because his role in the Conflagration is the largest.

I wait for pedestrian traffic to dissipate, then I approach the parked car from behind. The engine is still idling; is he hoping to run one of them down? I carefully take off my jacket and drape it over my arm, then I remove the gun from its pocket, keeping it hidden. I open the hag's unlocked passenger door and slide in.

"Keep your hands on the steering wheel," I tell him. The jacket conceals the gun from everyone's view but his—the barrel is staring at his chest. He stares back at it, then at me. With my right hand I pull the door shut.

"You can have the car, I just—"

"Shut up. I know who you are. Drive south, now."

He stares straight ahead with wide, panicked eyes. Maybe he's trying to trick me into thinking he's a contemp. I cock the gun to scare him into action and he pulls onto the road. He looks to be in his midtwenties; he sounds congested and his eyes are red, as if he's having a hard time adjusting to the new beat.

He manages to drive, slowly and hesitantly, and I direct him through a few residential blocks and beneath the highway underpass. Beyond this is a series of construction sites; older neighborhoods are being dynamited and bulldozed to make way for progress.

I tell him to pull over in a narrow side street, where we're boxed in between the last remaining brick wall of an almost demolished apartment building and a stretch of dumpsters filled with debris. "Turn off the engine and put the keys on the center of the dashboard."

He obeys, and then he gives up the innocent-contemp act. "You have a very strange job." He still stares ahead, as if unwilling to look at me. "You're killing everyone around us."

"They're already going to die. I'm not the one doing it."

"Except, if you stepped back and let us do what we're trying to do, they'd all live."

"You want to have a philosophical argument? Fine. You can run around this time thinking you're a savior, but all you're doing is prolonging an awful era, decades and decades of war and strife. Hatred begetting hatred. The Conflagration accelerated things—it was terrible, yes, but the end result was our Perfect Society. *That* is what I protect."

"You're delusional, like the rest of them."

"*Who's* delusional? You and your little martyrs are fools pretending to be heroes."

"The Perfect Society, huh?" He finally looks at me. "The land of milk and honey? Where no one wants for anything, and people dance in the streets holding hands?"

"We've come a long way. There are difficulties sometimes, but try comparing it to anything else you can imagine. Compare it to anything else that came before and—"

"I would *love* to make comparisons, but we can't, can we? Because all records of the past are kept under lock and key by your bosses. So whose word do we have that our society is so perfect? Oh yeah, the Government's word."

"If you're trying to recruit me, you're wasting your time."

"*Wasting time*—what a funny concept."

"Let's pretend for a minute that I can see your side of the argument," I say, the gun still pointed at him. "Let's pretend that our Perfect Society isn't worth the sacrifice. Or that I'm sick of doing this, and I really *want* to believe you. I could prevent the Great Conflagration, could remove billions of lives from a cauldron. I could stay here in the hate-filled 21st century and try to enjoy it, try to incrementally, painstakingly build a better world the way these people think they're doing. But that would negate everything I've already done: my career in Security, the missions I've done for the Department, all the other disasters I've helped protect."

"And that's too much for you."

"Maybe it is."

"And maybe that's why corrupt regimes like yours live on."

"Have you read their newspapers since you got here? Seen the TV news? Maybe you should leave this city, go to Iraq or Afghanistan, or Sudan or Kashmir. Maybe you need a better understanding of the world you're trying to save."

"You like to condemn. You see faults and decide that it can't be saved. Everything should just be wiped out."

"This *will be* wiped out."

"I don't think so." He shakes his head. "We know what we're doing this time. We've learned from our mistakes. There's a moral there, if you care to look for it."

I wish he would just shut up so I can get this over with. "Open the door and get out of the car," I tell him. "Keep your hands up."

He waits for a second, and when he finally opens his door I do the same, mirroring him. I don't do this well enough, because suddenly his hand is emerging from his pocket and there's a gun in it.

I fire first and his body spins.

He lands on his back, his gun hitting the pavement. I scramble around the car and kick his gun away. His eyes are wide, and sweat streaks down his face, his hair a wet mop. There's a hole just off the center of his chest.

"Where are your friends?" I kneel by his side and look through his pockets but find nothing useful. "Tell me so I can get this assignment over with and go home."

"Go to hell," he chokes.

"I'm already there, thanks." Then I snap. It's the weight of another murder, and all the murders to come. "Why do you people keep doing this? When will you all give up?"

I hear sirens. This area isn't as abandoned as I'd hoped—one of the last residents in the crumbling neighborhood must have called the authorities.

"Thanks for the memories." I plant a Flasher on his chest and back up three steps. He clutches at it, tries to tear it off, but they're not removable once set. I turn around and there's a burst of light for a second, my shadow stretching halfway down the alley and along the wall of the dumpster, and then it's gone again. I turn back; beside the car a wide, black circle has been burned into the broken asphalt, revealing an underlayer of century-old bricks. (I've certainly left a trace, but one that fits in with this rundown neighborhood.) The hag, his gun, and his blood are gone.

I walk to the edge of the alley, then down a short block until I emerge on a main road. Remembering my Customs lessons, I raise my hand for a taxi. The sirens are getting louder. A few empty taxis pass without stopping, and I wonder if I have this wrong. Finally one stops.

The driver is very dark-skinned and asks me a question with so strong an accent I barely understand him. I tell him to take me back to the Starbucks, where I've left my car.

He mutters something and shakes his head and I realize he's listening to a voice on the radio that's speaking in British-accented English with a calmness that belies the subject matter. "More than three hundred Hindus have now been killed by Muslim mobs in the Pakistan province of Swat in retaliation for the burning of two mosques last Thursday." The voice details beheadings, rapes, children trapped in collapsed buildings. I'm almost sick to my stomach at the thought of it all, so incomprehensible, but the announcer sounds bored.

The next report describes a "flaring of tensions" between Ethiopia and Eritrea, new skirmishes between two nations that only recently stopped fighting a war.

"Where are you from?" I ask the cabbie.

"Nigeria."

"How long have you lived here?"

"Thirty years, man."

"You came with your parents?"

"That's right. After the Biafran War."

I don't know that one, and I think about running it through my Historical Events file but ultimately decide not to bother. There were so many wars. Do the details even matter?

The British announcer is now talking to a woman, American, who is explaining the pros and cons of confronting North Korea on its rumored designs to build nuclear weapons. Which is quite relevant to my mission; I listen intently. I realize I've heard this exact report before, during my training—it's one of the news items the Archivists were able to recover. Then the announcer moves on in the great global banquet of conflict and atrocity, begins discussing heightened tensions in Palestine.

"This is quite a world you live in," I say.

He glances at me in the rearview and doesn't respond.

The cabbie pulls over across the street from where the men had done their coffee-shop conspiring. As I expected, the business meeting has concluded and the men are off to the next stage in their geopolitical adventure.

I walk south one block and turn west along a neighborhood of stately row houses with perfectly tended garden plots. I parked my car at the end of this street, which, I see, was a stupid decision. The area was quiet then, but now there's a swarm of people marching along the sidewalks in that quick, purposeful gait of Washingtonians. I realize (via my GPS) that I'm only a block away from both a Metro stop and one of the Senate office buildings; apparently a train just got in, or a congressional workday just ended, or both. This is not a good environment for someone who wishes to leave no trace, but at least they're all so busy trying not to bump into one another as they chat on their phones that it's unlikely anyone will notice me.

My keys are in my hand and I'm only a few feet away from my car when someone says my name. No, not my name—my cover's name.

"*Troy!* Hey, Troy."

I look up as a white man with short silver hair approaches me. His unbuttoned suit coat flaps around his thin frame.

"What are you doing here?" he asks, nearly in a whisper.

I'm running his image through my databases in search of a match. *How does he know my cover?*

The people in Logistics try to find covers whose racial backgrounds are more mixed than typical contemps' so our skin shares the same general hue as the people's we're replacing. In addition to that, the Engineers surgically alter our appearances so we can resemble the covers as closely as possible. But they tell us it's never an exact match— we may seem similar to the covers, but we aren't supposed to be such ringers that friends of the covers would mistake us for them. Yet that seems to be what's happening right now.

I shake my head at him. "I'm sorry, I—"

"You need to get out of D.C." He's standing just a bit closer to me than people in this time usually do. "Your little mission's been blown. I'm putting myself at risk just telling you this, but I—"

"I'm afraid you have me mixed up with someone else." The databases find no match, but he seems weirdly familiar. Have I seen him before during my time in D.C.? Or do I recognize him from the Perfect Present, or from some other beat?

The Department always assures us that we won't be placed near where the covers lived, that the odds of any of us crossing paths with someone who knows the cover are minuscule. Troy Jones is from Philadelphia, hours away from here. So who is this person, and how does he know Troy?

"*What?* Troy, listen to me: They know what you're doing. They're looking for you, and they'll find you soon enough. Do you hear what I'm saying?"

"You're confusing me with—"

"*You're* the one who's confused, and it's going to get you *killed,* do you see that? You think you're stopping them but you're only *leading them* where they need to go. You need to *leave,* and get as far away as possible."

I wait a moment, staring into his eyes. It sounds like he's talking about the hags, my mission.

"Are you with the Department?" I ask. We're not even supposed to say *the Department* out loud.

He puts his hand on my forearm, but I shake him off. A bit more violently than I meant to. He steps back, nearly falling as his feet get tangled, and people walking past us turn their heads. I'm leaving a trace, and badly. He stares at me in shock or maybe anger, then he hurries away, toward the Metro station.

I feel the gaze of security guards, police officers, sundry other professionals, and their ubiquitous hidden cameras as I open my car door and do my best to disappear from their memory.

7.

The alarm was an electric charge flaying the nerves in Sari's brain. She opened her eyes and already felt hollowed out.

It was 5:15. Her employer left each morning at 6:00 and expected his breakfast to be ready for him in the kitchen. The rice must be freshly prepared, not microwaved leftovers.

She crept past the twins' room, careful not to wake them, and went into the bathroom. Back home Sari hadn't always showered every day, but here she craved the peace it afforded, even if it only lasted a few minutes. Above the wooden blinds, the top half of the bathroom window was black. When she'd moved to Korea, it had taken her months to get used to the shortness of the days in autumn and winter, so unlike Indonesia. Here it seemed worse.

She showered in lukewarm water and was shivering before she even turned it off—Sang Hee had complained a few days earlier that there was never enough hot water left for her showers, so Sari had to be sparing. She dressed while standing on the narrow bathroom mat and she brushed her hair, long and thorough strokes, like rowing. Even after so many years, she missed the ocean.

After putting on gray sweatpants and a matching sweatshirt that she'd bought at a Marshalls during one of the few shopping excursions Sang Hee had granted her, she turned off the bathroom fan and already she could hear the babies crying.

Jung and Seung were ten months old. They were just starting to crawl—a little late, she gathered from what the parents had said, but they'd been born early, the result of a challenging pregnancy.

At Sang Hee's behest, Sari had spent much of the previous day rearranging pieces of furniture and electrical appliances for the newly mobile babies' safety. Then the husband complained about the unfamiliar layout of his home and insisted that everything be put back. *Babyproofing?* he had scoffed. *If you're doing your job, the babies won't hurt themselves.*

Her tiny room was next to the twins' far more spacious one. Sari bumped her head against a red modern-art mobile (*a gift from an American diplomat,* Sang Hee had said, *very expensive*) as she bent down to change Jung's diaper. Sang Hee forbade the use of pacifiers, so Sari tried to tune out their cries. She picked the babies up one at a time, then sat on the sofa, where with the help of some strategically arranged pillows she'd found a position in which she could feed both of them simultaneously. Jung's immense head leaned into Sari's left funny bone; two of her fingers were numb by the time they finished.

She heard movement above. Hyun Ki Shim, the diplomat, tended to glide like a phantom, so this was his wife announcing herself. A hole tore open inside of Sari.

When she finished giving the twins their bottles, she carried them into the kitchen and set them up in high chairs so she could prepare breakfast. Seung started to cry, so she picked him up and held him with one arm.

"They were crying for minutes before you did anything about it," Sang Hee said as she walked into the kitchen.

"I'm sorry, ma'am. I was in the shower."

"I told you, you take too long in there."

Sang Hee was wearing her emerald robe, pinned at her armpits by the crutches she'd been using since breaking her ankle a week ago. She had come down only to ensure that the maid was not murdering her infants. This had become her routine, except for those mornings when Sang Hee slept late after drinking too much. She was short, two inches or so smaller than Sari, and her curly hair was cut severely, in a way that reminded Sari of a bush.

"Give him to me," Sang Hee said, and Sari obeyed. Sang Hee

leaned her crutches against the kitchen counter, sat down, and held the baby with both arms. Sari saw the mother offer a quick smile to the little boy, who as usual reached for her necklace.

"I wish he wouldn't do that," Sang Hee said, the smile gone. She handed him back to Sari. The babies' fascination with jewelry had been established for weeks, yet Sang Hee was never without one of her gold necklaces.

"It's a very nice necklace," Sari said, compelled to explain the baby's thoughts.

"I'm sure you think so."

Later in the morning Sari spoon-fed the babies. Sang Hee had already taken her tea into the parlor to read the *Washington Post*. When they entertained American guests, Sang Hee spoke little, deferring to her husband, and Sari wondered if she spoke much English. Yet every morning there she was, staring at the *Post*. Sari herself studied English by watching television with the babies when she could, which was seldom, so she hardly knew a word of the language.

Hyun Ki walked into the room, his wingtips barely tapping the linoleum. He was tall for a Korean, yet his movements were spare and calm. The first time he'd raised his voice to her, it was as startling as seeing the sea rise up in a tsunami. It had become far less surprising.

He did not say good morning, merely glanced at her to let her know he was aware of her presence. He read a file he'd carried with him and ate the kimchi and rice Sari had placed on the table. Sari needed to hurry and finish feeding the babies before Hana, the rambunctious elder sister, woke up.

"How did they sleep?" he asked.

"Very well," she lied. They had in fact woken four times, another horrible night for her, as it often took more than an hour to soothe them back down. But she'd learned not to mention this, since she would be blamed.

"I heard them at three," he said. "They should be sleeping better." It was unclear what font of paternal wisdom he was drawing from.

Sari had never seen him hold either baby, and he acted as if Hana, the four-year-old, were a strange pet whose bleats perplexed him.

While feeding one of the babies, she glanced at Hyun Ki's cup to see if he needed more tea, and she saw that he was watching her. He'd been doing that lately. She looked back at the baby.

Hyun Ki left his plate on the table and walked out, off to the embassy. She cleared his plate and noticed he'd left the file there. The characters typed on the page weren't Korean; they were probably English. Before she could decide whether it was worth the effort to chase him down and tell him he'd forgotten it, he was there in the doorway, staring at her in an altogether different way than he had before.

She backed away and he stepped forward, closed the file folder, and picked it up. "You are not to look at my things. I thought I made that clear."

"Yes, of course." She looked away, at the babies, and grabbed one of their spoons as if for protection. It was so absurdly easy to offend these people. She held her breath and fed one of the babies, and the diplomat silently left.

Soon she could hear the rubber gripping of Sang Hee's crutches as the mistress slowly made her way to the kitchen.

"Stop shoveling the food into them," she said. "My God, are you trying to drown them? That's how they do it in Indonesia? No wonder so many of your babies die."

Sari clutched the plastic spoon an extra second before extending it to a gaping mouth. The twins gazed at her longingly, four brown eyes, two pates of dark hair tousled this way and that, two frowns surrounded by lips caked with sweet potato and carrot.

From behind Sari, Sang Hee sneezed, and the babies startled, then stared up like they'd never seen her before.

Washing the babies' bowls and spoons in the sink, Sari looked out the kitchen window. She could see the small yard and the backs of the houses on the next street. Oak branches shook off red and gold leaves, casting sharp autumn shadows on the lawn. A cardinal alighted on a wooden picnic table the family never used, twitching his crown.

Sari had been in Washington for seven weeks and had spent fewer than six hours out of the house. She had been permitted out once to rake leaves and help Sang Hee garden in the back, twice to shop for warmer clothing at Marshalls (with Sang Hee as an escort), and, now that Sang Hee was hobbling on crutches, once to buy groceries alone. She had overheard the master and mistress discussing the possibility of grocery trips the night before they sent her—Sang Hee had been concerned about Sari's being unchaperoned and had asked her husband to accompany her, but he'd been insulted by the idea of running a domestic errand. *Don't worry about her,* he'd said. *What will she do, run away? Where would she go?* They had taken her passport, after all, and she spoke no English.

Just as Sari was wondering if she should wake Hana, the young girl walked into the kitchen, wearing only a pink nightie.

"Good morning," Sari said.

Hana didn't respond; she'd learned that from her mother.

"You know you need to wear something warmer in the morning. You'll catch cold."

"I can wear what I want." But if her mother saw Hana like this, Sari would receive a tongue-lashing, or worse.

She gently took one of Hana's hands. "You won't be happy if you're sick all week. Come, let's find something warm." Hana yanked her hand away, but she followed and didn't talk back.

On the way to the stairs they saw Sang Hee sitting in the parlor, her fingers viciously poking at her laptop. She was writing a book, she had told Sari. Sari had asked what it was about and was told, "Things you wouldn't understand." Sari wondered what a mind like Sang Hee's saw fit to share with the world through writing.

Hana's room was a yellow zoo of stuffed animals. The girl sifted through her bureau until she found something that met with both her approval and Sari's. Unlike Sang Hee's hair, Hana's was straight and long, hanging well past her shoulders. Sang Hee was her *omma* now but she hadn't always been, Hana had explained once. Her first *omma* had gone to the land of ghosts when Hana was still a baby, and then *appa* had married Sang Hee, so Sang Hee was now her *omma*. This had been news to Sari. Perhaps it explained Sang Hee's distance around the girl, her seeming inability to play with her the way a mother should. But then again, Sang Hee was equally cold with the twins, her own flesh and blood—she never sang to them, seldom held them. Sometimes she would speak affectionately to them, coo at them, but then something would pass over her face, a sudden shadow, and she would hand the babies back to the maid and leave the room. *The woman is cursed,* Sari had thought the first time she saw this. *There is something wrong with her; I need to make sure the curse doesn't wander over to me as well.* She worried about the babies. They were probably doomed.

Hana liked Sari to comb her hair as she stood in front of the mirror and imagined herself a princess, or a movie star, or a president. She had said she was going to be all of these things when she grew up, and Sari never knew how to respond. Such confidence. To imagine the world as a series of banquets to which one is always invited. And to be right.

The previous night, Sari had spoken to her own mother while she was sleeping. Her mother had not come in days, and Sari was beginning to worry she had done something to offend her, had dreamed unclean thoughts that pushed her away. But while she was dreaming about being in Java, the background suddenly turned to sand and fell away, the grains cascading down, and all was dark except for her mother's unmistakable form in the middle.

Well, she said simply. *Are you doing better, daughter?*

Sari thought about this. *Yes, Mother.*

Don't lie.

I didn't think it was a lie, Mother. I wanted it to be true.

Do you think I liked working for those Chinese people? she asked. *I hated their filthy shop. No matter how many times I cleaned it, it was still filthy.*

The Mings were not charming people, Sari, but neither were they terrible employers. I managed.

And died for them, Sari almost said, but she kept it to herself.

Yes, so I did, her mother said. Sari had forgotten that here her mother could hear her thoughts. *They aren't the ones who killed me, of course. Don't forget that.*

Yes, Mother.

Listen: You had the wrong expectations when these people invited you here. You thought working in America would be different from working in Korea, but that house is Korea.

It's worse than Korea. I could come and go in Korea. I knew other Indonesians in Korea. I could quit my employer if I needed to in Korea.

True. But you took the job, so you have to get through it. His appointment is only two years.

Her mother's face was no more wrinkled than the last day she had seen her; in death she did not age. But it had been so many years now (Sari had no photographs of her) that she wondered if she had the face right at all.

I met a man yesterday. A white man who spoke Bahasa.

I know, child. I was there with you.

I want to try talking to him again.

Are you asking my permission? You don't need that.

If Sang Hee were to find out, she'd never let me out of the house again.

True. You need to be careful. And you need to be quick; her ankle will heal eventually, and she won't need to send you out anymore.

I know. I think I'll call him tomorrow, after everyone is asleep.

I'll try to watch Sang Hee for you. I'll let you know if she's spying.

Thank you. I wish sometimes her ankle would never heal.

Her mother issued a mischievous smile that Sari had never seen on her face before. *I'll see what I can do.*

Sang Hee usually typed on her laptop until lunch, in the parlor or in her bedroom. Then she would leave to visit with other diplomats' wives or to get a manicure and shop. If she came home early enough, she would sit in front of the television and watch DVDs of Korean soap operas that she had someone mail to her.

At eight thirty each morning a man in a Lincoln Town Car pulled up in front of the house, and a woman got out of it and took Hana to preschool.

Later that morning Sari was in the kitchen warming bottles; the twins were napping, and Sang Hee was upstairs showering. Sari hesitated, then picked up the phone. She'd been afraid the slip of paper with Leo's name and number would be discovered, so she had memorized the number and thrown the paper out the SUV window on the way home that night.

It rang five times, then his recorded voice said something in English. The machine beeped at her, and she hung up. He must be at work during the day; she should have expected that. She returned to the bottles and ran hot water over them, wondering what she would say if she reached him.

The first few days had been so strange, passing in a blur of jet lag and sleeplessness, that Sari barely noticed the restrictions they placed on her. The fourteenth day had come and gone, and so had a few more, when she finally asked about money. Wasn't she supposed to be paid every two weeks?

"Don't trouble me with your complaints," Sang Hee had said. Sari had just finished feeding Seung in his high chair while Jung entertained himself with plastic blocks on the kitchen floor. Sari stood to address Sang Hee. This was before her mistress had broken her ankle, and she was wearing sweat clothes, having returned from a jog through a park Sari had never seen.

"I'm sorry, but it's been more than two weeks, ma'am," she said. She hated conversations like this but had learned to stand up for herself through her other bad jobs in Seoul.

"We'll pay you when we pay you," Sang Hee said, then took a long drink of water. "Are you implying we're cheating you? Is that what you're saying to me?"

Sari considered for a moment. Seung coughed in a small orange burst, then smiled even as his eyes watered.

"No, ma'am. But I do worry about my sisters in Korea, and I was planning to send some money to them. So if I could—"

She had been looking at one of the babies while she spoke, so she didn't know what happened at first, only that she had to blink and gasp, and she was wet. Water ran down her face, soaking her shirt. Sang Hee's glass was empty.

Then Sang Hee put her glass down and slapped Sari's face. Sari gasped again; her hand covered her cheek. Only later would she wonder, *How did she know it would hurt so much worse on a wet cheek?*

"Shut up! If it's so important, I'll talk to my husband about it. I'll tell him you think we're cheating you. I'm sure he'll love to hear what you think of him. And I don't want to see you wearing those tight pants anymore, always bending over for things around him. Do you think I don't know what you're doing?"

She didn't respond, just kept her hand on her cheek to ward off another blow. The babies were staring but seemed not to have formed an opinion yet.

"There's water on the floor," Sang Hee said as she left the room. "Get the mop."

Two days after that incident, Sari had accidentally knocked over a glass vase she'd been dusting. Sang Hee had rushed in at the sound. Sari was kneeling on the floor, trying to pick up the pieces, when Sang Hee started cursing and hitting her. The first blow landed on her shoulder, startling her more than hurting her, but the next one found her neck. She hunched defensively and slipped on the hardwood floor, gashing her knee on one of the shards of glass. Sang Hee was strong for such a small woman. Sari was too stunned to even say *Stop*. Sang Hee finally decided Sari had been punished sufficiently, and she left the room, telling Sari to clean her mess.

She was slapped other times, once for spilling some juice on the newspaper Sang Hee had been reading, once when Sang Hee declared that one of her blouses had been destroyed in the laundry, other times for indiscretions Sari couldn't remember. She was more and more nervous in the mistress's presence, making mistakes, becoming clumsy, inviting the attacks.

Sang Hee got at least one manicure a week, sometimes more. Her nails were always new colors, always shining, her skin smelling of mangoes or strawberry or lavender. It took a while for Sari to see that the hands themselves were calloused and scarred. A line ran across the knuckles of her right hand, and her left pinkie finger didn't seem to straighten all the way. She sometimes wore thin blue or white gloves around the house, something Sari had initially thought was an odd stylistic affectation, but now she wondered.

Sari had no one to explain her situation to or ask for advice. Time passed and her mood darkened.

She could fight back, of course, but she worried about what would happen. Sang Hee reminded her that they had her papers, that she had even less status here in America than she did in Korea, where she'd been a reviled "guest worker." Sang Hee dropped hints that if they weren't pleased with their servant's work, she could be sent back to Indonesia, or even to some sort of detention camp. As could her two sisters.

Two nights after meeting Leo, Sari put Hana to bed. Sang Hee was upstairs writing, and Hyun Ki was working late, as he often did.

Hana pulled the covers to her neck, her fingertips slowly peeking out like worms after rain. "Tell me a story."

"All right," Sari said, willing her voice not to sound tired. Sang Hee sometimes stood outside the door to listen, so she could not afford to be short with the girl.

"A story about the ocean."

Lately Hana's requests had become distressingly specific, flitting about in accordance with her whims. Sari had been asked to tell a story about a butterfly and a monkey, a story about a little boy with a kite and a panda bear, a story about a comet and ice cream. In these brief, soft minutes illuminated only by the night-light, Sari's story-telling skills were taxed as much as the rest of her was during the day.

"A story about the ocean. All right." Sari missed the ocean, missed the way sunlight moved upon its breathing body like a sheet over a sleeping child, missed the salty brine and the cry of birds circling the fishing boats. She had recently spied a map of Washington in the newspaper, and if she understood it correctly, they were not far from the ocean. But even if this house were half a kilometer from a beach, she would still be living in the middle of a desert.

"Many years ago, like now, the ocean was rising," she said, re-membering something she had seen on television in Seoul only a few months ago, about South Pacific islands that were disappearing as the polar ice caps melted. She remembered the faces of the islanders as they spoke in some jibberish language to the camera, the look of people who were being erased. She understood them now. "Because of this, many islands were being flooded, as each day the waves rose higher and higher, covering first the beaches and then the dunes and then the woods. The people on one island had seen this coming, but they hadn't known what to do. The ocean continued to rise, so the people left their houses to move as many belongings as they could carry to the mountains. But the ocean rose higher still."

"What happened to their houses?"

"They were consumed by the ocean. One day the people on the mountains could still see their old houses' roofs, but then the next they were covered by waves."

"I don't like this story."

"Wait, you will." She couldn't tell the truth about the island from the television show, of course. What had the island been called? she wondered. What vanishing language had those people spoken? "One day, a young girl whose family had moved to the mountain had an idea. She thought that—"

"What was her name?"

"It was Oogaloogamoogadooga."

Hana laughed. "No, it wasn't!"

"It was a long time ago, so the people had very funny-sounding names to our ears. Anyway, the girl had an idea. The mountains were getting crowded and the ocean was rising further. Soon they would have to live on the lip of a volcano, which no one wanted to do. And everyone was sad because they'd had to leave many of their things behind. So Oogaloogamoogadooga thought of all the things that the people still had. One thing they had—though they were running out—was hope. So she and her friends traveled to all the people on the mountains and asked them to put their hope together and put it underneath the island, because hope is buoyant—that means it floats. So they all—"

"How did they get it under the island?"

"They had special underwater boats. The people pooled all their hope together and were amazed at how much they had after all, and when they put it under the island, the island rose a bit. Their houses were still underwater, but they could see the roofs. Then Oogaloogamoogadooga went to all the people on the mountains and told them they needed to get rid of their fear—fear is very heavy, and it was weighing down the island. So all the people, before going to sleep that night, took out their fear and gave it to some fishermen, who then put the fear in boats—they needed many boats for all the fear—and the fishermen let the boats sail away without any captains. The boats drifted, and before reaching the horizon they sank into the ocean. They're still there now, many leagues beneath the surface; giant squids live in them. And without all that fear weighing the island down, it rose again. Now the people's houses were not underwater, though the beaches and some of the low areas still were."

Hana's eyelids were heavy, but she wasn't asleep yet.

"Then the next day Oogaloogamoogadooga told everyone to have a good, full dinner so they would have many wonderful dreams at night. The next morning, she and her friends collected all the dreams, which are like kites, attached them to strings, and tied the ends of the strings to the island's four corners. The wind was very strong that day—a typhoon had passed nearby—and the wind blew the dreams so forcefully that the island was raised up higher still. It was now the way it had been before."

"Were the houses okay?"

"Yes. It was sunny for many days, and they dried out just fine."

"Did their pets drown?"

"On this island they had no pets. The fish and dolphins were like pets to them. Anyway, now everything was back to normal, but because the people had survived such a difficult ordeal, they felt even stronger than ever, and had more hope than before, more than anyone really needed, so Oogaloogamoogadooga decided that each week she and her friends would collect all the extra hope and have the special boats put it under the island, in case the oceans ever rose again. With more and more hope, the land was lifted higher and higher, and the island grew and grew and grew. It became nearly a thousand kilometers long."

"What's it called?"

"Java. Where I was born."

Hana's voice was heavy, sinking into sleep. "But Omma says people in Java are lazy and stupid."

Sari's mind followed the silence through the open crack of the bedroom door, along the hallway, and down the stairs, searching for Sang Hee.

"Yes, I know she does. Now go to sleep."

Hours more were spent doing dishes, cleaning, preparing bottles for the morning, and then soothing the twins, who woke again. Afterward, Sari made her way to the kitchen. She stood at the phone, listening for any sounds of movement from above. The oven clock told her it was past midnight; master and mistress had gone to sleep an hour or two ago.

She picked up the phone.

He had followed her around two grocery stores—clearly, he was interested in her. She was used to fending off clumsy advances, and despite the joy of being able to speak her language with him, she'd felt she had to dispatch him and get back to the house before she roused Sang Hee's suspicion. Only at the end of her shopping had she realized that, at worst, he might provide a badly needed distraction from her predicament, so she'd asked for his number.

Maybe he could offer even more than a distraction.

She dialed Leo's number, each press of the receiver's buttons too loud. They glowed so brightly, half the room was illuminated a sickly green, but when she held the phone to her face the room disappeared.

After three rings, she heard a man's voice harshly demand "Hello?," one of the only English words she knew.

His tone gave her pause. Maybe this was a mistake? She should hang up. No, she needed to be brave, and friendly. *More* than friendly. She steeled herself, then said, in Bahasa, "Hello, is this Leo?"

"Yes," he replied in Bahasa after a pause. His voice softened with the language, the inflection rising. But it wasn't just the language. She could tell already that she'd been right, and he was delighted she'd called.

"I'm sorry to call you so late."

"That's okay."

She was nervous about being overheard and wondered if she should try to sound less nervous. Or maybe he liked nervous women? "It was good to talk to you the other day. If you'd . . . if you'd like to work on your Bahasa sometime, maybe we could meet again?"

"That would be great."

"How about on Wednesday evening—can you meet me at the same place at seven o'clock?"

"Yes."

She felt so self-conscious, but he was responding naturally, as if he received such calls every night. Or dreamed of them.

"Okay. I must go, sorry—I'm not supposed to be on the phone. But I'll see you on Wednesday?"

"Sure. Great."

She smiled, hoping she would also *sound* like someone who was smiling, and said, "Good-bye."

She hung up and stood there listening, her heart loud, surely so loud she wouldn't have noticed the sounds of Sang Hee creeping around a corner or eavesdropping on the line. Maybe she'd made a horrible mistake. What was she really expecting from the American?

But still, there was this: her quickening heart, the feeling of flight beneath her toes as she stepped to her room, the fact that she *existed,* and had proven this existence to another person. It gave her something to look forward to, a horizon. And beyond that? She wasn't sure yet. But she was close to something, and she needed to get closer.

8.

Leo's parents lived in Bethesda, less than two miles from him, in a smaller, empty-nester version of the house where he'd grown up. He saw them about once every other month and spoke to them on the phone only slightly more often. He didn't think of this lack of communication as unusual; it was how they'd always lived their lives.

He met them one night for dinner at a sushi place they'd been patronizing since he was a kid. As was his personality, and as had been drilled into him by his time at the Agency, he was five minutes early. His father, Alan Hastings, was deposited by cab ten minutes late. Leo already had a sake in him by then, and he figured his dad had picked up a little something in whatever business meeting he'd just left.

"What's new?" Leo asked.

"Prices up, panic up, desperation up. I'm a busy man." Alan's Italian suit looked splendid; it was reassuring to see the way the old man kept his physique despite his rarely having time to hit the gym. Hopefully Leo would be as fortunate.

Alan was an energy lobbyist, which meant that he had a lot of energy and a lot of money. He never seemed to sleep much, except on the occasional weekend afternoon when he was home sitting in front of a sports game that bored him into narcolepsy.

When Leo had started work for the Agency, he'd given his parents the standard speech about his inability to disclose details of his job to them, but neither had fully accepted this need for secrecy. They both told him how proud they were that he was working for the government and possibly traveling the globe. Yet, as the weeks and months passed, they were increasingly miffed that they weren't bene-fiting from his new knowledge.

"But there's hardly any oil in Indonesia!" Alan had said when Leo completed his training and was able to pass some basic information (and some basic disinformation) to his parents about his upcoming post. "Come on, if I worked for the *coffee* industry, then Jakarta would be great, but, Jesus, Leo."

"It's my job, not yours."

"I know, but I was expecting a little quid pro quo for the family estate."

"You were hoping they'd send me to Saudi Arabia or Iraq?"

"Yes!"

Leo hadn't known how to respond.

"Well, look, I know they're dangerous," Alan had said, backpedal-ing a bit. "Venezuela has a lot of oil too, and South America in general is big with the lithium trade—that's going to be huge for laptops and phones. Can you ask for something in South America?"

"It doesn't really work that way."

"I can talk to some people."

"*No.* And I'm an Asian specialist. I like the assignment."

Alan had spent the next few weeks researching the various energy possibilities in Indonesia—there were some interesting developments in Irian Jaya—dropping several unsubtle hints and requests for in-formation the relatively few times Leo called home. Leo soon stopped calling.

At the sushi restaurant, they waited fifteen minutes before de-ciding to order for Leo's mother, Joyce. They knew what she liked anyway.

"What's new with Mom?"

"Don't mention the word *Microsoft,*" Alan said. "It didn't go well, and she was blamed."

"Got it."

"Technology in general you shouldn't discuss. The administration is bringing down a bunch of new rules that make life hell for her clients. Which I suppose is good for her, in some ways, but it's ruining some of her cases."

Dad was a Republican, Mom a Democrat. They bantered about politics only occasionally and with only as much emotional fervor as they exhibited when deciding which take-out place to order from. At this point in their careers they knew so many top politicians that they weren't picky about who won what election; they hedged their bets and would profit either way. Leo remembered when D.C. was the murder capital of the world, when the idea of going downtown seemed borderline suicidal for the white suburban kids, and the extent of the city's cultural life was a few punk bands. Now condos were rising everywhere, developers were filling old crack houses with granite countertops and stainless steel appliances and reselling them for half a million each, five-star restaurants and new theaters were opening in every other neighborhood, and the exurbs were busily cloning themselves all the way to the Shenandoah foothills. The capital was a bank, and everyone withdrew.

Joyce arrived, dropping her purse and cell phone and apologies just as the waiters were bringing the sushi. A peck on the cheek, a comment on Leo's apparent weight loss ("Have you lost your appetite for American cuisine?"), and then on with the food.

"Your new company's Web site is rather vague," she told her son after the basic pleasantries and some tuna.

"We're not really in the clarity industry."

"But you're no longer with *them*." *Them* was what she always called the Agency in Leo's presence. "What exactly are you doing?"

She didn't so much mean "doing with your day" as "doing with your life." Low-paid government work was one thing, but they'd assumed he would parlay that into profit eventually.

"I'm leveraging my taxpayer-funded skill set for private gain." He let himself smile.

"Do you like it?"

Leo was still thinking up an answer when his dad said, "Leo never likes new things. Give it a few months."

Leo realized his dad was right. Maybe this funk he was going through had nothing to do with the new employer and less than he'd thought with the sour end to his time at the Agency. Maybe in a few weeks he'd grow to love following war protesters around at the behest of unknown clients.

"But if you decide it's the wrong place," Alan continued, "remember: Energy companies need risk analysts. They'd love someone with your experience."

"I'll think about it."

The waiter had poured him more sake but he told himself not to touch it, that it would only cause problems. And he actually had a date, or a pseudo-date, after this.

"And who are we seeing these days?" Joyce asked as if reading his mind. She asked that every time, just to see what dodge her son would come up with.

"An HIV-positive drag queen."

"Well, don't do anything you can be blackmailed for, in your line of work."

Then the check, and a quick discussion about where to go for Thanksgiving (the islands, maybe? Or just stay home? Or ski?), which would likely be the next time they saw one another. Hugs at the curb, and Alan walked home while Joyce hailed a taxi back to the office for what would be, she warned her husband, another long night.

Leo rode the Metro back into the city and thought about what Bale had told him that morning. According to Bale's sources at State and the Agency, Sari's employer was Hyun Ki Shim, a thirty-seven-year-old diplomat. He'd started work at South Korea's embassy in Washington six months ago, following five years with South Korea's state department. Shim had a fabulously wealthy uncle in the telecommunications business and had enjoyed an uninteresting upbringing. He was once married to a history professor in Seoul, but she had died of complications from minor surgery a year after they had their daughter, Hana. He remarried, and his new wife and their children had lived in Seoul until two months ago—she had given birth to twins and didn't want to travel until they were older. No one had any dirt or unusual suspicions about this particular diplomat.

His wife was where things got interesting. Sang Hee was born in North Korea. She'd defected seven years ago—the story that she had told the South Korean state security was that she was a nurse living in Pyongyang until the fateful day her first husband said something about Kim Jong Il he shouldn't have. The family was sent north to a labor camp in an unnamed town. According to her, her husband and kids died at the camp, and she—by some unexplained miracle—escaped to China and defected to the South. She was vetted by South Korea's national intelligence service and was relocated to Seoul, where she had distant relatives from before the country's civil war. A few years later she met a dapper widower. They soon married, which won her a ticket to Washington.

"The idea of a high-status South Korean diplomat going for a North Korean woman who'd already supposedly been married and had kids," Bale said, "doesn't exactly fit the stereotype. And the South Koreans' current process for vetting defectors does not inspire confidence. Their president is pushing his 'sunshine policy' and keeps talking about improving relations, opening up the North, blah blah blah. They're getting weak and sloppy, and the result is we have a North Korean woman with a fanciful life story staying just up the road from the White House. My guy says he warned State about it, but they just said he was being paranoid. Meaning, they agree but have other problems. Meaning, she doesn't wear a burka and blow herself up at intersections, and they can only fight so many wars at once."

Bale had also managed a check on Sari. She'd given Leo her real name; she was twenty-two and an Indonesian citizen, had obtained a South Korean work visa a few years back. From what State could gather, her visa had expired but someone in South Korea had pulled some strings for her—which might be a sign of covert activity, but was probably just a result of her working for a rich guy who had connections. If she was a double agent trying to ensnare Leo in something, they'd covered her tracks well, both in South Korea and in her native land.

"Plus, you're just a private contractor, not a government officer," Bale added, seemingly unaware of the insult, "so the odds that they're trying to ensnare you are minimal."

Leo had been thinking of her almost constantly. For not entirely business-related reasons. And he was thrilled to have something to work on that didn't involve tailing peace activists.

Bale reminded him that he had "no official mandate, responsibility, role, or even legal right to do anything," but he nonetheless exhorted Leo to investigate. Leo's primary focus should remain the knoweverything.org project, of course, but any extra time could be devoted to recruiting Sari to spy on the Korean couple and seeing what she could find. Eavesdrop, tap into their computers, and/or take embarrassing photos that could be used to place either the diplomat or his wife in a delicate position where they could be further exploited. South Korea's sunshine policy was dangerous to American interests, so they needed to know how much of it was political posturing and how much was genuine.

Leo felt proud of himself for finding Sari, for uncovering information that had impressed not only Bale but "his guys" at the Agency and at State, whoever they were. Yet he felt a twinge of sadness at how quickly she was transformed from an alluring young woman into an asset.

The small bistro where he met Gail was close enough to Dupont Circle to have its fair share of yuppie couples flirting over martinis and close enough to Foggy Bottom for some suits from State to be conspiring in a corner booth. Gail had already eaten at some official function she couldn't talk about. They sat at one of the small tables off the bar.

They had trained together a few years back, although not nearly as long ago as it felt. They'd bonded during the experience and ever since had kept in as close touch as was possible for people in their line of work—the occasional e-mail, regards passed through various intermediaries, a brief lunch or drink on the rare occasion they both happened to be in the same city. She'd sent him a line telling him she'd be in D.C. for a few days, and he'd pounced.

"Do you like what you're working on these days?" He phrased it in a way that made it clear he wasn't asking her to divulge anything. Only her feelings, which by their nature could never be classified. Right?

"I do. It's great." She smiled and shrugged, as if she felt guilty.

"Good." He tried not to look jealous.

Leo had wanted to sleep with her since the first day of training and felt proud of himself for not acting on it, thought of his Agency-enforced chastity regarding his fellow trainee as his first step in the self-abnegating life of an operative. Or maybe he was just trying to make himself feel better for not having the nerve to make a move.

But now he could sleep with whomever he wanted, at least in theory, so he'd been thrilled to see her name in his in-box. He hoped she felt the same way, and nothing was disproving it yet: the strong drink she ordered, her low neckline, the way she smiled as they rehashed stories of their training. Drinks were dutifully refilled.

"How's life after the Agency?"

He chafed at the comment. "I like to think of it as being on hold."

"Oh." She watched him for a moment. Was that pity? "Good."

"I'm doing similar work as a green-tag," he lied, to both of them. She asked what sort of work he was doing and he described his latest assignments in terms vague enough to render them potentially interesting: the tracking of dangerous radicals, investigations into breaches of classified information.

"Very domestic," she noted, not fooled. "I mean, you have foreign experience, languages, counterterrorism. There are dozens of other firms that could use your skills."

"I guess I didn't want to deal with a long, protracted job hunt.

You know, take the first job that comes along, stay busy. I can always switch again."

She sipped her drink. "You didn't like it, did you? Being there."

"I did. Most of it."

"Look, Leo, just between us, I think what happened to you was rotten."

"It *was* rotten."

"I don't think people should be punished for what they say."

"But that's what we do, isn't it?"

"I mean internally. Just because you were a whistle-blower doesn't mean—"

"I wasn't a *whistle-blower*. Who said it like that?"

"I just meant—"

"A *whistle-blower?* That's how they talk about me?"

She gave him a look. "No one talks about you, Leo."

Twist the knife a little, thanks, he thought. There was a new distance in her eyes, and he felt the picture of her bedroom slipping away.

"The shit I saw, Gail, was not right." He slowed it down and said it a second time, his finger tapping the table with each syllable: "It was not right." There was more he could say. Descriptions, details. The sounds they made. Instead, he said, "I did what anyone would have done."

"Except plenty of other people haven't."

"And they get to look at themselves in the mirror. I look at me."

"And you like what you see."

He couldn't tell if there was a question mark there. He turned it around on her: "Do you?"

"I do," she said. "I love the job. I feel needed. It's hard as hell, but this is what I want."

He'd meant *Do you like what you see when you look at me?* not when she looked at herself. She'd missed the sad attempt at a come-on and instead preened in her own mental compact, admiring her accomplishments. He was angry at himself for getting defensive and uptight, for making the mistake of thinking that this was an appropriate time to vent about the things he couldn't mention to anyone else. *There* is *no appropriate time. Get used to it.*

"They all look so happy, don't they?" he asked, motioning to the people around them, eating large, getting drunk. He'd glanced at the menu, duck here and braised spare rib there, the seventy-dollar and beyond bottles of wine. "No clue what's going on."

"You have to enjoy yourself somehow."

"But doesn't it piss you off? The things we do, and the people we do it for, and they're here partying like it's still 1999? Did they miss something, or have we?"

Her glass was empty. She was putting cash on the table.

"It was good to see you, Leo." Then they shared a brief farewell hug, and off she went, he trying not to check out her ass, the ass he wouldn't have, the ass that was off to important geopolitical adventures. He sat back down, his glass half empty, and ordered another drink. Might as well make it official that he was here for the night.

Z.

Dwelling on the past is unhealthy and dangerous. It leads to self-perpetuating hatred, to Unclean Thoughts and Malicious Motives. We're taught this in school, and in all levels of the Perfect Society. Hope for a better future can be washed away by excessive thoughts about harmful pasts. I know this, yet I've found it harder and harder to obey the rule since my family's accident.

I first met Cemby at one of the Unification Day rallies, held in the cities every hundred days. We all held our flags and were silent at the beginning, when they showed old images from the wars on the giant screens, the speakers echoing short clips of people's cries. The Government probably didn't realize it—and no one would have dared admit it, as it was borderline illegal—but many of us found these glimpses titillating. We'd been told so little about what had happened, we were given such cursory summaries in school and in the occasional backward-looking Daily Missive, that these brief video clips were fascinating. *What had it really been like back then? How bad was it?* We didn't want to know, and yet we did.

We had the requisite moment of silence for all that our ancestors had lost, and for the successes of the Phoenix Generation, our forebears who learned how to lay down their arms, how to cobble together the few survivors into a new society. We applauded as our most recent advances were announced. Scientists were making new discoveries, re-creating the best of the old world while taking bold steps forward. Government Archivists were continually studying the pre-Conflagration period, passing on information when it was deemed beneficial. The most recent outbreaks of influenza and other viruses had been better contained than in previous years; the Agriculture Division was repairing the soil, making more areas fertile.

We cheered and waved our flags and sang the slogans. The pageantry always felt a bit much to me, but it was a good excuse to get out in the sun—on Unification Days, the atmospheric barriers were stretched across the tallest buildings, providing shade, which was a welcome rarity. The rallies usually devolved into free-floating picnics after the speeches, most people taking the rest of the afternoon off. I was sitting with a few friends, other officers mostly, and beside us was a group of young professionals distinguished solely by the fact that one of the women was stunning. I decided it was my patriotic duty to introduce myself and get to know her.

Wings were the style that year. Every jacket seemed to have them, sewn onto the shoulders, some of them hanging forward and others flapping in the back. Extra cotton and synthetics, a waste in my opinion, but it was the fad, everyone was doing it. Some were angular and spiked, metallic devils' or demons', others were curved like angels' wings or birds'. No one really knew much about angels or devils anymore; the stories were gone and all that was left were rumors, whispers. But here they were, reincarnated as fashion. I knew a little about the original stories from my classified research, had heard of Lucifer and Gabriel and a few others, and was surprised the Government allowed such fetishism. Maybe they considered it an allowable manifestation of something latent in us, a harmless commercialization of a part of ourselves we'd forgotten.

She wore a jacket with smallish black wings on the shoulders, barely visible, suggesting a willingness to go along with the trend and also a certain conservatism I appreciated. Her name was Cemby, she said. Short for December. I didn't know the word at the time and she told me it used to be the name of a "month," a twelfth of a year. I commented on how unusual a name it was, how surprising that the Government hadn't objected to the choice.

"My father's a level-five Archivist, so they gave him a pass. I think he told them it was *poetic*." She wore her hair long then, and it seemed to change colors when the sun emerged from the clouds. "He said his grandmother had been born on the last day of December, so it's an homage to her."

That too was odd. References to the past—even oblique ones—were too freighted, and I was surprised she would say this to someone she'd just met. She was nervous, talking without thinking. It was the first clue that she liked me.

She was a financial analyst, a few years out of school and working for one of the HumanTech firms. Her company had made a breakthrough on skin protectors, something to help block the sun. If everything went well, we'd all be receiving injections of her company's product in a year or two, but that was the extent of what she could tell me. "Proprietary information." She smiled. "Corporate espionage is out of control these days."

She asked what I did.

"I work with the Security Department."

"So neither of us can say much about our jobs. That doesn't leave us with much to talk about." That could have sounded like a brush-off, but she said it differently.

"I suppose we could just make things up."

"Okay. If you weren't in Security, what would you be?"

I thought for a moment. "An astronaut."

"Huh." I'd bored her. I was predictable. Plus, there were no astronauts—there hadn't been any since before the Conflagration, though more than a few scientists were arguing for a new space program now that our planet was in so much trouble. "Why?" she asked.

"I heard we used to send people to the moon, to Mars, to Pluto." We all trafficked in rumors, false snippets of history. Gossip became legend. But I really had seen an image of a man in a ballonish metal suit, a human zeppelin, standing on the moon beside a flag, hadn't I? Or had I only imagined it? "It would be fun to get back there, see what we left behind. Maybe we have colonies there that got cut off during the Conflagration."

"You think it would be interesting to get back in touch?"

"Unless they've all starved to death."

"In which case, being an astronaut would be rather bleak."

"Good point. All right, if you weren't a financial analyst, what would you be?"

"A writer."

"What would you write about?"

"Maybe I'd write about a Security agent who becomes an astronaut and travels to a cold, dark world populated by corpses."

"And the masses would flock to read it."

We did have writers and storytellers, yes, but most were employed by the Government. Their stories were vetted for intergroup bias, past fetishizing, that sort of thing. Most of what people knew or thought they knew about the past came from the stories. A good writer used just enough of the real past (writers had low-level clearance, could get access to some parts of history) mixed in with his nonsensical fictions. It made things seem real. Even though the readers themselves didn't know the past, they all thought that they *understood* it somehow, on some innate level. You'd read a story about two young lovers on a doomed vessel in a northern sea, or a tale of a couple reunited at a North African bar during a world war, and there was something in there, something indefinable, that felt true to you, that seemed like it had happened in your own life, or maybe in the lives of your subconsciously remembered ancestors. It reminded you of half-forgotten bedtime stories your grandparents had told you. It reminded you of yourself.

Every now and then a writer would be accused of writing real history, of only pretending that it was made up. The writer's story would surge in popularity for a few days, everyone reading voraciously to steal this glimpse of the true past before the Government deleted the story. Then (if you bought the rumors) the writer was arrested, and the literature officials who had negligently vetted the story were arrested as well. There were cynics who didn't believe this, who thought the Government actually started these rumors to make people *think* they were getting access to real history when really it was all untrue, propaganda. Were the lies truth, or not?

When Cemby was alone, she would scribble her stories, little pieces of herself. Even after we were married, she never let me read them, said they were too personal; she made empty promises to show them to me when they were "finished." But they were never finished—eventually she deleted them (or the Government did, if the expiration period had passed) or burned them, saying they weren't any good, that it was more like therapy, something for herself. Occasionally, she'd gaze off into space and I'd ask what she was thinking about and she'd say it was a story she'd written a while ago. It was actually pretty decent, she'd say. *Then let me read it.* I can't, she'd reply. The time ran out, I had to delete it—it's gone. A piece of me, somehow, but vanished forever.

So, I'd say to her, *tell me what you remember.* And she'd try her best.

At the time of the accident I'd been promoted to intelligence officer. I raided the secret libraries of rebels who wanted to disseminate their stories, poison the society. We shut down publishers and pulled the plug on writers who were sending out missives on the Net and the wires; we tracked down extant copies of texts that were supposed to have been burned long ago. As a result of that privileged position, I knew more than the average citizen about the past, but only so much. Sometimes on raids I would pore through the materials before the Elimination and Deletion crew arrived, would marvel at the wars, the exterminations, the genocide. The things we had been capable of—no, *were still* capable of. That's why my job was important. These evils were buried inside us, and it was my duty to keep them dormant. I protected people from themselves.

One day my wife went to pick up our daughter at school. Two hours passed. I did a quick scan for them and turned up nothing. Surprising, but not totally unheard-of, as some buildings had walls specially designed to prevent scanning. Another hour passed and she wasn't answering her wire. Then someone buzzed in, and the monitor showed three men waiting to come up. Three men I had worked with in my Security days.

They came up and I knew why they were there the moment I opened the door. An accident on the thruway, they said. Possible error by the other driver, maybe a pod malfunction.

I felt dizzy. Someone leaned me against a wall. Then I ran to the bathroom and threw up. Afterward I felt hot, like my body was being pulled through a tiny opening from one world into another. I didn't want to leave this world, wanted to stay in this place where I'd been so comfortable, but there was nothing to keep me tethered here anymore.

They said they were very sorry.

I don't remember much of the next few days. My memory blessedly wiped clean. I received calls and wires, words of encouragement. The funeral service passed in a blur, images without sounds, leaving no impression, just a heaviness. Old friends of my wife whom I'd forgotten about, parents of my daughter's playmates. Many people I didn't even know, and I began to see the different life Cemby had led, the mysteries I hadn't known about, the coworkers and jogging partners, the elderly cashier from her office cafeteria who said my wife had always been so friendly. I was given two weeks off, two weeks with nothing to do. I walked the city, going nowhere, returning home without any recollection of the preceding hours. My mind had been with my family the whole time, hiding in memories.

Once I was back at work, people didn't talk about it. I noticed that the guys didn't invite me out the first few weeks, as if they were afraid of what I'd say.

Two months passed and I received the dreaded visit.

I would have known it was coming even if I hadn't received the official memoranda reminding me of my duties and obligations. I'd ignored them. I'd felt I deserved special treatment.

"No," I told them at the door.

"Zed, you know how this works. We understand the difficulty, but—"

"I just need a little more time."

"We did give you a couple of extra days." It was one of my first bosses, from Security. At least they'd sent important people for the job. It was a show of respect. "Come on, you know the protocol. It'd be best if you left the apartment."

"I'm fine right here."

"Very well." He walked in. The other three followed, two men and a woman, and set up their devices and detectors. "We'll try to be quick."

They dispatched the obvious items first. The framed images of our wedding, a few of Cemby years ago when we'd first met. The tech waved her wand and the images went blank, then the tech packed the frames into her case. They would be disposed of at headquarters, and I would receive remuneration for them in my next pay. I followed another tech into our bedroom and more images were erased. I watched them go through the file cabinets. It was a long process. Paper records were rare but I had saved some notes she'd written to me, mostly from our younger days when we weren't as harried, when we weren't raising a daughter who consumed so much of our lives. Love letters, or quick scribbles left on the kitchen table before going to work, tiny mementos I had saved. Some were notes I had written to her; the techs were going through her cabinet now. Cemby had saved more than I had. She was always the more sentimental one. I hadn't realized how many notes I'd left her, so many pieces of myself, like molted skin. I stood there as they were destroyed.

They took her clothes and her other belongings. They found the perfume I had hidden in my own bureau. One of the techs booted into my account and busily stripped it of every wire and image of my wife and daughter. They cross-checked my other possessions against my wife's purchasing records to determine which of my clothes and what decorations in the apartment had been gifts from her, and these too were removed.

It was when they walked into my daughter's room that I snapped. Seeing a tech pick up one of her old toys—a stuffed bear that she hadn't played with in years; she'd outgrown it long ago—I clamped a hand on the tech's shoulder. He was so small, a rookie, no idea of what he'd just walked into. I punched him in the face.

"Get out of her room!" The tech bounced off the wall, his head knocking down an image of my daughter smiling in her grandfather's arms.

I woke up two hours later, in bed. A bed stripped of sheets, as Cemby had bought those too. My head didn't hurt, which meant they'd used a relatively weak Stunner. It had probably been done by my former boss, who must have known this was coming. I myself had done it to countless grievers. Later, I was embarrassed when I realized how stereotypically I'd acted, as if I were following a script. Are we so predictable? Are our actions and emotions so fated?

I walked through my suddenly less decorated, more spacious apartment. They'd even rearranged the furniture so that my daughter's room wasn't empty; it now contained a chair from the living room and a writing desk I didn't recognize. They did that sometimes, brought in new items to remake the space, no charge, courtesy of the Government. They'd fumigated the place too; the old scents were gone.

They had been thorough, as they always were. I had hidden a few things behind a fake panel in the kitchen—my favorite image of my wife, laughing while holding a wineglass, a crescent moon visible over her shoulder; one of my daughter's favorite shirts, which I had buried my nose in to smell just the other night. They both were gone.

I sat in the living room and stared out the window. It was dark out, or what passed for dark in my ceaseless city. Pod lights glittered at me as they frantically rushed about; beacons atop construction cranes and new buildings blinked warnings to the aircraft that disappeared into faintly glowing clouds. I was ashamed at how I'd acted and would have to apologize.

The past was gone. It was time to move forward.

PART TWO

REVISIONISM

10.

After Tasha sent the GTK files to the *Times,* nothing happened. And then more nothing happened. Until too many things started happening.

The worst part, at first, was when she thought she'd had no effect. Realized that the nerves that had plagued her, the added degree of tension and borderline nausea she'd felt anytime she had to work on a GTK-related task over the ensuing days, had all been for naught. The *Times* reporter apparently had not been impressed, or had other stories to write, or was too busy sending his résumés to PR firms in anticipation of the next round of journalistic layoffs.

Tasha—disappointed, saddened, and finally enraged—pondered her next move. Should she try someone at the *Post* or maybe the *LA Times?* Then she got another idea.

T.J. had invited her to join him and some friends for a party/poster-decorating event; there was a big pro-immigration rally at the Mall the next weekend, and they were designing eye-catching signage. Tasha didn't have much of an opinion on immigration, honestly. Or maybe she had two: she felt bad for the black folk in her old neighborhood who couldn't get jobs because the new Latinos were happy to do the work for slave wages, but she also felt more than a bit sketched out by the very white, very angry nativists who claimed that the influx of darker-skinned people was ruining the country. So she wasn't planning on attending the rally, but she went to the party because she wanted to ask T.J. something.

The party was held at an unkempt three-bedroom apartment in, appropriately enough, Columbia Heights, a neighborhood whose occupants were workaholic Salvadoran immigrants, multigenerational black families, and white professionals whose lesser pigmentation was leading to greater real estate prices and property taxes for everyone else. Tasha wasn't sure if the other activists, all of whom, except T.J., were white, saw the irony.

The activists were sprawled on furniture claimed from Salvation Army and Goodwill and local street corners; an upholstery-spewing chair here and a saggingly invertebrate sofa there. More people were spread out democratically on the floor, kneeling on bedsheets that they were decorating with slogans, the smell of permanent ink thick in the air. Also patchouli. All of them clad in Converse and Docs, jeans and cords, dyes and hennas.

While helping T.J. design and print some pamphlets, she asked him if he knew of any ways to create an untraceable e-mail account. T.J. told her yes, and he knew people who could do it; the hacker crowd and the activist crowd were tight, at least in D.C.

"But why do you ask? You making me party to credit card fraud? Or some underground kidnapping ring?"

"I need to contact someone anonymously. It's a good deed, I promise."

The next time he saw her, a few days later at a coffee shop near her office, he handed her a yellow Post-it with a password and an e-mail address: notreally.aname@carsonsgillem.com.

"What's carsonsgillem?" she asked.

"Hedge fund. Guy I know hacked into them, decided not to take them down but play around with them instead. He created a few e-mail addresses on their server; they'll never know, at least not until he comes up with something really crazy to do to them. He told me the account should work for at least a few months. You're free to use it as long as it lasts. Just don't say anything identifying on it, and don't access it from your home or office computer."

So she'd waited in line one lunch break at the Martin Luther King Jr. Memorial Library, basically a homeless shelter in downtown D.C.

where people occasionally checked out books. The wait time for a computer almost took her entire lunch hour, and the kiosk stank of the previous person's BO when Tasha finally logged into the hedge fund's site. She e-mailed the *Times* reporter. *Hello,* she typed. *I do not work at carsonsgillem but am accessing this account to reach you. I recently sent you information pertaining to GTK Industries which I had hoped would provide material for an important exposé. I was wondering why you have not written about it. Please write back to this address.* She didn't bother inventing an alias to sign off with.

The next day she returned to the library, this time at four thirty, just in case varying her routine was important. As it turned out, Notreally Aname had mail; one e-mail from the *Times* reporter. Yes, he had received the files and was very grateful for them. Much time and effort had been spent studying them, and various attempts had been made to verify certain bits of information. GTK was proving most unhelpful in their responses, he explained. Tasha's stomach tensed with the realization that while she'd thought nothing was happening, GTK's public relations department was receiving prying calls from the *Times*. That meant someone at the firm might already know about the leak, even though no story had broken yet.

The only reason the *Times* hadn't run a story, the reporter explained, was that a few issues were still confusing him. There followed a long list of follow-up questions and requests for clarification. Tasha's heart was pounding now, sweat on her back. They *were* going to run the story, so long as she could answer their follow-ups. She read through his questions, committing them to memory; a few would require a bit of digging into the files. Which she would need to do with extreme care, especially if anyone at GTK had tipped off her firm about the company's receiving alarming questions from the *Times*.

She spread the research out over the next week. Worked late every night (not that that was unusual) so she could access the GTK files when no one was around. One of the reporter's questions, which asked her to identify herself or at least explain her relationship to GTK, she chose to leave unanswered.

* * *

The next time Tasha saw T.J. (at a meeting to plan the candlelight vigil in front of the White House), she told him to ask his hacker friend to kill the account and delete the e-mails.

"You gonna tell me what it was all about?" he asked.

She realized that the hacker friend could just read them himself. Who was this hacker friend? Would he read the e-mails and tell T.J., or someone else? She'd taken such care to cover her steps; maybe there truly was no way to move without a trace. She'd make a lousy criminal.

"No," she told T.J. "Maybe one day. You'd approve, trust me."

The reporter worked fast; the article appeared three days after their last e-mail exchange. Tasha had opened her paper one morning and there it was, on page A-3. Not a front-page story? She seethed for a moment, then read it through. He'd done a good job, even finding a former GTK employee (unnamed) who said, "I'm not surprised to hear about shenanigans like this," and posited that this could be "the tip of the iceberg." But Tasha's documents provided the bulk of the story, and she felt a surge of pride that what she'd done did indeed matter to someone—hopefully, to many hundreds of thousands of someones. Including the important someones, the someones who had the power to stop such awful machinations, the someones who would now be roused by popular outrage into action.

People at her firm saw the *Times* story, of course, and an internal audit was launched; junior associates were questioned by the most court-savvy of the partners. But Tasha was cool and had rehearsed her answers many times; at the conclusion of her own thirty-minute inquisition, she felt she'd eluded the firm's suspicions. On coffee break with her pal Jill one morning, Jill asked Tasha point-blank if she was the leak, and Tasha confessed that the news story had made her happy, even thrilled, but she swore that it wasn't her; she still remembered Ethics 101, thank you very much.

The *Times* story instantly went viral. It hit on all the major liberal news-segmentation sites and countless like-minded blogs, which used it as evidence of the war's inherent illegality. Conservative and military bloggers touted the story as well, as proof of a bureaucratically mismanaged defense policy and an industry that cared less for patriotism than profit. By the third day, the *Times'* competing publications, like the *Washington Post,* were augmenting the tale with their own investigations. Cable anchors were disgusted, op-ed columns employed angry adjectives from the back pages, and a couple of congressmen vowed a close audit of GTK's business dealings.

And then, just when Tasha was feeling most proud of herself for making a difference, the GTK story receded into the media netherworld. She Googled it daily and sometimes found a heartfelt open letter on the blog of another bereaved military relative or saw an angry new screed from some critic of global capitalism, but that was all. The cable anchors had moved on to other stories of injustice, the op-ed pages were incensed by something else, and the two congressmen turned to other tasks more compelling than launching some boring audit of a very connected company. GTK Industries weathered the storm. Barely a week after the *Times* story appeared, a subcommittee chairman lightly admonished GTK from the Senate floor moments before voting in favor of giving the company a vast new defense contract.

It dawned on Tasha slowly, the irrelevance of what she had done.

A few nights later was the vigil at the White House. Suddenly she was going to so many meetings and events, leaving the office "early" at seven to make them, running the risk that her billable hours would be too low, that someone in HR (or one of the partners) would put a black mark by her name, file her under Lacks Commitment. She'd almost skipped the vigil, wary of that black mark and figuring the event would be just useless symbolism. Which it was.

But she'd gone, and it hadn't been a total disaster, as that's where she'd met Troy Jones. Maybe she was confusing her mourning with her loneliness, her heart with her libido. She'd spotted him right away—how could she *not* have?—and had angled to talk to him. Brothers like this did not drop from the sky. His hair was cut short and was very dark against his skin, and his light eyes—were they green? or gray? possibly the lightest sapphire blue?—seemed somehow double-lensed, like he was observing things from a certain remove. She wondered if his mother was white, or perhaps a grandfather, and there seemed to be some Asian in there too, possibly Vietnamese—perhaps Troy's very existence owed itself to America's past military adventures.

He reminded Tasha of her brother. He seemed to carry himself like a soldier, a certain bearing and gravity, so unlike the typical guys who figured using slyness and humor was the quickest way into her pants. After the vigil, she'd returned home and studied Marshall's military portrait, which her parents had given her and which she'd hung on her wall. Years ago they'd given her his first such portrait, and Marshall in all that regalia had been almost unrecognizable to her. She'd since grown used to it, and he'd grown into it. This picture, taken just before his last deployment, was the Marshall he had always been fated to become.

The day after the vigil, she used a much-deserved sick day after working three consecutive seven-day weeks and spent much of the day sifting through Marshall's old journals and trying to contact his war buddies.

Then she'd received the phone call. A mystery man, telling her to meet him at the Topaz Bar the next day. Calling from a blocked number. Someone who knew her name, her home phone number, that she worked at the firm, and that GTK was one of its clients. Someone who implied that he knew even more.

She barely slept that night. Had distinct memories of rolling over and staring at her clock to see that the time was 12:01, 1:57, 2:30. Telling herself not to panic. Maybe it was only the original *Times* reporter, or someone who worked with him? Maybe the guy hadn't really been threatening her?

In her head, the law school professors were clearing their throats.

* * *

The Topaz was one of those so-called boutique hotels that had appeared in D.C. over the past few years like infiltrators from a trendier city. Tasha had gotten drunk here with law school friends once, had vague memories of the rotating red and blue lights that bathed the bar in alternating warmth and coolness. At two in the afternoon, the bar was bright and nearly empty but for a few lone men wearing business suits and jet lag, tapping messages in their PDAs or chatting on their phones in foreign languages between sips of coffee. None of them looked up at her.

Even the location of this meeting was disturbing, suggesting that the mystery caller knew it was close enough to the firm's office for Tasha to walk here on break, yet far enough from it that it was unlikely they would meet or be overheard by any of her colleagues.

She'd been sitting at a small table by the window for five minutes, nervously telling the server she was waiting on a friend, when a familiar man walked in. He came right up, said, "Hi, Tasha," and sat down opposite her as if he'd been expected.

Who was he? Wait, now she remembered; she'd seen him at one of the antiwar meetings she'd attended. Couldn't remember his name. Tall, built like a track runner, short light hair, and glasses. What was he doing here? He was years younger than the voice on the phone had been.

"Oh, hi," she said. "I'm sorry, but I'm waiting for someone."

"Yes: me." He sat there with an implacable face, waiting for it to sink in.

"You aren't—"

"I'm not who called you, no. He sent me here in his stead." She noticed that he was carrying a black man-purse, which he flung open now. He removed two manila file folders and placed them on the table between them right as the waiter appeared. He ordered a vodka tonic, and it took her a few seconds to realize the waiter was looking at her. She managed to utter a barely audible "Iced tea."

Things were slowly falling into place.

She tried to remember what they'd talked about during their five-minute chat a couple of weeks ago. He'd said he was a graduate student, something about Asian history. He'd recently returned from years teaching English abroad and he was incensed at the direction their country was headed in.

"I'm afraid I forgot your name," she said, trying to keep calm as everything shifted around her.

"Leo Hastings."

"And you want to talk to me about one of my firm's clients?"

"Yes, GTK. That was quite a story that broke in the *Times*. The reporter had access to all kinds of confidential information about a company that's represented by your law firm."

"That story very much angered our client."

"You're the lawyer here—I'm sure you could skew things any way you want. But all I have to do is pick up the phone and call one of your firm's partners and tell him that I represent the government and I happen to know that one of his associates leaked those GTK files. One of his associates decided that her political opinions were more important than legal ethics, more important than the firm's reputation for defending its clients. And then I'd say your name."

The glasses arrived and Leo informed the waiter they wouldn't be ordering any food.

"I'm not sure how any of this is your business, Leo, but here are the facts. The partners already interviewed everyone at the firm, including myself, about the leak. GTK performed its own internal review as well. We still don't know who did it, and I have no idea why you would think it was me."

He smiled. "I get it. You think I'm taping this, and you need to be circumspect. Which is smart. But here are some more facts: The e-mail account you used to contact the *Times* reporter was created by a hacker we've been following, a hacker who travels in the same circles that you've unfortunately started traveling in of late. Your buddy T.J. And when those e-mails were sent, the account was accessed from the downtown D.C. public library, which is a five-minute walk from your office."

She needed a few seconds. *T.J.* and not a friend of T.J. was the hacker? Which probably meant that T.J. had read those e-mails she'd sent and never said anything about it.

"The library's a five-minute walk from *thousands* of people's offices," she said, "and most of them are much more politically connected than me and must have had access to something about GTK."

His smile hadn't changed. "You need to scan in and out of your building at the security kiosk. Terrorism-prevention measures—aren't they a bitch? We can match the times you scanned in and out with the times those e-mails were sent. Three times, all perfect matches." He tapped one of the manila folders, then slid it closer to her. "This has the evidence that the e-mails were sent from MLK Library, and also the security scan times at your office building."

She opened the file and was confronted by pages of techie-speak—acronyms and long streams of programming code, like android haiku. "I'm supposed to understand this?"

"You don't have to, but your firm will, and GTK will. And the D.C. Bar will."

She skimmed more of it and found the entire e-mail exchange between her unnamed self and the reporter. She felt dizzy and hot, and took a long sip from her glass.

"This is all circumstantial."

He laughed. "That's the argument someone would have to make if she was fighting this in court. You really want to do that?"

She waited, trying to consider her options. "What do you want?"

"That's the good news—I'm not asking you for much. I need someone to keep tabs on different organizations, someone who can get in deeper than I can. Someone who's an old buddy of one of the ringleaders. Someone with a gold-plated biography, a grade-A reason to be so involved with the groups."

He opened the second manila folder and she saw a number of photographs of a familiar man. He was yelling in most of them.

"Thomas Jefferson Trenton, also known as T.J. Your old college boyfriend, now a radical activist with a long record of arrests for trespassing, destruction of property, computer hacking, and other acts of civil disobedience."

"You know that we went to college together?"

"Public records, Tasha. It's not that hard. Don't worry, it's not like we dug up dirty e-mails you'd sent to each other from your Oberlin accounts, though we could. But I respect privacy."

Sure he did. College attendance records wouldn't have told him that she'd slept with T.J.—Leo must have spoken to some mutual acquaintance at one of the meetings. She felt violated; her whole body was hot.

"I still don't know what you're asking of me."

"I have strong reason to believe that T.J. is one of the brains behind a certain Web site called knoweverything.org. They like to post confidential, classified information just for the illicit thrill it gives them— I guess he outgrew the Internet porn he was into a few years ago. I need you to help us find out if this is true. All I want you to do is keep going to those antiwar meetings, maybe spend some extra time with T.J. and his pals, talk to them about what great work they're doing, and what they should do next. And maybe, due to your insider position at a powerful D.C. firm with all sorts of clients in the Establishment, you'll be able to offer them other juicy bits of leaked information if they're interested."

"This . . . You can't do this." She stood up.

"If you think things will turn out better for you by walking away and leaving this information with me, that is a mistake." He tapped the table again and slightly softened his voice. "I'm sorry, I rushed things. You just got hit with a lot—sit down a minute. Please."

She obeyed and he leaned closer. "You've gone to a few of those antiwar meetings, but only a few, and even when you're there, you keep quiet. I'm willing to bet I know why: It's because you're smart and sane, whereas most of the people in those groups are crazies nursing grudges. You don't agree with them, Tasha—they just want to exploit the pain of people like you and use it for their own political agenda. So why is it a problem to let me know what they're doing?"

The pain. He knew about Marshall. That's what he meant by her "gold-plated biography." If Tasha did try to insinuate herself more deeply into T.J.'s life and whatever he was doing, no one would ever suspect she was a mole. It would fit perfectly into T.J.'s worldview that the sister of a dead soldier would want to join his crusade.

"Maybe I *don't* like some of them," she told Leo. "But they have a right to protest."

"I believe in the First Amendment too, thanks. I'm not here to run anyone in for saying they don't like this president or that war." He tapped the first folder. "Look, you sent those files in because the crooked bastards at GTK put their stock price and earnings reports above the lives of the soldiers those vests and ammo might have protected. Good for you; sincerely. I applaud that. The thing is, there are people on the opposite side, people like T.J., who find classified information about intelligence strategies or ongoing investigations, about diplomatic policy, and they publicize it, putting the lives of dedicated people at risk just so they can score some political points. Now, how is that any different from delaying a shipment of vests?"

She shook her head. "I see how this works. You'll hold the GTK thing over me forever. One day you'll tell me my little project's done, but then, a year later, maybe five, I'll get another call, *Hey Tasha, I need this favor.*"

He took a sip of his two o'clock vodka and leaned back in his chair. "I promise you, if there's any chance I'll still be working on assignments like this five years from now, I'll shoot myself."

Jesus, she was having a hard time figuring him out. "This is what you do, Leo? Blackmail, extortion? This is legal for you?"

He chuckled. "Feel free to sue me. I'm a government contractor, so I'm pretty insulated. Honestly, they're still writing the rules about what applies and what doesn't. But yeah, if you'd rather challenge this in open court, lay bare all of your secrets, go for it."

"*Contractor?* Wait, who do you work for?"

For the first time, he moved around uncomfortably in his seat. "It's complicated. But I am authorized by the United States government to be doing this, and I have its full protection."

She tried to think. There were great, gaping holes in what he was saying. "I want something, in writing, that spells out what you want me to do, so that *if* I agree, then when I do finish it—"

"In writing? Sure. One copy for you and one for me, only I'll need to make some extra copies for my boss and his boss, and then it'll get entered into the system, which really means thousands of people can access it, and it's in there forever. I wanted to make this as painless for you as possible, anonymous and off the books, but if you really want it to be part of the permanent record that Tasha Coretta Wilson assisted in the—"

"All right, all right." What she really wanted was to slap him. The lawyer in her had already prepared half a dozen retorts beginning with "You have no right to—," but she knew he'd deflect, counter, or ignore them all.

"I'm not angry at you for GTK," he repeated. "You exposed wrongdoing. If you want to stand up and publicly take credit for that, then do it. Meaning: disbarment, and prosecution for legal malpractice, and never being able to repay your law school loans. A life of poverty for following your ideals. That's your choice. But if you think you're worth more than that, if you think you shouldn't have to suffer for the rest of your life over one little ethical lapse, then help me expose a little more wrongdoing."

"By war protesters?"

"If peaceful opposition is all you come across, then this will be the world's most boring assignment. A lot of what I do is boring, Tasha. I can't even tell you how boring. It would be par for the course if this leads nowhere. I'm not asking you to wear a wire or get in the middle of anything dangerous. Just keep your eyes open, listen, and tell me everything. That last part is important. If I ever find out you knew about something and kept quiet, if I so much as get a sense that you're holding out on me, then you've broken our deal"—he rapped his knuckles on the first folder—"and you live with the con-sequences."

She tried to contain her anger while he turned his eyes to the window to admire two young Asian women bouncing past in sleek running outfits. Who the hell was this guy? What parallel universe had he transported over from?

The joggers passed and his eyes went back to her. The smugness there, the obnoxious confidence in his tone, and the way he hadn't even bothered to hide his ogling of those women, struck another chord in her. She realized that she was actually sitting across from someone from that much-imagined, never-before-seen world: the right-wing military-industrial machine that had consumed her brother. For months she'd been raging and raging at an amorphous, seemingly intangible foe, but here was one of its representatives in the flesh. Maybe this wasn't such a terrible thing.

"Well," she said, hoping her minor change in tone wouldn't be too obvious, "since you seem like such a well-informed guy, I want a lit-tle something from you too."

"We're prepared to pay, but that's—"

"I don't mean *money*—yours probably all comes from laundering Afghan drug deals, right?"

"Sure, that and overthrowing leftist governments and raiding their national banks."

So he had a sense of humor. "What I want is information, about my brother."

"Specifically?"

"How he died. Where, when, all the contributing factors."

"The army hasn't shared anything with you?"

"Let's just say I don't believe it. I want to *know everything*"—she raised her eyebrows at the pun—"such as why his blog was taken down a week before he died and why he never sent any e-mails that last week. I want to know if something Marshall posted online pissed off some commanding officer or some suit at the Pentagon. I want to know if anyone in the chain of command gave any orders that placed him in harm's way because of something he wrote or said."

Leo thought for a moment. Tasha knew she wasn't in a position to make demands, but part of being a good negotiator was acting as if you were.

"I'll try," he said. "But military intelligence isn't exactly my turf. Us spooks don't play together as nicely as we should."

"Yeah, we all noticed that with 9/11."

He eyed her for a moment, then grinned, as if granting her the point. "For the record, I was in a different line of work then. But I will see what I can do for you. Your brother was a hero, and if anyone in the army has lied to your family about him, I won't like that any more than you do."

"So we agree on something. How nice."

"I think we agree on more than you realize."

Her heart was still beating too fast but the sourness in her stomach was gone. She hated this guy, but she could use him just as he used her. She wasn't sure how yet—she'd need time to replay the conversation and figure the angles—but this was what she'd always excelled at, from debate club through law school and up to the few trials that the firm had let her handle: finding her adversary's weak points, the flaws in his logic, and outmaneuvering him. And just plain being smarter than him. Because who was Leo but some obviously low-level security-firm hack? If he were a superspy, he wouldn't be in D.C. tailing activists. Yet surely he had connections, and these she could make use of. She still felt violated by his entrance into her life, but her fear faded as she got a better take on him. She would play along with him to get what she needed, for a while at least.

Leo leaned back again and took a celebratory swig of his drink. Then he told her how he envisioned their relationship working and where he wanted her to start.

Finally, he looked at his watch and apologized for how long he'd kept her from her important clients. He put the folders back in his bag and said good-bye, dismissing her, but staying in his chair.

Apparently he wanted them to leave separately, her first, which seemed an odd bit of clandestine tomfoolery, considering they'd been sitting together in public beside a window for an hour now. Which only confirmed her opinion of him; he'd probably been a damned TSA baggage checker before winning a promotion.

It had started raining and she'd didn't have an umbrella. She hailed a cab, needing to be alone with her thoughts so she could puzzle out the immensity of her conversation. The middle-aged Eastern European driver stopped muttering into his earpiece cell phone and asked, "Where to?" She told him, and like that the guy pulled a U and resumed his call in some Slavic tongue, speaking softly, as if afraid she'd overhear his conversation and understand it. Asking after his kids or the political situation in Ukraine, maybe, or talking soccer, or complaining about work or the weather or this damn city where the spoiled kids drink all night. It was easy to tune it all out when you didn't know what they were saying.

11.

Sari was more nervous than usual as she wound her way through Washington's chaotic streets. The SUV was three times larger than anything she had driven before, and she thanked the gods for helping her steer it without running over another car. She also thanked her mother, whom she knew was watching her. At a red light Sari let her eyes wander, and there in the distance was the Washington Monument glowing in the dark; someone honked, and she saw that the light was green again. The wheel was too big for her hands—it would have been too big for an ape's hands, and she didn't understand how Sang Hee, who was no taller than herself, could enjoy handling something like this. No, of course she understood—the mistress loved power.

Sari didn't have an American or even a Korean driver's license, but Sang Hee said that didn't matter.

The other cars sped along with a sort of impersonal professionalism, hurrying to their important destinations. Frightened pedestrians huddled on street corners, aware of their low status. Still, it felt so *good* to be out, not just out of the house but here in a city, even if an unfamiliar one. She'd lived in urban areas all her life and was used to noise and commotion. The noise was different here—no whine from motorbike engines, no street vendors calling out—but still the vibrancy charged her.

She knew that Sang Hee was timing her, so she could not afford any wrong turns. She followed the primitive map the mistress had drawn, only the relevant streets noted, along with an occasional landmark. The drive from their house in Mount Pleasant was short, and the clock told her she had been gone only ten minutes when she pulled to the curb in front of the store. She had been told not to worry about understanding street signs, that the diplomatic plates gave her license to park anywhere.

She walked inside. The automatic doors pulled open and there Leo was, standing in front of a display of freshly cut flowers. She smelled lilac and rose, and he smiled.

"Good evening, Sari," he said in Bahasa. He wore a light gray dress shirt tucked into black slacks. He was even taller than she remembered, and just as handsome.

"Hello," she said, and realized she had no idea what to say next. She turned to free a shopping cart from the long chain while she tried to think. What exactly was she doing, and what was she prepared to do? Was she stringing him along for company and conversation, or for help? But what kind of help could some random American provide?

Or perhaps she was just attracted to him and acting stupid. Being in his presence again threw her, and she worried she was setting in motion things she couldn't control.

"So...you want to shop?" he asked slowly. She wondered if perhaps he wasn't as fluent as she had thought.

"Yes. I only have thirty minutes, and I have a lot to buy. They time me. Um...Would you like to shop with me?"

"They time you?"

"They are very strict."

He paused for a moment. "There's a café across the street. Let's just sit for a moment, then I'll help you shop so you aren't late. Okay?"

It was a reasonable request, but her situation was so unreasonable. She had heard that Americans were insistent; this was her first experience with it. Still, her initial plan of chatting with him while shopping now seemed absurd. It would be nice to sit and talk, if she could relax.

They stepped outside and she shivered. Despite her years in Korea she still had not gotten used to the cold. But the shiver felt welcome on her skin. It was proof that she was outside, proof that she existed. The pedestrians passing her on either side were talking in a language she didn't understand, but still it was wonderful to hear them: people in a city, running to countless adventures. She missed other people's voices.

The young black people behind the coffee shop's counter wore green aprons with matching visors. Up-tempo jazz played on the speakers but the customers at the tables moved with an air of lethargy if they moved at all; a few people sat alone, reading or typing on computers; two young lovers held hands while sharing a secret; an old man in a tattered gray coat sat with his eyes shut. Hanging on the wall above each table was a framed, colorful photo of smiling Filipinos selling their wares from narrow boats.

"Can I get you a coffee, or some tea?" he asked. His Bahasa was heavily accented and sometimes he used the wrong prefixes, but she always knew what he meant.

"Thank you, I'm fine."

Leo ordered his coffee and they sat in the back. He took the chair facing out, leaving her to face him and a brick wall. He asked her how she was, and she lied.

"How did you come to be working in America?" he asked.

"I lived in Korea for the last eight years. The family I worked for most recently didn't need me anymore, but they knew someone who did." She tried not to sound bitter when she added, "I was nervous about the travel, but the money they offered was good."

She hadn't put on any makeup, as Sang Hee surely would have been suspicious. And she wished she had something more attractive to wear than this baggy sweatshirt and these unstylish jeans. She reminded herself that she had looked just as disheveled the last time they'd met, and he hadn't seemed to mind then.

"So you must have left Indonesia right around when Suharto was overthrown."

It was always interesting to hear how people described it. Sometimes Suharto was "overthrown," sometimes he "stepped down," sometimes he was "exiled," sometimes he was even "voted out." She wondered what most Americans knew of the transition and the accompanying violence, if they even knew of it at all.

"A little while after."

"That must have been quite a time. I wasn't there yet, but I . . . heard a lot about it."

"It was difficult. Protests and riots and police everywhere. The students would come in and make noise and then the police would punish everyone else for it."

"Is that why you left?"

She didn't like to talk about these things, but it felt different to be asked by someone so removed from her past, sitting in a place so far away. Or maybe it was because she hadn't spoken about it in so long that retelling it finally made her feel some power over her own story.

"I left for many reasons. It's hard to give just one." Was that really true? There had been the one overpowering reason, but she couldn't confront this right now. "I followed my sisters, so that made it easier. We had some relatives who had moved to Seoul, and they told us good things about it."

"And they were wrong?"

"By the time we got there, the economy was slowing down. And they don't like non-Korean workers there."

She wanted to change the subject. She wasn't wearing a watch and couldn't see a clock from where she was sitting. She should tell him that she needed to go, but even though she was risking much just sitting there, it felt too good to get up. So she asked where else he had traveled in her country.

He described the tourist spots that everyone in Java visits, and it was like hearing a travel brochure of her homeland read aloud. She knew everything he was talking about better than he did, but she was happy to let him describe the golden shine of the temples and the acrid smell of the volcanoes, to reminisce about the street-side *warungs* selling *saté* and hot milk with honey. When she blinked, she let her eyes stay shut an extra moment so she could see it again.

"Do you miss it?" he asked.

"I miss the food. I miss the ocean. I miss many of the people I left behind. But there are things I don't miss." Then she asked him what time it was, and she recoiled at the answer—she had already spent half of her allotted time.

"I'm sorry, but I really need to shop. Want to come with me?"

"Of course." She thought he was going to stand, but he stayed still, looking directly at her. "You asked me to come meet you tonight. Was there something you wanted?"

Yes, but she wasn't sure what. There were too many answers. *I wanted you to describe that volcano. I wanted to hear you mispronounce our words for* automobile *and* financial. *I wanted to stare at your light hair and still eyes. I wanted to feel your eyes falling to my shoulders and chest, trying to find where my body hides in this ill-fitting outfit. I wanted to see your forefinger rub the bit of coffee that escaped onto the lip of the plastic lid over and over, the one sign of nervousness your body allows itself. I wanted to see if you remembered my name.*

Yet she was compelled to do her job and avoid a beating for tardiness.

"Can we talk while we shop? I really must hurry."

"Okay." He followed her out. She stopped for a moment in front of Sang Hee's SUV. The keys in her pocket suddenly felt so heavy. Then they walked into the store.

She pulled out a cart and Leo grabbed one of the plastic baskets. She translated into Bahasa the fruits and vegetables on her list; he grabbed some oranges while she looked for a grapefruit. Like the grocery stores in Seoul, the produce section amused her; it was designed to look like the outdoor markets she had grown up with, yet its quiet and orderliness emphasized how bad an imitation it was.

Several shoppers had headphone wires dangling from their ears and others were talking on their phones, everyone devising ways to pretend he or she wasn't actually here. Whereas getting out to the store was the highlight of Sari's week. "Do you see any durian?"

"That's difficult to find here," he said. "Americans aren't fond of it."

"How is that possible?"

"Really, Americans haven't heard of it."

She wheeled her cart into the next aisle. The signs were no help to her, so she had to glance at the contents on each shelf to get an idea of what she might find.

"The people you work for, what do they have you do?" Leo asked. He was so persistent, seemingly emboldened by her attempts at evasion. His American directness—homing in on the one thing she shouldn't talk about—left her unsure how to respond. And then suddenly it all came out.

"I'm their cook, and their maid. Also the nanny for their three children. Sometimes their gardener as well. And now, because the wife has broken her ankle, I shop for her. I work sixteen or seventeen hours a day. And I'm up half the night with their babies."

People were all around them, but because no one spoke the language, she and Leo might as well have been invisible. It felt both frightening to talk about this in public and liberating, the thrill of crossing an unguarded border.

"You don't like them very much," he said.

"I don't like them at all."

"Are my questions bothering you?"

"No. It's good to be able to talk to someone. To let someone know."

"Can I ask you another one?"

"Yes, if you help me find the fish sauce and shrimp paste."

He turned, and three seconds later the items were in his hands.

"Are you working there against your will?"

She pushed the cart and he followed. "I'm not sure of my will sometimes. I don't know what to do. At least I can talk and you can hear me talk. Maybe that's my will. Maybe I just want you to hear me. Where is the green tea? I couldn't find any last time and she went crazy."

He found it for her, and they walked to the next aisle, trailing another woman in headphones. America was invisible voices, singing.

"They have my passport, my papers. There's nowhere for me to go. Plus, they could do something to my sisters. The diplomat is important in Seoul, and he could get them in trouble."

Leo was watching her very carefully. She wasn't entirely sure if she was dodging his questions or doing the opposite, leading him exactly where she wanted him to go. For the next five minutes he stopped asking anything, obediently locating the final items on her list. But always she felt his eyes on her, even when he was facing away. How did he do that?

In the checkout line, he stood beside her like he was her husband. Surely people were watching them, the foreign woman with the tall white man.

"I'm sorry if I've acted strangely tonight," she said. "Maybe I've forgotten how to act with people I don't work for."

"Does she give you the shopping lists in advance?"

"I'm sorry?"

"The grocery list—does she give it to you just as you're leaving, or earlier in the day?"

What a strange question. But his voice was so calm and orderly, as if he weren't so much asking a question as telling her what to do.

"Earlier in the day."

"Once you have the next list, call me. You can read it to me, and I can buy everything in advance. That way you'll have time to meet me somewhere else, without her being suspicious."

She was confused for a moment. Then she thought she understood. Did Americans always proposition each other so bluntly? She'd made a mistake to call him.

Or maybe she'd picked exactly the right person? Because, yes, it was a tempting thought.

Still, she was about to object, for propriety's sake at least, when he noticed the expression on her face. Leo held out a palm and spoke in a gentler voice than before.

"I'm not planning anything"—he seemed to search for the word—"*wrong* by you. I'm trying to help."

It was almost her turn at the register. "I'm not even supposed to use their phone. If they had overheard me calling you . . ."

"You'll have to make sure they don't overhear you—call at night, when they're asleep. And don't use their phone. I put a cell phone in your shopping cart; it has my number programmed into it. It's turned off now. Just turn it on when you need to make the call, then turn it off immediately. That's important. Hide it someplace they won't find it."

She glanced at the cart and saw it there, nestled among packages of noodles. Its charging cord was wrapped neatly beside it. When had he put them there?

"I know this is difficult to understand," he said. "But it's the best way to get you out of this."

He stood there an extra moment, perhaps waiting for her to say the thank you that she was too shocked to say. Or perhaps he was equally unsure how they should part. "Okay," he said. "Call me. Good night." Then he leaned forward and kissed her cheek.

His lips were warm and dry. She was so startled she didn't move, and she felt the color rushing to her face. As if ashamed of his own act, he didn't look at her as he pulled back, just turned and walked past the other customers. The automatic doors pulled open and he was gone. Her eyes tried to follow him through the windows, but she could see only her own reflection and the dazzling colors of the store behind her.

Z.

Again night finds me a few blocks from the White House, surrounded by bland office buildings, their windows glowing yellow. Perhaps the local restaurants do big business on power lunches between lobbyists and their quarries, but the sidewalks are nearly empty as I take a preliminary recon walk.

It's only a few hours after my protection of the most recent Event. I'm still not sure what to make of the hag's warning that they had learned from their mistakes. I try to stay alert for tails, something I've lost the habit of doing in my time with the Department since I'm always the one following them.

Was that a hallucination I had, that man claiming to know who I was, even calling me *Troy?* Did something else go berserk when my GeneScan broke the other night? My head is pounding as I walk, a headache like the one I woke up with the day before yesterday.

The last thing I should be doing is going out on a date. But despite the Department's strict rules, I'm not the only Protector who's done this. The temptation is too great, after being trapped in these gigs long enough. You crave a human touch, something other than the violence of subduing your prey. So you find someone, someone your files assure you is not of historical importance—preferably someone who is going to die soon anyway. It's like setting up a perfect and untraceable crime, but really it's the opposite—it's a rare opportunity for a person in the Disasters Division to bring someone pleasure instead of pain.

The next Event I need to protect isn't until tomorrow afternoon, so I have time.

The restaurant Tasha chose is Middle Eastern in theme; the smell of hummus in the air, faint zithers on the sound track. I wonder if Tasha chose the place because it serves a cuisine native to the area where her brother died in battle but figure I shouldn't ask.

Tasha sits with the menu and a faint squint that tells me she needs reading glasses but doesn't want to use them tonight. She wears a bright red blouse, and her braids fall loose around her. If I've been doubting whether this is a good thing to be doing, those doubts vanish when she looks up and smiles. True, I already burned a similar image the other night, but the images we carry with us can do only so much. We need the real thing.

We chat about the weather, and she asks me how my work in the city is going. I come up with something, trying to make it boring enough to keep her from asking follow-up questions but not too boring. Which isn't easy.

After the waiter brings us some wine, I ask Tasha what kind of law she practices.

"Contracts law." She sees my blank look and adds, "Corporate law."

"What does that mean, one corporation suing another?"

"Basically. Or a corporation suing little people to crush them into even smaller pieces."

"I'm sure it's more complicated than that." Out of habit I look out the window to see if anyone is watching us. The street is clogged with traffic, the sidewalk a track meet of commuters running different routes. Yet the restaurant remains nearly empty—it's as if people know nothing of importance is happening here, best for them to move along.

"Usually it's the little people trying to sue the corporation, and my job is to contest and stonewall for so long they can't afford to keep going. Meanwhile lining the firm's pockets with billable hours."

"You don't sound very enthusiastic."

"I'm enthusiastic about paying off my debts. I'm gaining experience, you know, the whole corporate-slave thing. Just a few more years."

I've brought up a sore subject.

"I do have misgivings," she goes on after a pause. "Especially lately. I mean, my parents were very active politically. For a while, at least. I remember them taking me to the Mall for rallies against the contra war, or against slashing funding for city schools, or against the Gulf War, or in favor of AIDS funding, you name it. Me and the Mall go way back. But as I got older, I don't know, I guess I felt like protesting was their thing and I needed my own. I focused more on my studies, you know? I read the paper, I stayed informed, but I didn't want to be that... that stereotype, the angry leftist on the sidewalk. I told myself I was still being a good citizen, I was working hard, paying taxes, voting. But now..." Her voice trails off, the privileged early-21st-century American painfully unsure of the meaning of life.

"It's hard to know how engaged to be," I say.

"Yeah. And it's hard to have an airtight political opinion when mainly you're just worried about your brother's safety."

I assure her that I know exactly what she means.

Prior to coming here tonight, I searched the databases for a soldier named Jones who'd died recently so I could at least use a real name as my fake dead brother, just in case Tasha checked up on me. Fortunately (for me, not for him) there was indeed a soldier named Randy Jones who died in combat a few months ago. I won't tell Tasha that this particular Jones was white and grew up in South Dakota.

Letting her opinions guide me, I add, "On the one hand, I hate war. At the same time, I'm not naive enough to doubt that there are enemies out there who'd like nothing more than to wipe us out. Destroy our way of life, erase all of modernity and bring us back to some ancient past, or at least the particular view of an ancient past that they see when reading one old book. We need someone to stop them. My brother wanted to be one of those people."

"So did mine."

"So sometimes I think I shouldn't feel bad for him. He got what he wanted. He died a hero. But nothing's that simple."

"How are your parents?" she asks.

"They passed away before this all started."

"Oh, I'm sorry."

"How are yours?"

She sighs. "They wouldn't talk about it much when Marshall was alive, but I think they were against the wars. They'd just say they wanted their boy safe. They don't want to get into second-guessing the army, doubting the president—which is weird to me. They were members of SCLC in the sixties, and even though my dad owned a store here on U, they still managed to travel down to Montgomery for the protests there. Then their store burned down during the riots."

I nod, unsure whether I'm supposed to offer condolences.

"Everyone was having so much fun burning places down that eventually people stopped looking for those *Black Owned* signs and burned whatever they could, you know?" Tasha says. "The irony of my dad's place getting torched by the people he was spending all his time fighting for..." She shakes her head. "He's still bitter about it. I wasn't even born yet, but I can tell." She stares off for a moment. "Sorry, I'm going on and on. Are you from Philly originally?"

"We moved around a lot—I was an army brat." The Department provided me with some facts about Troy Jones's life, but not many; I have to make the rest up. "My father was raised in a bad part of Philly, but then he was drafted for Vietnam, I guess before the riots. Maybe in '65? He liked to say it was safer over there than back home. He did two tours, lived to tell about it. Also met a lovely young Vietnamese woman with pro-American sympathies, brought her home, and made some babies."

"I was wondering if you had some army in you."

"Some. My brother followed in his footsteps, but I was the family nerd."

She seems skeptical. "You don't look like much of a nerd."

"You should have seen my brother. Anyway, my dad stayed in the service after the war, so we lived in lots of towns in lots of states, mostly in the South."

"How'd your mom like living in the South?"

I try to imagine that, try to imagine a time and a place even more rife with racial animosities than this one. "I'm sure there were hard things about it, but she wasn't a complainer. We were a tight family. We stuck together." I wonder if something like this could be true. The cover was just something I read and memorized; I've never given it much critical thought. But what must it have been like for such children in a time that so derided half-breeds? Would the parents have been strong enough to endure it all? No, probably not. My story is too rosy. Maybe the father would have begun to feel ostracized by his fellow blacks for marrying a bride from a former enemy nation; maybe he would have started to drink; maybe he and his wife would have fought, and eventually divorced. Maybe Troy Jones had a rough time of it indeed. No sense burdening my date with this sad history, though, so I tell her, "My dad retired from the service and bought into a car dealership outside Philly when I was in junior high."

"How did he feel about the wars?"

"He passed away before they started." Cirrhosis of the liver, or a car accident? Possibly suicide. "But I'm willing to bet he would have been against them. He had mixed feelings about Vietnam. The army was good for him; it gave him a role to play that he wouldn't otherwise have been able to. But he discouraged me the few times I mentioned enlisting. It was more important to him that I be the first in the family to go to college. Once I did that, it sort of freed up Randy to enlist. My mother didn't like that, though. She'd lost a lot of her family during the war; some of them to U.S. forces, some to the Vietcong. At a certain point, the reasons a war started aren't important anymore, who did what to whom however many years ago. The faces behind the guns don't really matter. It's just a bunch of guns. All you want to do is get away."

"You ever go there?"

I'm confused; I let myself roam too many places. "Where?"

"Vietnam."

Funny how a dinner date can lead to a more detailed grilling than some professional encounters. I wait a moment, think. "Once, when we were kids. I don't remember much of it. I spoke very little of the language, and it was so long ago. And they weren't real thrilled about the mixed-breed kids over there either. My mom never went back af- ter that.one time. I think people might have said things about us— the kids—that she didn't like. I didn't hear anything myself, but I put two and two together. Also, she didn't have much family there anymore. So many people died then. I think that the whole country— the landscape, the language, the heat—only reminded her of what she'd lost."

Too much of the conversation has been focused on my constructed past. I don't know how much longer I can sit here inventing myself before such a perceptive audience.

Then a new voice asks, "Troy?"

I look up and there's a white woman standing at our table. She wears a sleek gray business suit and holds a briefcase in her finely manicured hand. Her long blond hair is pulled into a ponytail and she's smiling at me.

"Troy! How *are* you? It's been for*ever*!"

"Hi," I say, pausing for a second and then trying to return her smile. *Another one?* Who are these people who seem to know me? I burn her image, start scanning it against my databases. "Um, yeah, it has. How's it going?"

"Oh, good, busy, the usual. How's life up in the suburbs?"

"It's good," I say, trying not to speak too slowly, trying not to show how confused I am. The blonde is still smiling, but her eyes are steel. I feel taunted.

"Your daughter must *love* having all that space," the woman says. I don't turn up any matches of her face.

"She does, she does. We'll, um, we'll have to get her into the city soon so she can see all the old sights."

"That'd be great." The blonde pauses for a moment. "Speaking of which, I'm late for picking up Clara—I should run. So nice to see you!" She walks away, and I look at Tasha and try to put on a neutral expression. But over Tasha's head I can see the blonde moving toward the door and continuing to stare at me all the while. Her smile is gone, but the steel in her eyes is still there.

"You okay?" Tasha asks.

"Yeah, it's just..." I make myself smile. "I really have no idea who that was." And suddenly I'm laughing. I need another drink.

"Sounds like it was the mom of some kid that played with your daughter?"

"Yeah, I guess it was."

I look outside again, hoping for obvious signs of surveillance. The man at Capitol Hill, who also called me Troy, seemed to be warning me that I was being watched, that I was only leading the hags to their targets. But how? Are they following me in hopes of finding a safe moment to eliminate me? *How* are they following me? Maybe one of them has a GeneScan. Then why don't they just show up at my motel in the middle of the night and kill me?

Tasha looks at my hands, then at me. Her expression has changed.

"I guess I missed the part about you having a wife and daughter." She sounds like she's barely holding in a sudden anger.

"I don't have a wife and daughter," I say.

"Just a daughter, then?"

"I did have a daughter. She was five."

I exhale those words and she breathes them in, where they thicken; they're like smoke in her lungs. She seems to have trouble breathing for a moment; she's unsure how to respond, trying to control her reaction. It's a relief that I'm not the one feeling that for a change.

I make myself continue. "And I did have a wife. They were in a...a car accident."

The Department, either out of some unexpected spite or because they thought it would be easier for me, found me a cover who had a tragedy similar to mine. The real Troy Jones also lost his family. Like a page torn out of a memoir and stuffed into a novel.

"Oh God. I'm so sorry."

"It was a long time ago."

She shifts in her seat, folds and unfolds her hands, her body moving every which way in search of the appropriate response. She starts to reach for one of my hands, but stops halfway.

"I'm so sorry, Troy. I hope I didn't sound . . . I was just confused."

"It's all right. I wanted to tell you." I finish my glass of wine, willing this to be a normal conversation again. But I don't know what normal is, in this time or any other.

"You, um, you lived around here with them?"

"Not far." I feel like I'm looking at pieces inside myself, trying to decide which ones to lift up and show her, which are worth the effort and which are still too heavy. "There's a lot you want to forget, you know? A lot you never, ever want to forget, but plenty you'd like to just let go of. And then it happens and you realize you have forgotten, you really have. And you hate yourself for it."

She nods as if she can understand.

Things get hazy here; I'm too distracted by the strange blond woman and my memories of Cemby and our daughter. Tasha and I talk, but it's like I'm not really here. A waiter has brought food and refilled my glass and I'm drinking deeply. I try to tune back in, remind myself of the Department's ridiculous credo to *live in the present.* Tasha's talking about her brother.

"My parents flipped when he enlisted. I mean, my folks worked hard so we could go to college. But Marshall, I don't know, he had to be the rebel. The more they told him that the army was just a place for poor folks to get sent because the system didn't give them any other options, the more appealing it was for him. He bought into all that honor and valor stuff, you know? He was seduced by that image of the hero, the good soldier. He did two tours and made it through unscathed, physically and mentally. But not the third."

"How did it happen?" I could look it up in my files, but I'd rather hear it from her.

"I'm still trying to figure that out. They told us he was ambushed by *insurgents,* whatever that word actually means, and that he and two of his soldiers were shot and killed. But I've been getting conflicting information, which only makes me more suspicious. I have a bad feeling that the deeper I dig, the uglier the truth will be, you know? It'll turn out there *were* no insurgents in the area, and it was friendly fire or some colossal fuck-up."

Then she asks, "What happened to your brother?"

"IED, under his Humvee. A supply run on a very bad road."

"Did you...investigate at all, ask around?"

"No."

She looks like she doesn't believe me. Maybe I've made a crucial mistake. I'm too good at concealing pain.

But her face changes, slowly, as if she's beginning to understand how two people can respond to the same tragedy in different ways.

"Maybe I'm too skeptical for my own good," she says. "I just have a hard time trusting that the government is telling the truth when it's already told so many lies. I mean, some PR guy in the U.S. Army press office told me how Marshall died, but I can't just believe him. I have to find the real story."

"War is awful."

She has nothing to add to that.

"And I believe we'll come to a point where we won't have it anymore."

She looks at me as if I've said something outlandish. "You do? I *tell* myself I do, but—"

"I do believe it. We'll figure it out eventually. A time will come when no one will have to tell the kind of stories we just did."

"You sound so sure of yourself." Being in the presence of such unfettered optimism is disorienting to her.

"It's not myself I'm sure of," I say. I wish there were a way to explain this to her, but there isn't.

"But...I mean, the political activism and this book I'm trying to write about Marshall—I'm doing all of this for the *future,* you know? Because I want a better future, I want my kids and grandkids to grow up in a world where they don't even have to *think* of enlisting. A world where we don't have all these wars popping up. But, honestly, when I sit down and try to imagine a future like that...A world where people aren't as petty as we are? A world where human nature is somehow different? I mean, that's science fiction. That's crazy. I'm working and working for a better future, but *I can't even imagine it.*"

Her eyes are tearing up. She has tried for so long to let her lawyerly combativeness beat down her emotions, but her emotions are waging a sneak attack. Their victory rolls down her cheeks.

I reach out to take her hand.

"But some of us can," I say. "And maybe that's enough."

My wife complimented me on being an excellent liar. It was one of the last things she ever said to me.

Lying for a good cause, committing indiscretions in the name of a greater good—these are equations I have plenty of experience balancing. I enforce rules I don't always understand. I deceive my targets, my friends, my wife. I need to lie, tell different stories, make things up. Provide excuses, justifications. Sometimes I think them up in advance, so they're ready to be deployed at various opportunities; sometimes I ad-lib, writing them as I speak. My voice becomes just a tool, inanimate. Not really a part of myself.

Cemby understood there were things I couldn't tell her. What must it have been like to live with someone she could never fully know? Someone who always had to hide things from her? Even if she knew I was lying because I had to, nothing personal, could she forgive me? Did it drive her a little crazy? Or did it seem to her that *I* was the crazy one, that she was the only sane person in an insane world?

Of course, I know so much about everyone else: their secrets, their goals, their hopes. And their pasts—the Government keeps track of citizens' pasts even after the people themselves delete their old records. Once I became a level-5 intelligence officer, I had top clearance, could find information on a mark that the mark himself had likely forgotten. *We know them better than they know themselves,* we always said. Whole parts of their lives had vanished in a tangible sense: no images, no relics, no receipts, no mementos. All they had were their memories, fragile, fading, altering in their minds with the passage of time. Polluted by wistfulness, by fantasies, by the ways they wished things had been. We intelligence officers had access to the real past, the real them. Or did we? What *was* the real them, the data and irrefutable evidence I could look up, or the constantly half-forgotten and revised fictions they carried in their own minds?

I was cleared for level 5 just after I married Cemby. Instead of investigating routine crimes—yes, we do have the occasional crime, albeit nothing like this anarchic 21st century—I was intercepting the few remaining rebel groups, clamping down on agitators. Society continued to function as intended, and most people had no idea of the threats that popped up now and again.

Most of my cases were standard detect-and-deletes on citizens who were illegally harboring historical information. I did it for years. I think I liked it. I'm not sure anymore. New events have a way of skewing everything behind them. I revise my own past as I go, have revised it so many times I can't help but doubt my own memories, or whatever these scenes in my head are.

It was a few days before my wife and daughter's accident that I discovered the existence of the hags.

We'd been running traces on a scientific researcher named Dalton. He was young, working for a bionetics firm. Something related to reversing dead seas, if such a thing is possible. It probably isn't, but that won't stop them from trying. Scientists of various stripes are given degrees of clearance regarding historical information—they need access to some of it to make progress and build on past discoveries. But they're closely watched.

Dalton wasn't deleting his files as quickly as he should have been. It's a common error, and one usually committed by a standard, patriotic, overworked citizen who lets things slide. It's a tier-2 misdemeanor and it lands you on the Lists for a few years.

These sorts of visits were once the bulk of my job—visits as minor and annoying as those of the taxation officers who noticed incorrect computations and hit people with audits—but I was doing fewer of them, usually just to train a rookie. I never expected trouble. A true criminal would cover his tracks better. He would never do something as stupid as allowing old files to accumulate, the way this Dalton had.

Still, there I was, knocking on the door to his eighth-floor apartment at 10:00 p.m. I always visited late, when people's defenses were down.

I was holding my ID up to his screen before his voice even came over the comm to ask who I was. He sounded nervous, but everyone did around us. Beside me was a rookie named Hyer, a big kid, too intimidated by the job to reveal any personality yet. I'd told him to speak as little as possible.

The door slid open. Dalton was paler in person than he'd looked in his files, which was never a good sign. The descendants of lines that hadn't sufficiently mixed tended to be the ones who harbored ill will toward society. I knew his height and weight, but he seemed shorter than the numbers, stooping from fatigue or fear. His eyes were red. It was obvious he had been staring at a screen for too long. Marks sometimes became suspicious, or were tipped off somehow, and deleted their files at the last minute. We'd recently developed ways to surreptitiously place holds on their accounts. I wondered if he'd been frantically trying to tap in while we were waiting at his door.

I told him we were coming in and we did. He stuttered, asking what he'd done wrong.

"You have several files that exceed the expiration limit. Several thousand such files."

He swallowed. Hyer took a few steps and stood at Dalton's side. The target had to keep turning his head to see both of us, adding to his disorientation.

We entered the standard lair of a well-educated scientific brat. Bright images of beaches and sunsets shone forth from monitors on the walls; the furniture was sleek and male. His vidder was in the back corner, near a window that offered a narrow view of the space between this building and the next. At that hour, the view was of nothing but darkness, reflections of ourselves, and the knowledge of a steep drop.

"I, um, I must have let it slip. I'm sorry. I'm at this new job and the stress is insane—I've just been bad about cleaning old files, that's all."

"We know about your new job. We know it's very important, and you've been working hard. You're a tribute to our society, Mr. Dalton. The Phoenix Generation would be proud."

He looked both flattered and scared. "Um, thank you."

"In my experience, though, people in such jobs tend to think they can get away with things."

"No, no!" I'd been speaking in even tones yet still I was terrifying him. It was so easy. "I'm not like that. Really, it was an honest mistake. I mean, a stupid mistake."

"An honest mistake, or a stupid one? Are you an honest man, Mr. Dalton, or a stupid man?"

He didn't know how to respond.

"Are you saying you're both, or that they're the same thing?" I looked at Hyer, then back at the target. "I'm an honest man—does that mean I'm also stupid?"

Dalton was falling to pieces; I didn't have to speak another word. But his manner was alarming. People were scared of us, yes, but he seemed more scared than usual.

"No, no, sir, absolutely not. I was calling *myself* stupid."

"Good, because I'm really not stupid at all. I'm quite bright. But I do feel a little dumb, just a tad slow, when I read your communications about the Revisions project. Could you help me understand that project better?"

Analysts had been watching his correspondence since his files backdated too far. Standard procedure, but usually there weren't enough analysts to keep up. They would just speed-read a few things, assume all was well, and pass the records on to Security for the standard visit. But the analyst on Dalton's case had been a voracious and

thorough reader. She'd noted that Dalton used strange diction whenever he wrote to a colleague about something called Revisions. It had
seemed like he was communicating in code.

I assumed there was a logical explanation. These leads never went
anywhere. Which was why I was surprised to see Dalton's face go even
paler. The room was cool, yet his forehead shone.

"Re-revisions?" he stammered.

"I called your boss this morning and asked her about it. She'd never
heard of it. So I called her boss. And do you know what he said?"

"No." His voice was shrinking.

"He'd never heard of it either."

"Um, I . . ."

Hyer folded his arms and lowered his head a bit. He had a dumb-
sounding voice but a great look for the part. If he kept his mouth
shut, he'd go far.

"Is there something you'd like to tell us, Mr. Dalton," I asked, "to
make things a little easier on yourself?"

He shivered as he searched in vain for a helpful word or two. I
looked at one of the images on his mantel, a girl about his age. "She's
pretty," I lied. "I wonder what she knows about it."

"Nothing!" he shouted. "She doesn't—she's not involved. She has
nothing to do with it."

I turned back to him and kept my facial muscles still for a few seconds while his did the opposite. He looked as if he might explode.
"Nothing to do with what?" I asked.

He sank onto his sofa. His head fell into his hands. I told Hyer
to tap into Dalton's account through the vidder, pull up the relevant
correspondence. I could have just asked Dalton to do it, but at that
moment it would have been too much for him to even turn on a light.

"I never wanted to get involved," Dalton said when he looked up.
His eyes were wet. "I'm not that kind of person, understand?"

"Of course you're not. Your files demonstrate that you've been a
class-A citizen. Someone forced you."

"Yes! It's just, my parents, they're very sick. They've been trying to get access to this new treatment that another firm's been pioneering. I, I tried to get a job there, you know, and see if I could pull some strings that way, but I...didn't get hired."

"So you started working at AdvanceSeaBio instead."

"And when I was doing my hist-search through Archives to lay the groundwork for my new project, my boss—"

"Ms. Carmichael."

"Yes, Ms. Carmichael, she told me to pull up some other files. They didn't seem relevant to what I was doing, but, you know, she's my boss."

"You were just doing as you were told."

"And then, I get these calls, and I meet this guy who tells me he can get my parents that treatment, he can move them to the top of the list, but he needs me to use my account to store some more files. He never even told me his name, only that he could get Mom and Dad into the trials. Honestly, that's all it was. I know it was stupid of me, and—"

"This started how long ago?"

"Um, about a year, I think?"

I waited. He must have been dizzy from darting his eyes to me, then to the floor, then to Hyer, then back to me again.

"How are your parents now, Mr. Dalton?"

His hands were clasped before him, the fingers interlocked, like images I'd seen of people praying. If history was any indication, it wouldn't do him any good.

"They're getting better," he said, quietly. *The next syllable,* I said to myself. *His voice will break on the next syllable.*

"That's good. Hopefully the treatment they've received so far will be enough."

"Please—"

I waited a moment for him to get control of himself. "I don't believe your story," I said. "I don't believe a reasonably intelligent person like you would put himself at risk that way unless he had something else in mind. I think that what you've just told me is a very interesting beginning—the opening sentence—of a much more complicated story that you're going to explain to us one way or another. But not here."

I nodded at Hyer. "Let's take him in."

Hyer restrained the crying young scientist, which mostly involved preventing him from collapsing. I called the office and told them to reserve a Dark Room for us, on hearing which Dalton gasped. I also told them to get an Intervention team here immediately, sweep the apartment for bugs. Whoever had recruited a fool like Dalton was probably smart enough to keep careful watch over him. For all I knew, everything we'd just said had been recorded by someone else.

At the station, Dalton broke easily, but too easily—into so many pieces it was left to me to put them back together, see what kind of whole they formed. It was messy and confusing.

I was washing up afterward, and my boss, Myers, walked into the bathroom.

"Big night," he said as I toweled off. "This is catching people by surprise."

"Me included. The kid certainly got himself involved in something."

Myers stepped closer, peering at the base of the stalls to make sure we were alone. He turned the sink on full blast.

"You look tired, but we need to talk." His voice was low. "Any of those names he mentioned register with you?"

I shook my head. "I figured the analysts would be looking into it."

"They are, but I recognized a few myself. They were aliases, and I've seen them in other correspondence we've been watching."

I didn't like his need for secrecy. This was my boss, a very exemplar of strict regulation and adherence to code, whispering beside the commodes.

"Great," I said. "We'll have a head start with them once we bring them in."

"The alias Echo didn't register with you?"

He was watching me as carefully as I watched a mark. I was still holding the towel, ratty and thin and tinted red from Dalton's blood. "No," I told him. Out of the corner of my eye I glimpsed my reflection as I tossed the towel into the bin.

He waited, a heavy pause. "That's an alias that's been used by your father-in-law."

I might have flinched. I probably blinked. I had been conscious of how I looked to his eyes, but that last sentence made me descend deeply into my own mind.

"Are you sure?"

"Of course we're sure."

My father-in-law was an Archivist, quite senior. That meant he couldn't say anything more about his job than I could about mine. I always figured that made it somewhat easier for Cemby to understand me; she was used to men who lived within the shadows they cast. My father-in-law, Joseph, had been talking about retirement for years but claimed his colleagues were always begging him to stay on for just another year or two. Cemby worried about his health, the stress, but he said he had little choice.

"How do you get on with him?" Myers asked.

"Fine. He's quiet, hard to get to know."

"But you've never reported any misgivings about him."

"I haven't had any. I'm ... stunned."

He nodded.

"And look, he's an old man. Maybe he just got confused and misappropriated a few files, or met the wrong person at a conference. This doesn't mean—"

"Zed, you were the one in there with that kid. This is more than just someone collecting an illegal library—people outside the Government are compiling a history, a vast one. They're collecting old files and trying to connect the dots. They're writing something, and they're being careful about it because they know what it means. What this kid was compiling wasn't the whole thing, it was a damned *footnote*. There's no telling how much information they've got their hands on. Now, you're saying that you're *certain* Joseph's never let anything odd slip around you? That you've never had the slightest inkling—"

"Are you accusing me of incompetence or conspiracy?"

He smiled awkwardly and looked down. When he raised his eyes the smile was gone. "Zed, there are reasons I'm asking you this in the bathroom and not in front of a roomful of counterintelligence officers. Ease up, all right?"

I nodded. "Sorry."

He turned off the sink and started speaking at a normal volume. "When is Cemby expecting you home?"

Something inside me started to die right then. I felt it in my stomach, a rotting. I'd been so shocked by the news about Joseph that I hadn't finished tracing all the possible ramifications.

"I told her I'd be all night. She probably figures I'll be back by lunch."

"Call her from your desk and tell her you'll be here for another day or two. Tell her it's nothing to worry about, but you'll be a while."

"You're bringing him in."

"Of *course* we're bringing him in. They're probably already at his office, so I want you to call her before she hears anything. Call her now, and if she calls you back later, do not answer."

"You don't trust me?"

"I have a wife too. I'm trying to make this as easy as possible for you."

I wanted to ask him if Cemby was suspected of anything. If she was on any Lists, if one of those other aliases was hers. But I would have looked like a fool to ask, would have brought more suspicion on myself.

He wouldn't have told me anyway.

My boss followed me to my desk and stood a few feet away. At the end of the hallway, a briefing room was filled with analysts who wanted to chat with me, presumably about things Dalton had said in his Dark Room, but I was wondering if I myself was a target now. Or

Cemby. I told myself not to sit there stewing, not to let myself get nervous. I picked up the comm and called her.

It was midmorning and she sounded tired, an extra exhalation when she said hello. Like she was letting go of something.

"How was Laurynn this morning?" I asked.

"Normal." Our daughter had developed an aversion to waking up on time; Cemby literally pulled her out of bed to get her ready for school, she told me. They'd had to eat breakfast in the pod.

I told her I was sorry she'd had to do so much on her own and that I loved her. I mentioned that the project I'd gotten sucked into was going to keep sucking at me for another day, possibly longer.

"They're letting you sleep at least?"

"A little. In shifts. I'm okay, it's nothing serious. They just want me here until it's over. I'll get a few off days next month in return. Maybe we can escape the city for a vacation."

"Are you all right? You sound sad."

"Just a temporary crash." I wondered how long it would be until she found out about her father. I wondered how quickly she'd realize that I had known during this call.

I wondered what she knew about what her father was doing, and I hated myself for thinking that.

She said she had to go, she was late on a deadline of her own. On my vidder was a still image of her from a few weeks earlier—video calls were banned in the office, for obvious reasons. In the image she was smiling, her arm around Laurynn, who grinned beside her like a miniature, idealized version of Cemby.

I told her, "I'm sorry."

"It's all right. I understand."

I couldn't tell her what I was really apologizing for. One of the analysts was already walking to my desk to hurry me along.

She told me she loved me too, and I didn't realize that I'd never hear her say that again.

* * *

After dinner (I surprise, and borderline amaze, Tasha by confessing that I'm vegetarian) and a gratuitous dessert, we step outside, the air cool and the wind surprisingly strong. Her braids snap against my face for a moment. We walk alongside each other and she holds my hand. I hadn't expected that and I tense up despite myself.

"We should do this again sometime," she says. I'm not even sure where we're walking.

"That would be great." Wanting to tell her, *You have so little time. But thank you for tonight just the same.*

Traffic is sparse and the only pedestrians on the street are hurrying toward the shelter of a Metro station or an ATM kiosk. No suspicious watchers are loitering anywhere I can see.

"Do you have a phone number yet?" she asks.

Technically I don't, but I've trolled the network for dead numbers and have appropriated one for my own use, linking it to an internal switch in my brain. I even set up a voice-mail greeting, so I give her the number. She says she'll call me soon.

She leans in and kisses me, a peck, but not a quick one. Funny how similar certain rituals are through time. I wonder if it's attraction she feels or just pity, if she sees in me something she needs, or if the story about my wife and daughter has made her feel sorry for me, sorry enough for this consolation prize. But I do feel consoled.

And then she's stepping into a cab that has magically appeared before us, and she's gone. I stand and watch the taillights fade.

"Enjoying yourself, Zed?"

I must have been standing here and staring for longer than I thought, because I didn't even hear him coming. He's good at what he does. We all are.

"Having fun with all that 21st-century womanhood has to offer?" he continues, not smiling. I don't recognize the face—he too has had his appearance altered—but I do recognize the voice. He has a not entirely time-appropriate fedora pulled low over his eyes, and a dark trench coat. I've seen a few of the black contemps dress like this, but not many.

"Wills?" If I look closely into his eyes, I can recognize him, despite what the Engineers have done to the rest of his face. "What are you doing in my beat?"

"Funny," he says, glancing up and down the street. "I was about to ask you the same thing."

13.

When Leo's cell rang at 11:45 one night, he knew who it was before he checked the caller ID. He answered with hello in Bahasa.

"Hello." Her voice quiet, as it was the last time. "I'm sorry, am I calling too late?"

"No, no, it's fine." He'd been staying up late all week, hoping she'd call. "How are you?"

"I am well." She was a good liar—that would help. "Um, I was wondering if you'd like to meet me again tomorrow?"

"Of course. What time?"

"I think it will be three o'clock. The mistress wants the shopping finished before dinner—she'll probably send me when the twins are napping."

"Has she given you the grocery list yet?"

"No. But she'll be away in the afternoon when I leave, so she'll have to give it to me before then, sometime in the morning."

"Call me as soon as you get the list. If I don't answer, leave a message and read the entire list—call a second time if it cuts you off. I'll buy everything and have it ready in my car." He'd already bought four large coolers and ice packs to keep things cold.

"She always asks me for the receipt."

"I'll give it to you. Does she give you a credit card or cash?"

"Cash."

Perfect. He'd just tear off the bottom of the receipt where it showed time of purchase.

"What if someone sees me driving where I'm not supposed to?"

He assured her he'd thought everything out. He told her to get a pencil and paper, then told her she should drive the first few minutes as if heading to Whole Foods. Next he narrated a detour to a parking lot near Logan Circle, where they'd be able to talk. He told her not to bring her phone, and reminded her to turn it off as soon as they finished this call.

"I'm still not sure this is a good idea," she said. "I, I appreciate your concern, but if she were to find out—"

"You have to trust me. This is the best way to get you out of there. That's what you want, isn't it?"

Another pause. He worried he'd overplayed his hand. Slow down, he reminded himself. Let her think she's the one coming to you.

"Of course."

"Good. Just call me as soon as you get that list."

"All right. Thank you."

He hung up. They'd been on the phone for three minutes. His heart was pounding and he had too much adrenaline to think about sleep. He poured himself a bourbon. It was too late to catch the Wizards or the Caps, so he turned the TV to cable news and watched some war.

He followed her to the parking lot the next day. He'd already shopped at Whole Foods, put the perishables in his coolers, and driven back to Mount Pleasant, where he waited two blocks from the diplomat's house. After twenty minutes he saw the familiar black SUV with diminutive Sari visible through the windshield. He let her pass and waited for another car to fill in between them before he pulled out, curious if anyone was following her. No one was, other than himself.

Traffic was thickening, the long bell curve of D.C.'s rush hour beginning to spike two full hours before its peak. The drive took fifteen minutes, exactly what he'd thought it would. He had timed her departure and knew when she would be expected back at the house.

His chosen parking lot was in the back of an elementary school that had recently closed due to a collapsed roof. Utility trucks and a crane sat outside the building, but there were no workers and hadn't been for days—the school system's limited repairs budget had been diverted to a high school in Northeast that had caught fire last week. Leo·parked his Accord alongside Sari's SUV. He smiled at her, then motioned for her to get in shotgun of his car. He doubted the SUV was bugged, but there was no reason to chance it.

Her hair was pulled back, and again some of the strands had broken free. She was wearing a black hoodie and matching sweatpants, both of which actually fit. She looked like any Asian American student at Georgetown or GW, rushing from class to the gym in mommy and daddy's eighteenth-birthday present, just off the phone with her buds to coordinate which bars to hit that night. He wondered if she had any idea how stunning she was. And he wondered how much longer she'd look this good with a life like hers.

The last time he'd seen her, she had seemed less nervous around him. Her black eye had completely faded, though a certain puffiness of exhaustion had been evident. Still, he had been struck by her beauty. Simply getting to sit with her, being allowed to look into her eyes for those few minutes, felt like a gift he didn't deserve. He'd had to tell himself to stop leering, to stay focused.

His good-bye kiss on her cheek had been pure impulse. And desire. It was stupid, as it risked scaring her away. He'd spent the next few hours of that day regretting the kiss. And then later, trying to fall asleep, he'd spent the rest of the night imagining all the other things he would have liked to do afterward.

So, in his car with her now, he was relieved by the genuine smile she wore when she said, "Hello, Leo."

She was brave to be doing this. Or stupid, or desperate. Getting in the car of a man she didn't know well, in a country she didn't understand. He tried to imagine what it was like to be an immigrant, one of the only people of your kind in this vast and challenging land, always in the midst of situations whose designs perplexed you. Spooks were supposed to be trained for exactly this kind of disorientation,

but they had no idea. Those classes should be taught not by case officers but by first-generation Americans: This is how it feels to stumble
off the boat. This is how it feels to smile dumbly when someone says
something you don't follow. This is how it feels to have no friends.

He asked how she was, what she thought of the encroaching winter. He noticed that she sat with her hands pressed together tightly,
her thin fingers obviously chilled even though the air felt comfortably
crisp to him, football weather.

One of the plastic grocery bags settled behind them, and she
turned her head at the sound of the crinkling. She thanked him again
for doing her shopping.

"How much did she give you to pay for them?" he asked.

She told him, he did the math, then he handed her some change
and told her to keep what the mistress had given her. She looked
frightened by the offer.

"I shouldn't keep that. If they found it . . ."

He nodded, told her to forget it. She handed him the grocery money.

"I have a question for you," he said. "You told me you're working
for that couple against your will. I want you to tell me what you'd
want if you could have anything. Anything at all. Do you want to be
back in Seoul? Do you have family in Indonesia you want to be with?
Any family you need to care for?"

She gazed outside. "It's complicated."

"Do you want to go back to Jakarta?"

She thought for a moment, then shook her head.

"Do you want to go back to Seoul?"

She waited again. "It's where my sisters are, but . . . I don't really
know them anymore. Soon they'll marry anyway, and I'd be on my
own there."

"Do you want to stay in America?"

"I don't know anyone here."

This was going to be harder than he'd thought.

These sorts of barters required clear goals. Even if the other side's
goal was obscured by lies and subterfuge, even if you didn't truly

know what they wanted, you knew they wanted *something.* Something they figured you could provide. Money was the obvious goal with poor agents, but sometimes people could be so poor, so beyond hope, that they didn't even know what to ask for. It was hard for Leo to trust such people because he didn't understand them.

"What do you know about your employers?"

"I know what they like to eat, what they wear, how they like their house kept."

"What does Sang Hee do most days?"

She seemed surprised he knew her name. "She writes on her computer."

"Is she sending messages or typing a document?"

"She said she's writing a book. But she doesn't let me get close enough to see, even though I don't read Korean very well."

"What does she do other than type on her computer? Take me through her day."

"She goes visiting most of the afternoons—other diplomats' wives, I think."

"How do you know? Does she use names?"

"No. Or sometimes she does, when speaking to her husband, but they don't mean anything to me."

"I need you to start paying attention to the names. What else does she do?"

"She shops a lot. Or she used to, before she broke her ankle. It's hard for her to get around stores with the cast."

"What does she buy?"

"Clothes, perfume, electronics. Things to send back home."

"Does she mail things very often?"

"Once a week, I think. She doesn't take me with her to the post office; I just see her with packages sometimes."

"Okay. Her computer, is it a laptop or one that's on a desk?"

"A laptop."

"Where does she keep it when she isn't using it?"

"Her room. Sometimes downstairs, if she writes there at night, when she's drinking. Sometimes she's very drunk and she leaves it there. I brought it up to her room once but she said she didn't want me to touch it. Why are you asking all this?"

"I know some people in the government here, in our Immigration department. I've told them about your situation and asked how we could help you. Because your employer is a diplomat, he's protected from most of our laws." He paused for a beat. "But I talked to my friends and I said there must be *some* way we can help you. They said there was, but they'd need to get something from you first."

She looked at her hands for a moment. Leo was used to the reticent, deferential behavior of Indonesian women, but it was hard to tell what effect his words were having on her. "What do they want from me?" she asked.

"They're very interested in your employers. Especially Sang Hee. Because you work in their house, you can learn certain things."

"My Korean isn't perfect. They don't talk to each other much in my presence, and when they do, I don't always understand what they're saying."

"But even if you don't understand them, we can." He turned to reach into the backseat, leaning toward her a bit, and she leaned back, surprised or uncomfortable to have him so close. He took out a small cardboard box. "This is a digital camera, this is a portable copier, and these are flash drives," he said, opening the box. He explained how to use them.

"I don't... I don't understand."

She wasn't stupid; she was nervous. Now was the time to press. "They've hit you, haven't they?"

She looked out the window.

"Has Hyun Ki Shim ever touched you?"

Her head snapped back. "No. His wife is the evil one."

Part of Leo felt disappointed. Sexual abuse would make their leverage on the diplomat all the stronger. But part of him—a much greater part—felt relief, for her sake. And for the sake of his own fantasies.

"Sari, you are in danger. They can do anything they want to you; they can keep beating you like this, can even kill you if they want, and there's nothing anyone can do. You are their slave, and we can't protect you from them. *Unless* you help us with this."

He was trying to keep his voice calm and steady. Here was the key moment, the point at which this would be consummated or not. At the same time, he saw the look in her eyes, the sadness and fear, and he felt the awful knowledge that all he really needed to do to save her was drive her to the Indonesian embassy. He could drop her off and they would likely repatriate her, even without her passport, and protect her from her employers. Hell, she could drive to the embassy herself; all he had to do was tell her where it was, less than ten minutes away. He couldn't let her know how easy it was. He had to limit her world, limit her possibilities. Luckily she seemed familiar with such constraints.

"I know you're scared of them. But the longer you stay there, the worse they will treat you. I've seen other situations like this. If you do what I'm asking, we can get you someplace else. Maybe to another city in another country, if that's what you want. Or American citizenship, and some money, and you can start over. People like Hyun Ki and Sang Hee will never be able to hurt you again."

He had no friends in Immigration and no right to offer her citizenship. Maybe, if this went well, he could ask Bale to talk to someone, inquire if any strings could in fact be pulled. But he doubted it. At the Agency, dangling false promises like this could get him seriously reprimanded, but at TES anything seemed allowable.

"What is this building?" she asked, looking straight ahead.

"A school."

"What are they doing to it?"

"Fixing it. The roof collapsed."

She looked horrified. "On top of children?"

"No, it happened over the weekend, when no one was inside." Actually, he had no idea. It might well have taken out a handful of the District's seven-year-olds; he didn't keep up with local news.

"This is what happens to schools here?"

"In this city, we spend most of our time worrying about other places instead of taking care of ourselves."

"If I had a child in America, would the roof collapse on him?"

He looked at her—at the wide eyes he wanted to see himself reflected in, at those full lips that he wanted to gently take between his teeth—and tried to control his expression. So hard to present yourself correctly when all these cultural cues are different. And when you've forgotten who the correct you is.

"I will keep the roofs from falling on you and anyone else, I promise."

Z.

The next morning Wills and I stake out a downtown hotel where he tells me he tracked some hags earlier. They're relatively safe from us so long as they stay inside. If we tried to storm the place, we'd likely do more harm than good; a firefight in such a sensitive building would cause too many historical disruptions. Our best option is to wait for them to come out, where we can dispose of them more discreetly.

After Wills approached me on the sidewalk the previous night, he led me to his car (a nondescript rented Civic) so we could talk while he drove. He'd tracked me to the restaurant with his GeneScan, but he had as many questions as I did. Why would the Department send two of us here? They'd never done that before. Having a partner would be helpful, sure, but the Department has always figured that doubling the imprint left on the beat was too big a risk. What was going on?

We downloaded files from each other as he drove. Our intel didn't match; some of the Events he was protecting weren't rated as important in my files, and vice versa.

"I was afraid of this," he said. "The hags must have so many plots back here, the Department didn't think one Protector could handle them all."

"But why didn't they warn us about each other? We might have killed each other by mistake."

I silently processed his intel, then stopped at an image.

"This contemp," I said, weighing what to explain and what to hold back, "Tasha Wilson. She wasn't in my intel."

"That doesn't quite explain what you were doing having dinner with her, Zed."

"All right, I had a date. Report me if you want to. But it shouldn't matter, since she'll be dead soon anyway."

"Yes, but not as part of the Conflagration. She goes sooner. And she's a target, Zed, which means you need to stay away from her."

I was reeling; Tasha *was* important after all? I downloaded the rest of Wills's intel, checked the dates against my own. The diplomat, the product, the underground journalists. Pieces of the narrative jibed with my own, but some of the characters seemed rearranged, the causes occurring after effects, the wreckage preceding the accidents. How could the Department get so much wrong?

Missions are simplest when the people in Veracity can provide the Protectors with clear, concise information on what happened historically. But this isn't always possible. Records are incomplete, inaccessible, or damaged. History as recorded may contain flaws, omissions, and biases. There may be competing versions of history. It's hard to protect what actually happened when you aren't entirely sure what happened. Whenever the data is less than complete, or when it's contradictory, the brains in Veracity are supposed to resolve the discrepancies, fill in the holes, before passing the intel to the Protectors.

I've grown used to the process of sifting through competing narratives, but this beat is the muddiest of any I've been sent to, the theories most divergent, the passions strongest. The bombs in America started the Great Conflagration, sure, but who set them off? Was it terrorists, and if so, was it international jihadists or domestic anti-government radicals? Was it the calculated act of a rogue state, an attempt by a small nation to cripple the hegemonic U.S.A.? Or was it an isolated move by a deranged individual or a small group that sparked reprisals from so many sides so quickly that the violence overwhelmed any possibility of determining the origins? The counterstrikes came so rapidly and apocalyptically that little was left of a press or news media. Analysis was impossible; guesswork was accepted without evidence. Conspiracy theories were touted as gospel; fact merged with fiction. No one really knew what was happening, survivors whispering in the dark. Then came the long migrations to unscorched earth, the disruptions and dislocations, the new alliances. Which is when it got really messy, each side clinging to its own story of what had happened and why, each side blaming someone else, each narrative of blame taking on the power of a founding myth. They were all zealots digging in their heels and aiming their weapons.

There's a saying that dates back even before this time: *History is written by the winners.* So what happens when everyone has lost?

"The hags are hedging their bets—I've never seen them send so many operatives back," Wills said as we sat at a red light outside one of D.C.'s many traffic circles. "They're trying to prevent numerous different Events, cut as many arteries as possible. Maybe Veracity started prepping one of us for the mission, then uncovered more data and realized it was more complicated, and instead of adding all the extra work to one Protector, they prepped a second."

That would be unfortunate, but believable. Some underling in Veracity could have uncovered a few pieces of data at the last minute—from rediscovered newspaper stories, restored audio records, unearthed diaries. Wills's information made sense, but it was a lot to absorb. The bottle of wine I'd split with Tasha wasn't helping.

I thought about the man on Capitol Hill and the blond woman from the restaurant, both of whom approached me and called me Troy, one warning me away and the other acting nice, but maybe only because Tasha was there. I chose not to mention them to Wills.

"If they sent both of us," I said, "do you think there could be…others too?"

"Maybe. I hope not."

I'd never considered this possibility before. I'd always thought I was a lone gunman, but maybe I was part of an arsenal. Or part of a scroll, the paper unspooling, more words crossed out and rewritten and revised and recrossed out, paper falling to the floor in an illegible mass.

"The hags are staying in the Mayflower hotel, just south of Dupont Circle," Wills said as he drove. "They're learning, doing a better job of insinuating themselves into the era, making it harder for us to take them out so surgically. I'm worried about how many there are this time. Must've gotten their hands on more machines than we realized, or maybe they even built some themselves. We're going to be busy."

I didn't bother telling him how unfocused I'd been—the walks to the playground, the drinks at the Anonymous Source. The wine on my breath was probably a good enough hint.

"I can't believe they didn't tell us about each other," I said. "We're being strung along by bureaucratic morons. I'd like to see any of *them* try to do what we do."

"You're funny, Zed. One minute you're the burned-out vet drinking on the job, and the next you're the passionate warrior."

"Maybe the passion's faked. Maybe I'm all burned out."

"Maybe you're not the only one." He pulled into a parking space on Connecticut. "Everyone who's been doing this as long as we have feels the same way. This is my last mission—I'm not supposed to be saying that, but they promised me, and I'm going to hold them to it—so we just need to hang together until this is finished."

"It's my last one too."

"You know what happened to Derringer after his little tirade?"

"I have an idea."

"Yeah, well, I plan on enjoying my retirement."

"Me too." I tried to imagine that.

"That's the hotel there," he said, pointing across the street. From here we could just see the grand entrance, the over-uniformed men beckoning taxis and carrying suitcases for the important guests.

I could tell from his suddenly glazed eyes that he was checking his GeneScan—I can't describe my relief at knowing that I was with someone whose GeneScan functioned properly. "They're in there—at least four, I think. The fourteenth floor."

I felt for the gun inside my jacket. "Let's go in, wipe them out. However many there are. Get this over with and go home."

"Make a raid on an expensive downtown hotel full of diplomats and politicians and celebrities, kill as many as four hags, and do it without affecting the upcoming Events? If you can think of a way to do it that won't cause chaos in this city, I'm listening."

He was right. "What do you suggest?"

"We stake it out, see if they're planning anything tonight. My intel says no, so does yours, but we wait just in case. When they do leave the building, we take them down, one by one."

It was a smarter idea than mine, and I resented him for it.

"The sooner we can end this job, the sooner we can get back to"— he shook his head—"whatever the hell it is we left behind."

We stay in the car all night, one of us at the wheel and the other sleeping. A few times we have to move the car after a cop or security guard or local contemp takes too much notice of our presence—we just drive in a circle and park in a different spot, and that works until sunrise. At six o'clock, when a coffee shop across the street opens, we get out and buy some stimulants.

The fedora Wills leaves in the car after I convince him it's wrong for the time and only makes us memorable.

"Do you ever wonder," he asks when we're well into our second coffees, sitting at a table, "if this job could actually be a punishment?"

"It's definitely a punishment."

"I'm serious. They told all of us it was an honor, the most important job anyone could have. But I've been running through a few things in my head. You and I both worked in Security for a while, right? We didn't know each other, different squads, but still. Maybe someone important got tired of us. Maybe we got blamed for something, and they decided this was the best way to get rid of us."

I try to look at him without letting my eyes stray from the Mayflower for too long. Half the cars that pull up in front of it are Lincoln Town Cars, limousines, or SUVs with tinted windows. Important people with secrets to hide.

He continues, "Because, here's the thing: Can you really go back and alter history? Can the hags actually do that?" He's speaking softly, and with the Muzak and the cacophony of customers and espresso grinders, no one can hear him but me. "They think they can, but what if they're wrong? The Perfect Present—can they really undo that? We have our memories, the basic facts of our lives. These things *exist,* if only in our minds. If the hags manage to do what they're trying to do, stop the Great Conflagration, then sure, they'll change the course of history, but it'll just go down an alternate path. It won't change the future that you and I are from, and it won't change what we carry in our memory."

"So you're saying that what we do here makes no difference."

We're sitting as far back in the coffee shop as we can without losing the view through the window. We know we'll be spotted by contemps—so many of them that we could never get their names or samples or even images—but we've decided we have no other option. We can't sit in a parked car on this avenue by daylight, not in this age of "orange alerts." The only other option is staying in our motel until the time of the specific Events that our intel claims the hags are trying to disrupt, but we don't fully totally trust our conflicting intel anymore.

"I'm just wondering," he says, as if the coffee-house environment has unleashed his inner philosopher. "I'm opening it up for debate."

A homeless man staggers past the window, drops a plastic bag on the ground, stares at it for a moment as if wondering where it came from, and walks away.

"But we've done other missions. We've gone to the past and been recalled again."

"And didn't you find it a little suspicious that they kept us on campus between missions? That we weren't allowed to leave, walk around, see our families?"

I have no family, I nearly say. But I swallow this down.

"Maybe this is a new kind of prison we're in," he continues. "They send us back, we do a mission, and, if we survive, great, they recall us and just send us on another one. Over and over. It will never end, whether we stop the hags or not. We could cause an apocalypse here, spread some horrible disease, kill vital historical figures, and it wouldn't matter. The ramifications would all occur on alternate paths, and our superiors would still recall us afterward." He shrugs. "Or maybe this is all some elaborate computer program they've plugged our brains into, or a drug trip."

"We wouldn't have the same trip. And that back-and-forth idea, that can't be right either. Because this is our last mission."

"Sure, they *said* that, but what if we go back and they say, Oops, sorry, some things have come up, the hags have a new plot, we need more help from our loyal soldiers." He leans closer. "Don't you find it odd that this time, on what are supposed to be our last missions, they sent us *here* instead of to our usual beats?"

"So this is a purgatory we're in."

Odd how natural it is to talk in the contemps' terms for fate, for afterlife. The beat seeps into you.

"And nothing that we do matters," I say. "No control over our fate or anyone else's."

"It's just a theory."

One could say the same thing about life in general, right? That we run around in frantic circles, directed by those more powerful than us, having an effect on nothing. Wills's existential wonderings are only making me more depressed.

"Let's just say I hope you're wrong."

Three women in long jackets pass on the sidewalk; the one in the middle is pointing with her finger like a conductor as she issues commands.

"Me too. Me too."

"And you're giving me a headache. Look, the Engineers can play with the theories. I just want to kill some damned hags and go home." We've each had two coffees by now, and so many pastries I'm tense from sugar and caffeine, not to mention sleeplessness from the night in the car. "Let's go in, get it over with. I'm tired of waiting, tired of being *back here*."

"We need to be smart about this. I'm sorry if what I said upset you."

"What you said didn't *upset* me. I just think you're a little crazy."

"I don't think anyone expected us to emerge from this many gigs with our heads straight." Then he sits up, distracted. He's seeing something on his GeneScan. "They're moving," he says. It's not quite eight in the morning; the sidewalks are manic with activity. "No, only one of them—the others are staying put."

As the hag descends the elevator, we flip a coin—trusting at least something to fate—and I win. I'll follow the hag, and Wills can wait for the next one.

I cross the street, hands in my pockets against the morning chill, engulfed in a mass of office workers. I stand outside the tie shop at the Mayflower's entrance, glancing at the headlines of the *Post* through the glass of a dispenser ("Defense Budget Passes," "Wizards Blow 4th-Q Lead," "10 Best Cocktails in D.C."), and then watching Wills, who's moved to the front of the coffee shop so I can see him. When he gives me a faint nod, I turn to the door and see a young man emerge from the hotel. He's wearing a long, charcoal-gray topcoat over a suit with cuffed pants, and I wonder if he visited a tailor here or if they somehow managed to construct a contemp wardrobe back in our own time. I wait a few seconds, then follow him south on Connecticut.

I keep just far enough away, lingering at intersections and waiting for lights. He never talks on a phone or to anyone else.

We walk east for twenty minutes. We've apparently reached the outer edge of the city's commercial core—the crowds are thinning, the buildings shorter, the ground-floor delis and snack shops more rundown. Cranes in the distance are struggling to expand the white-collar reach. The hag turns north. On one side of the street is a long line of row houses in desperate need of paint and gardening and new roofs, or maybe just bulldozers. Looming above them on the other side is a concrete monstrosity that stretches as far as I can see. My GPS informs me that this is the Washington convention center.

I know the convention he's heading to—it was in my intel. Rather than follow him too closely, I loiter at a street corner and pretend to be very interested in the list of bands that will soon grace the nearby tiny club, at least until the bombs hit.

The hag walks into the entrance and I watch him chat with a man at the front desk. I don't know how he gets past security, but he manages it. I check and there are no metal detectors, a good thing, since I'm armed. The hag likely is too.

A taxi pulls up to the entrance and a small entourage of businessmen carries briefcases and the leftovers of their conversation into the building. I walk in thirty seconds later. The man at the front desk wears a light brown jacket with the crest of a security firm sewn on the sleeve.

"I'm not on your list, actually," I say after he asks me for my invitation. I show him, but don't hand him, one of the extra IDs that the people in Logistics gave me for just such a purpose. It has my cover name, Troy Jones, but it's not a driver's license; it's a badge from the Federal Bureau of Investigation. I don't know how realistic it is, but I assume that this guy doesn't know what a real one looks like anyway. "I need to hunt around for someone."

"Oh. Um, who are you looking for?"

"Don't worry about that."

"Sir, um, we have some rather important people here today, and I'd—"

"*I'm* rather important," I tell him, surprised to be getting such pushback after showing him the badge. Perhaps the authorities aren't as highly regarded in this time as my training has led me to believe.

"I'm sorry, it's just . . . I wasn't told anyone from the FBI would be coming today."

"We're not big on prior announcements. And no one from the FBI *did* come here today, understand?" I wink at him, burn his image into my drive, and walk away.

I stroll down a hallway wide enough for two tanks. In the center, a hundred yards up, a swarm of business-suited middle-aged and elderly men and a few token women buzz around a breakfast buffet like plump bees attracted by the piles of sliced pineapples and strawberries. Name tags dangle from lapels. To make myself less conspicuous—I'm darker-skinned, slightly younger, and less formally dressed than anyone here—I grab a stack of papers and a thick white binder from a kiosk. I skim through the agenda, the lectures with titles like "Investment Opportunities in Newly Opened Nations" and "Putting Advanced Surveillance Technologies to Work for Your Company." Last night's keynote speech was delivered by a senator from South Carolina; a congressman from California will close the sessions at six o'clock tonight.

I've let the hag lead me to a meeting of key figures indeed, a convention of CEOs and elected officials. This city is a nightmare to operate in.

Placards set up at the doorways tell me which lectures will be occurring inside. I walk into the room for "Beyond Automated Ticketing: The Future of Privatized Police." It's crowded, but I don't see the hag.

At the third room ("Making Your Workforce Kidnap-Proof: Best Practices for Human-Asset Protection"), I see the hag in the third row. I sit in the back just as a portly man in a light gray suit makes an introductory joke about their country's president then notes that the agenda has a typo and that the demonstration project on disaster evacuations and triage of wounded will be at 11:30, not 11:00. He introduces the speaker to light applause. I check the agenda, and I recognize a name. In less than two hours, one of the hag's targets will be giving a speech in this very room.

The target's name is Randolph McAlester. He is a former head of Britain's MI5 and worked closely with America's National Security Agency. He now runs a "clandestine training firm," whatever that means, based in London but with offices in Dubai, Tokyo, and Johannesburg. He's scheduled to present new findings about digital surveillance technology and its amazing possibilities. He will never finish his speech.

Flight data tells me he will land at Washington National Airport in twenty minutes. He'll no doubt take one of those tinted-window SUVs to get here. If the hags were smart, they would intercept him at the airport, or they could have tried to get to him in London. Instead, they think they're going to save him here.

When the session ends, I return to the lobby, then pretend to consult the agenda as I walk into a corner. I place the binder and paperwork on a small table and watch the room's door as everyone files out, including the hag. I turn around, face the wall, and follow his reflection in an ornate mirror hanging there. McAlester's plane landed two minutes ago.

The hag goes to the men's room. I wait a few seconds, then walk there as well. Before opening the door, I see, hidden behind a potted plant against the wall, a yellow janitor's DO NOT ENTER sign. I step inside, see a man at the urinal. It's not the hag. There's a pair of feet in one of the stalls. I wash my hands, slowly, and wait for the contemp to finish his business and leave. When he does, I walk out the door and set up the janitor's sign. Back inside, I kick a rubber doorstop in place.

There were no security cameras in the hallway and there are none in here, so I take out my gun and fasten on the silencer. I cough as I pull back the hammer, then I walk up to the front of the stall. What an embarrassing way to go.

I kick the door open just after he flushes. He's standing, and thankfully he's all buttoned up. His eyes are wide.

"Digestive troubles getting in the way of revolution?"

"You..." He's stunned by my appearance. Why are they always so surprised?

"I have a question first. Before we make things even messier." My gun is aimed at his head. He's too far away to knock the gun from me, and my body pins the door to the side wall so he can't try to kick it shut.

"Are you one of the religious cultists?" I ask him. "This isn't an overtly religious mission you're on, not like some of the others I've had to deal with. But still: Do you believe in fate? Or in God? If there's fate, if we're being pulled along on trajectories that are beyond our power, then there's nothing we can do to change that. Right? Which means that your whole mission, disrupting the Perfect Present, is impossible."

"Why don't we have this conversation somewhere else?" He's about my size and looks like he could be trouble if I didn't have a gun on him. But his voice is tiny.

"You're not going anywhere. But you can buy a little time with an interesting answer." *Buying time,* there's another good one.

"This isn't about fate. This is about freeing ourselves. This is about—"

"But freeing yourselves from what, fate? Or God? That's my question. I'm betting you don't believe in fate. You think we can step outside our boundaries, do whatever we want, have an effect on the larger forces. Am I right?"

"Yes. I might feel that way even more if you stopped pointing that gun at me."

"But I'm doing my job. I'm fulfilling my fate, and the fate of all the people around us. What is going to happen to them has *happened to them.* If you go back and undo it, if I *let* you undo it, or if I suddenly decide to undo it myself—*Sure, why not, let's disrupt things and see what happens*—then I've imposed my own moral judgment on millions, billions of people. The rest of humankind, really. I would *be* God, wouldn't I? And so would you."

"I...I guess that's one way of looking at it."

"But here's the problem: If there's fate, then there's no God. Because the whole idea of God is that there's free will, right? That we can make our own decisions and live with the consequences, that there *is* no fate, and anything is possible. If I let you disrupt things, though, I make myself God, but we've already established there is no God. So the whole thing just collapses. It's a mess. A *goddamned* mess, as the contemps would say."

"You're right to question what you're doing, Zed. If we could just talk a little more, I think you'd begin to understand what we're trying to—"

"Flush the toilet again."

"What?"

"The toilet. It stinks. Flush it again."

He still looks confused, but he slowly turns, daring to take his eyes off me, and he bends down a bit to flush it. During the loud *whoosh* I shoot him twice in the back.

His body slumps awkwardly. There's not enough space for him to fall, and he's still slightly alive as I pull him down, hitting his head against the commode. I plant a Flasher on his bubbling chest—the bullets went straight through—and step back. The silent blast melts the walls of his stall and the ones flanking it, everything within six feet is blackened, the horrid pipes exposed. This clearly will perplex people—I've left more of a trace than I should have, as is becoming alarmingly typical on this gig—but I tell myself it's the best I could do given the circumstances.

I walk out, leaving the janitor's DO NOT ENTER sign in front of the door. Hopefully no one will walk in for a few hours, maybe not even until the convention ends. I walk back through the hallway to pick up the binder and other paperwork, then I walk down one of the long hallways, past the meeting rooms, and find an empty spot. I sit on a couch and read through the binder in hopes it will help explain the holes in my intel.

When it's time for McAlester's speech, I slip into the back of the assigned room. It's standing room only, but I'm tall enough to see over other people's shoulders. The introducer finishes regaling the crowd with a list of McAlester's many achievements in the service of international peace and diplomacy, then the great man himself ascends to the podium amid the applause. He looks unusually sweaty and a little gray.

He starts with a joke, badly delivered. Wins a few awkward laughs. He begins his speech, with weird pauses that grow in length. Heads in the crowd turn to each other, perplexed. Then McAlester's voice trails off and he falls before anyone can catch him.

People stand, voices compete for volume and clarity. I wait for an appropriate moment to leave, realizing that a hasty exit would arouse suspicions. Behind me, they're all wondering what happened, a heart attack or a seizure, maybe exhaustion or a blood clot from the long flight. Only I, and a few others, know that Randolph McAlester has had a heart attack as a result of a refined and untraceable poison put into the coffee that someone handed him the moment he arrived here, poison the hag never had a chance to intercept.

I'm back at the hotel; Wills is gone. I tap my appropriated line and call him—we swapped numbers last night. I can talk to him without actually using my voice, almost a form of telepathy.

I'm at the Mayflower—where are you? I ask.

Tracking another hag. He left the hotel about thirty minutes after the other one did. I think he's tailing the Korean diplomat.

Interesting. That Event is still a few days away. Maybe I should take things from here?

No, I'm fine. I downloaded everything from you last night; I know what's happening. How did yours go?

The integrity of history was preserved. I left a mess in a public bathroom, but no body.

We decide I'll stay outside the hotel in case I spot any other hags leaving, but without my GeneScan, it's pointless. Going back to that coffee shop to *kill more time* would start to look suspicious, so instead I buy a vegetarian empanada at a vendor's stand and eat it in a tiny triangular park surrounded by busy roads. The only other people in the park are two homeless men; I give them some money and keep my eyes on the hotel.

15.

For the second time in a week, Tasha left work early, passing through the electronic scanners on the ground floor at 7:30 (her billable hours would be suspiciously low) and emerging into an unusually warm autumn night. The leaves that had begun turning colors refused to fall, as if wondering if they'd been mistaken about winter coming. As if they could hang on, maybe turn themselves green again, reverse nature's clock.

Tasha wasn't working as late as an associate was expected to because she was hurrying to T.J.'s anti-recruitment meeting. Her excuse the previous night had been a dinner date with Troy—it hadn't necessarily been the greatest first date of her life, but guys who were great on first dates usually turned out to be guys uninterested in relationships, the ones who viewed life as a nonstop cocktail party and were frightened of serious conversation. Troy was a serious one.

She was still figuring him out; all she knew for sure was that he was that rare man who didn't seem to realize how good-looking he was. And he had an air of preternatural calm. He'd said he was a health statistician, so maybe this was just his scientific nature, doing calculus in his head while he pondered questions like fair reimbursement rates for city hospitals and the societal costs of obesity, hiding in his mental laboratory and observing the world from a distance.

She liked him. Maybe starting a relationship now was exactly what she needed. But she was worried about his being a widower. Having lost not just a wife but a little kid—*Jesus*. She couldn't imagine that. He had been vague about the details, said it had happened a while ago (how old was he, thirty-five, forty?). But there was no mistaking how present the pain was.

Regardless, she realized that she was thinking about Troy and the too-brief kiss she'd allowed him mainly to distract herself from what she was about to do.

She'd had a few days to digest everything Leo had told her. Though the evidence he possessed wasn't as rock solid as he'd acted like it was, it was probably enough to get her fired. She had known the possibility existed that someone in the firm might think she was the leak; none of the other hundreds of lawyers at the D.C. office had any family members who'd been killed overseas, though a few secretaries and paralegals did. All Leo really had to do, as he'd said, was place a call to one of the partners, and the suspicion he planted (even without those computer-speak files he had) would lead to a confrontation that Tasha was no longer sure she could talk her way out of.

On the one hand, maybe Leo was right when he said he wasn't asking her to do anything terrible. T.J. was a big boy and could take care of himself. He projected an awareness that he was constantly surrounded by powerful enemies plotting against him—something she had considered self-aggrandizement at best and paranoia at worst. (Now she wasn't so sure.) But whether T.J.'s politics and personality were extreme or not, that wasn't the point. He was a friend, a friend who was trying to do some good in the world. Whereas Leo represented everything about the world that needed serious fixing. A power structure gone mad with paranoia of its own. A national belligerence that took out its grievances on its own citizens just as thoughtlessly as it took them out on Third World nations. An abject moral blindness.

True, her enthusiasm for T.J.'s brand of activism was waning, but she would keep going to the meetings as a cover for her own ends. Leo would think she was doing his dirty work, but she wouldn't be. She would stall him long enough to get information from him on Marshall, and maybe even learn more about who Leo was, who he worked for, and why the hell he was monitoring innocent civilians like some

21st-century Stasi. This wouldn't be easy—he would likely require her to provide something on T.J. before he gave her anything on Marshall. She probably couldn't make something up (Leo might catch her, and she wasn't sure she could lie *that* well), but she could feed him just enough information on some of T.J.'s various activities to make Leo think she was holding up her end. She wouldn't even need to act like she enjoyed it—she could show Leo that she hated herself for playing along with him, and maybe that would incent him to give her information on Marshall as a way of winning her loyalty. *I appreciate your hard work, Tasha; check out what I learned from army intelligence.*

Unless she was just in denial, and her plan to stall Leo was in fact her way of putting off a real decision on how to deal with the mess she'd gotten herself into.

She got off the Metro at Shaw and walked a few blocks to a Howard University classroom building, where T.J. had parlayed some connections (probably involving a smitten underclasswoman) into the use of a lecture hall for the launch of his guerrilla campaign against the United States military.

The plan, T.J. explained from the podium, was to offer a message to counter "the siren song of glory and triumph that the army uses to seduce teenagers into carrying arms in the name of U.S. hegemony." Tasha found herself wondering what it was that had initially attracted Marshall to military service. Their parents' idea of heroic conflict involved getting blasted by fire hoses wielded by racist Alabama cops, and yet Marshall had joined the most powerful fighting force ever assembled. To Tasha (and, she could tell, to her parents), this represented a symbolic switching of teams, from the righteous underdog's to the thundering bully's. But to Marshall, it was a logical continuation of his parents' activism: they had fought to ensure that democracy would exist in a true form here in America, and Marshall would do his part to protect that democracy and to extend its reach into oppressed nations. She still wasn't sure who was right.

Scattered about the lecture hall were two dozen people, most of them college students but others old enough to remember earlier wars. T.J. wore a long-sleeved black tee proclaiming EVOLUTION IS JUST A THEORY / REVOLUTION IS INTELLIGENT DESIGN. He explained to his listeners that military recruiters focused their efforts on the very people that the capitalist system ignored, the kids in violent inner cities and meth-ridden rural communities whose only options were jail and war. The people gathered in this room, he said, would offer these kids another solution. They would show up at high schools and community centers armed with information the recruiters didn't want the kids to know, news from the front lines and the VA mental wards. "We'll hit them with the truth so they can make informed decisions and not be led to the slaughter. We're here not just to spread truth but to save lives."

T.J. peppered his speech with terms like *imperialist regime* and *warmongers*. Tasha found herself wondering if Leo was right, if T.J. was just someone with a permanent grudge, spoiling for a fight; whatever society he'd been born into, whatever conceivable utopia, he would have found reason to object, incite, attack. She had tried to focus on their common ground these last few weeks, but the earth was always slanted with T.J.; he was always dangerously pushing everyone into a crevasse. Guys like him gave the political Left a bad name.

During a break in the consciousness-raising, while some of the college students distributed articles and statistics among the believers, T.J. walked up to Tasha.

"Do you want to take the podium for a bit?" he asked her.

"Me?" She'd never promised him she'd participate in the group; only after frequent needling had she consented to even attend the meeting. "Why?"

"So you can tell your story, you know. Having the sister of a veteran on our side, that'd mean a lot, carry real weight with the kids."

"My brother is not a rhetorical device, T.J."

"I didn't mean it like that," he said. "I just figured, maybe you could get things off your chest, and at the same time it would rally people to be a part of this. That's all."

She tried to breathe slowly, concentrate on not lashing out.

"I don't feel comfortable doing that right now."

He nodded, then returned to the podium to discuss who would start calling which high-school principals.

After the anti-recruitment meeting ended, she and T.J. went out to Busboys and Poets for a drink.

"I'm sorry if what I said about your brother was out of line," he said after they clinked pint glasses.

"That's okay. I can be touchy about it, that's all."

"And I can be tactless, I know. I'm working on it."

This was one of the many reasons she'd chosen not to tell him about Leo. *Maybe* T.J. would have some good ideas on how they could both string Leo along, but more likely he'd go public with the information and land Tasha in even worse trouble. She would tell him about it, she promised herself, but not until she'd gotten what she needed from Leo.

Her phone buzzed and she excused herself to check who it was, hoping it wasn't someone at the office demanding her return. No; it was her parents. She didn't feel mentally prepared to deal with them right then. She stared at the phone for an extra second before silencing it.

While she'd been distracted, T.J. had picked up a *Post* from the empty table beside them. He seemed particularly engrossed by whatever he was reading.

"Holy shit, I know this dude," he said.

"Who?"

He told her there was a story about a reporter who'd recently gone missing. Allegations were made that he'd been kidnapped, or worse, to silence an investigation he'd been reporting on, something to do with intelligence matters. Tasha couldn't tell how much of that was in the story and how much of it was T.J.'s conspiracy-minded editorializing.

"How well do you know him?" she asked.

"No, I just meant"—and he looked up—"like, I've read his stuff. Jesus."

Was that what he'd meant? At the office, when she was working on a GTK-related matter, she found herself overanalyzing comments her coworkers made. She obsessed over anything any of the partners said about the *Times* story, wondering if the remark had been made for her benefit, to goad her into a confession. When someone voiced a criticism of U.S. foreign policy, Tasha held her tongue, worried that a similar comment coming from her would mark her as a dissident, a disgruntled American who might have leaked documents.

What if someone at the firm was still investigating, checking computer records to see who had accessed which files when? What if she played along with Leo (or *pretended to* play along with Leo) only to have the firm nab her anyway? She was battling on two opposite fronts: pretending to be innocent at work and pretending to act with deceit for her spymaster.

As if reading her mind, T.J. asked what kind of law she practiced. He'd never shown any interest in her work before, had been happy to let his activism dominate the conversations.

"Corporate law. I admit it's not very edifying. But I have so much school debt, I have to do this for a few years until I can move on to something more... worthwhile."

"That's it right there. They rope us in with our debts and our 401(k)s and our property values. Make us vested participants in shit we don't like. Because we're *American,* we *deserve* all this. Everything done in our name, for our own good, and we're supposed to smile and thank them with our votes."

"Not that you vote."

He made a distasteful face. "I try not to do things that can be stolen. Democrats and Republicans are pursuing the same agenda."

"Uh-huh."

"Seriously. Republicans believe that the scariest thing in the world is an all-powerful, unfettered government crushing their freedom. Right? And Democrats believe that the scariest thing in the world is a group of all-powerful, unfettered corporations crushing their rights. What they don't want to admit is that the corporations and our government are completely intertwined: the modern corporatist state."

"Is *corporatist* really a word?"

He shrugged. "If it ain't, you can file a petition for me with the relevant office."

Then he glanced at the cover photo on the newspaper between them, the president smiling while making some doubtless important announcement from the Rose Garden.

"You know what a president actually is?" he asked. "An unreliable narrator."

"Really." She sensed a speech coming.

"He's the one who tells us how it is, right? And we fall for it, we read along with his story and let him construct the reality around us. We want to be entertained, soothed. Until one day, we hit that certain chapter, right, and suddenly we see the light and realize, *Holy shit, we've been lied to the whole time. Reality ain't like that at all. His story was bullshit.* But by then, it's too late. We've all been suckered, and we just have to follow along with his little plot."

"You really believe that?"

"You don't?"

"Look, I have friends who are journalists, and they're hardworking, level-headed people. They do their best to sublimate their opinions and tell a story objectively. I don't think that makes them 'tools of the Man' or whatever you want to call them."

He watched her for a second. "So why are you here talking to a freak like me?"

A damn good question. Was she here for Leo or for herself? For Marshall or for T.J.?

This was the best segue she was going to get. She told herself she wasn't actually doing what Leo wanted, she was only pretending she was. She would simply gauge T.J.'s interest. Stringing T.J. along now was practice for deceiving Leo later.

"Sometimes the freaks like you are right about some things," she said, "but no one'll listen to you unless you have someone like me to lay it out for them."

"Well put."

"Speaking of which. You know that GTK scandal that hit a few weeks ago?"

T.J. nodded. His eyes, she thought, suddenly seemed more professional than friendly. Leo had told her that T.J. himself was the hacker who'd created the e-mail address for her, which meant he had most likely read her correspondence with the *Times*. Or had he kept his word and stopped himself from e-eavesdropping?

She leaned closer, and he seemed happy to do the same. "Someone at GTK or my law firm must have leaked it. We still don't know who did it. But it got me to thinking. I mean, do you know who some of my firm's clients are?"

"I don't keep up too well with legal rosters."

"Well, one of the firm's clients is Consolidated Forces, a private police group, like Hellwater but smaller, and worse."

"I know who they are."

"Break into their training camp to shoot any documentaries?"

"Not yet, but I'd love to try. They're way out in the middle of the Nevada, so they're hard to get to. Some groups based in San Francisco have tried it, but they have guards at the outer perimeter."

She had rehearsed this, telling herself it wasn't wrong, that she wasn't setting up a snare for someone she considered a friend because she would in fact free him just in time. Legally speaking, it might seem that she was entrapping T.J., but ultimately she wouldn't let that happen. She was doing this in the name of finding out the truth about Marshall. T.J. had his cause, and she had hers. He'd understand.

"Charges have been brought against Consolidated for some shootings last March," she said, "when their guards, who are just supposed to provide protection for diplomats, opened fire at a market. There weren't any diplomats nearby, so they had no reason to even be there. It was a vendetta or something; they killed the relatives of a woman the guards had raped."

"I've seen a few stories."

"The other night I had some drinks with a couple of the associates who are working on the case. That company is crooked, T.J., and the guards are guilty as hell. They'll never get punished, though. The U.S. is pressuring the local government to drop the charges, tying it in with aid packages. But what if the public learned more about what really happened?"

Leo had told her to be vague, sketch things out slowly. She was only supposed to have talked to people over drinks; her knowledge should have holes in it. Leo's story, more or less, was that her law firm's defense of Consolidated had turned up troves of files relating to *other,* as-yet-unreported crimes. Shootings, kidnappings, rapes. All perpetrated by the company's mercenaries, and all pretty much sanctioned by the U.S. government.

These crimes were fictional, Leo had explained. The files that he and his nameless colleagues would soon give to her, and that she was to pass on to T.J., contained detailed information about imaginary events and nonexistent people. A real news organization would discover this when it tried to corroborate the story, but an enraged, politically motivated Web site would rush online without doing its homework. Once readers learned it was all a hoax, the site would be discredited, Consolidated would have all it needed for a libel suit, and Leo and his associates would know for certain that T.J. was behind the Web site.

She would have to hope she could bleed information about Marshall out of Leo before T.J. did anything with the fake story.

"So you're thinking of leaking it to a reporter?" T.J. asked after taking a moment to digest what she'd said.

He still wasn't tipping his hand about GTK. Maybe he was wondering why *she* wasn't.

"No. And I'm surprised to hear that from you, Mr. 'The Mainstream Media Is in Cahoots with Washington.' You saw what happened with that GTK story—whoever leaked it sent it to the *Times,* mainstream media outlet number one, and it was instantly absorbed into the Establishment's story line before vanishing again. The only way to truly influence things is to go outside the system. I'm thinking something edgier, maybe a Web site."

She felt dirty to be borrowing his own language and ideology like this. If he noticed her appropriation, he didn't show it.

"Would those associates who told you about this be willing to dig up some more?"

"I don't think so. I mean, they're disgusted by it, but it's the kind of disgust people just suck up and live with."

"As so many millions do."

"But *I* could dig around."

"It would be a hell of a story. How long would it take you?"

"I don't know. It's not my client, so I'd have to find a way into the files. Pull some later-than-usual nights, tap into someone else's PC." In truth she could never do something like that in an office like hers, but she was using T.J.'s ignorance of standard office culture against him. "Even if I got some kind of smoking-gun document, what would I do with it?"

"Give it to me."

She raised a skeptical eyebrow. "Why you? I came to you for advice, not to get you—"

"I know some people, all right? If you got this to me, we would find a way to use it in the most effective way possible."

She paused. "I'll look into it. I can't even promise I'll be able to access anything. This is my career we're talking about, remember."

He said that he understood. "Don't do anything you're not comfortable with."

She wished she could tell him just how far outside her comfort zone she already was.

16.

Sari kept thinking of the word *slave*. Leo had said she was their slave, but that wasn't right. The diplomat was still sending money to her sisters in Korea, wasn't he? He claimed he was, though there was no proof yet. She wanted to write to her sisters, tell them of her plight and confirm they were getting the money, but she wasn't sure if there was a way to mail it—if the Shims weren't sending the payments, then they would certainly intercept the letters. And they never let her online. Maybe she could give a letter to Leo. If she ever found time to write one.

Had she been a slave back in Seoul, a new arrival from Jakarta, scared of a new country that seemed so different, so mechanistic, so cold? Had she been a slave when she'd been a night janitor in those offices, or when she'd worked in that plant assembling toys for children she would never meet, and her fingers were slashed by the machines and her back ached from stooping for hours? Had she been a slave as a girl, helping her mother work in the Mings' store? The Mings had worked them hard, had not been terribly kind, but surely her family hadn't been *slaves*. They had been paid for their labor, had managed the rent for their apartment. Part of her hated Leo for using that word, hated the way it made her look back at her own life, and her mother's. Perhaps someone like Leo was simply so free that anyone else's life looked like slavery.

She hid the cell phone he'd given her beneath her mattress, and every third night she left it plugged in under the bed so it would have power if she needed it. He had asked her what days she took the garbage and recycling out (which she did twice a week, a former annoyance that now would come in handy). He told her how to leave notes for him and what signals to put in the windows, the sash here or the sash there, a lamp moved to this side or that. But her employers were sticklers for order, and she interrupted Leo many times—*No, they would never let me move the lamp there, they would suspect something*—before they finally found a manageable solution.

It all seemed so bizarre. Was this how newcomers became Americans, by betraying others?

She couldn't figure Leo out. She'd never known an American, so maybe this was how they acted. That kiss at the grocery store, delivered stiffly and quickly, not so much a formality as something stolen. He'd left the store immediately, as if worried the shoplifter alarm would go off. The next time they'd met, in the parking lot of that destroyed school, she wondered if he would try for another one.

She wanted him to. He was nothing at all like the boys she'd spent time with—schoolboys in Jakarta and coworkers in Seoul, jokers who tried to impress her with their silliness, by acting as if they didn't care whether they impressed her or not, which fooled no one. She had never imagined herself with a white man—at least, not until the past few days.

Her own motivations were confusing to her. She wanted out of this house, yes, absolutely, but she hadn't been sure it was truly possible. So when she'd called him that first time, all she'd dared hope for was someone to talk to. That kiss in the grocery store, as hurried and surprising as it had been, had been the best gift she'd received since coming to America. She craved another kiss, a real one this time. Not stolen but given, freely and slowly.

But when they met at the parking lot, instead of getting a caress, she'd gotten an assignment—a potentially dangerous one. All day and night she did other people's bidding, and now she had to add another layer to that. But he was offering her an escape, and *this* was exactly what she'd wanted, what she'd been too afraid to even hope for. Wasn't it? Maybe she was confusing the need to touch someone with the need to be released. They could be so similar.

First she would have to find the information he needed. The devices had to be hidden somewhere; Sang Hee seldom entered Sari's room, but how could Sari be sure she wouldn't decide to? She left Leo's electronics in the garage at first, stuffed in the bottom of a box of gardening tools. Late that night, after the twins' feeding, she snuck out to retrieve them and stashed them in her closet. At least they were small.

Maybe she never should have called him. What had she been hoping for, that they would fall in love and he'd carry her away to some perfect American existence? She was ridiculous.

Then again, wasn't that exactly what he was offering? This handsome American, living in their capital, surely with an important job—he was taking a risk by helping her like this. Why? Maybe her hopes weren't so ridiculous. Maybe he did want to carry her away. Or maybe they were both ridiculous. Which made them either perfect for each other or a dangerous pair indeed.

Sari altered the timing of her chores, dusting or tidying the living room when Sang Hee was typing on her computer on the off chance the mistress would receive an interesting call. If one of the Shims were in their bedroom with the door open, she would clean Hana's adjoining room, lingering by the doorway. But Hyun Ki received few calls, and Sang Hee almost none. She was oddly reclusive. Before her injury she ventured out occasionally, and she still managed to go out for lunch now and then, but Sari noticed that she never made plans with anyone by phone. Either she went to lunch alone or she communicated with her lunch dates through other means. Maybe Sari should mention that to Leo.

Hyun Ki rarely took calls at home, in part because he was seldom there. If the phone rang at night, he would take it upstairs. Sari was usually busy with the twins then, but even if she hadn't been, picking up the downstairs line to eavesdrop was too frightening.

The couple didn't even seem to talk to each other much. There was precious little to overhear. Surely they spoke at night, in their bedroom—but even so, it must have been done in whispers, because Sari never even caught any mumbling. She didn't think they really loved each other. She seldom saw them kiss or embrace; Hyun Ki administered the occasional peck on the cheek with ambassadorial formality. The more she forced herself to watch them, the odder they seemed. The only conversations she overheard were trivial—a doctor's appointment for Hana, a restaurant recommendation he'd received from a colleague.

Very late one night, Sari walked out of the twins' room after consoling them and noticed that the kitchen light was on. Hyun Ki was talking on the phone.

"She's making things difficult," he said. "I'm not sure what to do."

Sari made it as far as her bedroom doorway and then stood there, leaning against the wall. Hyun Ki was not a loud talker even in the daytime. His voice seemed sad, or frustrated, and given the hour, she assumed he was talking to someone in Korea.

"She wasn't like this before. I knew she had a short temper, but still...It's different now."

Sari could see the kitchen from there but not the table at which he was sitting.

"No, it's not Washington. If she's lived in North Korea, she can live anywhere. That's not it—it's the twins. They've changed her."

The kitchen floor creaked, and the sound frightened her into her room. Had he heard her in the hallway, or was he just standing to get a glass of water? She crept back into her bed, lay down, and pulled the covers up. She couldn't hear him from here, not even any mumbling. Eventually she fell asleep.

And the next evening, after tucking Hana in, she entered the hallway and heard the Shims talking in their bedroom. They'd been out for dinner and must have returned while Sari was reading Hana stories. The diplomat was scolding his wife.

"You need to stop hitting the servant. I know you don't like her, but it doesn't look good for us."

Sari was stunned, never having expected Hyun Ki to defend her. It was true that he'd never raised a hand against her like his wife had, but he'd never treated her with respect either.

"She's lazy and stupid and she keeps ruining our things," Sang Hee said. "And one of the twins still isn't growing as fast as the other."

"Then we can fire her and get someone else."

Sari hadn't thought of this possibility. Being fired implied a more normal work arrangement than what she currently had. Could she really get herself fired? That would be perfect! But how? What could she do wrong that would merit firing, not just more abuse?

"My point," Hyun Ki said, "is that it will not do for a servant of mine to be seen, in the city, or by guests, with bruises. How do you think we look if our servant has a bruise?"

"Who cares how we look? And who knows she's ours?"

"I care how I look. I am paid to care how I look."

"The cast comes off next week, so we won't have to send her to the store anymore. I'll be able to get around for myself."

"Good. But we'll need groceries before then. Figure out how to order them online if you can't keep from hitting the girl until then, all right?"

Their conversation turned to other complaints, and Sari felt she'd been standing there long enough, so she lightly stepped down the stairs.

An hour later, after the babies woke again and she rocked them back to sleep, she went into the kitchen to get some water. Hyun Ki was doing the same. She lowered her eyes as he turned to face her.

"They're still waking a lot, aren't they?"

She could smell alcohol on his breath. "Yes." She dared to lie. "I think it's getting better."

He stepped aside so she could use the faucet. She started filling her glass.

"Sometimes I myself have trouble sleeping," he said. Then his right hand was on her forearm. She froze as his fingers lightly stroked her skin. He was standing just behind her, closer than he'd ever been.

She didn't know where Sang Hee was. She remembered Leo's words: *They can do anything they want to you.*

She dropped the glass. It was full and heavy, and it landed with a loud clang but didn't break. She hadn't meant to do that, but it worked; he backed off. Water had splashed on her shirt and maybe gotten him as well. She apologized for the mess, but he was already walking away.

That night she dreamed of her mother again.

I don't know what to do, Sari said. *The situation in this house is horrible, but if they catch me sneaking around on them . . .*

You've always been so cautious. But maybe it's time to take a chance.

Mother, am I their slave?

If you're trying to break free, if you believe you can escape, then you won't be a slave forever.

But I'm one now?

Don't waste time wondering about this. You should be planning how you're going to get the information the American wants.

I want to see him again, but Sang Hee's ankle will heal soon. She's already out of her hard cast. Then the only way I'll be able to communicate with him is through notes in the garbage.

There's one more thing I need to tell you.

What is it?

Wake up!

Sari sat up in bed at the sound of the crash. Then came the screaming.

She hurried out of the bedroom, hitting the light switch. At the end of the hallway, by the front door, a reflection of the light moved along the floor. A glass, empty and thick enough to have survived the fall intact, rolled to a stop at the fallen Sang Hee. All Sari could see of the mistress was a pile of purple bathrobe, a white knee, and a foot with green-painted toenails. The fabric thrashed, and Sang Hee screamed again.

Hyun Ki ran down the stairs and bent over his wife. They spoke so quickly and angrily that Sari couldn't follow everything. Something about trying to fetch water, the crutch getting caught in the banister. He tried to help her up but she howled in pain.

The diplomat looked at Sari and told her to tend to Hana. Only then did Sari realize the little girl was crying in her room. Hyun Ki helped his wife hobble to the living room, and Sari smelled alcohol on her mistress's breath as she passed her. Sari ran upstairs and into Hana's room, her shadow cast faintly on the wall by the night-light. "Everything's all right, go to sleep." She rubbed Hana's back and spoke softly, making herself into a fragment of a dream. The tiny clock on her bedside table said it was half past two.

She was still sitting there minutes later, and Hana was softly sailing back down her nocturnal river, when Hyun Ki's silhouette appeared in the doorway. He whispered that he had to take Sang Hee to the hospital—it looked like she'd rebroken her ankle, or worse. He told her to take care of the children while they were gone.

Sari watched through the window as the SUV pulled out of the driveway. She prayed that the twins wouldn't wake up, and then she walked into the hallway and saw that in the Shims' panic they had forgotten to close, let alone lock, the master bedroom door.

Was it really this easy?

She crept downstairs, entered her room, and opened the closet. Beneath a stack of extra blankets was the scanning device Leo had given her. Then she walked upstairs, holding her breath as she passed Hana's doorway. She quietly closed the master bedroom door behind her, turning the lights on but keeping the dimmer low. This was the only room in the house she did not clean, as Sang Hee had made it clear she was not allowed inside. Entering their matrimonial space felt alien, and as she stood looking at the unfamiliar photographs and decorative fabric, she realized how little she really knew these people whom she'd been living with for weeks. She was exhausted, and the usual heaviness behind her eyes was there, but her heartbeat was fast, and she realized her hands were shaking.

Where to begin? There were two desks crammed in the bay window, as well as a tall filing cabinet whose doors were locked. Surely there was a key somewhere.

She opened his unlocked desk drawers, flipped through some papers. She tried to make note of the exact arrangement of everything she touched, but she worried that she was so tired and nervous that she'd botch this, that they'd know instantly what she'd done. She saw Hyun Ki's computer on one of the tables and turned it on. Leo had told to her what to do; she had some experience using computers but none doing the bizarre copying that he required. She tried to remember the steps, nervously pressing the keys and inserting the flash drive he'd given her.

Only the next morning would she realize she could have called Leo, asked his advice while she fumbled along. But what she'd felt more than anything at that moment was alone, alone in other people's words, in their language, in their sparsely decorated little world. She understood little, but she grabbed what she could, hoping it was important, hoping this mattered.

Sari was sitting on the living room floor with the babies when the Shims returned. Sang Hee was still on crutches, and the soft cast had been replaced by a harder one, larger than before, extending almost to her knee. She made eye contact with Sari and wordlessly handed the crutches to her husband, then hopped up the stairs on her good foot.

Sari was more nervous than before, afraid they could somehow see the guilt in her eyes. But mixed with that was an undeniable pleasure at seeing pain in Sang Hee's face.

While the shower ran upstairs, Hyun Ki barked at Sari for not having his breakfast ready. Carrying one of the little ones with her, she hurried into the kitchen and made it for him.

"My wife is in a lot of pain," he said between bites. His eyes were red and his hair was badly combed. "You are to take her meals upstairs, as she's less mobile than before. Do whatever she asks and don't give her any lip, understood?"

She said of course, and then he was gone. The flash drive was hidden between the mattress and box spring of her bed, where it would stay until that night, when she would hide it in the recycling bin for Leo to retrieve.

"How were the children last night?" Sang Hee asked as Sari carried her lunch into the bedroom.

"Fine, ma'am. Hana woke briefly but fell back asleep right away. She probably doesn't even remember it."

"You think a daughter could forget the sound of her mother crying out in pain so easily?"

She hesitated. "Of course not."

Sang Hee watched her for a moment as she placed the plate and glass on the bedside table.

"You're a very careful girl, aren't you?"

"Ma'am?"

"Nothing. You can go."

The rest of the day was normal, task after task after task, occasionally interrupted by tense moments with Sang Hee. After Hyun Ki came home and the couple ate dinner, Sari put the babies to bed, then took out the garbage and the recycling. She hid the flash drive in an empty can, placing it exactly where Leo had told her to. She felt nervous as she did this, but surely no one could tell this was different from any other garbage night. While crouching there at the sidewalk, she gave the briefest of glances down the street, the rows of cars parked on either side. Was Leo sitting in one of them right now? Was he watching her?

She walked into the house through the back door, resisting the temptation to look over her shoulder at the innocent-appearing trash and recycling bins. To her surprise, Sang Hee was sitting at the kitchen table, alone, with a bottle of whiskey and a glass.

"Excuse me," Sari said, lowering her eyes.

"Sit down," Sang Hee said. "Have a drink with me."

Sari had never received anything remotely resembling a social invitation from Sang Hee before. She took a glass from the cabinet, fully expecting the mistress to laugh and rescind the invitation. As Sari filled her glass at the faucet, Sang Hee said, "No, I said have a *drink* with me. You aren't Muslim, girl, right? You can drink?"

"Yes," Sari said, emptying her glass in the sink and sitting down hesitantly. Sang Hee poured her some whiskey.

"Tell me, what do you think of my family?"

"It is a beautiful family, madam."

Sang Hee's face was a mask. "What else do you think?"

"I think Hana is very precocious. I think she will be a diplomat like her father, or whatever she wishes to be."

"What would you do to have a family like mine?"

"I . . . I don't understand what you mean."

"It's perfect, isn't it? Two cute babies, a sweet little girl. An attractive husband. Don't blush—I'm only stating a fact. He is a good-looking man. I've done well for myself, haven't I?"

"You have, madam."

"You haven't touched your drink."

Sari touched it, barely.

"One day maybe you'll have a family for yourself. After our stay here is finished, after we've all gone back to Korea and you've scurried off to some other job. Maybe you'll meet a nice young immigrant, some handsome dark-skinned man, who will take away your maidenhood and offer you something in return."

Sari stared at her glass.

"And you'll bear him children, and they'll suck on your round breasts and grow fat, and they will be so cute. You at least will think they're cute, even if others don't. So, you'll be happy. Imagine that for a moment. Are you imagining it?"

"Madam?"

"You need to imagine it." Sang Hee's voice hardened. "Close your eyes. This only works if you really, really imagine it."

Sari was afraid to close her eyes around Sang Hee but more afraid of disobeying. She closed her eyes.

"Imagine your dark-skinned man. Maybe it was someone you knew back in Indonesia, or maybe someone you saw in the slums at Seoul. A construction worker, a janitor, I don't know. Imagine him, and imagine him taking you, and imagine the family you create. Now imagine a few years later. There are times you feel tired of him and unappreciated, yes, there are times you wish you could return to the happy courtship days, but overall you're happy. It's life. It has its trials and its pleasures."

There was a pause as Sang Hee sipped, and Sari wondered if she was allowed to open her eyes yet. She was about to ask when Sang Hee continued.

"But then things change. I forgot to tell you, you aren't in South Korea, you're in North Korea. It's different there. People think they're in paradise but they're not. They're brought up to believe that it's heaven on earth, but it's not, and it only gets worse. One day your husband is angry with you because of something you did— nothing terrible, just some trivial thing, that's how marriage is—and when he's out with his friends he gets carried away and says things he shouldn't. Not about you, but about the Dear Leader. The Dear Leader is what we call God over in North Korea, only it isn't God, it's a man, and he is not dear. Your husband says things he shouldn't, and a few days later the government sends people to your home and they take your husband away. They don't say why. The night passes and he does not return. All night long you are terrified. Your children—two little girls—ask where he is and you lie to them. You say he will be home soon. But you assume the worst, because this is what happens to people who say the wrong thing. You don't sleep for two days, and you don't leave the house, because you can't bear to tell any of your friends. You're afraid that if they find out, they will shun you. You would do the same thing to them, after all, and you have.

"One week later he returns with the government people, and his eyes are black and his skin is sickly and he looks so much thinner. After just one week. He tells you that the family is moving out of the city, to the north, to work new jobs. Are you imagining it?"

Sari told her that she was.

"So you go north, with your cute children, and you live in a shack with no heat in a destitute little village. Not even a village—a camp, and surrounding it are walls and big ugly guards with guns who call you names and say they'd love to fuck you sometime when your dark-skinned man isn't around. So you never walk near the walls again, and you warn your cute little girls to stay away too. Your new shack has thin walls and the only heat comes from a small stove—it's very cold in autumn, and winter is unbearable. You are told that you are a miner now, and they make you crawl into caves and smash a hammer against stone until your fingers feel that they're breaking off. This is important work for the revolution, they say. Your husband does the same job, in a different mine. You only see him at night, when you're too tired to talk to each other. You eat thin broth and less than a handful of rice every day. Your children are sent to a special school in the camp where they are told that you and your husband are traitors, evil people who think wicked thoughts and cannot be trusted. Your children stop talking to you. You lose ten kilograms, then fifteen, then more. Your children look terrible. They get sick a lot, and you try to treat them, and it's the only time they don't yell at you and call you impure. But the camp doesn't have any good medicines, so their illnesses linger. You almost prefer them when they're sick, because at least they let you hold them again. Are you still imagining this?"

"Yes." Sari's voice was faint. It was like she barely existed. Sang Hee's voice blotted her out.

"You're a liar. You *can't* imagine it. It's impossible. It's something that just *happens,* and even then you can't understand it. There is no way a pretty little thing sitting in a clean kitchen with a full stomach can imagine it." Sari heard Sang Hee pour more whiskey. "But keep trying. And stop ignoring your glass."

Sari took another sip.

"The other thing you can't imagine is the *time*. Years. You think you will go insane, and then you do go insane, but it keeps going on. And I forgot to tell you: The people in this camp do not talk to one another. You have all been warned. You are impure elements and cannot be allowed to exchange information, share your dirty germs. You are allowed to speak the bare minimum of words while working in the mines, but that's it. The isolation is unbearable. To see so many faces and never know what their voices sound like. Now and then there are mine explosions and people die. Now and then people try to escape, but they're always caught. If they aren't shot during the attempt, they're brought in for a public execution. You lose track of how many of these you've had to watch. Your little girls have to watch too. After the people who tried to escape are killed, their families are too."

Sari could feel the drink affecting her, making her head heavy and her toes warm. Fear kept her awake, yet she felt herself descending into a nightmare. She wanted Sang Hee to stop and let her sleep.

The mistress told her to drink more.

"Then something happens. Something you had not expected, because you had stopped expecting things. One of the new functionaries in charge of the camp is someone you knew from the city. Back when you were a human being. He has just been sent to replace someone, and he sees you walking toward the mine. You look away, ashamed and afraid. The next morning, on your way to work, he summons you into his office. It's a dirty old building with flimsy walls, but compared to your shack it feels luxurious. You walk past the other clerks, people who have spat at you, and you keep your head down. Then you are alone in his office and he closes the door. He offers you tea. You are too scared to refuse. The two of you knew each other growing up. You went to school together, and you liked him. Only after his family moved away and you grew older did you realize that he'd liked you too but had been too shy to tell you. His family would visit the old neighborhood every now and then, which is the only reason you recognize him now that he's a man. You're surprised that he recognizes you, because you are so much thinner and uglier than before."

Sari heard Sang Hee take a sip. She told Sari to do the same. It was smoky on Sari's lips, numbing on her tongue.

"You sit there as he pulls a file and reads, and you know he is reading about you and your husband, about what your husband said."

Then there was proof that the drink was affecting Sari: she asked a question. "What had my husband said?"

"It doesn't matter. Whatever they say he said. You sit there while the functionary reads about your life, your rotten and tiny little life, and then he talks to you and asks how you are. You lie, of course. You tell him the Dear Leader provides all that your family needs, you thank him for his beneficence, you say that you are so fortunate to have been granted all this despite the horrible act your husband committed. Then he sends you back to the mines. You wonder if you were rude not to inquire about his own family, but you'd been too nervous. The overseers at the mine punish you for being late—two slaps in the face, and you aren't given any lunch.

"Three days later the functionary summons you again. The door is closed, and he sits closer to you than last time. He tells you he wants to know how you really feel. You're frightened, but you remember to ask about his family. His parents have died but he says they lived well. His brothers were once important Party officials like him, he says, but they recently have all been put in charge of camps like this, far away from Pyongyang. He says this is because relatives of the Dear Leader consider his family to be rivals, and want them removed. He says he is lucky that he was sent into the mountains and not simply killed.

"People do not talk like this anywhere in the country, and especially not in this camp. It makes you more nervous. He scoots his little chair closer to yours, and your knees are almost touching. You haven't been looking at him this whole time, but you do now. He is not too handsome, but not ugly either—a perfectly average man. He has good hair and you haven't seen teeth that clean in a long time. Your husband hasn't touched you in weeks, and the last few times were not fun at all, no joy in it. Almost wrestling. You've been turned into an animal, do you understand? A filthy animal. Try to imagine that; but you can't—it's impossible to imagine being something that itself lacks imagination, has had imagination beaten and starved out of it. But my point is that to be this close to a not-unattractive man, it does things to you."

Sari swallowed. Her hand was still holding the glass; she was afraid to let it go. It was something to cling to.

"What he does is this: He asks if you want to get out. He tells you that he too is a prisoner here, in a way; the Party will never call for him, never give him a better posting. He has been put here to rot. The difference, he says, is that he at least will die an old man, but you will die very soon. He says he can help. Things are happening quickly, and if he doesn't act soon, his connections will disappear as these people too are banished to distant posts. He says he knows how he can get you out, but it will be difficult. He tells you he's crazy to offer you this, but he wants to. You say no. This is all a test, you realize. A trap. You tell him no, you have all you need here. Then he says you can go. He tells you the overseers won't punish you for being late this time, and you are surprised to find that he is right.

"But one week later, it happens again, the same way. He tells you this is not a loyalty test and he really wants to help you. All week you have been thinking of his offer, assuming it was a test but wondering *what if* it was genuine. And now, here he is again, making you the same offer. You dare to ask him what he wants in return, and now you're staring down, looking at his hands. They are so fine and soft— you forgot that adult fingers could look so white and pure. He sits up straighter and tells you that you have misunderstood. Your heart races and you think, *It was a test, and I have failed.* He says he doesn't want anything. He only wants to make the most of this brief opportunity to do something good."

Then Sang Hee laughed. "Can you believe that? He actually uses the word *good.* Because here's the thing: He can only let one person escape. His plan, which he can't tell you until he puts it in motion, can only work for one. Two would be impossible, let alone four. You shake your head and say no again.

"Imagine how hard it is to sleep, to even *think* about anything other than escape now that it has been offered to you. And you turned it down! You are a fool. Every time you smash your fingers in the mine, every time one of the guards harasses you, every time you *shiver,* you think to yourself, *It doesn't have to be. I could escape.* But you missed your chance. Two nights later, when your husband returns from work, he hits you. He's done that before, a few times. He tells you that he heard about the new functionary inviting you to his office. The guards told him, made obscene gestures. He hits you again until you tell him that if you show up to work with bruises, he'll be punished. It's true—only the guards are allowed to hit you. Abusive husbands are counterrevolutionary. After you tell him that, he stops. But he refuses to speak to you.

"Your children watch this, of course. They watch everything. You still aren't sure if the authorities will ship them off to some other town once their schooling finishes or if they too will have to work the mines as punishment for what your husband said. You are afraid to ask.

"Two weeks go by, and your husband still will not talk to you. Finally you can't take it anymore, and after your children are asleep, you tell him what really happened in the functionary's office. Your husband, your once-beautiful, once-dark-skinned man, says he doesn't believe you, that it doesn't make sense. *If someone made that offer to me,* he says, *I would take it in a heartbeat.* But then they would kill me and the children as punishment, you remind him. He simply says, *For freedom from this, I would do it in a heartbeat.* He falls asleep.

"The very next day, when you are raw and bleary from not sleeping that whole night, the very next day the functionary calls for you *again.* Can you resist yet again? He tells you, once more, that he could set you free, that he could get you into China, and from there you could find a way to South Korea, where perhaps you have extended family, people left behind from before the war. He tells you he brought you in this morning because one of the people he would need to call on for help will only be at his post for one week longer, so he's running out of time. You ask him why *he* doesn't escape, and he says he isn't ready. He still has hope. He still believes he can return to the Party and make a difference. Besides, he says, he'll still be alive in two or three years, but you won't be. People only survive at the camp for so long, and you're nearing the end.

"You accept his offer. He says that after you have escaped and an investigation is made, he will do what he can to protect your family, and you pretend to believe him. Open your eyes."

Sang Hee had to repeat herself before Sari understood. She had become immersed in the tale, and her head was heavy with drink. The light was harsh, and everything before her looked wrong, too shiny, almost glistening. Nothing more so than Sang Hee's eyes.

"I know what you think of me," Sang Hee said. "But let me tell you something. What you think of me is *nothing* compared to what I think of myself."

Sari managed to look away from her and at her own glass, which, to her surprise, was empty again.

"I want you to remember that, to keep that close in your mind at all times. *This is a woman who killed her whole family. That is what she is capable of.* Don't you ever, ever forget that."

"Yes, madam."

"Now go to bed. Dream about your dark-skinned man and your little girls. Do that for me, please, because I don't know how to anymore."

Z.

Over the next two days Wills picks off a few more hags while I tail some others, but we don't feel much closer to accomplishing our mission. The hags have indeed learned from their mistakes; instead of all of them coming back on the same date, a few of them come one day, a few the next, et cetera, making it impossible for us to wipe them all out. No one at the Department thought the hags were capable of sending so many, and so frequently—at least, no one told us to suspect this. It makes us wonder what else we haven't been told.

This afternoon I'm tailing another hag through the city. He left the Mayflower hotel—still their rendezvous spot—an hour ago and is walking downtown. It's raining, and my umbrella provides me perfect cover, though his makes him harder to follow. I stay closer than usual. He's short and thick, a human bollard. Dark hair is going gray along his temples, and his skin, though pale to my eyes, isn't quite as pale as some of the other white people's here. Like the previous hags I've followed the last few days, he wears a well-tailored suit.

While I'd been waiting outside the hotel, my internal radio connection picked up a live story from a local station that mentioned one of the earlier Events. The news announcer noted the suspicious disappearance of a young Washington-based reporter who worked for an international wire agency. He explained that the young reporter, Karthik Chaudhry, covered the U.S. intelligence beat. Implications were made that Chaudhry—who had dual American and Pakistani citizenship, was a graduate of George Washington University, and had lived in D.C. for the past decade—had stumbled onto something dangerous. Chaudhry's employer was asking several governments for their assistance in locating him, and the D.C. police were appealing to the public for information.

The announcer gave statistics from a global journalism organization showing that murders and kidnappings of reporters and photographers had skyrocketed in recent years, though for the most part those occurred in countries considered less stable than this one.

Finally, a commentator noted that it was possible the young man had run off and committed suicide, or, more thrillingly, perhaps he was not a journalist but an undercover operative for another country meddling with U.S. affairs; the supposedly sacrosanct boundaries between intelligence and the media had long ago been violated. Had the "journalist" been removed by U.S. counterintelligence officers, or had his native country abruptly called him home? Then there was music and a segue into a story about a shooting at a D.C. elementary school, and I'd spotted the hag leaving the Mayflower.

(The death of Mr. McAlester at the convention center received only a short paragraph in the following day's *Post*—"Former Brit Spy Chief Collapses, Dies in D.C."—and was blamed on a weak heart.)

The radio report is a well-timed reminder that what I'm doing matters, that the integrity of history has thus far been preserved. Still, there are so many ways for me to blow this. I'm overtired and bored, and last night, when Will and I were heading back to our terrible motel after keeping watch for a few hours, I stopped and bought a bottle of vodka from one of the many liquor stores. I lost track of how much I drank—Wills criticized me for drinking on the job, but then he asked for some—and my head is pounding today. I just want this job over with, want the hags to stop their ceaseless parade into the past.

I tail the hag for twenty minutes, then he stops at a street corner. I stop at an earlier one, a block away from him. I lift my umbrella enough to get a look at the sidewalk, the pedestrians coming and going, and I see someone I recognize. Tasha, walking into a restaurant. She's a block ahead but the entrance to the restaurant is well lit, and I see her shaking her braids out as she retracts her umbrella; she enters and sits at a table. The hag is still standing at his intersection.

A few minutes later, a thin black man with strange hair bicycles his way down the street, managing to avert death three times in the one block that I see him. He looks up to check the street, as if he suspects he is being followed, and I recognize him from my intel: T.J. Trenton, a key player in the final Event I'm supposed to protect, though that's not for a few more days.

This is one of the discrepancies between my intel and Wills's: The Department told him that Tasha plays a role in what will happen to T.J., but there was nothing about her in the narrative they provided me. Why not? Did I just *happen* to stumble onto a person who turns out to be important? Did something that I myself did alter her path and put her life at risk?

T.J. locks his bike to a streetlight pole, shakes water from his poncho, and enters the building. I can barely see into the restaurant from here, but I see him greet Tasha and sit at her table.

I stand there in the rain, my shoes and the bottom of my pants soaked as I try to determine the best ways to eliminate the hag before he makes a move. Wondering if whatever I do will only create more problems—for myself, and for Tasha, and for everyone else.

I wasn't the one who had to interrogate Cemby's father, fortunately. But I listened to the playback afterward. It was bad.

He gave up a little of the Revisions plot, but he held most of it back. He was very prepared, seemed to have known this moment would come.

They're always caught. So why do any of them pick a fight in the first place? That's what I've never understood. We are so, so good at what we do. Even if someone feels he has a legitimate grievance against the Government, how can he be so deranged as to act on it, knowing what he is up against? That kind of fatalism is a mystery to me.

Joseph sounded like a different person in the Dark Room. Everyone is a different person when going through that. Or maybe he finally had the false layers of himself stripped away and was showing who he truly was for the first time. Maybe everything else was falseness, the father-in-law I thought I had. He'd seemed a kind man, loyal, loving to his daughter and granddaughter. Quiet, a bit of a recluse—the consummate Archivist type, I'd always assumed. But maybe he'd been that way only around me. Because he didn't trust me, because he was already walking his fated path when I first met him. He had counseled Cemby against marrying me so quickly. He'd been smart about it, dropping subtle hints, offering only minor pressure, knowing that an outright objection would have had the opposite of his intended effect. Back then, when she told me about his concern, I wrote it off as typical of a protective father, or maybe he was uncomfortable about my job. Now it seemed more the latter, in a worse way than I'd imagined.

Still, it hurt to listen to the interrogation. I couldn't stop thinking of Cemby, of the things she'd told me about her father. He'd walked her to school when she was a kid, taught her to play the guitar, had helped her through the death of her mother years ago. All that dreamy and placid and difficult family nonsense I'd never had. He was a great granddad too—always sprawled on the floor playing with Laurynn when she was a baby, and as she grew older he called her once a week to chat. How was I going to explain this to my daughter?

In the Dark Room, he used my name a few times. First in anger, as if blaming me for this. Later in desperation, as if I were on the other side of the door and could have intervened. At one point I was worried he would point a finger at me to distract the investigation, a final *fuck you* to the son-in-law he'd never trusted. But he didn't. He protected his daughter and her family until the end.

After his interrogation, I was brought into a room for the first in a series of long conversations with counterintelligence and teams of analysts I'd never met. *We understand you've given many years to Security,* they all said. *We just need to be sure of a few things. You'd do the same in our place.* I told them I understood, no hard feelings. *Ask whatever you need to ask. Look through whatever files you care to.*

I was in the building for three days and didn't sleep except during a few brief breaks. I knew this was how they wanted it. When it was over, when I had passed their tests and was allowed to return to my desk, I was surprised to see there were no messages for me.

"We deleted them," Myers told me. Wearing a different suit than the last time I'd seen him, days ago.

"How many times did she call?"

"Enough. She even tried to come into the building and look for you." He sighed. "You should probably sleep here before you go home. Clear your head a little."

That wasn't an official order, so I didn't obey. I wish that I had.

Tasha and T.J. either are very quick eaters or are meeting only to talk, because after fifteen minutes, they leave. He unlocks his bike and heads off in one direction while Tasha walks in another. To my surprise, the hag follows Tasha instead of T.J. I follow the hag.

Her bright red umbrella is like a beacon we're homing in on, the hag about half a block behind her, me maintaining a similar space from him. After three blocks, Tasha walks into an alcove of a building, shakes out her umbrella, and takes an escalator down to the Metro.

My Customs lessons fortunately covered public transportation; the Department doesn't want me riding crowded Metro trains, but they know emergencies may require it. I buy a ticket downstairs, hurrying to keep pace—Tasha already had one, and so, to my surprise, did the hag. I realize with shame that he's more prepared than I am. Wills is right that I'm slipping.

After sliding my card into the machine, I spot the hag and ride another escalator down a level. I don't see Tasha and have to be careful I don't look around too obviously. There she is—a good thirty feet beyond the hag. He's going to board a different car than hers, one back, and view her through the window. It's as if he's done this before.

The platform is crowded, meaning that countless people see me. I tell myself this isn't a problem—in such a vast crowd, I might as well be invisible.

Lights at my feet blink, and the train approaches with a long sigh. People push forward as the doors open. The hag is one of the first in; I'm one of the last.

The train is astonishingly humid, rain from all the passengers' shoulders and feet and umbrellas evaporating into a heavy torpor. Elbows and forearms intertwine as people reach for the slick metal bars above. Beside me a young black man in a black 76ers cap (even their sports teams celebrate history) holds a sleeping infant with his free hand. By the doors a white-clad colonel checks out the reflection of his epaulets in the window. Someone is laughing; someone else's child whines faintly. A voice advises us not to leave any items unattended on the train and to alert the station chief if we see anything suspicious. The hag is standing sideways at the very back of the car so he can check the small rear window—I see him do it at least twice—and keep track of Tasha.

With each stop, the crowd thins; after three stops, the hag and I have both found empty seats. We're leaving downtown's offices and cultural sites and entering Capitol Hill.

Most of the advertisements on the train aren't for products or services the way they are in my time; they're political in nature. Apparently everyone in this city is deeply invested in the bureaucracy of the state. One ad exhorts them to oppose the repeal of the Wildlife Protection Act, one encourages them to support their teachers' unions, and another celebrates Toyota's long track record of providing jobs at its U.S. factories.

Another ad warns me to BE PREPARED, recommends that I heighten my vigilance around people wearing "unusually baggy jackets." It occurs to me that most of the young black people on the train are wearing exactly such jackets. Everyone here is afraid of something.

* * *

When I finally made it back to my apartment after being interrogated by counterintelligence, I had not seen my wife and daughter in three days.

Our apartment was a mess. Plates were piled in the sink, jackets lay on the floor. Some food had burned, but hours or even days ago, just a faint note of its despair lingering. Cemby called my name and ran from the bedroom.

She hugged me. It was the last thing I had expected. I felt a tightness in my throat.

"Are you all right?" she asked. "I've been *terrified*. Is Dad with you?"

She looked like she'd slept as little as I had. Her hair was frizzy and uncombed, her eyes red and puffy. She'd been staring into the face of something she couldn't understand. I was the one who had to explain it to her.

I asked her where Laurynn was. In school, she said—she'd be home soon.

"What happened?" I asked. "How long ago were they here?"

"Who?"

"No one from Security came?"

"*No one* from *anywhere* came. I've been here for days with no word from you, no explanation from anyone about—"

"No one's questioned you?"

"Stop asking *me* questions, and tell me what's going on!"

My head was pounding. I kept hearing the voices of the counterintelligence officers, all seven or eight of them—they'd gone at me in shifts, taking breaks and sleeping and coming back refreshed while I festered in that tiny room. *Tell us again about the day you met your wife. How did she strike you then? How long did you date before you proposed? What was her father like? What sorts of questions did he ask you about your job?* Their suspicions became my own, an osmosis of fear pulling at me.

"Where's Dad?"

She had received a call from her father's assistant, then calls from some of his friends. She tried to reach me but couldn't. She assumed that he had been taken in and so had I, and that soon they'd be coming for her. She thought I was here now because Security had finally realized it was all a misunderstanding, and her father would be right behind me.

"Cemby, if you know what Joseph's been doing, you need to tell me now."

"What are you talking about?"

"He's already made . . . certain confessions. This will be much easier on us if you can tell me whatever you know about it."

She was shaking her head.

"Even if he never told you, you must have *noticed* something, some stray comment, maybe new friends he wouldn't introduce you to?"

"What's happening?"

I held up a hand. "Look, this could have been a lot worse. We just need—"

"Worse? *Where is he?* Take me to see him *now*."

"I don't know where he is! Do you understand how serious this is? He's admitted to being a part of a conspiracy to . . . circulate historical information, anti-Government propaganda. He and a handful of other Archivists, and people in the scientific sector. He's had contacts with rebel groups in the Outer Regions."

Her whole body was shaking, and there were tears in her eyes. "*What* rebel groups, Zed? The ones your bosses make up to keep everyone in line?"

"*Don't* say that." Recently, there'd been reports that rebel groups had established a base in the previously uninhabitable Outer Regions, an area where the Government's reach did not yet extend. I'd heard a few people whisper that those reports were untrue, political fabrications; such accusations were treasonous. Weeks ago, Cemby had implied that she agreed with the doubters, and I'd snapped at her.

Of course, the interrogators asked me if she'd ever said anything like this. They would have found out anyway.

"You need to be very careful about what you say." I tried to suppress my emotions. If our apartment hadn't been bugged before, it certainly was by then.

She started to laugh, but it wasn't a laugh. It scared me to hear it. "What did they do to you in there?"

The analysts kept asking their questions in my mind. *Tell us more about this friend of your wife, the one she meets for lunch every other Tuesday. And that friend, the one who made those comments you didn't approve of last winter—you filed the report but never followed up. Why was that? Your wife's seemed depressed lately, hasn't she? What do you think is troubling her? Does she confide in you the way she did when she was younger?*

"I know this is hard," I told her. "We need to rest, we need to calm down and pick ourselves up. Because of your father, people will be watching us for a while. People will feel uncomfortable around us. I'll probably be put on temporary leave. We need to be calm and smart, and not do anything—"

"They can't do this. Someone in this family still has some decency." She started putting on her jacket. "I'm going to wherever they have him and I'll sleep on the damned sidewalk if I have to."

In your wife's vid-diary, what do you think she meant when she said, "Sometimes I wonder if we're all being pushed to buy this delusion that used to make us happy but doesn't anymore"?

I grabbed Cemby's arm and told her she couldn't go back to my office, she would only make it worse. "You need to tell me everything you know about this," I said. "Immediately."

"So now *you're* questioning me?"

"Better me than them! If we can get everything into the open, there's a chance—"

She slapped me with her free hand. Instinctively I squeezed the forearm I was holding. Finally I released her. She backed up and stared at me, rubbing her arm. Her cheeks were wet, her eyes shimmering with hatred.

I told her we needed to calm down and clean up, act normally. Laurynn would be home soon.

"Is this normal for you?" she asked in a whisper. "Is this what you do?"

I tried to explain. There were layers to this. Things were going to be difficult but we'd make it through. She walked toward the door.

"I told you not to—"

"I'm going to pick up Laurynn!"

I told her she didn't seem in any condition to drive, but she only laughed. I told her to please watch what she said while she was out. She suggested I follow her and record all her statements for my superiors. I let her go.

I pull the bill of my Nationals hat lower and slump my head as if I'm just another dark-skinned man falling asleep on the Metro as the car empties out. I don't think the hag has noticed me yet, and from here I have an idea what he'll do. Tasha's house is close to the next stop, Potomac Avenue, so I play dead as the train slows toward the station.

The window beside me offers just enough reflection of the rest of the car for me to see that the hag is standing at the doors now, waiting for them to open. At the *bing,* I look up and he steps through. Then I rush out the back door and step onto the platform behind him, hoping he won't turn around. He doesn't, and I stand behind a thick pole that displays a map of the subway lines as he follows Tasha up the escalator.

I tap my line and call Wills.

Are you sure the guy you sent me after is a hag? I ask him.

Of course I'm sure. I'm the one with a functioning GeneScan, remember?

He's not acting like a hag. He's just following her. Watched her have a meeting with Trenton and then go home. It's not like them to do recon like this. They come and they attack their Event, that's it.

I slide my card through the slot, the mechanical doors let me through, and up ahead I see Tasha opening her red umbrella at the top of the next escalator. Rain cascades through the night; the metal teeth of the escalator shine as they're pulled along on their endless circuit.

Maybe he knows you're tailing him, Wills says.

I'm better than that, thanks. Something's wrong. Something is definitely wrong.

Then stay with her. Keep watch at her place. You'd like to do that anyway, wouldn't you?

We can't hear each other's voices—it doesn't work that way, it's more electronic, ones and zeros processing through our brains—but I can almost feel him smiling at me.

Something isn't adding up. The hags tried to prevent the disappearance (and likely murder) of the reporter Karthik Chaudhry. They tried to prevent the murder of former spymaster Randolph McAlester. They will soon try to prevent the murder of T.J. Trenton and several of his associates—an Event that, unfortunately, will also involve Tasha. But why are they following her *now?*

I ask Wills what he's doing.

Hags just tried to stop the Korean diplomat from meeting with contacts from Zaire and Sierra Leone. I didn't let them.

I'm glad one of us is doing something right.

Relax. See what your guy is up to, and, if you get a chance, take him out.

The escalator deposits me on the sidewalk and I let my feet take it from there, unwilling and unable to stop the momentum.

The night after my argument with Cemby was when I received the visit from my former boss at Security and some of my ex-colleagues. I thought they'd come with news of Joseph or some update on my own status. Instead, they told me about Cemby's accident.

We had nothing to do with it, Myers told me when I called him. *She'd been driving too fast and made a wrong turn into traffic, the other driver said. It's being looked into.* Whatever else he told me vanished, just like Cemby and little Laurynn, who are now relegated forever to the realm of my memory. The sparks that flare and linger but will one day fade completely despite my attempts to keep them vibrant and alive.

* * *

This part of Capitol Hill is quiet at night, though there are enough pedestrians returning to their homes from work that the hag and I can follow our respective marks without attracting attention. The rain has stopped; some people have lowered their umbrellas, but others still hold them as if they don't quite trust the night. They also carry handbags or groceries, push strollers, or cradle phones. Some of them manage to do all these things at once. Tasha walks alone, red umbrella at her side, her ears phoneless, the noise of the world not reaching her, at least not at the moment.

She's a block from her house when the hag stops at a street corner and takes out a cell. I back into an alley and focus on his lips while my internal microphone does the rest.

"Affirmative. She met with him and went straight home. Nothing doing tonight."

I can't hear the voice on his line.

"Got it. I'll pick up tomorrow." Then he puts the phone in his pocket and heads back to the Metro.

The so-called Revisions project, which we'd discovered thanks to my initial pursuit of Dalton and that began to come to light with the interrogation of my father-in-law, produced a trove of information on what the rebels were plotting. No one had seen anything like this, not since the Government had been established. There'd been warnings to the public to be vigilant against agitators, but no one on the inside had thought such well-orchestrated resistance was possible.

The investigation merged with an internal one that the Scientific Explorations Agency had been conducting; apparently, the rebels had stolen the technology for time travel, which the Government had recently discovered and barely understood (and had, of course, kept secret from the public). Only preliminary tests had been run. The Intelligence Department was informed of this a few weeks after my family's accident. I was still in shock; everything seemed equally stunning and impossible. My too-large bed; my daughter's dusty bureau; the possibility of time travel; the sickness in my stomach; the fact that someone could change history itself; the awful silence when I woke in the middle of the night.

The clandestine Department of Historical Integrity was formed to institute new safeguards. Only the finest, most trustworthy officers were recruited to join the team of Protectors. No one was more highly regarded than myself, they told me. I had assumed the Joseph situation would blacklist me, shunting me to dead-end assignments in windowless rooms. But the very opposite occurred: my superiors, colleagues, and countless bureaucrats I'd never seen before shook my hand and impressed upon me the gravity of the situation and how much they needed men like me. I was someone who had sacrificed all he had for our society. A lesser man might have stepped in and interfered with the investigation of Joseph, might have tried to pull some strings. I, however, had allowed parts of myself to die so that our Perfect Present could continue, exemplifying all that was good about what we did.

I was a hero.

Tailing the hag back into the city is trickier. At this hour, few people are boarding inbound trains. I follow him to the Potomac Avenue station at double the previous distance. I take an escalator down to the platform opposite his, and I linger behind what used to be a payphone stall but no longer is. Everyone has a cell phone now; the kiosk has a large hole in the center where the phone was once affixed, and old wires capped with plastic dangle from it. A bumper sticker taped beneath the hole tells me to FREE D.C. FROM WASHINGTON, whatever that means.

A Blue Line train tiredly rolls in. I board after the hag and sit in the same row as him, across the aisle. There are only five other people on this car, and three of them appear to be sleeping. I check for security cameras, but there are none. We reach the stop for Eastern Market and two more people get on, a young white couple, holding hands. They sit a few rows in front of us.

I get up, cross the aisle, and sit directly behind the hag.

"You're good at following people," I say just loudly enough for him to hear over the voice of the driver, who's naming the next stop.

"Excuse me?" He turns his head.

"Tasha Wilson. Unless your intel is wrong, nothing happens to her for a few days. If you were smart, you'd come out only when you need to."

He scowls at me. "Do I know you?"

"No one knows me."

He smiles at that. "Well, you're butting into something that doesn't concern you."

I remove the gun from my jacket's inside pocket and, holding it low, angle it so he can view it from the direction you never want to see a gun.

"Whoa," he says, eyes wide. "You have the wrong idea."

"Then give me the right one." I check the faces of the other people on the train. No one's watching us, and we're talking too quietly to be overheard.

"I'm just following her. It's a simple job, man. Come on, put that away. They're not paying me nearly enough for—"

"Who's paying you?"

"I don't even know. It's all thirdhand. I was told this was simple, noncontact. Whoever you are, I don't need to know. Really."

It's customary for cornered hags to pretend that they're just contemps. But I find myself believing this one—he's taking risks by putting himself out in ways hags usually don't.

If he isn't a hag, then why did Wills send me to follow him? I can think of some answers to that, and they're not reassuring.

I ask him his name, and he says Larry Ansler. I look him up in my databases and there he is: age, forty-five; residence, Alexandria; family, none; occupation, private investigator; past occupation, Metropolitan Police Department.

"You don't know who hired you to follow her?"

"No." He tells me he has a buddy who came to him as a middleman and said there was "a company" that needed this woman followed. He gives me the buddy's name, but that's all I get.

"All right, Larry. Maybe I do have the wrong idea. I'm sure your following Ms. Wilson around is perfectly harmless. You can go back to your job tomorrow and forget all about this conversation."

"You got it, pal."

I slip the gun back into my pocket as the train reaches L'Enfant Plaza, an intersection of three subway lines. It's a convenient place to escape, so I hurry off the train, taking a quick glance back to make sure he isn't following.

Some game must have ended downtown; people passing me to board the train all wear matching jerseys and jackets and hats and look dazed and happy, drunk on other people's success.

18.

At eleven o'clock on garbage night, Leo left his apartment to see if Sari had tossed anything interesting.

He walked north on Mount Pleasant Street, past the commercial district, and the houses soon became grander, looking down on the cluttered streets from the wizened visages of their stone steps and Southern porches. He turned west, and the canopy of trees thickened as he approached Rock Creek Park. Hyun Ki Shim's house was on a quiet side street from which the hustle of 16th and the flow of traffic on the Rock Creek Parkway seemed farther away than they actually were.

Leo had driven through the neighborhood often to get an idea of when Hyun Ki and Sang Hee retired for the night. Sari had told him that their bedroom was in the front of the house, second floor, and he'd noticed the lights were usually out by ten thirty. There was no traffic here; the streets were so quiet Leo could hear what sounded like an owl or maybe some exotic wildlife from the nearby National Zoo.

Leo had tailed Hyun Ki as the diplomat went to and from work, even staking out the embassy for a few hours here and there, though doing so was tricky, as he didn't want to run the risk of being observed himself. He'd seen nothing odd, but then again, any savvy spy would have ways of meeting with people or doing unsavory things without being noticed. And Leo was on his own; if he saw Hyun Ki meet a man for lunch, Leo would have no way of knowing who the man was, and there was no institutional knowledge to fall back on.

Sang Hee rarely left the house. The two of them were, thus far, a completely vanilla diplomatic couple, if a bit cruel with their domestic help.

Leo walked slowly and naturally, passing stinky garbage barrels and recycle bins crowded with their owners' sad hopes for a better future. He was wearing an old jean jacket he usually found too unstylish, and a blue Nats cap; he'd forgone his glasses in favor of contacts, and he had eschewed his preferred shoes in favor of quieter sneakers. He tried to step around the acorn caps and dry leaves scattered on the sidewalk.

The lights in the houses of the diplomat's immediate neighbors were off, but across the street a few were on. Crouching in front of their trash barrel, which blocked him from the house's view, he fidgeted with his laces as if he were retying one of his sneakers. Then he carefully reached into the recycle bin. This was hardly the way the Agency had taught him to do dead drops, but given Sari's restricted movements, it was the best he could come up with.

He had told her to put whatever items she had for him in the side of the recycle bin closest to the street, to save him the trouble and the noise of rummaging through the whole thing. He found it on his first try, in an empty can of baby formula: a flash drive. He was impressed.

He stood up and continued the way he'd been going, taking a meandering route home. Once there, he immediately uploaded the files onto his computer, erased the drive, and walked back to the Shims'. Decorative white stones were laid at the edge of their property; he lifted the second stone from the right and slid the drive beneath it. He nestled the drive into the dirt so the rock wouldn't crush it.

The data on the drive had all been in Korean, of course, which Leo didn't know as well now as he had in his grad-school days. He wasted a couple hours scanning different files before conceding that he needed a translator. The next morning he handed it to Bale, who said he'd get some people to work on it.

Late the next night, another quick call from Sari: grocery run, tomorrow. Evening this time, as Sari was needed around the house during the afternoon. He gave her new instructions, annoyed by the call. Maybe he hadn't been clear enough; that last grocery run was supposed to be their last. Once you established the relationship, you weren't supposed to meet with your spies any more than necessary.

Of course, he *wanted* to see her. For not entirely professional reasons. Hell, for totally unprofessional reasons. But she sounded nervous on the phone, so he told himself the meeting would help calm her down; he could reassure her that she was doing a great job.

Bale's translators were quick; the following day, Leo was told by his boss that the drive had contained "some useful information," but, though the translators hadn't quite finished everything yet, most of the data seemed to be little more than "diplomatic dick-fondling," as Bale described it—nothing important enough to be important. Try again, he said. And this time get Sang Hee's computer, not her husband's.

At nine thirty that night he met Sari at a small parking lot beside empty fields in the northern finger of Rock Creek Park. The city's light pollution made the sky above the spindly branches glow movie-screen gray.

"Thank you for getting that flash drive," Leo told her after she got in his grocery-laden car. He noticed she was wearing only sweats and had no jacket or gloves and that she was holding her hands together tightly. He turned the heat on full blast for her sake, and unbuttoned his jacket. "But we're particularly interested in what's on Sang Hee's computer."

"I'm sorry—I assumed his information was more important."

Leo had told her otherwise, hadn't he? "We're very interested in Sang Hee. What you did was helpful, but I want to focus on her."

"She hurt her ankle again. She'll be on crutches for a while longer, otherwise I wouldn't get out like this."

"Good. You're doing an excellent job."

"I can't do this much longer. She suspects something."

"Why do you say that?" He tried to sound calm and natural. "Has she said something?"

"I don't know. She watches me, all the time."

"You said she did that before."

"I'm afraid something is...going to happen."

"What do you mean?"

Sari started rambling. She was scared and seemed convinced that Sang Hee could read her mind or something. She told him about some story Sang Hee had spun, about Sang Hee's being a prisoner in a North Korean work camp, and how she'd murdered her family. That's probably when the woman became possessed by demons, Sari explained. Leo would pass that on to Bale, not that it made sense.

"She's a mean lady, you're right." He had to redirect her. "What you're doing is the best way of getting away from her permanently. You need to remember that."

She stared out the windshield. Looking over her shoulder he saw headlights as another car made its way down the curving narrow road. He watched it, then reached forward to adjust his rearview mirror so he could see the car drive away. No one should be on this dead-end road, as the park grounds were closed. Hopefully the driver was just lost in the labyrinth of Rock Creek Park. Or maybe some congressman was looking for a good place to dispose of an intern's body. The car was getting stuffy but Sari still looked cold.

"We should get the groceries out of your car," Sari said.

"If you focus on the good that will come from this, it will make it easier."

"The good. I don't know what that means anymore."

He waited. "Why did you leave Jakarta? Why don't you want to go back there?"

She seemed prepared to dodge the question again. He was being too direct with her, overlooking the cultural differences, the power imbalance. He would scare her away if he didn't change tack.

To his surprise, she looked up at him. "They burned my mother alive."

"Who did?"

"All of them. All of them." Some leaves landed silently on the windshield. "I don't even like to think of myself as Indonesian or Javanese anymore. I'd rather be something else. But I don't know what. Everything else seems just as bad."

"What happened?"

"When Suharto fell, all the riots. The people in the city hated the Chinese, said they were leeches, they ran all the businesses and loaned all the money and we Javanese were their slaves. So they rampaged through town, attacked Chinese, burned their shops and homes. My family worked at a store owned by a Chinese couple. People chased me and my sisters, but we got away. My mother stayed in the store, and they burned it to the ground."

"I'm very sorry."

"We looked for her for days. My sisters didn't want to admit she'd been killed, thought maybe she was hiding somewhere in the city. But I knew she was gone—she was in my dreams that first night, and she hasn't left them. After a couple of weeks the police got around to pulling all the bodies out of the rubble."

He searched for something to say, in any language.

"My eldest sister went to Korea first, then the middle one. First I lived with some friends of my mother's, but eventually they told me I had to leave, they couldn't afford to keep me. I nearly starved. There were rumors some people in the city refused to hire anyone who'd worked for Chinese, as punishment. As soon as I got my chance to go, I took it."

"It was a...a bad time. There are other places, safer ones, where you could start over."

"Safer places?" She looked insulted. "That was my home. I grew up there. It felt safe to me, until one day it wasn't. That's the funny thing. Everyone knew he was a horrible tyrant—you weren't supposed to talk about it, but people would say things when they felt they could trust you. But then when the horrible tyrant was finally stepping down, look what we did to each other. Maybe all those students and protesters were wrong. Maybe it was good to live under a dictator."

It was so hot, he wanted to turn down the heat but he saw that she was still holding her hands in front of the vents.

"Well, it seems to me you're living under one now, in that little house of theirs. And you don't like it very much."

"I'm learning that everywhere is just as bad as everywhere else. Sang Hee hates me just because I'm not Korean. In North Korea they hated her just because her husband said something good about South Korea, or something. And here in America they'll hate me because I'm not American."

"We're not like that. Some people are, maybe, but most people—"

"Do you believe that? Or are you just trying to cheer me up?" She'd never been this direct before.

"I do believe that. I do believe that people can improve. That's what my country's all about, finding a better way, a noble experiment." Jesus, he couldn't believe he was giving her a civics lecture. But what she'd said made him feel defensive about his country, about his job. "There are bad people in the world, yes, I'm not naive. But when you finish this job for me, when my friends say they have everything they need and they can pay you back, you'll see that life doesn't have to be as hard as it's been for you."

She watched him for so long he felt uncomfortable.

"I don't know if you really believe that, and you are naive," she said, "or if you're just trying to trick me into doing you more favors."

"I'm not trying to trick you."

"Then why did you tell me you work for a bank?"

She said it so naturally, in the same blank tone she'd been using, that it took him a second. "I used to work for a bank, in Jakarta, like I said, but—"

"And now you read the computers of Korean diplomats and have well-connected friends who can help foreigners with no passports."

He waited, reassessing her, then said, "If you don't want to do this anymore, I won't force you. I can just walk away."

"Then I'd have no one to speak Bahasa with."

He could feel sweat rolling down the small of his back, it was so goddamned hot in there. The windows were starting to fog, and he feared some park cop might come knocking on their windshield, hoping to get a glimpse of a half-naked Bethesda cheerleader.

"I'm sorry we can't talk more," he said. "I wish there were another way to do this. It would be great if I could take you out and show you the city. Maybe when this is finished..."

She surprised him with a smile. He hadn't seen her do that very often. "A date? A date with an American?"

Oh, Jesus Christ, was he *blushing?* He hated himself. He reached for the heat, turned it down a bit, as if this action might make her think the redness on his cheeks were something else. He needed to remember that she was not as meek as she sometimes seemed.

"Is that so hard to believe?" he asked.

"Not so hard." She was still smiling, but he found her face inscrutable—yet more evidence that this was not the best line of work for him. There were too many mysteries he couldn't begin to puzzle out. "What would we do? On our big date?"

"Well, that depends," he said. "What kind of food do you like?"

"Anything but Korean."

"There's a great Thai restaurant not far from my house, near Dupont Circle." He allowed himself to wander down this fantasy, inviting her along. "We'd have dinner there, then see a movie at my favorite theater, and—"

"I wouldn't understand a word." She laughed.

"I'd translate."

"I don't think the other people would appreciate that."

"Then I'd rent out the entire theater just for us."

"This sounds like a very big date." She raised her eyebrows, impressed. "But I don't think I'd believe your translation. I'd wonder if you were just telling me the best parts and making up the rest."

He didn't know what to do with that. "And then we'd take a taxi to the Washington Monument and ride the elevator to the top and see the city sparkling below us." He hoped that wasn't too phallic a reference.

"And I would see all the happy Americans, holding hands." She rolled her eyes. "It sounds very nice, like the fairy tales I tell their daughter every night."

Maybe she was right; his translation wasn't all that believable.

"I want to help you," he said, trying to appear earnest. Then he reached out and took one of her hands in his. It was cold, the fingers narrow and hard. He felt her tense up and worried he'd made a mistake again. "Please stay with me a little longer." He gave her hand a gentle squeeze before releasing it.

"Okay. But we're running out of time. Can we move the groceries now?"

After placing the last of the bags inside her SUV, they stood beside each other like a couple at the end of a date. And because he was still living in that little fantasy he had sketched for her, and because they both wanted to believe his translation, he stood closer to her than he otherwise might have. She looked up at him, and it seemed she was leaning toward him, or maybe he was only hoping she was—he wasn't sure. When he leaned down to kiss her, she did not laugh at him or recoil. Perhaps his translation wasn't as bad as he'd feared.

Then he stepped back, and she smiled at him before getting in the SUV. Neither of them said good-bye.

He should have gone straight home.

Instead he drove slowly through the park, finally emerging near Chevy Chase, far from not only her house but also his own, to foil any potential watchers. The kiss, and the way she'd looked at him, and their strange, topic-spanning conversation had him too amped up. This was a ridiculous operation—it wasn't even an operation, strictly speaking, just a blind trolling for anything of interest. He never should have told Bale about her. He should have just driven her to the Indonesian embassy, told her what to say. She would have had to go back to her homeland, which she didn't seem to want, but surely that would have been better than where she was now. He had told her he'd help her even though he probably couldn't. The more he thought about her, the worse he felt about the deception, and the more he wanted to deliver on his promise.

At a red light, he looked at his empty passenger seat. The vinyl still bore the slight imprint of her thighs. He let his finger glide there. He breathed in and thought he could smell her.

There was no practical reason for him to drive back to the diplomat's neighborhood. It was counterproductive to risk being seen. Yet after driving into Maryland and coasting through Bethesda, watching the couples strolling to this Lebanese restaurant or that sports bar, and then winding his way back into the city, he pulled into an empty spot a block away from the Shims'. His windshield was just beneath the low bough of an elm tree, and he could barely see the dark windows of the house. He turned off the engine.

He found himself yearning for another a glance, hoping she'd raise the window shades or maybe step outside. I'm a stalker, he realized. That's all he'd ever been, really, and at least now he was being honest. He was a low-level errand runner, a pawn of secret machinations he would never fully understand. He knew this, and he hated it. He should be doing something else with his life. This was not the way to make a difference.

The passenger-side door opened. He'd been lost in thought and was jarred by the sound and by the internal car light and by the way the vehicle sagged with the added weight of this unexpected stranger. He saw a pair of knees entering his car, and then a torso, and then a gun.

"Keep your hands on the wheel," the man said. "Look straight ahead. Now."

Leo obeyed. The man closed the passenger door and the light slowly faded. Leo could peripherally see the man holding the gun in his lap, aimed at Leo's midsection. It was a black automatic. He had seen the man for only a second—somewhat dark-skinned, ethnically ambiguous; short hair; dark jacket, maybe leather; and black slacks. He seemed big, but maybe that was just the gun.

"You can take the car and my money—"

251

"Who are you," the man asked, "and why are you tailing Mr. Shim?" The man opened Leo's glove box, passed his hand through the stack of oil-change receipts and AAA maps, then closed it. Leo's mouth went dry.

"I don't work for anyone. I'm just sitting here waiting on a friend, and—"

"Spare me the innocent contemp act. Who do you work for, and where are the rest of them?"

The man cocked the hammer of his gun. Then he started moving his hands, doing something Leo couldn't discern from the corner of his eye. Another dark object was in the man's hand. Leo could hear the sound of metal fitting atop metal.

"No one ever seems to walk down this block," the man said. "You would be amazed by the things I can do inside a car. If you don't give me answers, I'll start with your kneecaps."

Leo tried to swallow.

"That a wallet in your pants pocket?"

"Yes."

"Take it out very slowly, and place it on the seat between us. Keep facing forward." Leo complied, and the man flipped it open, removed the driver's license, and dropped the rest. "All right, *Leonard*. Tell me about yourself."

"Look, I don't know what I've stumbled into here, but—"

"You don't need to know. You only need to answer questions. Do you work with Wills?"

"Will who?"

"How long have you been back here?"

"Back where?"

"*Here, now.* How long have you been in this beat?"

Whatever jargon this guy was using, it was new to Leo. "Look, this isn't an operation. This is . . . my own thing."

The man seemed to consider this for a moment. "I'm asking for the last time: Who do you work for? Try to dodge that and you'll never walk normally again."

Leo breathed. Who was this guy? He talked like he was an insider but he was threatening to *shoot* him. "Targeted Executive Solutions," Leo said.

"And you have no actual client, you just took it upon yourself to tail a random diplomat?"

"I was...approached by someone with access. Someone I could run. I'm just...following up."

"Someone in the house, a maid?"

He nodded, hating himself.

"This has been going on how long?"

Leo lied, shaving the time in half. His hands were sweaty, his fingers so slick on the wheel he had to tighten his grip to guard against their slipping suddenly and causing the man to shoot him.

"You said *them*. Who are your targets?"

"It's, um, it's pretty vague."

"Clarify it for me."

"The diplomat's wife is a person of interest."

"But not the diplomat himself?"

"Thus far, no."

The intruder thought for a few seconds. "Tell me, Leonard Hastings: Do you believe in God?"

Leo had heard of people feeling cold shivers run down their spines, but he'd never before experienced it. "What?"

"I've been thinking about this a lot lately. In your opinion, how much of what we do is truly up to us? How much of it is predetermined, or at least dictated by larger forces we can't control? Have you ever wondered that?"

Leo's voice was a rasp as he said, "Existential thoughts are beyond my pay grade."

"As is so very much. But it's been puzzling me. All this activity, all this running around. Whatever intent we might have, not that someone like you seems to have much. But people in general. We try and we try, we work so very hard, we seek to control our own destinies. Isn't that hilarious? We control nothing. Well, one another, maybe.

We enslave one another, conquer one another—that's the closest any of us get to God. We use the word *God* to make ourselves feel better about how tiny and insignificant we are."

Leo was slick with sweat. All the oxygen had been sucked out of the car.

"Maybe you should think about these questions sometime," the man said. "Like when you're sitting in a car alone, watching people."

"Okay."

The man laughed and leaned back. "You really thought I was going to shoot you, didn't you?"

"I'm...having some trouble figuring out your motivations."

"Get used to being confused. I'm going to go now, Leonard. Do your best not to remember this conversation."

Leo kept staring straight ahead as the man kicked open the passenger door and started to slide out. "Can I have my license back?"

"Call your DMV."

With that the man left, leaving the door open, which again triggered the internal light. Leo looked at his mirror, but the glare obscured his view. He leaned over and pulled the door shut. The man was gone. Leo sat there, defeated, and gave his nerves a moment to settle before checking his wallet to make sure nothing was missing other than his license.

He started the engine and pulled onto the road, wondering if he was being watched even now. The intruder had moved with such effortless confidence that surely he hadn't acted alone. They might even be renting one of the houses on this block; they'd no doubt filmed Leo's recent recycling pickup. He decided not to drive home yet and instead found himself taking Prospect Street over Rock Creek Park and onto Connecticut, scouting for a place to pull over so he could get a drink, figure this out.

It didn't make sense.

If Leo had accidentally stumbled into the surveillance net of some other agency—CIA, NSA, DIA, FBI, Homeland, whoever—they wouldn't have been so brusque as to point a *gun* at him. Turf battles were one thing, but death threats were a bit much. Did the man work for a different country or some stateless group? Did he merely want Leo to *think* that he worked for the U.S.?

He hadn't been wearing gloves, had he? Leo wasn't sure. God, what a failure he was, not even to be certain of that most basic fact. It was his job to observe, but add the specter of bodily harm into the mix and his panicked eyes turned inward. Maybe Leo *did* deserve the Knoweverything assignment; maybe he was no better than a mole sent to kvetch with lefty dreamers. He couldn't handle the dark side. He replayed the scene in his head: he had told the man everything he'd wanted to know, had ruined his little operation in thirty seconds.

At least he could check for prints on his wallet and glove box, try to identify the stranger. He would sit in his apartment and recollect every step he'd taken to this point, try to figure out where he'd gone wrong.

His fingers weren't shaking anymore by the time he parked his car. He looked at the passenger seat. Sari's imprint had been obliterated by that of the mystery man.

Z.

I've never been so confused about a mission before. Maybe that bump on the head affected more than I thought; maybe those strange people who claimed to recognize me were warnings. Or maybe it's simply that I've never been in a beat for this long—I've let myself get comfortable here, let myself care too much about what happens to the contemps.

After questioning the man on the Metro—not a hag, just a contemp investigator tailing Tasha, although I'm not sure why—I switched lines and took a train up to Mount Pleasant, to case the diplomat's house. Which was where I found Leonard Hastings, another contemp playing shadow, another man who couldn't identify his client as he spied on key targets. It made me wonder if that was how life worked in this beat, if everyone spied on everyone else, if parked cars were full of cops and feds and dicks, if on every Metro ride you were subject to the gazes of paid informants.

I pore through my intel again. Scan it backward and forward, look for the pieces I might have missed, extrapolate what the Department itself might have missed or willfully left out.

Then I catch a cab so I can get back to the motel Wills and I have been using as our home base. After hearing the unappealing destination, the cabbie grudgingly takes me there.

Wills's light isn't on. I knock on his door loudly. I hear him stumble out of bed, then he opens the door. Like me, he sleeps in his clothes.

Before he can ask me what the trouble is, I walk in and tell him

256

there's been a development with Tasha. I pace the room, glancing at him quickly to gauge just how unsettled he is.

"I messed up," I tell him. "They got her."

"They got—who?"

"The hags took out Tasha Wilson," I lie. "I was watching her place, like you said, but without a GeneScan I couldn't tell that another hag had snuck in the back. I heard the shot, and I broke into her house as they were leaving."

"Oh." He's trying to think fast. "That will...definitely create some complications."

"Yes. But maybe we can fix them. I have one of the hags."

"What?"

"Tied up, in the trunk of his car. Here in the parking lot. I thought we could interrogate him together."

"Wow. Good. Has he...said anything yet?"

"Not yet. I stunned him; he's still out. Want to help me carry him in?"

"Yes, definitely."

"It'll be tricky to get him in without being seen," I say, watching Wills carefully. He's telling me plenty without saying a thing.

"I need to go to the bathroom first," he finally says. "Wait a minute."

I wait for much less than that. After he shuts the bathroom door, I lightly walk up to it, listen for a moment, take out my Stunner, and kick the door open. He's standing in front of the toilet, loading a gun. He looks up at me and extends an arm, but he isn't fast enough and I've already taken three steps toward him. I hit him with the Stunner, and his head snaps back from the shock. His fingers loosen around the gun barrel, and I take it before he can drop it—I don't want a round to go off accidentally. For a second his hand stays in the air with mine even as the rest of his heavy body falls to the floor.

When Wills wakes up, he's naked in the bathtub. I've bound his hands and feet, and the base of his head is leaning against the hard lip of the tub, the spigot scraping his temple. I've taped his mouth and he breathes loudly through his nose. I run some water on him, and his body tenses from the cold; he turns his head away to keep his nostrils clear. I shut off the water and sit on the toilet, gripping the Stunner, waiting for a moment so he'll understand.

"You played me very well," I say. "You weren't sent here by the Department. The Department would never send two Protectors to the same beat—I knew that, but I was so thrown to see you here that I figured there must be a reason. I overlooked the most obvious one."

I tear the tape from his mouth. He inhales deeply, then says, "What's wrong with you, Zed? *Think!* We're on the same—"

I hit him in the chest with the Stunner, set relatively weak. His head jolts back and snaps against the tub's wall behind him. Fortunately the tub's not porcelain, just plastic, otherwise the impact might have knocked him out.

"This will take a very long time if you don't start admitting things."

"Zed, I was sent here same as you. I've been—"

"You've been working for the hags, keeping your eye on me. The hag that I got at the convention center, he looked so shocked to see me. I wondered why. It's because you were supposed to be stalling me, tricking me into following random people around, telling me they were hags doing recon. You didn't do it well that first day. But ever since, you've been pointing me in the wrong direction while you *claimed* you were eliminating other hags. The only thing I'm still trying to figure out is why you didn't just kill me."

I stun him again.

After a few seconds, he says, between pants, "I know you're going through a hard time, Zed, but you've got to forget about—"

Another shock convinces him, finally, to stop denying it.

"You've had me staking out a hotel for nothing; you knew my GeneScan wasn't working, so you lied about what yours said. You must have gotten a real kick out of playing me like that. Now it's my turn to get some kicks."

"I haven't been the one playing you, Zed," he says after catching his breath. "The *Department's* been playing you—been playing both of us, this whole time."

"How did the hags get to you? Did they use your family?"

"I don't have one." His eyes are cold.

"What, then? They offered you something the Department didn't?"

"Yes: the truth."

"Just tell me where the other hags are, Wills, and maybe we can still part friends."

He doesn't answer.

"Okay, I'll give you an easier one: Admit that Tasha has nothing to do with the Great Conflagration. You just had me follow her to distract me."

He laughs. "You *wish* she weren't important—that's obvious. The job hurts a lot worse when you get to know the people that our bosses have already written off, doesn't it? History's losers. But maybe they're *all* important, Zed. Ever think of that? Maybe everything's important, everything matters. What if the Great Man theory is a myth, and everyone can be great, and there's no way for you to tell which person might one day make history?"

I stun him out of his philosophical reverie.

"Zed," he says, biting his lips so hard he draws blood, a line of it dripping down his chin, "*listen* to me. What you and I have done for the Department, it's all lies. We aren't preserving the integrity of history, we're *rewriting* history, remaking the world in the regime's image. There was no Great Conflagration, not originally. But they've sent so many of us back, and they've tinkered, they've eliminated the people who opposed them and eliminated the Events that went against their worldview. *All the conspiracy theories are true, Zed.* This is our opportunity to make it right, and—"

"You've lost it. The time travel, adjusting to the beats, avoiding contemps—it's hard, I know. You couldn't handle it, and they got to you at the right moment, spun your head around."

"No one ran me, Zed. No one recruited me. They tried to tell me the truth, plenty of times, when I was the one with the Stunner in my hands. But I followed orders, *preserved the integrity of history*. I kept lying to myself, just like you are. Still, all those dying words echoed in my head. They sounded *eerily true*, you know? When I was back home, I started digging around. I noticed the changes, changes that *we* had made. Entire peoples had disappeared, areas had completely vanished. Society not quite the way I remembered it. *That's* why they keep us sequestered on campus, Zed—they don't want to let us see the world that we've helped them remake. You saw how they reacted when we left campus that one night."

"That was Derringer trying to recruit us. I see that now."

"*Wrong*. Back on campus, I looked into the background of our superiors, the ones we've been serving so faithfully all these years, and—"

I hit him with the Stunner again, square in the chest. His teeth chatter for a few seconds afterward. I might need to stuff a cloth in his mouth soon.

"This is going to take a very long time," I say. "But time is the one thing we've always had a lot of, isn't it? Come on, no more of your hag stories. I want facts. I want the exact number of hags who are back here, and where they are right now. And where they're really coming from, so I can stop them as soon as they appear."

"There are millions, Zed. They're everywhere."

I laugh. "Great. Thanks."

"Everyone is a hag to the Government, don't you see? Not just the rebels who send themselves back, but everyone ever born, in any time. Anyone who dares to see the world in a different way than—"

I stun him again.

After recovering, he's back at it: "We believed we were working for our Perfect Society, Zed, but we weren't! We're just doing it to keep a bunch of bastards in power! They use us to turn their fictions into reality—I know you've thought this too. They told us we were part of the Disasters Division, right? Well, there *is* no other division, Zed—it's all disasters! All we do is ensure disasters for everyone else!"

He's getting too loud, so I fasten the gag on him and stun him again.

I exhale deeply, lean against the wall. Suddenly feel overcome. Hopefully he's in too much pain to notice. He's spinning stories, I tell myself; he's trying to confuse me. I won't get anything out of him; I should just kill him now. There was a time I would have done that, quickly and without overthinking. I hate that I can't do that anymore and hate how horrifically true all of his stories sound so far.

I tear off his gag.

"Zed. Let me ask you something." He's speaking through gritted teeth, his voice a thin whisper hammered flat. "If everything is so perfect in our time, then why are you in so much pain?"

"*I'm* the one in pain?"

"You're a walking sympathy card."

"What happened to my family . . . has nothing to do with our job."

"Really? Why is it that—"

"It was an accident! Some idiot spun out of control on the thruway, and suddenly my life is different. That has *nothing* to do with—"

"But it does." A line of bloody drool hangs from his chin. "What's the point in going to such trouble to create, to protect, this supposedly *perfect* order if it *isn't* perfect, if it *can't be* perfect? Because we ourselves are so damned imperfect. Even if our pasts are erased, even if every group forgets what horrible things it did to every other group, even if all those hatreds and vendettas and grudges are wiped clean, we'll still make messes. We'll still have accidents. We'll still insult each other and irritate each other and sleep with the wrong person and grow to hate each other. We'll still want what the other one has."

"You're talking about two different things."

"Fine, keep living in their dream world. Be their slave a little longer." Then he laughs—an impressive feat at this point—and there's a condescending tone to it. "So, did they make you the promise? And you believed them?"

"What promise?"

"They made me the promise too. That after I fulfilled my quota, after I performed enough missions and the trouble with the hags was over, they'd send me back to her." His eyelids are drooping from fatigue, but his eyes shine. "And I believed them too."

"Why don't you just——"

"Has it occurred to you how odd it is that all of the Protectors are widowers or have lost children? Or maybe you didn't realize that, because they did their best to prevent us from getting to know each other. That's one of the ways they recruited us, Zed. Sad men who'd do anything to have their pasts back. They knew we wouldn't care about the irony. None of that political nonsense matters when it's your own family."

I feel heat behind my eyes, spreading down my limbs.

"They're not going to save your wife and daughter, Zed! If that's why you're doing all of this, if you're still holding out hope that after you finish your missions they'll send you back to save them and live happily ever after, then you're——"

I pull the trigger of the gun I hadn't even realized I'd picked up and blast the rest of his sentence through the back of his skull.

Trying to breathe, I place the gun on the lip of the bathtub.

He only said that to force me to shoot him, to spare himself what I was planning to do next. He was lying—he didn't have a dead wife; he must have gained access to my file and learned about my family, then tried to get to me through them. He discovered their promise in my personnel file somewhere.

I tell myself these things as I clean up the mess I've made.

PART THREE

GREEN-TAGS

20.

Tasha hadn't expected so many checkpoints at Walter Reed. It was as though the military had brought all the security from the Green Zone back here to northwest D.C., where the biggest danger was being hit by an SUV driven by a texting soccer mom. She wanted to blame the military for this new life of having her bag and purse checked everywhere she went—not just airports but Wizards games, the Smithsonian museums, her own office building—even though she knew the military was hardly to blame. This was America, and for once she didn't want to be treated like some potential assassin, would appreciate a smile from a stranger, would like people to remember how it felt to live in a city made up of neighbors rather than spies and informers. She knew it was petty to feel this way, knew that some of these guards themselves might have returned from the desert, might battle nightly memories of explosions from queues just like this one. Perhaps she was angry only because all these men in uniform made her miss her brother more.

When she reached the front desk and finally got to a person who did not want to x-ray her or examine her belongings, she told the woman whom she was here to see. Then a call was placed, a pen was tapped against a desk, a message was relayed, and Tasha was asked to wait.

A few days ago she had finally reached Sergeant Velasquez, one of the only soldiers from Marshall's company who'd been willing to speak to her. It was unclear whether the silence she'd otherwise encountered was due to some nefarious plot or to collective survivors' guilt or to the practical difficulty of getting active-duty soldiers to reply to a stranger's phone calls or e-mails during a war. Her hopes that Leo would be able to leverage his contacts for information were proving equally fruitless—she'd met with him a third time now, and he'd told her only that he had "some people" looking into it. She had the uncomfortable feeling that he was trying to wait her out, the same thing she was doing to him, all the while knowing a timer was getting closer and closer to zero, and she'd soon have to either deliver T.J. to Leo or tell Leo that she would never entrap her friend, regardless of the consequences.

She waited in the hospital lobby for another ten minutes, then saw a man wheeling toward her. She'd been seeing a lot of wheelchairs lately, it seemed—an unusual number of young black men in her neighborhood and on the Metro sat in the contraptions, and she often wondered who had been shot in a street dispute, who was a returning veteran, who a slow victim of diabetes. The man before her looked to be in his early twenties, had the standard military haircut, and wore a ratty gray Oakland A's T-shirt stretched tight across his chest. He was handsome and too young.

"Miss Wilson?"

"Tasha." She smiled. "Pleased to meet you, Sergeant."

She shook his hand. His left foot wore a red Nike, and she could see a glimmer of white gauze just inside the right tails of his shiny black basketball shorts.

"I could've picked you out of a crowd," he said, smiling. "You two have the same eyes, same cheekbones—it's eerie."

Velasquez recommended they talk at one of the tables on the patio outside. Other recovering soldiers and Marines were sitting alone or in groups; some of them were working through basic stretching exercises, their therapists instructing them as they retaught their arms and legs how to move. Tasha had an aunt who was a physical therapist, and the whole profession seemed to her a gathering of saints, patient do-gooders spending their lives working with broken people, endlessly toiling toward small victories: standing up, tying shoes, taking a shower.

Clouds of cigarette smoke blew in the autumn wind. One of the soldiers wore a white T-shirt that read THE PRICE OF FREEDOM and had an arrow pointing to his left sleeve, which dangled empty. The skies were dim, and Tasha zipped up her coat. She saw how underdressed Velasquez was and asked if he wouldn't be more comfortable inside.

"Nah, this is nice. Oakland weather. I don't get out much these days."

"How long have you been here?"

"Coupla months. I was in Germany for a while before that, though I never really saw the place. Just the inside of a hospital, then the inside of an airplane."

"I'm sorry about your leg."

"Yeah. The weirdest thing? When I hear music, like especially when I'm sitting—what do I mean, when I'm sitting? That's all I ever do now"—and he laughed at himself—"anyway, I used to play drums, and my right foot was the bass foot. So I sit here listening to my iPod and I'm tapping my foot and then I realize *there is no foot*. That's the weirdest thing. I'm like grooving to a beat, and I'm subconsciously tapping a foot that ain't there. But I can feel it tapping, y'know? If I was sitting at a real drum kit and hearing a song right now and tapped my little mental foot, I swear to God that bass drum would go *boom*. I know that sounds crazy."

"Not crazy at all."

"They had this neurologist talking to a bunch of us the other day. He said that kind of stuff, and the phantom pains you get, they literally *are* in the mind. Like, usually when you say something's all in your mind, you mean that it isn't real. But it *is* real—the brain actually has these like neurons or something, and they're still convinced that the foot is there. So I have the memory of my foot, physically, inside my brain, and it won't go away. A part of our therapy is to get the brain to forget the foot. Which is so weird. You'd think that after all the hours of me staring at my lack of foot, my brain would get it already, but no."

She nodded. She couldn't tell if he'd always been a rambler or if this was the new him, if this was the way he was dealing with it, and she wanted him to feel comfortable. Marshall hadn't been a big talker, but she wondered: If Marshall had survived, if he'd lost a leg instead of his life, would his personality have been transformed, would he too be going on and on about neuroscience and percussion? Can personalities change as quickly as lives can end?

"Marshall played guitar," she said.

"Nah, he didn't." And Velasquez laughed.

"What?"

"Dude *owned* a guitar. But he couldn't play a lick. Tried to teach himself—tortured us with it at Fort Benning. I'm sorry to say, miss, but your brother had no musical soul."

She laughed. "You're right. He had the thing forever, but he never really spent the time on it."

"Oh, man, I don't even like *thinking* of him working on his scales. And don't even ask me about him trying to rap."

She laughed again, trying not to show how desperate she was to hear whatever else he knew of Marshall. The scenes, conversations, the way they'd passed afternoons and nights. It was memory porn—she craved it. She wanted to reach inside this stranger's brain, tear out everything he had of Marshall, take it for herself. But she feared that if she revealed the extent of her needs, he'd turn silent.

"How are your folks?" he asked.

She thought for a moment. Why lie? "Bad. We all grieve in different ways, you know? How are yours? They must be pretty relieved to have you back."

"Yeah, they're good. They were out here for a while, the army put 'em up nearby. But I told 'em I was good and, you know, they have jobs, grandkids. I didn't want 'em here doting on me while bills were piling up."

She nodded, and they waited a moment. Then she asked, "Did you ever read Marshall's blog?"

"He had a blog?" He looked genuinely surprised.

"Yeah. He didn't use his name on it, because he...was afraid that if he said something the army didn't like, he could be disciplined for it. He didn't talk about it?"

"No, ma'am. At least not to me. What, uh, what kinds of things did he say?"

"It was like a journal. Here's what I did today, here's what I've been thinking. The irony is that when he had a lot of time to write, there wasn't as much to write about. And then he'd be busy and couldn't post for a while, and suddenly one day he'd get to the computer and he'd post these long stories..."

"So...He said things he thought he might get disciplined for?"

"I didn't see anything objectionable. But I'm not an army censor. In the beginning, it was all rah-rah, go-army stuff, lots of details on what it was like to be there. But it sometimes sounded...critical of what we're doing over there."

He was watching her carefully.

"Anyway, by the time my family and I got word of what had happened, the blog was down. Meaning, the site was gone and everything had been deleted. I'm wondering why that happened, and so quickly."

"Like I said, he never mentioned it."

"I was wondering if you wouldn't mind...I was wondering what you might be able to tell me about how Marshall died."

He looked away for a moment.

"Or maybe that's the last thing you want to talk about."

He shrugged. "The last thing and the first thing, you know? Same as you, probably."

"Yeah."

"I don't remember much about it. It was the same day as this." He motioned to his phantom limb. "They tell your family anything about it?"

"They did, but from the ten-thousand-feet perspective. I was hoping to get the view from the ground."

"Where things blow up, right?" He smiled. He seemed to swing

between amiable and brooding, and she couldn't tell if she was pushing certain buttons or if the randomness was self-programmed. So she
waited, unsure what to say next, hoping he would continue.

"We'd gained control of the city after a real nasty week. We'd
lost a lot of guys, but we'd pushed the hajjis out by the sixth day. So
we were doing different patrols, making sure everything was locked
down, that there weren't any neighborhoods where they were hiding
out to hit us later." None of this contradicted what she'd been told.
"Anyway, things had calmed down when three soldiers on a supply
run vanished. I mean, they came under fire, but before they finished
radioing, we lost their signal, and when more joes got there, they
were gone. No bodies, just a shot-up truck. Couple hours later, we
got word that some American soldiers were being held in this old
warehouse. Lieutenant Wilson led a small group, and we stormed
it. I was one of the guards outside it, and when the guys went in,
there were shots, something was going down, and then me and the
other guard saw activity across the street. That's pretty much all I
remember.

"Well, not really, but it's the only stuff that makes any sense. I
remember an explosion, not from inside the building but outside,
someone firing RPGs, and one of them hit close to me. Then I was
just on the ground and things get, you know, disjointed and stuff.
Eventually we controlled the area and they got me out of there. From
what I been told, he didn't make it out of the building."

She nodded, watching him. She tried to replay what he'd said,
tried to let the images unfold, see if she'd missed anything. Her family had been told that Marshall died leading his men to safety, that
he died trying to rescue other soldiers, but they hadn't been told
anything about people being held hostage or any search-and-rescue
mission. Was it standard procedure for the military to fail to mention
that, or was it suspicious?

"Don't they usually send in special teams of Rangers for rescue
missions?"

"For something planned in advance, yeah. But word had barely gotten out that the soldiers had been taken before the lieutenant got a tip on their location, and we moved immediately."

"Did you save the hostages?"

"Yes, ma'am. The tough thing for me was, you get injured, you get medevaced out, and then you're detached from your unit. You're in another world. I was finally able to get some messages out, and yeah, they say we saved the hostages. The hajjis were planning to execute them on camera, had a little TV studio hooked up and everything."

"Do you know their names?" She hadn't brought a notebook, hadn't wanted to put him off or alarm the guards by looking like a journalist. She was memorizing as much as she could.

"No," he said, and he seemed to be looking back at himself for a moment. "I never thought to ask. They weren't from our platoon, so I probably wouldn't have known 'em anyway."

A therapist wheeled another patient toward the building, a young white man missing his right leg and right arm. Velasquez broke from his reverie to call encouragement to the kid, who smiled and nodded, his eyes wandering quickly to Tasha. Once they were gone, she looked at Velasquez again, trying to be patient, to see what else he might offer her. His eyes were filling up.

"I was guarding the perimeter. If I had seen things, if I'd picked up on a detail better, we could have gotten them out quicker. Or told the team to wait." He nodded, his voice growing tight. "It's my fault things got out of hand. Said they're gonna give me a Purple Heart for this, but I'm the one that fucked it up, and guys died." He wasn't looking at her. "I wanted to tell you...that I was sorry."

"No." She shook her head, only now realizing what she'd done. "Please don't feel that way. I'm sure that what happened—"

"Thank you, but you weren't there."

She hated herself; why hadn't she realized that all she was doing was adding to someone else's pain?

"Whatever they told you," he said, "whatever the official story is, they're lying, sure. That's why you're here, right? You don't trust the official line and you want to know what really happened. The official line should be: *Sergeant Velasquez's failure to secure the perimeter and failure to notify his forward soldiers of imminent danger resulted in loss of life*. I mean, Marshall was the lieutenant, yeah, but I was the sergeant; those were my boys in there. My boys that died. Army isn't saying all that, to protect me, because they don't want to hang me out like that. They see I lost a leg and figure I suffered enough. But it's the truth."

She'd come in search of a grand conspiracy, something that would implicate sinister and powerful forces. The last thing she'd wanted was to point a finger at a young man in a wheelchair, lost in the cold.

She took his hand and tried to tell him that he wasn't the reason Marshall died. She said she wouldn't have come if she'd realized he would say or even think that, and here they were, two mourners trading apologies, each unburdening him- or herself of things the other didn't want either. So she tried to sound stern, telling him that the last thing Marshall Wilson would want was for any of his comrades to castigate himself like this.

Velasquez nodded like a petulant teenager who knows that faking an agreement is the only way to get his parent to shut up. Hell, he practically *was* a teenager. He rolled his shoulder to wipe at his cheek with his sleeve.

"Yeah," he said. His eyes were glassy, staring straight ahead. "You know, I am getting kinda cold. I should head in."

His hands started spinning the wheels and he turned toward the door. She had to hurry to keep pace with him. She thanked him for meeting with her, asked him if there was anything he needed, anything she could pick up for him.

"Nah, I'm good, thanks."

She wasn't sure how to say good-bye, whether a handshake would be too formal or if bending over for a hug would make him feel pitied, and while she was wondering this he leaned on his back wheel to turn and face her. As if he had one last important thing to tell her. But all he told her was to take care and she'd barely replied when he spun around again, his wheels taking him past another guard station and down the long hallway.

Z.

Timelines have grown confusing to me, cause and effect reversed and turned inside out, stories mixed with the wrong endings. Without my GeneScan I can't track any hags, and I can't help but wonder which other parts of my perception have been blurred or simply wiped clean.

I wonder if Wills was right, that this a purgatory for me. And I've dispatched the one person who might have understood what I'm living through.

The day after shooting Wills—and using a Flasher to eliminate his body, then leaving and checking into a new motel before the manager of the first found an enormous hole in the bathroom—I'm staking out the Korean diplomat's place. Nothing happening, no obvious hags about. I linger outside his office at the embassy, but here too all seems normal.

Then I get a call from Tasha coming in through the line I'd tapped for my personal use. She asks me if I'd like to meet for lunch downtown. I was about to check on her, actually, so this is the perfect excuse.

Wills never really answered my question about Tasha. My intel didn't say she was important; his did. Was his intel faked, to throw me off? Or is she in fact slated to be killed with T.J.? If so, is it because of something I've done? Is there a way I can undo it, erase my own accidental imprint on history? Or would that too be a violation, and she's already damned, and there's nothing I can do to save her?

I opt for a cab ride instead of the Metro. Better one contemp silently driving me around than countless others glancing at me.

She'd said to meet in the sculpture garden at the National Mall. There she is, standing in front of an optical illusion: a fifteen-foot-tall painting of an almost two-dimensional house that seems to bend and open as I approach it. She stands at the center of it, the fulcrum where the two panes impossibly move, the house seeming to grow and shrink with each of my steps.

"I love this Lichtenstein," she says. She's actually standing a good ten feet away from it, but from a distance she seemed to be inside of it. "When I was a kid, me and Marshall would try to play in it. We didn't understand why our parents wouldn't let us until the time a security guard saw us and started yelling."

"A metaphor for the flatness of domestic life?" I wonder, reassessing it now that I'm closer. "Or how the people you love are never what they appear to be?"

"You've never seen it before?" She's shocked. "And you used to live here?"

"I'm...not much for art."

"I'll have to work on that."

A gust of wind blows her braids across her face. She asks if I wouldn't mind a bit of a walk before lunch or if I need to rush back to the office.

"No, I have time," I say. "I've been wanting to skip work for a while now."

"Things bad at the office?"

I look around at the other sculptures, giant spiders and vulvic metal installations lurking among the trees. What am I doing here? Is anyone actually interested in interfering with Tasha's life, or is it just me?

"I think things have been bad at the office for some time and I'm only beginning to notice."

She smiles like she knows exactly what I mean. Then we walk toward the Lincoln Memorial. The skies are gray, the grass ocher. Far fewer tourists around than the last time I came here, when I saw that doomed little black girl with the pink sweater.

It's a long walk, and Tasha asks me about my job, forcing me to make up more lies. I try to change the subject. Finally she explains why she wanted to see me so suddenly.

"I talked to one of the soldiers who served with my brother. I figured you might be the only person who'd understand what I'm thinking."

The wind seems to calm as we approach the Lincoln, the tall fortress providing sanctuary.

"I was thinking about what you said to me the other day," she continues. "About how you weren't trying to learn more about what happened to your own brother. I couldn't understand how you *wouldn't* want to find out *everything* you could. I figured maybe we were just in two different stages of grief."

I keep careful watch for strange loiterers or suspicious movement. She notices my preoccupation, her gaze following mine a few times. I try to act like I'm just admiring the sights, but I can tell she's wondering.

Camera flashes strobe the marble as we climb the steps. Tourists stare in awe at the speeches etched on the walls, puzzling out meaning.

"I just wanted to say"—and we wander closer to those two enormous white loafers, resting grandly yet casually behind the red velvet security rope—"that I think you're right. That I've been pushing my anger onto other people. My suspicions. I've always had that tendency, and this only made it worse."

"It's natural to feel that way. We need people to blame."

"That's the thing. When I talked to this soldier, this kid who's never going to walk again and who loved Marshall like *they* were brothers, I could see all I was doing was blaming him. Blaming anyone who had anything to do with the war. I wanted answers, and I figured everyone must be hiding one. And I ruined this poor guy's day."

"I'm sure it didn't work out that way."

She looks at me for a moment. "You are the calmest person I've ever met."

"I've just . . . seen things that most people don't have to see."

Avoiding the questions in her eyes, I turn to read the inscriptions, the great man's speech made in the middle of a war that must have seemed like the very end of civilization to people alive then.

"I wanted to say thank you, for the things you said."

"You're welcome."

She asks me if my parents ever dragged me to Gettysburg or Harpers Ferry and I say no, quickly running searches on my databases so I can follow the conversation. She says I was lucky, and she tells me stories of awful family vacations, her father lecturing them on the importance of history, their heritage as African Americans. The long walks with weird tour guides across sacred battlefields where countless lives were lost in a war against slavery, when all she and her brother wanted to do was go home and watch television.

"I don't think I've ever had so many serious conversations with a guy," she says as she reads one of the speeches beside me.

"Should we be talking about hip-hop and movies?"

"That was a compliment. Usually guys try to act all funny and sly. You don't do that."

Nearby a tour has ended and people are applauding.

"Maybe I'm so sly you don't even notice."

We take a cab back to her apartment after a long lunch at a Spanish restaurant, a meal involving small plates, plentiful garlic, and strong drinks with apple chunks floating in them. She calls her boss at one point and says she's ill and won't return for the day. And I've all but done the same thing; I've dropped all pretense of why I'm with her. This isn't about upholding the order of history or the sanctity of a Perfect Society. I just want this one moment to be perfect.

A few times I worry that I've given myself away—*No, I don't know that TV show; Sorry, I haven't heard that album.* I fear she thinks I'm a freak, some cultural outsider. But the way she looks at me is something I haven't seen in so long.

It's still light out and she's barely opened the door of her row house—I almost forget to check for solo men sitting in parked cars—when she turns to kiss me. We stand in her tiny vestibule like that for a while, my first kiss in I don't know how long. I can't remember the last one, though I know it happened. No file or image of it, but I can still feel it, and when her tongue glances off my teeth I remember more, and I hope Tasha wouldn't hate knowing that I'm not thinking of her just now, or maybe I am, but of Cemby too, two people rolled into one. I hope she can forgive me that.

Inside, while she's pouring us glasses of wine, I stand in her living room and gaze at the book spines—so many books!—and the images on her shelves. In some of the images I see the young man who must be her brother (the eyes and the cheekbones are so similar); one is an official image of him standing in uniform before their flag.

She walks into the room, hands me a glass. Smiling as if at a joke.

"What?" I ask, afraid I've done something un-contemp again.

"No, it's just, I was thinking. How weird it is that we met. How unpredictable. I mean, of all places."

"I always pick up women at political rallies. It's a good way to meet the committed type. Or the crazy ones."

"Seriously, though. Almost makes you wonder if someone was guiding us, strange as that sounds."

I feel a swelling in my chest, and I honestly don't know if it's pity for or jealousy of her belief that God or her dead brother can reach out and affect her life like that.

I take her head in my hands and hold her closer, wondering which of us is lost and which is guiding the other someplace new.

22.

Leo found it surprisingly entertaining to concoct imaginary smoking guns for Tasha. He wrote up false memos about Consolidated Forces, typed fanciful e-mails sent from one fictional character to the next, and used his scanner and small copier to create documents that seemed aged. It felt weirdly like being in grad school again, crafting a paper for some obscure journal, the two key differences being that this time he didn't have to feel bad about making parts of it up, and he was working on something that would actually have an impact on the world.

Tasha had impressed him already by dangling the fake scandal story to T.J., who predictably asked her to bring more information the next time she met with him. Leo had expected more pushback from her, but apparently she was bright and pragmatic enough to see that she had no choice but to obey. The only potential problem was that she'd asked him at their last meeting if he'd found out anything about her brother. He'd forgotten all about his vague promise to look into it (because how the hell would he have any way of finding out how an overseas soldier died?). She seemed to think he had access to all levels of intelligence, a ridiculous assumption that at least allowed him to feel more important than he was. There was no harm in stringing her along, and he'd recovered in time to tell her that his nameless contacts in army intelligence were still looking into it and that such bureaucratic file-sharing took time.

Meanwhile he worked on more nefarious file-sharing. He'd researched Consolidated Forces and was employing enough real names to provide his fake docs with an aura of truth, just in case T.J. or his fellows in guerrilla journalism tried to verify any of this. Which he knew they wouldn't. They would eagerly take the information, which confirmed all their worst assumptions about the U.S. government, and post it on Knoweverything immediately.

Once that happened, Leo's client would have proof that T.J. was involved, and Leo could start identifying the rest of the network. The false story would discredit the site in the eyes of the mainstream media and most of the country. Their most extreme adherents would no doubt sense a plot against them, a new, grander conspiracy, but that would be their little shared delusion while the rest of the world moved on.

The previous night, he'd retrieved another flash drive from Sari and had sent it on to Bale. He had been more cautious than before, approaching the house from a different direction and much later, at two in the morning. Again, there had been no sign that anyone in the neighboring houses was even awake. The mysterious stranger did not make a repeat appearance.

Leo couldn't wait for the Knoweverything operation to be complete. He was tired of following people who only knew how to complain and tear down. The truth was, you could find fault in anything if you tried hard enough. That was the modern condition, especially in his generation. What is *irony* other than pointing out the flaws in something while wearing a superior smirk on your face? The unstated always being *I'm better than this thing I'm making fun of,* whatever the thing was. A new movie, a pop singer, the president, patriotism, the American Dream, faith in God or country or things larger than oneself. Larger than one's ability to make snide comments. Why were people willing to settle for the easy laugh? He'd had people tell him he had no sense of humor—usually this came from disappointed, soon-to-be-ex-girlfriends. But the truth was that he saw *past* humor, at least the modern, ice-pick-thin version of it. Everyone else wanted to show off how smart they were.

Because here was what none of them wanted to admit, Leo

thought, the thing they were simply too blind or angry or spoiled to realize: this life was the best it could possibly be. There were flaws, yes, and the world might not work for everyone all of the time, and innocent people occasionally suffered due to the callousness of fate or their fellow citizens, but what were the alternatives? What utopia were people like T.J. dreaming of when they railed against the minor problems of capitalism and democracy? Had they taken a look at the world around them? Didn't they realize how much *better* this was than any other country, any other system, any other way of life? Had they failed to notice that every time some mad dreamer took the reins of a country by revolution and promised his people a paradise on earth, he delivered the opposite? T.J. and his pals reminded Leo of the academics he'd grown so tired of; they'd been too busy lining up for Abuses of the American Empire 101 to bother learning about Stalin's gulags. They'd been too busy mocking Oliver North and Reagan to read about the Sandinista death camps. They'd been too taken with the romance of the Black Panthers and the Weathermen's heroic post office bombings to take heed of the warnings in Pol Pot's exterminations or Mao's purges. They had so much fun pointing out all that was wrong with the closest thing to *perfection* that any of them would ever see in their angst-ridden lives.

Didn't people like them realize that if they lived in almost any other country, they would have already been arrested, tortured, and discarded? No, they would doubtless take Leo's very involvement in their lives as evidence that the system was corrupt.

Leo read through his false documents one more time, then turned off his computer. He needed to sweat this insanity out of his system, so he threw on his running clothes and sprinted from his apartment.

He was jogging along Rock Creek Park, nestled in late-afternoon shadows, when an SUV pulled over beside him. The hazards were on, and two men stepped out of the backseat and into the bike path, their palms held out. One was white and bald, the other Asian with graying hair at his temples. They wore dark suits and sunglasses and were straight out of central casting.

He slowed to a trot and pulled the buds out of his ears. Garage rock dangled from his fingers.

"Leo!" one of them shouted over the traffic. Cars honked, outraged that the SUV was blocking a lane, and during rush hour no less. "We need to talk. C'mon."

"What about?" He'd been running for twenty minutes and it was all he could do not to lean over and put his sweaty hands on the knees of his running pants. He didn't want to look weak in front of whoever this was.

"Those fingerprints you lifted."

He nodded. He figured his asking *Who are you?* would only lead to evasive answers, so he didn't bother with questions as he followed them into the back of the SUV. They had him sit in the middle. Ah, the memories. Backseat briefings in Indonesia or Thailand or Hong Kong, sometimes by people he knew and sometimes by total strangers he never saw again but who knew the code words. You learned to pay attention to what was being said as well as where you were going, since you never knew where you'd be dropped off and you weren't always left in a city you'd been to before. It made him nostalgic, again, for what he'd lost.

The two at his sides looked to be in their early forties, tall and athletic. Even though they kept their shades on, Leo was confident he'd never seen them before.

"We'd like to know how you came upon those fingerprints," said a man riding shotgun, who faced forward. He had silvery-gray hair, and Leo could only occasionally catch bits of the man's face in the mirror, a pale cheek here and a bushy gray eyebrow there.

"You work with Bale?" Leo asked.

"We move in similar circles."

Leo had passed the mystery man's prints on to Bale, telling his boss that they belonged to a man who'd been at a couple of the peacenik meetings lately, a possible agent provocateur sent by another entity.

Later that day, Bale reported that the prints hadn't turned up any matches. Had he been lying? Had he passed the prints on to these men, or had his search unknowingly tripped some silent alarm?

"Listen, Leo," the man in shotgun continued. "Sometimes people who have been on the inside but no longer are, they tend to feel they're still protected. They think they're comfortably nestled under the government's blanket. But it's a cold world, and you're alone, and there are werewolves everywhere."

"I was always more afraid of vampires." He was still catching his breath, panting loudly and drenched in sweat while the others sat motionless and silent in their suits. But he would not act intimidated. He'd had plenty of time to steep in the shame of his speedy disclosure to the mystery man, and he was determined to handle himself more professionally.

"Where did you meet the man you lifted those prints from? Your little story about him attending some antiwar powwow doesn't add up."

So, these men said they weren't with Bale, but clearly they'd spoken to him—or spoken to someone who'd spoken to him or had listened in somehow. Too many possibilities.

"Who am I talking to?"

"Allow me to explain things to you more clearly. You're a civilian who erroneously believes that he has the power and might of the U.S. government at his back. You have nothing at your back. That little breeze you feel there? That's the wind from the cliff you're standing at the edge of. Any trouble comes your way, you think someone like Bale will vouch for you? And you think anything in that little head of yours will be considered valuable enough for you to barter your way out of trouble? No and no. I hate conversations like this, because I'm talking to a destitute man who thinks he's independently wealthy. You green-tags are all the same."

"What trouble would come my way?"

"Use your imagination."

Rock Creek Parkway curved and bent vertiginously, and Leo's shoulders rocked against the two other men's.

"I met this individual while I was performing research as part of an operation for my employer."

That won him laughter.

"Leo," the man to his left said. "We're not asking you anything difficult. And your man Bale won't care what you tell us, since he'll never know anyway. So stop worrying about the integrity of your precious operation and tell us about your conversation with the guy. What he told you, what if anything he asked you, how he acted."

"I already told my boss."

They crossed the river and headed north on the GW Parkway. This was the way to Langley, but he still wasn't sure if that's where they were going.

"Tell us what you left out," the back of the gray head in shotgun said. "Such as where it really was."

"We know you hate the work you're doing," said the man on his left, who was actively campaigning for the role of Good Cop, if only these guys had been cops. "I would too. It's beneath you. So you're trying to make a little rain, prove your resourcefulness. Hoping to impress someone important, someone with connections."

"And the good news"—the guy riding shotgun took the baton—"is that you are now in a car with precisely such individuals. The meter is running, Leo. If you want to impress us, start impressing us. Maybe you'll never have to tail a hippie again."

Leo thought for a moment.

"I was told those prints produced no matches."

"Which is mostly true," Shotgun said. "They did not match up with any identified person, any name, date of birth, et cetera. But they do match the prints of an as-yet-unidentified individual who's been causing us some trouble."

Maybe sharing a little would yield a little. "I've been surveilling the residence of a South Korean diplomat. It's in its early stages. There isn't much to tell."

The SUV climbed the hill, and Leo caught glimpses of the Potomac below.

"And you approached this gentleman, or he approached you?"

"He'd seen me observing the man's house. He approached my car and implied that I was disrupting another operation." He left out the gun, the threats, the weird existential questioning. And he didn't mention Sari. No one seemed to be taking notes, so there must have been a recorder somewhere.

"So he was watching you while you were watching the diplomat," Shotgun recapped. He'd said it like he already knew which diplomat Leo was talking about.

"Maybe. He was acting pretty randomly. I know people on long stakeouts can get a little unhinged, but it seemed more than that. And I don't necessarily think that what I was doing had anything to do with—"

"You're probably right," Shotgun said, too quickly.

"So who was the guy?" Leo asked.

"Someone we're trying very hard to find," Shotgun said.

"He works for . . . ?"

"That's not yours to know, I'm afraid."

"Look, I've given you—"

"Stop thinking like a case officer, because you aren't one. Remember? This is not a meeting of equal minds. You, a green-tag, do not have clearance to know *anything*. You're fortunate you aren't having this conversation with a black bag over your head."

Leo seethed. But they were right.

The car exited at one of the scenic overlooks. A station wagon with Minnesota plates had been idling there, but it pulled away when the SUV entered, as if sensing danger. Leo and his interrogators were alone with the view and the circling hawks and the falls far below.

"So," Shotgun continued, "you, Mr. Hastings, are a former government operative playing amateur spy games with a South Korean diplomat. Last I checked, that country was a staunch ally of the United States. I'm sure any number of people would be happy to lock up a loose cannon who's trying to jeopardize our sound diplomatic relations with the people of South Korea."

The way they traded sticks for carrots and back again was disorienting. And he was sick of their belittling tone. "I haven't done anything illegal or—"

Everyone laughed again. Leo sat there and tried not to let his face turn any redder than it already was. The SUV leaned as gusts blew along the ravine.

"Leo, allow me to explain a few things about how your world will exist from this moment forward. You, your employer, and your nonexistent client will cease and desist from whatever you're doing and will henceforth pretend you've never heard of this diplomat. Never even heard of South Korea. You can't find Asia on a map, understood? Failure to obey these instructions will affect you so unbelievably adversely that I'd like to pause here for a moment of silence while you imagine it."

Leo didn't grant the man his silence. "I've been threatened by old men in suits before."

"And the last time it happened, if memory serves, they followed through on their threats and kicked your whistle-blowing self out of the Agency. Next time you give someone a reason to follow through on their—"

"I wasn't a whistle-blower."

"That's not the word on the street. And you're lucky that information wasn't made public. You could have been *prosecuted*, Leo."

"I *did not* leak that story." His hands were fists in his lap. "I filed official reports through official channels voicing my concerns about what was happening. When my superiors ignored the reports, I went a rung higher. That might piss off bureaucrats like you, but everyone on the ground knows it's how things get done. The black-sites story hit the press *two months later*, the Agency needed someone to blame, and they chose me. If they'd had any evidence I'd leaked anything, yes, I *would* have been prosecuted. But it *wasn't me*."

"I think you found his soft spot," Good Cop said to Shotgun.

"They had the best people in counterintelligence investigating me. So either you believe it when I say it wasn't me or you think I'm the most brilliant spy in the world for leaking a story like that without leaving a trace."

They seemed to ponder that a bit. Or maybe they'd just wanted to get a rise out of him and were already through having their fun.

"All right," Shotgun said. "Maybe I do believe you. And maybe I will tell you, out of the utmost professional courtesy—which a green-tag like you does not deserve, even if you weren't a whistle-blower—that the Korean diplomat you have been tailing is an asset. And that your surveillance of him, which evidently isn't all that good, will cause him to panic and stop the helpful stream of information he's been providing to us. Which is why we are humbly requesting, in the nicest possible way this time, that you stay the hell away from him so you don't jeopardize our valuable relationship."

Leo thought this over. He could see his chagrined expression in the rearview but still couldn't glimpse his interlocutor.

"You could have gotten around to saying that a lot faster."

"And if you were still a case officer, I would have. I just gave you much more than you're entitled to. Now, hopefully, you'll never see that strange individual again, and you'll never even need to remember this conversation. But if you should see him, you will refrain from contacting him and will instead call us." On cue, the silent man to Leo's right handed him a business card. It had nothing but a phone number on it. "Understood?"

"Sure."

The silent man got out of the car and motioned for Leo to follow him. Leo was almost out when Shotgun said, "You really didn't leak that story, did you?"

"No. Not that anyone cares anymore."

"How long did you work at the sites?"

"That's classified." It felt good to turn it around on him. "But long enough. Long enough to figure right from wrong."

"That's funny. In my experience, the more you do this work, the *less* you can figure those two terms out."

"I guess you and I are different types of people."

"Apparently. Good-bye, Leo."

Leo exited, and the man who'd been sitting beside him on the right patted him on the shoulder, smiling somewhat tauntingly. "Sorry to interrupt your jog. You can resume it here."

The guy got in the car, which pulled back onto the parkway. Leo memorized its Virginia plates, knowing it was probably worthless to do so, then tried to replay the conversation in his head. But he kept focusing on the whistle-blower taunts. Which, he realized sadly, was exactly what they'd wanted: He was so angry and had expended so much energy defending himself that he couldn't remember everything they'd said earlier about the diplomat and the mystery man. If they'd accidentally given anything away, if there had been any subtle slips, he'd been too worked up to notice.

All he really knew was he was a long way from home.

He was not terribly surprised to find two voice mails from Bale when he finally made it to his apartment. *"Where are you that you aren't answering your cell? Call me immediately."*

Leo's shins and knees were throbbing; he felt light-headed and was famished—it had taken him nearly two hours to make it back home, jogging partway and walking when he couldn't jog any farther. He hadn't been dressed warmly enough for the drop in temperature at sundown, and he felt fevered, his skin cold but his insides overheated.

It was past nine o'clock. He chugged two glasses of water, then called his boss.

"Where have you been?" Bale asked.

"Running an impromptu marathon."

"Well, I just got the translations back from the files on her laptop."

"Great." So the second flash drive from Sari was indeed from Sang Hee's computer—she'd done a good job. But he was surprised Bale would call him with this rather than tell him in person.

"No, not great. Her correspondence turns up nothing, and the

287

only documents she has in there is a fucking *novel*. Or a memoir, or whatever you call them. What's the difference? It's this tear-jerking bullshit story about a poor woman in North Korea who gets sent to a labor camp and loses her family, blah blah blah. Jesus. The guys who translated said Oprah would love it. What the fuck? Why did I let you con me into spending all this time and money to get some analysts to read an Oprah book?"

He'd never heard Bale like this. Disappointment would have been an appropriate response, but this was more.

"I never said I knew what would be on it," Leo said. "You're the one who said she was a person of interest, so—"

"Do not even think of pointing a finger at me, Leo. This was your initiative, and it's failed."

"Understood. I'm sorry it didn't work out." He said that while expecting Bale to reel himself back in, say, No, no, it's not over yet, but Bale didn't.

"Me too. We wasted time and you put yourself out there to this maid, but it's over now. I want you to stop all contact with her, immediately. You never met her, and you certainly never promised her anything."

"Isn't that being a little hasty?" He hadn't yet decided if he was going to tell Bale that the diplomat was an Agency asset. "So the info on her laptop wasn't interesting, but maybe there's something else, something in hard copy or on her husband's computer that—"

"No and no. I let you follow a hunch, and now I'm following mine: it's over. Return your energies to the assignment you're supposed to be focusing on."

Bale hung up.

Leo collapsed into a chair, way too exhausted to even begin sorting this out. Those men had dumped him far from home not just to be cruel but to buy themselves time, so they could lean on Bale while Leo was gone, and so Leo would be too tired to make sense of this. His pride hurt a lot worse than his feet.

But if those men really were CIA, wouldn't Bale have said as much? *Leo, we're stepping on someone's toes.* Short, sweet, cryptic. Why all the drama?

He hated them all. All the people who got in the way of his simply trying to do some good. The constant reminders that there were things he was not allowed to know, and that if he ever brushed up against that knowledge, he would be severely punished. He wanted to tell them all to fuck off. He wanted to hear Sari's voice, see her face. She wasn't his asset anymore—well, fine. Then maybe he could help her now the way he should have from the beginning. Maybe it had been fated this way.

His phone rang. The caller ID said it was one of the Latino grocery stores on Mount Pleasant Street. He'd never set foot in it—wrong number?

But somehow he knew. Maybe because he was thinking of her, maybe because he knew the place was just down the street from the diplomat's house. Maybe because grocery stores would, for the rest of his life, always make him think of her.

"Hello?"

He was right. "Leo, please, please help me." She was panicked and out of breath. "Please."

23.

Sari had been washing dishes when it started. A bedtime story about a camel who wishes he could learn how to fly had lulled Hana to sleep, and miraculously neither of the twins had woken yet. Sari had almost come to enjoy washing dishes at night, because at least no one was crying or demanding anything of her, and she could stand in one place and let her mind go blank.

She had now sent two flash drives in the recycling to Leo. She managed to get at Sang Hee's computer late one night, after the mistress had gone to bed drunk and left her laptop on in the living room. It had been in sleep mode, and no password was required to start it up again. Sari looked over her shoulder every few seconds as she moved as much data as she could. She left the laptop exactly as she found it.

Sang Hee had spoken only a few words to Sari since the night she'd told her about North Korea. She seemed even quieter than usual, as if she were ashamed of what she had disclosed. Sari had seen little of the diplomat, who had been working late for much of that week.

As she washed dishes now, she heard them yelling in their bedroom. She turned off the water and walked down the hallway. As if the two sensed her, their voices grew quiet. She remembered, last night or the one before, waking up to the sounds of something similar and then falling back to sleep. She'd thought it was a dream, but perhaps not? They always acted so formal in each other's presence—at least, when Sari was there to observe them. It was disturbing to hear them like this.

Five minutes later, Sari was almost finished with the dishes, and

Hyun Ki came downstairs. She didn't say anything and kept facing the sink, though the window in front of her displayed his reflection. Without greeting her he took a highball glass from the cabinet, then went to the liquor cabinet. He opened the freezer door and she heard the music of ice cubes dancing in his glass. They both drank a lot, Sari noticed, and they seemed to be picking up the pace of late.

She heard him pull up a chair and sit at the kitchen table. She couldn't see his reflection from here.

"Leave the dishes for the morning," he told her.

"I'm almost finished," she said. But she still had to clean the counters, and take the trash out to the garage, and make up some bottles for the babies' overnight feed.

"I want to be alone. Go to bed."

She shut off the faucet. This only meant she'd have more to do in the morning, when the kids were awake, or in the middle of the night. But at least she could go to bed early. She untied the apron and put it away, then left the room without looking at him. She felt him watching her.

She was nervous around him. Leo had even asked if he had ever touched her, which bothered her, as it confirmed her fears that such a thing was indeed a possibility. And then that recent night, when he'd stroked her arm . . . She had wanted to sleep with her door shut that night, but Sang Hee had long ago ordered her to keep it open so she could hear the twins, even though she had a baby monitor by her pillow. Each night after, she lay in bed wide-eyed for a good while.

So on this night, after being sent away from the kitchen, she hurriedly brushed and washed, then got in bed. Wearing her sweat clothes, the blankets pulled to her chin. She could hear the occasional clink of new ice in his glass. Light from the kitchen kept the hallway brighter than she wanted, so she closed her door almost all the way.

She had a harder time than usual falling asleep. The forced-air heat switched on and off sporadically, and the accompanying change in air pressure nudged her door the slightest bit open or shut. The light from the hallway crept closer, then backed up, then crept closer again.

* * *

She wasn't sure what time she was roused. It happened softly, almost delicately, fingertips light on her cheek. Dreams melting off of them. Her eyes were open, yet everything was dark. Her mother had been visiting her again, and Sari heard her voice.

"*Shhh.*"

No, that wasn't her mother's voice. She tried to sit up, but the hand slid over her lips and jaw, holding her there. She couldn't see him. He had closed the door.

Then he was climbing into the bed, her small twin bed, pressing her into the wall. She could smell the whiskey on his breath. His other hand was on her belly, searching for the bottom of her sweatshirt. He'd taken the covers off while she was sleeping.

Get away from him, her mother said. The dream still lingering, none of this seeming real. *Get away from both of them, now.*

He moved his hand from Sari's mouth to support himself as he tried to get on top of her.

"Go away," Sari said, pulling her knees together and pushing at his hand. She was whispering too. Maybe she should yell? What would happen? But what would happen if she didn't? "Please."

She put a hand on his chest, trying to hold him off as he settled on her raised knees. Even though he was a slight man, she realized how easy it would be for him to overpower her. His weight pressed her knees down, so she tightened them again and she heard him grunt as the ridge of his ribs bumped against her kneecaps.

Then a hand tight at her throat. "Stop fighting. Or it will be worse."

But it was impossible not to fight with the hand gripping her like that. Even if she hadn't wanted to resist, something primal prevented her from letting his hand stay there. She dug the nails of both hands into his wrist. She could see only shapes of blackness moving against the dark background as a bit of city light bled through the window blinds. She imagined her nails tearing out small chunks of flesh. She heard him suck in his breath. Then he hit her in the face. Her knees pushed up against his now-unsupported body, toppling him onto the floor.

It was even louder than she'd expected. The sound widening somehow, making echoes in this room and in others. She was reacting to everything, unable to think clearly, her arms now covering her chest as she sat up in bed.

Then the light burst on.

Sang Hee was in the doorway, screaming at them. *Bastard* and *whore* and both of them *damned to hell*. A white robe was barely cinched around her waist, the pressure from the crutches loosening the belt. Then she hobbled away as suddenly as she'd appeared.

Hyun Ki slowly rose from the floor, his expression more chagrined than ashamed. As if this had happened a few times before and was just an inconvenience he needed to steel himself against. Sari watched him for a moment, half afraid that he would close the door, lock it this time. Then they heard Sang Hee screaming again. She was in the kitchen, slamming cabinet doors, throwing glasses. The world was exploding, and in between pops Sari heard the twins crying.

She started to get up, the sounds of the twins' cries reminding her of her duties, as if this were any other night. If she rocked them back to sleep and did her job, she told herself, maybe it would be.

She realized she was shaking when she stood. The diplomat stood too, and he turned to her, his face stern, a warning that didn't need to be voiced.

The smashing of plates and china ceased, but the silence lasted only a moment, because there was Sang Hee again, screaming at them. Moving much faster than either of them thought a woman with a broken ankle could.

"You bastard! You rotten disgusting pig!" She ran at him and he turned just in time to absorb her blows, deflecting a few with his forearms, evading others.

His scream was far louder than Sari expected. And at a very different pitch.

And though Sari was unquestionably wide awake now, she heard her mother's voice again:

Get away from her, quick!

Sari saw the glint of the metal and realized Sang Hee wasn't hitting her husband but stabbing him. He pushed out against Sang Hee, and her body spun to the side as she pulled the blade out. The next blow was meant for Sari. She raised her arms in time and felt the heat along them. She was screaming now too, they all were, and she heard rather than felt the next strike as Hyun Ki lashed out at his wife, knocking her down. Sang Hee was still holding the knife, but she landed in a heap, the blood-streaked white robe fluttering and opening as if she were some fairy princess crash-landing in the real world.

Sari didn't know where she was going, only that she heading down the hallway. She looked into the kitchen, but the shattered glass glittered everywhere, and she was barefoot. Where were her shoes? In the bedroom, with the two of them. She ran to the front door.

And take his briefcase, too, her mother said.

"Missy! Missy!" She turned at the sound of Hana's voice. "Missy, what's wrong?" The little girl was standing at the top of the stairway in her pink nightie. It was darker here but still Sari could see the tears on the girl's face. More screaming from the other room, although this time it was only Sang Hee, with Hyun Ki's quieter voice occasionally snapping at her. Sari could barely hear the twins; they were separated from her by so many crises now.

She didn't know what to tell the little girl. *You live in a cursed house, and there's nothing I can do.*

Her hand was on the doorknob when she noticed, amid the neatly arranged shoes, his briefcase. It wasn't like him to leave it here; maybe he'd intended to work in the kitchen but had been waylaid by his whiskey. Or by the sight of Sari's backside as she washed dishes. In the middle of all the yelling and crying she heard her mother's command again, echoing.

(Later she realized she should have slipped on a pair of his loafers while she was taking the briefcase, but she hadn't been thinking clearly then.)

She ran outside, down the walkway, and onto the sidewalk. She remembered that a few blocks away were some markets. Surely there would be a phone somewhere. She kept running until she couldn't hear the screaming anymore.

She was limping by the time she made it out of the residential neighborhood and onto the main road. She'd stepped on acorns and branches and bottle caps and probably even worse things, and even her calloused feet could feel the cold of the November sidewalk. She hugged herself, the adrenaline and panic not quite enough to counteract the frigid air.

She stood at the intersection a moment, her hair blown across her face by the wind. It was the coldest weather she'd felt yet. A group of black men in colorful sports jerseys were standing in front of a convenience store, their conversation no longer interesting them as they watched her silently. A crazy young barefoot woman with a briefcase. Her arm stung, and she looked at it quickly, saw and felt the blood. The sweatshirt she wore was dark blue so maybe they couldn't see how hurt she was. Even she wasn't sure how hurt she was.

She turned right and headed toward a small grocery store. The people at the cash registers were neither as white as nor as dark as some of the Americans she'd seen; they must be some other race she wasn't familiar with. She had no idea what the neon sign above her said.

The girl at the register looked about Sari's age, her eyes wide. Sari asked for help in Bahasa, then in Korean. The girl stared an extra moment, then turned and yelled something. A much older woman emerged from one of the aisles and stared at their bedraggled customer. Strange music played overhead.

Sari mimed a telephone. Even asked for one, again in a language she knew they couldn't understand, but she couldn't stop herself, she needed help, please, could they help her?

There was cold judgment in the old woman's eyes, yet the hand on Sari's shoulder felt warm and gentle as she guided her to the front corner of the room where a white telephone sat beside a pile of newspapers. The old woman picked up the receiver and dialed three digits. Sari shook her head, assuming the woman was calling some official police or hospital line. The woman looked at her another moment and seemed disappointed. Then she put her finger down again, killing the call. She looked at Sari, opening her palm as if to ask, *Who do you want to call, then?*

He was there in ten minutes, pulling in front of the store and turning on his hazards as he'd explained he would. He did not honk the horn. He had told her not to talk to anyone, as if he were concerned that someone fluent in Korean or Bahasa might suddenly materialize in this grocery store filled with sweet-smelling baked goods and huge bags of multicolored beans. The old lady had sucked in her breath when she noticed Sari's wounded arm and yelled something at the young cashier, who'd run off and then reappeared with a paper towel. Sari nodded her thanks, then pressed the towel to her arm, which burned.

She nodded thanks to them again when Leo arrived, then she ran outside. He pushed open the passenger door, and they were driving away before she could say anything. He turned left at a light and told her to put on her seat belt.

"What happened?" he asked. She hadn't said much to him on the phone.

"They attacked me."

"What do you mean?"

"I was just doing the dishes, and Sang Hee started yelling at me for something. I don't even know what." She was staring out the windshield, afraid to look at him. They were driving on a wide avenue, down a hill, the same way she'd driven to the grocery store. Buses and taxis sped by on either side. "Then she hit me, and took out a knife. She hit him too."

Apparently he was a very cautious driver, as he was looking in his rearview mirror a lot.

"She stabbed you?"

She nodded. They were at a red light now, and he really looked at her for the first time since she'd gotten in. "Are you hurt?" he asked.

She pulled the paper towel off her right forearm and glanced at the wound for only a moment before her eyes refused the assignment and went to the window instead. Her stomach turned, and she closed her mouth.

He said what was probably a swear in English. She felt dizzy; the world vibrated at the edges of her vision. She wished she could lie down.

"Breathe through your mouth," he told her, "and try to slow your breaths. Just be calm."

He pulled off the main road and drove what seemed to her like a long circle through a neighborhood of multicolored row houses and young white men walking dogs. He looked in the rearview almost constantly. Then he pulled into a parking space. He turned off the lights but left the engine on as he reached past her and opened the glove box.

"What is that, his briefcase?"

"Yes."

"Did he see you take it?"

"I don't know. I don't think so."

He unzipped a small red pouch and removed some gauze and medical tape. She closed her eyes, tried to follow his instructions about breathing. As if it were so easy. She could still hear Sang Hee yelling, could still see Hana forlorn on the steps. Would both parents have to go to the hospital? Who would take care of the children? She doubted either of the parents had the faintest idea how.

She gasped as he rubbed something into her arm.

"I'm sorry," he said. "I need to clean it. I'd rather take you to a doctor, but I'm not sure if we can do that. Tell me again what happened."

"What?" She squirmed as he rubbed at the wound, but he held her tight.

"She just attacked you, and him? Where was he if you were doing the dishes?" He didn't believe her. He was staring into her eyes. He was hurting her on purpose.

"He was just sitting there! She's crazy! She's hit me before, and this time she decided to use a knife too! He got in the way, and then she started stabbing him! That's when I ran off."

He stopped cleaning the wound, if that's what he'd really been doing, and taped the gauze onto her arm, which throbbed. "Is he hurt as bad as you?"

"Worse, I think. She stabbed him a lot. In the arms and the chest."

He pressed her left hand against the dressing. "You need to apply pressure." Then he held four pills in front of her. "Open; it's for the pain." He placed them on her tongue. He held a water bottle to her, and she took a drink, some of it spilling down her neck.

"Do you have your cell phone with you?" he asked.

"No. I left it there."

"Where exactly?"

"Between my mattress and the box spring."

He didn't say anything for a moment, but the way he breathed told her he didn't like that answer. "How about the flash drives, the other things I gave you?"

She told him where she'd stashed them, in her bedroom closet, and when he asked if there was any new data on them she said no, they were blank. Then he put on a pair of leather gloves and pulled the briefcase onto his lap and opened it. There were some files inside, and a notebook, and he quickly flipped through them, not even skimming them but checking to see if anything else was inside. He leaned back and carefully placed the paperwork in the backseat. It seemed like he was moving too fast, like an old movie with the wrong-size reels, or maybe her perceptions were just slowing down. He checked the other pockets, removed some pens and clips and a flash drive. Then he pocketed the drive, rolled down his window, and dropped the other things outside.

"What are you doing?"

"Taking precautions."

She closed her eyes for a moment, willing the world to resume its normal speed, and when she opened them he was holding a small retractable knife. She shuddered at the sight and turned away, telling herself surely he wouldn't do anything to hurt her. She stared at the front door of an attractive row house, the door painted red and the bricks white, a grand chandelier visible through the foyer window. She heard tearing, and she turned back to see him eviscerating the briefcase. He checked between the layers of leather, looking for God knew what. It took him less than a minute to shred the case in every imaginable way. Then he turned on the lights, pulled out of the parking spot, and drove farther into the city.

At the next red light, he punched the top of his steering wheel, three times. The entire car shook. She was surprised the wheel wasn't dented. She closed her eyes and hoped he was finished.

"I'm very cold," she said after a while.

He hit a button and the sound of the air through the vents grew louder. "You're getting the chills. Your body's just reacting to what happened." Keeping one hand on the wheel, he reached behind him and handed her a blanket. "Here. Try not to get any blood on it or on the car."

"I'm sorry about the car."

"It's not the car I'm worried about. I just don't want to leave any evidence."

Evidence? Is that what was bleeding out of her? Is that what she had become?

He pulled suddenly into an alley behind some storefronts, stopping next to a dumpster. He rolled down his window and underhanded the torn briefcase, whose pieces fluttered like the pages of an open book, into the garbage, then drove on.

"Where are we going?"

"I need to get you someplace safe until I know what's going on. I would take you to the Indonesian embassy, but the Shims might go to the police and say you stole something from them and ran off, or worse. The embassy might not shield you if they think you attacked a diplomat."

"Why would the Shims say I did that?"

"Do they strike you as the type of people who will be honest?" His voice sounded calm, cold, professional. He'd acted this way before, and she was glad he was helping her, but she found herself wishing he were more like the vision of him she'd had when they'd first met, in the grocery store. Friendly, trustworthy.

She thought for a while. They were on a winding highway, cutting through a swath of forest that seemed misplaced in the city. She had no idea where she was.

"You're saying I should have just stayed. Let them do this to me again, so I could get whatever it is you want from them."

"No. I'm not saying that. I'm just saying that I don't have all the answers I wish I had, at least not yet." They weren't at a light, but he still managed to take his eyes off the road and look at her. "I'm going to get you out of this."

She believed him about as much as she believed that any of this was really happening to her, as much as she believed that she'd followed an evil couple to another country and had fallen into some incomprehensible trap. Nothing made any less sense than anything else.

His eyes were back on the road. "Are you going to be able to walk?"

"What?"

"I know you're tired and you're hurt, but if we're going to get you someplace safe, you're going to need to walk a little ways. And be seen in public without seeming injured. Do you think you can do that?"

She didn't answer. They reached another light and he leaned closer to her. "Come here," he said. She looked at him, confused, and he put his hands on her cheeks—cautiously and gently, but the last thing she wanted was someone touching her. She tried to pull back, but his hands were too strong. He was staring into her eyes like a doctor. Then he released her.

"You're going to be okay."

He was driving again when she mentioned she didn't have any shoes.

It seemed that enough events for several nights had already been crammed into one, but the night only got longer. He drove to a suburban strip mall, parked on the street, and told her to wait while he bought her some shoes. He told her to honk the horn three times if anyone approached the car. He was nothing if not prepared—in his glove box was a tape measure, and he used it to measure her foot. He was in the store less than five minutes before returning with a box of plastic-smelling blue-and-white Nikes, some socks, a black sweatshirt, a black baseball cap, synthetic track pants, and a matching zippered jacket. He pulled back onto the road immediately, dropped his wallet and some loose bills on the gearshift between them, and asked her to put the bills away for him so he could focus on driving. She did so, gingerly, with her injured hand, so the other one could keep applying pressure. As she folded the bills into his thick wallet— he had so much cash!—she thought of something. He was watching the road, and he didn't notice that she took a twenty and put it into her own pocket. Just in case.

Ten minutes later, they parked in the second level of a tiered garage.

He reached under his seat, and when his hand reappeared he was holding a gun. She'd never seen one in real life before, at least not this close. It was surprisingly shiny, like some giant precious object recently extracted from a riverbed. It looked heavy, yet he slipped it into his jacket quickly and smoothly. Then he nodded to her as if that hadn't just happened, as if he'd done something as natural as combing his hair.

"Change into those clothes," he told her. "I'll stand outside and block the window. Put your old clothes in the bag and give it to me when you get out."

She sat there after he closed his door. Change here, in public? She looked out her window and saw the seat of his jeans casually leaning into her door. He had wisely parked in the far corner. Still—maybe this was perfectly normal for Americans, but it wasn't anything she was in a habit of doing.

Sensing her lack of movement, he rapped at the window twice with his knuckles. "Come on. You have to do this, and hurry."

She finally obeyed, angrily. She remembered to move the twenty dollars from the old pants to the new ones. When she got out of the car she handed him the bag of old clothes; they started walking and he threw the bag into a garbage bin two blocks later.

They took the subway, her first experience with American public transit, the station's egg-carton ceiling high above them as they waited for the train. He kept his head down, almost staring at his feet, and told her to do the same. He also said to avoid eye contact with anyone. What faces she did allow herself to glimpse belonged to so many different races, she had to wonder about this city and this country, if it really was a place where all these different types of people could coexist peacefully. They rode the train for a while, a computerized voice telling them sweet nothings in English, and then Leo told her they were getting out.

They walked two blocks, past new apartment buildings, six stories tall, some of them displaying banner-size ads with large numbers and dollar signs. The sky glowed gray above the rooftops, and airplanes blinked in the blacker dome above. Leo reached up and hailed a taxi, not even telling her his steps in advance anymore, and they got in.

A short ride, maybe five minutes, and when they got out it seemed like they were on the same street of modern towers. Had he told the cabbie to drive in a circle, or was she just confused? He held her hand, asked if she was all right. He told her to walk faster.

Ten minutes later, as they carefully avoided puddles beneath a highway on-ramp, she began to wonder for the first time if what he meant by "a safe place" was perhaps a safe place in which to imprison her, or worse. Why was she running around with this man?

302

Just because he spoke Bahasa and was handsome? Just because he had pretended to be friends with her before asking her to spy on her employers?

She saw a figure in a sleeping bag lying against the concrete supports of the highway, the wind pressing plastic shopping bags and other garbage against him. Graffiti was sprayed on the underside of the road—she wondered if it was his name, something claiming this territory. She remembered what she told Leo in his car a few days ago, that every place was as terrible as every place else. She'd spat those words out, half hoping that the insulted world would do something to prove her wrong. She was still waiting.

They emerged from beneath the highway ramps and saw before them, cowering like a relic of an earlier time, a dingy motel. Two floors, all of the doors facing the outside. Soot from millions of automobiles caked the gray windows and once-white doors. The sign was neon, and though she couldn't read the English she recognized the blinking American flag beside it.

"Where are we?"

"Virginia. Just a few miles from where you worked."

It was wonderful to hear that in the past tense: She didn't work there anymore. She would never see them again. She hoped he was right.

"This place is safe?"

"It's not much to look at, but, yes, it is. No one will think to search for you here."

She waited by the entrance as he went in and paid for a room. Then he walked her upstairs, along the outer hallway that was serenaded by the sounds of cars rocketing by on the highways. She could still hear them after he'd closed the door.

The room smelled of mold and Chinese food. It felt as though someone else had been in it only a few minutes ago. Surely Leo wouldn't bring her to the sort of place that you paid for by the hour?

Cigarette burns measled the tan walls, and water damage paisleyed the ceiling. She saw some pills on the floor, scattered into the corners by a halfhearted sweeping. There was no phone, and the small TV was mysteriously unplugged. At least the bed was made.

Leo locked the door and turned the dead bolt. She faced him, more frightened than she'd been since she'd leaped into his car. He walked past her, businesslike still, to inspect the bathroom and closet. He even looked under the bed. Then he sat on it, letting his head fall into his hands, and exhaled deeply. Other than those three punches he'd thrown at his poor steering wheel, this was the only time she'd seen him act anything other than completely in control.

She found herself sitting beside him.

"Okay," he said after a little while. Around them was the constant sound track of car horns and velocity. "No one followed us, so no one knows you're here. I need to go to my office in the morning and find out what the Shims are saying, how badly he's hurt. Do a little research. Until then, you cannot leave this room, for any reason."

She was used to prisons. This one was a little smaller than the last, but at least there were no screaming kids.

Then he asked about the Shims. What they had been talking to each other about lately, if she'd noticed anything different. He was very interested in the fact that they'd been bickering, though she did not mention the approaches Hyun Ki had made to her. He asked if there had been any visitors, any change in Sang Hee's routine, and whether Sari had ever seen a tall man who looked perhaps part black and part Asian and part white, but she shook her head.

He told her there were towels and soap in the bathroom, and he opened his messenger bag and emptied it onto the bed. She saw what looked like candy bars and packages of nuts. "I know it's not a lot, but it will keep you going for a little while. I don't know how much time I'm going to need. I'll try to come back within two days—hopefully tomorrow, but I'm not sure. And you absolutely cannot call me. Someone will trace the call and figure out where you are." She realized he was awaiting a reply, so she nodded.

"How's your arm?"

It was throbbing worse than before, but she lied and said she would be fine.

"Let me look at it again." He rolled up her sleeve and took off the dressing. She sucked in her breath; the wound glistened red, but there was less blood on the gauze than she'd expected. "Good," he said. "It's better." She hadn't noticed him packing the first aid kit, but there it was; he applied a new bandage and handed her pills for later.

The alarm clock beside the bed claimed that more than three hours had passed since she'd left the diplomat's house.

"What's going to happen?" she dared to ask.

"I'm going to come up with a brilliant idea, and you're going to be fine." He said that as if he were reading a newspaper's synopsis of the plot of some outlandish new movie he was not terribly interested in seeing.

She asked him one of the questions that had been echoing in her mind for days. "What did you really do in Jakarta?"

He stood up and paced.

"I would like to know," she said, "that I can trust you. Was what you did there so terrible that you can't tell me?"

He stopped pacing. "It wasn't terrible."

"But it wasn't a bank."

"I went to Jakarta," he said slowly, as if trying to construct the sentence in his head before he lent it to his tongue, "to write. I helped write stories for a newspaper based out of Hong Kong. While I was there, it was also my job to . . . to make friends. To make friends with people who might know about certain activities in Indonesia. People who recruited angry and confused young men and tried to talk them into blowing up hotels and killing Western tourists and attacking my country. It was my job to watch people like that, and write about them, but not for the newspaper."

"And that's what you're doing here, with me? Making friends? So things won't blow up?"

"It's different."

"What happened to your 'friends' there?"

"They didn't get to blow anything up."

"But they would have if not for you?"

"Yes. Some of them. Maybe not all of them. But that was one of the lessons, that you have to watch who you become friends with."

"That's good advice."

They looked at each other. If he had been two paces closer to her, she would have felt that he was looming over her. As if mindful of this, he stayed where he was.

"I am trying to do the right thing," he said. "I have always tried to do the right thing. I could be living a very different life right now. I could be making money and raising my little family and telling myself I'm a great person for doing nothing." Yet he sounded like he regretted his choices.

Not that *she* had a choice. She had had one, once, and she'd made it, and that choice had led her here. To a motel room with a bed and a locked door and a man who seemed part chameleon.

"So, the people you work with, they can help me? You're a . . . a spy, and your group can help clear all of this up?"

"I don't work for them anymore."

This was as alarming as anything he'd said. "Why not?"

"They didn't think I was good at what I did. And I didn't think they were good at what they did."

She ran her fingers through her hair and pulled at it for a moment, stopping herself before the pain became too intense. "I'm tired of you talking in riddles."

He sat down beside her. She exhaled, brushed the hair out of her face.

"When I decided that people were doing wrong, people that I'd been following and reporting on, we took them," Leo said. His hands were folded in his lap and he was staring forward at the blank television. "Sometimes we had evidence and could give it to the local police; sometimes we didn't. So I had to be sure, sure that they were the right people to target. I didn't know what happened to them afterward, where they went. I didn't. Then a couple of years later, I found out. I'd heard stories but didn't believe them. Then I saw it for myself, and I didn't like it. It didn't feel...like something my country should be involved in. It made me feel even more pressure to get things right, to make sure I was targeting the right people. If I made a mistake, I would have to live with that forever. Live with knowing a person would be kidnapped, locked in a box somewhere in Thailand, and tortured, maybe for years. I would have to live with that. So it got much, much harder to know when I was sure I was targeting the right people."

He spoke slowly and almost tonelessly, as if he had rehearsed this in his mind but never said it out loud. And certainly not in her language.

"It went on like that for months, and I wasn't sleeping very well. There were other things bothering me too, but..." He didn't continue with that. "There was this one man; not really a man, I think he was seventeen. Funny, smart, the kind of guy who could make everyone his friend. But there was another side of him, and he was talking to the wrong people, and I told my bosses to target him. That's how it worked: I sent a note with someone's name on it to a person I barely knew, and I'd never hear anything else. That way no one person had to be too involved. But after I had this kid targeted, I learned some more things about him that made me reconsider. I kept thinking of him in that box. Just a kid, the wrong kid, and I'd ruined his life. Or worse.

"Now I couldn't sleep. I drank a lot. Finally I found a way to tell my bosses that I'd made a mistake, that it was the wrong kid. I tried to explain my case, show them more evidence. I begged and pleaded for them to let him go. I threatened to quit if they didn't.

"So they let him go. Back to Jakarta, to his family. I wanted to visit him, see how he was doing, but that would have been a mistake. He would have put two and two together. And I didn't want to see what had become of him, what my mistake had done, what had happened to him while he was in that prison for five weeks. But at least, at the very least, I could look at myself in the mirror and know that

I had undone my mistake. That I'd managed to wring some good out of the bad."

He sighed deeply, as if he'd just dropped a weight.

"Three weeks later he blew himself up at a hotel in Bali."

Leo looked at Sari and went on. "So, the questions. Had I been wrong to tell them to release him and right to have him targeted initially? Because he really was bad all along? And I'd set free a man who would kill forty people and maim dozens more? Or had he been a good person before, until my people got their hands on him and turned him against us because of my mistake?"

He was staring at her so intently that she felt he needed an answer. "I don't know," she said.

"Neither do I." Then he smiled, and it was frightening to her. "And I never will."

He looked away and exhaled deeply a few more times, and she realized he was trying not to cry. That explained the scary smile, all the jumbled emotions coming out wrong.

"I'm sorry that happened," she said.

"I'm not even sure if I should be sorry. Maybe it all happened for a reason. Maybe it was necessary for me to make a mistake like that so they could weed me out. So they could clear away people like me and make room for men who really know how to do that job." He shook his head. "You wanted to know if my old employer can help you, and that's why the answer is no. But you can trust *me*. And you can trust that I do know enough, that I can do enough, to get you out of this."

"I trust you." Thinking, *Do I? Or do I just want him to stop talking?*

He looked at her. Then his hand was on her cheek again. It felt less clinical this time when he looked into her eyes. Her leg was pressing against him. She had thought before of being alone with him, but not like this. There were too many other things in her head now.

"You're very brave," he told her. It was about the last thing she'd expected him to say. She had just been thinking of how scared she was, too scared even to move his hand away. Too scared even to look at him, so she closed her eyes.

Misinterpreting, he leaned forward, and suddenly his lips were on hers. All she could think about was waking up in the bedroom those three hours ago.

He stopped when he noticed she wasn't responding.

"I'm very tired," she managed to say.

He stood and told her not to answer the door unless she heard a series of three hard knocks followed by two quick ones. He demonstrated his code on the tiny table that the unplugged TV rested on.

"Lock the door after me," he said, then walked out and left her to her new prison.

24.

Tasha sat at her kitchen table the next morning, her hands cupped around a warm mug of coffee. The wonderful sound of a shower running, the knowledge that a gorgeous man was in there. She did have a bit of a headache, further proof (not that she needed any) that she'd drunk too much. Still, no part of the previous day was regrettable. Her colleagues would no doubt be suspicious about yesterday's early exit, but she'd make up for it. Lord knew she felt energized.

She was staring off into space when she glimpsed, in the corner of the room, Troy's briefcase. He always carried it with him, which was one of the stranger things about him. Who carried a briefcase anymore? Troy was a throwback to an earlier time—no shoulder bag or man-purse for him. She found that traditionalism endearing, even though she figured that if she mentioned it, he might take it as an insult. He had this strange innocence to him, a lack of awareness that so many of his mannerisms were slightly off. Maybe it came from having an immigrant mother, or maybe it was his scientific background—he really was a nerd, if a six-two nerd cut like a cornerback. And, damn, his clothes—she'd started to wonder how many outfits he had here in D.C., if he was one of those traveling businessmen who simply alternated between two shirts and two pairs of slacks. Still, if that was the worst of his faults, she'd found a keeper. His fashion sense she could always work on.

She looked at the briefcase again.

She knew it would be wrong to go through his things, but a girl could never be too careful these days. You were allowed to look through a guy's medicine cabinet, so you should be able to look through his briefcase—it was permissible under the single girl's rules of self-defense.

To her surprise, the inside of the briefcase was quite unlike the orderly Mr. Jones. Pages everywhere, some upside down, some horizontal, some even torn. Indecipherable scribbles in the margins, black ink blotting out entire lines. File folders had been bent in half and crammed in. For a moment she wondered if he'd picked up the wrong briefcase at a meeting—surely this couldn't be Troy's. Also inside was one of the smallest laptops she'd ever seen, barely an inch thick, and three flash drives.

She picked up a random sheet of paper, read it, and started to feel dizzy.

She was standing by the front window, after pacing in the living room, when he finally descended the stairs. He took a while to get going in the morning, which was good, as it had allowed her time to move from shock to confusion to hurt to rage. And here he was, in yesterday's clothes and jacket, but looking so good she wanted to slap him. The living room was cluttered, her shoes everywhere, magazines on the floor, the wastebasket full of mashed Kleenex. She was a terrible housekeeper. And a terrible judge of people, apparently.

"Health statistics, huh?"

He looked at her blankly. Then he noticed the briefcase in her arms. She underhanded it; one of its corners hit him hard in the chest as he managed an awkward catch.

"That was very enlightening reading. Normally I'd apologize for going through someone else's things, but it looks like you of all people would understand."

Still he was silent, shifting the briefcase to one hand. She took a few steps toward him but went no farther, kept her distance.

"Who *are* you, Troy?"

"I'm not that person, Tasha."

"Don't even say my name. Jesus, you conned me pretty good.

What, was I a test subject for what you assholes can do? You pretty proud of yourself?"

"I'm not proud at all."

She was so angry she almost didn't notice his expression—he looked not just stunned but disappointed, like he was as hurt as she was. She'd assumed he would have ten lies ready to deploy in case of emergency. "So, what, you guys spy on political activists? A little domestic surveillance to make sure people stay in line? Is Leo your boss, or are you his?"

He shook his head. "I'm not a part of that."

"The hell you aren't—I read the files, Troy!" Document after document about surveillance, how to watch people, how to filter through their e-mail and Web browsing, listen in on their cell phone calls, decode their texts. T.J. had been right all along. "You photocopy my diary while I was sleeping? What, you decided to take it to the next level by getting me in bed?"

"That briefcase isn't me, Tasha. You have to believe that."

"Oh, you saw the light when you were fucking me, that's your story? What about the health-care-consultant bit, you remember that one? You getting confused from all the different lies you've been telling?"

"I think everyone's confused right now." His calmness only made her want to hit him more. This was so cerebral to them, so analytical. They didn't understand how *personal* this was, and that's how they were able to play games like this, manipulate people. She had thought he was one of the few who understood this when in fact he was the opposite. "I know this is a difficult time for you," he said, "but you need to understand that—"

"Stop it! You can stop acting now, *Troy,* or whoever you are. Jesus Christ, that story about your wife and kid wasn't even true, was it? Just part of your con?"

"I wish it weren't true."

"And your brother?"

He didn't answer.

312

"I cannot believe this. I can't believe anyone would be so low." Her voice broke, goddamn it. Her anger had initially overpowered the hurt, but the hurt always won eventually. "You are fucking scum. Get out of my house."

He watched her for a final moment, and the look in his eyes again was so unexpected, a look of sadness, of empathy even, as if he wanted to come forward and wipe the tears from her eyes, as if he had that right. He didn't seem capable of acknowledging the fact that his game was over. She hardened her face, willed the hurt away, made herself a wall.

Finally he walked past her, toward the door. She looked out the window.

"You shouldn't tell anyone what you saw in here," he said from behind her.

She spun around. "Don't you *dare* tell me what to do!"

"Tasha. For your own good: Don't tell anyone about this. Don't tell anyone about me." That could have sounded like a threat, but he said it differently. Sadly. Like he was trying to explain the concept of death to a child with a sick parent.

"I wish I could tell you why," he said, "but..."

Without further explanation, he opened the door. She let him go, just stood there at the window and watched Troy Jones walk south until the diagonal line of row houses on Potomac stole him from view.

A good while later, after she had taken some time to compose herself, she called Leo. He'd given her his number, telling her she should call only in an emergency. She reached a generic voice-mail box, and a computer recited the number she'd reached and advised her to leave a message. Did she ever.

He called back in less than five minutes. The caller ID was blank, just like the time she'd received a ring from the suspicious voice that had roped her into this.

"You have some goddamn nerve," she said as soon as she picked it up.

313

"What's wrong?"

"We're through, Leo, or whoever you really are. *You* blew our deal. If you ever call me again, I'm going media crazy with this story. I'm calling every reporter on the East Coast with the scoop of a lifetime about domestic surveillance and—"

"What are you talking about? Calm down. What happened?"

"Your little lover boy blew his assignment. He got a little sloppy with his briefcase. I don't like what I've been doing for you, but I thought that at least we had an understanding. I didn't think you'd have a partner following me. And I didn't think your observations would extend to the bedroom, you sick fuck."

Silence for a few beats. "I don't have a partner in this. And I don't know what you mean by a lover boy. I know this kind of work can make a person a little overly on guard, but—"

"You people are unbelievable. I read his files, Leo! I know what you're doing, who you really work for."

He exhaled. "Maybe I'm the one who's confused. Tell me who you're talking about. Please."

"Troy Jones."

"I don't know a Troy Jones. He said he works with me?"

"Of course not. But he fell into my life right around when you did, and now I find that he's in the same line of work."

"Describe him for me."

She did, though a lot less flatteringly than she might have a few hours earlier. Leo was quiet for so long she thought he'd hung up. "Leo?"

"I think I know who you mean."

"What a shock."

"He and I do not work together."

"You know what? I don't really care. Whether he's your partner or your rival or some other spy from another agency or country or company, I do not fucking care. I am tired of being played by boys who think that treating people like pawns makes them kings. No, Leo, it makes you a fucking child playing with toys. Go unleash your imagination on someone else, because we're through. You even think of using what you had on me, I will visit it back on you tenfold, I promise you that."

"Do you still have his briefcase?"

"I gave it back to him. I don't want that kind of poison on my hands."

"What did you see in the files? What made you think this guy works with me?"

"He told me he worked in health care and instead he has a briefcase full of memos about spy technology and telecom contracts and computer codes. And detailed bios of journalists and activists, including *myself*—scary shit, thank you very much. I might not have understood it all, but I'm bright enough."

"Did it have the name of his company? A letterhead or anything?"

He really didn't seem to know Troy after all. But he was awfully interested.

"Enhanced Awareness. Somewhere in Maryland."

"You have his phone number?"

She gave it to him, pausing a few seconds for him to write it down before adding, right before hanging up, "Oh, and Leo? Get a real job."

25.

Leo's cell phone had woken him at seven. He'd left the device in his apartment the previous night so it couldn't be used to track his movements with Sari. As he reached across the bed for it, his first thought was that it was her calling, that she was disobeying his instructions already. But it wasn't her—it was his boss.

He took a sip of water before answering, said his name three times to clear out his throat. "Good morning," he said into the phone, hoping he didn't sound as if he'd just woken up.

"We need to talk, at the office, immediately."

"Sure. What about?"

"Your little side project."

"I don't have a side project." Not in a smart-ass tone but flatly stated. *You told me it was over last night, so it is. Sir.*

"Just come to the office, immediately."

He showered quickly, wishing he could draw it out so he could think more. But he'd thought plenty last night and hadn't had any epiphanies then either.

Who the hell were Sang Hee and Hyun Ki? That's what it kept coming back to. His agent had successfully loaded a couple of flash drives from each of their home computers, and the information had turned up nothing (if Leo believed what Bale had told him). Then why had Leo twice been warned away from them by people who refused to identify themselves? People who acted like intelligence officers and dropped just enough signifiers to imply this, but who backed away from anything concrete. Why were they so worried about Leo tailing the couple?

He'd barely slept. He put some drops in his red eyes to disguise the fact that he'd been running all over the D.C. metro area last night with a fugitive. He took some coffee in a travel mug and zipped along on his reverse commute to the antiseptic Virginia suburbs. Targeted Executive Solutions' office was barely a mile from the hideous motel at which he had stashed Sari. The motel was also fewer than twenty blocks from the Pentagon, and a short drive from the Agency. Chances were, countless case officers and even military personnel used the motel to stash a variety of agents, witnesses, felons, spies, and prisoners. It had seemed like a good place at the time—he'd needed something fast, something without cameras or credit card scanners, something he could walk the last few blocks to so that no taxi driver would recall bringing him there—but now he was worried. For all he knew, she'd been picked up already.

The offices were as abandoned as always when he walked in. He proceeded straight to his boss's door, knocked, and was told to come the hell in already.

"Anything you'd like to tell me?" Bale asked when Leo sat in the uncomfortable chair.

Life at the Agency had given Leo an aversion to open-ended questions. "I'm sorry?"

Bale watched him an extra second. It occurred to Leo that he knew precious little about his boss. Bale acted as if he had Agency experience, but did he really? And if so, what exactly had he done? Analysis, fieldwork, administration? What parts of the world had he worked in, and for how long? Who else worked here?

"Your little agent snapped," Bale said. "She attacked Hyun Ki and his wife with a knife last night, sending them both to the hospital. The wife has lacerations on her hands and a few bruises, but he has numerous stab wounds in his chest and back, as well as defensive wounds all up his arms. He called 911 at nine twenty-seven, they were taken to Sibley's ER, and he was in surgery for two hours. He'll live, but he isn't saying anything now. The wife was stitched up and immediately picked up by staff from their embassy. What little info we're getting from them is that their maid grabbed a steak knife and went samurai."

Leo decided not to tell Bale he was mixing up his Asian cultures.

"I was afraid this might happen." Leo tried to appear analytical and calm. "She seemed meek enough to me, but they were pushing her awfully hard."

"Where is she?"

Leo looked confused, then surprised. He tried to remember every nonverbal tip-off that showed someone was lying so he could avoid all of them. "Wait, you mean she wasn't arrested?"

"*Where is she,* Leo?"

"I never contacted her again after your call. Jesus, this was probably happening at the same moment you and I were on the phone."

He knew that someone eventually would find the cell phone stashed in her bed and see his number in it—D.C. police, or maybe the CIA; hopefully not the South Korean embassy or some other spy group, but all were possibilities. And there was a strong chance that someone on the American side would look at Leo's phone records and see the surprising fact that just minutes after Hyun Ki called 911, Leo received a call from his neighborhood Latino grocer. He supposed he could claim the call was to tell him that the empanadas he'd ordered were ready to be picked up, but someone would no doubt interview the Latin American staff, who, after being threatened with deportation or health-code violations, would be happy to talk about the frantic, wounded young Asian woman who'd used their phone that night.

He had very little time. Waiting until morning like this to see what tack the diplomat and Sang Hee would take had been a mistake.

"Where do you think she would go?" Bale asked. Leo couldn't tell if his boss believed what he'd said so far.

"The only place she ever went was Whole Foods, as far as I know. She doesn't know anyone in the country and only speaks Bahasa and some Korean." He shrugged. "How hard could it be to find her?"

"If the cops or someone else finds her, is there anything that connects her to us? Does she know your real name?"

"Yes." When he saw Bale's expression, he said, "Look, when I met her she was just a pretty girl in a grocery store. I didn't realize she was going to turn into an asset. When harmless strangers ask me my name, I tell them."

"One of your many mistakes. Look, I don't need to tell you that if the Koreans piece together the fact that you were spying on their diplomat, you are in serious trouble. We had no authority to do anything, and my friends at State will suddenly forget they ever knew me. My company will be eviscerated. I will not allow that to happen. You need to find this girl, immediately, and silence her."

Leo crossed his legs. He hated how easily he showed physical signs of discomfort, but he hadn't been expecting Bale's implication. "That's very far above my pay grade."

"Are you *listening* to me? You could go to jail; I could go to jail. I'm not going to let a fuck-up by a new hire who can't even successfully tail a bunch of peace activists ruin *my* career too."

Leo was very still. Then he asked, "What are your other operations and relationships, if you don't mind my asking?"

"I do mind." Bale stared him down for a moment. "It goes without saying, Leo, that you'll be fired when this is over. But if you want to have any chance of doing even remotely similar work ever again, you will get this taken care of. Immediately."

It wasn't difficult for Leo to figure out he was being followed. He'd noticed the silver Jetta behind him on the Rock Creek Parkway that morning on the way to work, and again ten minutes later as he navigated the tangled highways of Northern Virginia. And there it was again when he drove back into the city a couple of hours after his meeting with Bale.

The Jetta followed him into the city, finally fading when it became clear that Leo was driving back to his apartment. Which he was until he got the voice mail from a raving Tasha. He pulled into a space on 16th, called her back. She knew the guy, the strange guy with the gun. Had slept with him, apparently. Jesus Christ. Leo tried to calm her down as he worked through what she was telling him. Troy Jones. Enhanced Awareness.

Where had he heard of Enhanced Awareness before? He opened his shoulder bag, removed the files he'd taken from Hyun Ki's briefcase. He had skimmed the contents the previous night before collapsing into bed. Mixed in with a number of diplomatic cables and forms that were very illegal for him to possess but nonetheless seemed uninteresting was a memo addressed to Hyun Ki from a James Harrows, director of business development at Enhanced Awareness LLC, based in Laurel. Leo reread it: Harrows was following up on a meeting they'd recently had and was excited about demonstrating some of his company's new products. Leo wasn't sure if the vague business-speak was hiding some code or if it really was that boring. No mention was made of the government of South Korea; no proper names at all were given. Harrows looked forward to hearing from Mr. Shim and further discussing how his company could meet his and his colleagues' needs.

Finally a connection, though Leo still didn't understand it. Troy Jones worked for a company that was trying to do business with Shim, and therefore with the government of South Korea. At least, it looked that way. It was very possible that Enhanced Awareness was just a front, that Jones and this Harrows person worked for some government agency (which agency, and which government?) that was trying to ensnare Shim in something. But if they were trying to recruit him as an agent to spy on South Korea, they wouldn't put anything in writing.

Leo pulled back onto the road and headed east, trying to make sense of this. The Jetta reappeared somewhere around Foggy Bottom. Two men were inside, both of them white, but he couldn't see much else. No hats or striking hairdos.

They were two cars back as he drove down the M Street corridor of clothing chain stores and tourist restaurants. Then he wound his way through Georgetown's brick row houses, so tiny and tidy they seemed like stratospherically expensive dollhouses for particularly powerful dolls. He found street parking, tried not to look over his shoulder for the Jetta again. Carrying his shoulder bag, he jogged up the tall stone steps to the library at Georgetown University.

This is what he'd been reduced to: doing intelligence research at a college library. He knew he had better resources at the office, but he didn't trust Bale anymore. Any Web site he visited or call he made would be monitored, and he still wasn't sure why or by whom. When he'd returned to America he'd bought himself a guest card for the Georgetown library for emergencies like this. He found an unoccupied computer and surfed the Web, then checked Nexis for articles on Troy Jones and his employer.

The annoyingly common name led to numerous stories on professional and college athletes, drug dealers, a city councilman in Seattle, and an author of sexually explicit novels for black ladies. Nothing on a Troy Jones who might have been involved in intelligence work. Leo had expected that result, but he'd still needed to check.

Enhanced Awareness did not have a Web site. He did find a few newspaper articles mentioning the company; it was described as an intelligence contractor in a long and amorphous story about the recent privatization of government work. Then Leo noticed a byline; one of the stories had been written by Karthik Chaudhry. The young journalist who'd gone missing a few days ago.

He detoured his search, looked up more information on Chaudhry.

He was confident that his shadows were not in the library—everyone there looked like either a typical wildly privileged college student or a harried professor. He asked one of the librarians, a cute brunette born when Leo was a college student, if there was a pay phone, and she pointed him to the third floor. Once at the phone, he dialed the number on the otherwise blank card that the men in the SUV had given him yesterday.

"Yes?"

Leo recognized the voice.

"Hello," he said, raising his voice an octave, "I'm trying to reach James Harrows."

"To whom am I speaking?"

"I represent a client interested in doing business with Enhanced Awareness."

"I don't really handle sales, but if you'd like to talk to—"

Leo hung up, having gotten the confirmation he was looking for. The men in that car weren't with the Agency after all but with Enhanced Awareness, meaning they were Troy Jones's colleagues. Or maybe ex-colleagues. Unless, again, the company was a front for the Agency.

Outside, crossing the quad, he couldn't see his tails, though he knew they were out there. Using his cell this time, he called Gail. Her voice was decidedly neutral. Yes, she was still in D.C. He asked if she could do him a favor, quickly.

"Not if it's the kind of favor I think you mean."

"I just need you to look up information on a company, and one of its employees." He assured her he wasn't trying to use her to get classified information (though he was hoping that that might happen). He just needed the basics, and he wasn't in a position to find them. Could they get a drink tonight to discuss it?

Gail didn't sound enthusiastic, but she didn't say no.

Leo walked down to M Street and into a sporting goods store, bought some gym socks and running shoes that he didn't bother trying on. The salesperson, a young guy with a thick Indian accent, seemed personally insulted about this, insisting that Leo try them on first to make sure they fit well, but Leo said he was in a rush. Finally the clerk took his cash—which he viewed warily, as if a customer who didn't use plastic for an eighty-three-dollar purchase merited suspicion—and rang him up.

Three doors down, Leo bought a new wardrobe at a Gap. Jeans, a long-sleeved waffle shirt, a lightweight nylon jacket, boxers, socks,

and a blue baseball cap with a capital G. The shadow had not followed him into the last store, and Leo didn't think he was being
watched here either—they were most likely outside—but still, he
couldn't risk being seen buying clothes for Sari. She no doubt could
use new underwear, but she'd have to put up with that a while longer.

He paid cash (for a nearly two-hundred-dollar purchase, again
earning a surprised look from a clerk) and took the overlarge bag from
the young lady at the register. As he walked he carefully kept the bag
from brushing against his body.

Across the street was one of the locations of the Washington
Sports Club. It was the kind of overly sleek place that made him
feel uncool for not scoring dates at the elliptical machine—dozens
of flat-screen monitors pleaded for attention, house music played so
loud that bringing one's own iPod was redundant, and the staff at the
front desk were as stylish as the hostesses at the restaurants lining the
street. He waved his membership card and headed to the locker room.

He wasn't sure if any of his clothes or possessions were bugged,
but now seemed an appropriate time for extreme countermeasures. In
the empty locker room, he carefully stripped naked and placed all of
his clothes in his messenger bag. Then he put on his new, bug-free
wardrobe. He smelled like a shopping mall. The shoes were a little
too springy, but they fit—he'd asked for a half a size too big, just to
guard against getting a blister, as a limp would have been noticeable.

He placed his wallet and his cell phone, turned off, into the locker
and spun the lock's dial.

The locker room was at the end of a long hallway in the back of
the club. Across the hall was a fire exit, which he opened, guessing it
wouldn't trigger the alarm that its large sign warned people it would.
He was right. Then he was outside, in an alley. He jogged to the end,
then walked naturally through a parking lot and down to K Street,
which in this part of town ran in the shadows beneath the Whitehurst
Freeway. No one was watching him. He flagged down a taxi and took
a ride across the river.

* * *

After quick stops to buy the cheapest digital camera he could find—nearly depleting his supply of cash—and some groceries, he walked twenty minutes to the USA Motel. He gave his coded knock, holding his breath.

"Yes?" she asked in Bahasa.

"It's me. Open, quick."

The latches turned and she let him in. He closed the door behind him swiftly, even though he was confident no one had tailed him since he'd shed his outer skin.

They were alone in a motel room. He hated himself for thinking it, but she looked great. She had showered recently, and her hair was pulled back more tightly than before. The room felt warm to him, but she wore her track coat on top of the rest of the outfit he'd bought her last night. They both looked so ridiculously sporty in their new duds, a yuppie couple ready for their morning jog along the Potomac before they headed out for brunch or maybe just read the *Post* all afternoon.

Speaking of which, he wished he had something she could read or entertain herself with, but he didn't have any books in a language she'd understand, and it wasn't worth scouring the city for anything. The boredom and stress must be driving her crazy.

He had been exhausted and crashing from his adrenaline high when he'd kissed her the night before. At least, it was easy to blame it on those things. After what she'd just been through, romance obviously had been far from her mind. Why didn't his mind work that way too? He wasn't sure if this was a male/female difference, an East/West thing, a spy/agent power discrepancy, or something else.

"Are you all right?" he asked.

"I'm fine." Standing rather far away from him, as if the room weren't big enough for both.

"How's your arm?"

"Okay. I put a new bandage on. Did you bring anything to eat that isn't a candy bar?"

He laughed at that—he'd brought energy and sports bars the night before, but of course they were basically the same as Snickers to someone who hadn't been tricked by the marketing campaigns. So he handed her the grocery bag, and her eyes lit up at the pile of fruit. She started peeling an orange immediately; the citrus tang hit his nose through the motel funk.

"Are people looking for me?"

"I think so. I had to be very careful getting here." He took the camera out of its package. The salesclerk had promised it didn't need to be hooked up to a computer first and would work immediately. "I need to take your picture. For a driver's license—an ID card."

She thought about this for a moment while she ate. She was just dropping the peels on the floor, as if her weeks as a slave maid had made her swear off basic cleanliness from then on. "You don't have friends in Immigration, do you?"

"I'm going to get you out of here. I can get you to a safe place, where—"

"Safe like *this?*" She gestured to the room.

"No, something better. I can get you to a place in America where other Indonesians live, where you can find people who speak your language and can help you get by. Tell you where to work, where to get an apartment, that sort of thing. And I can get you some money to start out. But you'll need an ID."

When he saw that the walls were painted tan—he'd forgotten about that—he checked the bathroom; they were white. She stood beside the toilet and he leaned against the opposite wall, trying to fit her in the frame.

"Don't smile for it," he told her. "No one ever does."

She hardly needed to be told that.

Back in the main room, he told her his plan—at least, the part of it he had figured out thus far. When he got to the fact that they would never see each other again, she barely blinked. He felt a shiver in the bottom of his gut, a physical sadness. Maybe she was only trying to appear strong, not reacting because of the professional, matter-of-fact way in which he explained everything. He wasn't sure if she was a great agent or just terribly unromantic.

He found himself remembering that ridiculous date he'd described for her the other night, wishing it could come true. He was keeping careful track of how long he'd been gone from the gym, knowing a point would come when the shadow outside would start wondering how the hell long a workout Leo could endure. He'd hurried over here, had checked for shadows, but hadn't taken quite as circuitous a route as he should have, half hoping he could buy himself time to make more traditional use of this motel room. He was an idiot, led by things he should be suppressing.

She had flirted with him before, though, hadn't she? She had used her beauty to draw him to her. She didn't need to, of course—she was valuable for other reasons, but she hadn't known this. Now, though, when sex was at least plausible, she was acting more distant. He wondered if it was shock from the Shims attacking her or if it was from some of the things he'd said last night. Perhaps she'd seen him as some heroic American figure, calm and in charge, until his admission that he didn't have a ready escape plan—and his confession of his mistakes in Jakarta—had dispelled the illusion.

That was the other thing he'd always loved about the job, he realized. The ability to portray himself as better than he truly was. Now, sadly, he was just himself.

Her arms were folded, the injured one on top. She wasn't looking him in the eye any more than necessary. Maybe that kiss in Rock Creek Park had been offered only as a bribe, a plea for help, and she didn't feel like begging anymore. Maybe she'd been using him as much as he'd been using her.

"Are you all right?" he asked.

"You just . . . told me my future. I'm still taking it in."

It wasn't a very good future, was what she meant. He tried to reassure her, explained that what he was giving her was possibility. That anything could happen for her in the future. What he didn't say was that this was the best he could do, given the fact that she was wanted for attempted murder, and possibly espionage, by at least two countries.

"Just...think it over," he said. "It will sound better. Everything's going to be fine, really."

She nodded, but her eyes didn't seem to agree. Those eyes, and his watch, told him it was time to leave.

Z.

The dense trees along both sides of the Baltimore-Washington Parkway have lost enough of their leaves to reveal the houses and apartment buildings behind them, like a badly covered secret coming to light. People everywhere, even when you think you're free of them.

Now I understand why Wills's and my own intel deviated about Tasha. She wasn't historically important originally, but my own actions changed that. I selfishly got involved with her, and now that she's perused my files and come to the conclusion that I'm some government spy following her around, her anger at the world will only grow hotter. I've inadvertently pushed her deeper into T.J.'s ring of believers, and that's why she'll be with him at the final Event.

I could rationalize that this doesn't matter; according to my records, she was going to die not long from now anyway. All I've cost her is a bit of time. But even that much is unforgivable; what have I deprived her of? What joys might she have had, what discoveries and successes? When I spent time with her, I liked to think I was doing it partly for her, that I was easing away some of her pain in this difficult time, but really it was all for myself. More than anyone, I should realize how motives can become so confused, how actors can fail to know themselves. I've darkened her life, and shortened it.

I decide I need to do something that truly is for her. I tap into my databases and look for information on her brother, something she might not have been told by the unhelpful people in the army. It takes a while, but the records they loaded into me are extensive.

I do the research while hiding in yet another motel. The day passes in a blur as I sit impassively, gazing inward. I find a few things that might interest her—it's probably not what she's looking for, but it's what the record states. Which is a form of truth, isn't it? Or at least it's something that someone thought was true. More important, it's in Marshall's own words, which I know she'll appreciate. I'll need to go to an office somewhere and find a way to print out the files so she can read them—I can scan them into the ancient laptop they've given me, hook it up to a printer later. If I can get it to her apartment soon, she might read it before the final Event. At the very least, she'll know the truth about Marshall when she dies. At most—and I allow myself to hope this, even if it violates the Department's core principles—maybe it will keep her away from the Event. Maybe I can undo the historical changes I accidentally made, can return her to her original path and buy her back those few moments.

All this research gives me another idea.

Tasha was so enraged by what she thought she learned about Troy Jones. I decide that *I* need to find more information on who he really was and what he did. He keeps tripping me up, after all—those two strangers who seemed to recognize me as Troy still bother me.

I run checks through my databases, and at first I get nothing but error messages. The databases don't seem to understand the concept of my researching my own cover. Or maybe I'm only allowed to know what the Department already told me about him.

I—Troy Jones—am a defense contractor, I was told, so although I live in Philadelphia I have occasion to do business in Washington, which explains my presence here. Jones's firm is located outside Washington, which means there are colleagues of the real Troy Jones not far away. And as I've learned, the real Troy once lived here too.

The Department's surgical alterations to my appearance are supposed to create a strong likeness but not a perfect replica. The two people who called me Troy were both white, and I was briefed that the contemp white people weren't very good at discerning differences among darker-skinned individuals whom they didn't know well. For the sake of my sanity I'll assume that I don't look *too* much like the real Troy Jones, that the white people were just confused and made a mistake. But what are the odds?

I hit the files again, trying harder to uncover hidden documents, hacking into my own databases. The Department was trying to keep something from me, but they didn't count on my determination. And there, buried in the data on the many contemps who perish in the initial bombs, I find a misplaced file on Troy Jones.

He's dead. Well, of course he's dead; everyone's dead from a certain historical perspective. According to these records, though, as of today's date he was still only "missing." He would not be declared dead for a few more days.

Again, this is fairly standard as covers go. And all of the other information I turn up jibes with what the Department gave me in my briefings. His father was an "African American" who fought in Vietnam, his mother was a Vietnamese immigrant. Troy himself didn't serve in the army, but he had a successful career with an intelligence agency before going into related work for private industry. He, like me, had a wife and daughter once.

When talking to Tasha and mentioning my own wife and daughter, I was able to conflate my identity with Troy's. That's part of the job, an inevitability that makes it easier to play the role. You hold on to pieces of yourself, bring them into your new character. But I need to guard against the identities becoming too mixed, need to make sure it's not myself I'm confusing.

And then I find the first discrepancy: According to a file from the State of Maryland, Jones owned a house in the city of Laurel, fewer than twenty miles from D.C. He even made a mortgage payment a couple of weeks ago. Then why did the Department tell me he lived in Philadelphia? And why would they give me the cover of someone who lives so close to the area I'm patrolling?

There's only one way to solve the puzzle. I need to find the real Troy Jones.

* * *

330

After printing and mailing some records for Tasha from a pay-as-you-go office, I drive to Laurel. The rental car has its own GPS; this time I decide to use it instead of the one the Department implanted in me. I've learned not to trust what's in here. The bruise on the side of my skull is still sore. Maybe when it's faded I'll be able to think more clearly, but when *was* the last time I thought clearly?

I follow the small LCD screen's directions, the mechanized voice telling me when to exit and when to turn left. I pass through the commercial core of the suburb, the Home Depots and Walmarts, like the looming castles of feudal lords protected by their large lots and flanked by their usual cronies, the fast-food joints selling microwaved meat. Places like this are mostly vacant in my time, as everyone has crowded close to the urban centers. This road is choked with evening rush-hour traffic, cars and SUVs and shipping trucks inching along, brake lights crimsoning the scene. I pass some subdivisions, the buildings narrow and jammed together, as if by imitating urban row houses they can trick prospective home-owners into believing that this is a vibrant community. Then the voice tells me to turn right.

I ease off the accelerator and glide into what seems a conventional neighborhood. The houses two-story and unattached, the yards well tended, some of them strewn with children's playthings. Cars rest in driveways or inside garages whose open doors gape as I pass.

"Destination reached."

But there's no house. I pull over and look at the other side of the street, see the yellow police tape sagging in the autumn breeze like party decorations left in place too long. The tape stretches across almost the entire property. A half a dozen stone steps end at noth-ingness, as if they lead to a portal to another world. Beneath them is a pile of rubble, all of it blacker than the night sky above me, a total erasure. Beams poke out here and there, an old fireplace stands mostly intact at the rear, but everything else is ash and soot. A neighbor's white house, twenty yards away, has char stains from the blaze.

I sit in the Neon and watch the ruins for a while, as if I'm expecting some being to take shape out of the shards and fragments. As if, if I stare hard enough, I could look into the building's past, see how the fire started and why, and then see what happened in the preceding nights and days, the many events leading up to this disaster.

The road is curved, and a passing car casts its headlights on the rubble. I think I see a poster a little girl might have hung in her room, but I'm sure I'm only imagining things. Seeing things from my own past. My own emptied apartment. I haven't been inside it in what feels like years—my new home is the Department, and whatever beat they send me to. But no matter how hard the men in Security tried, carting out those images and gifts and old letters, there is no way to truly erase a past. I still carry it with me.

Where are you, Troy Jones? If you're not here in your home, if they didn't find your remains in the smoldering heap, then what became of you? And why are you haunting me?

I find myself getting out of the car and crossing the street. I stand on the sidewalk and I can still smell something, if not smoke then the relic of it, the lingering decay of ruins. How many days ago did this happen? The Department didn't load that file into me, or at least I can't find it.

"Are you okay?"

It's a tiny voice that I hear but don't acknowledge. I'm still staring at what used to be a house, imagining what happened here, and how it relates to me and what I'm doing. Whether a central plot ties this all together or if it's all just loose strings, and this really is the purgatory Wills fears it is, and I have no real job to do, and none of my actions will ever have an effect on anything.

"Mr. Jones, are you okay?"

He's a little white boy, maybe five or six years old. Looking at me with an empathy beyond his years, like he too has suffered and he knows the sting when he sees it. There are tears running down my cheeks. I don't know how long I've been standing here.

He reaches out and tugs at my sleeve, repeating his question. At his feet is a discarded bicycle. His cheeks are red from exercise.

I wipe my eyes and try to clear the knot from my throat.

"You should go back home," I tell him. "It's dark out, and not safe."

27.

Leo made it back to the gym in Georgetown less than two hours after he'd left. If any shadows were still watching on M, they wouldn't have noticed him going in; they would have been expecting him to leave, and not in the outfit he had on now. He went to his locker, put his old clothes back on, ran some water through his hair so it looked like he had just showered, and went out the front door.

He had a message from Gail, and she agreed to meet him for a drink in an hour.

An hour later they had drinks at Zola, the lavishly decorated bar that was attached to the International Spy Museum a few blocks north of the Mall. He'd picked the spot because he'd been unable to resist the irony, and because he, Gail, and some other trainees had come here once, many years before.

It was happy hour, and the people crowding the bar were either happy or trying very hard to convince themselves of the possibility of happiness. Leo ordered at the bar and brought two white cosmos to the small table Gail had staked out. She had cut her hair short sometime in the past few days, and also dyed it blond. It looked good. He resisted the temptation to ask if her new look had anything to do with an operation she was working on.

"I was worried at first that you wanted me to look into something relating to... what happened in Asia," she said after they'd toasted to nothing. "But this looks like something else."

"It is. I could have done this research with my company's resources, but I'm not entirely sure I trust them anymore. I'm worried they've been...setting me up for something."

She offered him a short, wry smile. "That sort of thing happens to you a lot, doesn't it?"

"What did you find out?"

She removed a file folder from her bag, placed it between them, and opened it. "Troy Jones, thirty-nine and a resident of Laurel, Maryland, was until recently an employee of the National Security Agency, and rather highly placed. From what I understand, he was part cryptologist, part telecom wizard for whatever the hell it is they do there." People in Leo and Gail's line of work tended to despise the techno-geeks at NSA, who were slowly co-opting the CIA's money and influence with their monstrously powerful ability to overhear and oversee pretty much anything on earth.

Jones had left the NSA seven months ago to go contractor, Gail explained, taking a job with Enhanced Awareness LLC, which was based at one of the anonymous office parks that surrounded NSA's heavily guarded headquarters in Fort Meade. His departure from NSA was particularly unusual.

"Jones's wife was Persian—that's how Iranian Americans describe themselves when they don't want to freak people out. She came from a wealthy family, so like a lot of the upper class they fled during the revolution, when she was a young girl. She grew up in California, public schools, then Stanford. Moved to D.C. in her early twenties, following a boyfriend—it didn't work out, but she stayed here anyway, working in PR. She first volunteered and later took a full-time job with a political organization dedicated to freeing the Iranian people from the tyranny of the ayatollah. She and Troy met at a party of a mutual friend, married two years later, bought a place on Capitol Hill, and had a daughter."

According to personnel files from a recent check the Agency had made—and here Leo knew that Gail was indeed showing him things she shouldn't—Mrs. Jones had become alarmed by the disappearance, about eighteen months ago, of one of her uncles, who had been residing in Frankfurt, Germany. Many of her relatives—Iranian expats spread across Europe and the States—felt that the uncle, a history professor who was involved in various Iranian political groups, had been kidnapped as a result of certain incendiary comments he'd made about 9/11. Authorities claimed to have no information on him.

"He'd been rendered," Leo said.

"Well, I didn't pull the uncle's files for you, that's for sure." Gail probably couldn't have anyway, and such a request would have been noticed. "But those groups he was a part of, and the things he said . . . he clearly landed on some lists. He was a bad guy, or he made the mistake of calling and e-mailing bad guys. Regardless, his niece Mrs. Troy Jones came to blame the U.S. government, particularly its intelligence agencies. Including her husband's employer. This led, as one can imagine, to some marital tensions at the Jones household.

"She left her husband just over a year ago, taking their daughter, and filed for divorce. A couple months later, she picked up the daughter at day care, then took an ill-advised right on red while talking on her cell, failing to notice an SUV that had the right-of-way. Troy Jones, beset with grief, took a leave of absence from NSA, then tendered his resignation."

Next Gail sketched out what little she knew about Enhanced Awareness: it was an intelligence contractor run by former NSA men as well as veterans of a variety of nations' intelligence agencies. Finding out exactly what they did and who they did it for, however, would have taken more digging than Gail felt Leo deserved.

"So now we've come to the part where you tell me why you needed to know this," Gail said. "And why you keep looking in the mirrors and out the window."

He thought for a moment. "Jones was following me. I didn't know his name. I managed to lift his prints and I got them to my boss, who claimed they didn't pull up any matches. Which can't be true. Which means this Troy Jones is someone my boss is protecting or trying to find without my knowing about it. So I wanted to know why."

"And do you?"

Despite Gail's criticism, Leo looked out the window again. There was the silver Jetta, parked at the end of the block. Also, waiting for a northbound bus—which would go through a predominantly African American neighborhood—was a young black couple in matching Wizards jackets and a tall white man in a black coat talking on a cell phone.

"Not really. But someone seems to think I'm getting there."

After finishing their drinks, they paid and split up—Leo would have been insulted at how hastily Gail had made her retreat if he hadn't been so busy running through his mental files of the past few days. He walked half a block, then stood at the foot of the wide stone staircase that led into the Hotel Monaco.

Looking back, he saw the silhouettes in the Jetta. He'd narrowed down the possibilities of who the men were and was confident he wasn't in danger. At least not at the moment.

It was nearing seven, and the sidewalks were filled with fans headed to see the Wizards game. The sidewalk at his feet glowed and flashed from the giant LCD screen down the street that showed highlights of the team's last exciting victory.

Leo called the number he'd been given by the men in the SUV, using his own phone this time. Ambient noise would make it easy for them to figure out where he was if they didn't know already, but he tried to tell himself this didn't matter.

"Yes?"

"Why did you lie to me about Troy Jones?" he asked the voice, which he was pretty sure belonged to the Good Cop from the backseat.

"Excuse me?"

"You knew his name—you worked with him. But you didn't want me to know this. Start filling in some blanks."

"You should talk to Terry Sentrick, our CEO." Leo recognized the name from Gail's report. Good Cop gave him Sentrick's number, then hung up.

Leo walked away from the noise of the LCD screen and toward the U.S. Navy Memorial. The fountain was turned off this time of year; there was just a large empty pool where a few bums lingered. This city was damn littered with memorials, as if its leaders were terrified that people would forget about their past if not provided with tangible reminders.

He got Sentrick's voice mail. Good Cop was probably talking to Sentrick, warning that Leo would be calling. Leo hung up, waited a minute, redialed. Sentrick said, "Hello, Mr. Hastings."

"I'd like to talk to you about your former employee Troy Jones."

"What would you like to know?"

"For starters, why did some of your employees fill my head with bogus stories about Troy being some mysterious agent disrupting a spy operation on South Korea? And why did they try to deceive me into thinking they're government officers when in fact they're lowly green-tags like me?"

"Lowly is all a matter of perception, Mr. Hastings."

"My perception's been getting a lot clearer since I talked to your associates."

"First of all, it would be inaccurate to call Troy my employee. He doesn't really work for us anymore. I don't think he's capable of working for anyone at the moment. He needs to be institutionalized. Also, he's disappeared."

Leo had thought the men in the SUV were either hunting Troy or trying to protect him; maybe both. "I'm listening," he said.

"You asked me what Troy used to do for us. We do a lot here, Mr. Hastings. I worked for a long time at the Agency, and some of my partners were in Mossad. We have guys from NSA, from FBI, from British intelligence. We develop various systems patterned on what we've learned in our myriad experiences and shape them to our clients' needs. I didn't know Troy personally then, but other people here did, and when they heard that he'd left NSA, they asked if he'd be interested in a job. I met with him then, and Troy seemed to be rather...confused. He said that he'd stepped down at NSA to clear his head and he wasn't sure if he wanted to get back to work so soon. Frankly, I didn't want to hire him, but the feeling from my partners was that he would be invaluable despite his...eccentricities. He's something of a SIGINT savant, well versed in the kind of systems we use. Sort of like he has computers in his head, and he'd done extensive development for NSA in phone lines, telecom, new media. My partners explained that Troy had always been a bit off, you know, the fine line between mathematical genius and what have you, and that he was dealing with a family tragedy, but what he needed was to be put back to work."

"And they were wrong?"

"He worked here for about six months and did work that my more technologically savvy partners tell me was quite extraordinary, helping us design our newest product. But also acting even more odd. Just as we're getting ready to take it to market, I found out from an old buddy at NSA that Troy had basically been diagnosed as a paranoid schizophrenic a year earlier during a standard psych eval, but someone had overruled the diagnosis so he wouldn't have to step down in the middle of a key project." He chuckled. "Makes you feel safe knowing such decisions are made, doesn't it? Anyway, right around then, Troy stopped coming in to work. He didn't return e-mails, calls, texts. We kept trying to reach him, but after a few days his phone was out of service, e-mails bouncing back. So we sent someone to his house. They peeked in the windows, saw empty rooms. *Completely* empty—nothing on the walls, no furniture, no desks or bureaus or bookshelves. They climbed his fence to check his backyard, and a patch of grass was burned black, a heap of ashes scattered in the middle."

"He disappeared and destroyed all record of himself."

"Or as much record as one can in our digital age. And the very next night, by wild coincidence, the house itself burned to the ground. Ask me why he would do that, I have no idea."

Leo had several. "Who have you reported this to?"

"No one. He hasn't broken any laws. Well, except maybe theft, because he did disappear with a laptop chock-full of proprietary information, but I'm willing to forgive him."

Leo ruefully noted the word choice. "*Proprietary* or classified?"

"What's the difference anymore? We work for government clients, that makes us the government, doesn't it?" Sentrick chuckled. "Look, I'd be lying if I told you I knew exactly what information Troy went off with, whether it was Enhanced Awareness product information only or whether he also had government files there too, private citizens' data; who knows. There's no reason for us to tell anyone, because it appears that he simply decided to run off, and isn't that his right as an American?" Another empty laugh. "He kind of screwed us on a project or two, but we'll be all right."

"You said you once worked for the Agency?"

"Fifteen boring, bureaucratic years."

"So did I, for less than that. But obviously a man of your background has to at least suspect that your Mr. Jones—"

"Was a spy? Had been a plant at NSA and was suddenly ferried back to whichever sovereign nation had been employing him? C'mon, this guy had top clearance for years."

"And maybe he sold some of his information to the highest bidder, or he was just bitter about something, or he craved a sense of adventure?"

Sentrick gave a condescending sigh. "I know it can *appear* that's what happened here. But I don't buy it. Troy wasn't a mole. I think he just snapped. He'd recently lost his wife and daughter—a little kid, four or five, I think. He and his wife had separated, but that doesn't make it easier. Sometimes it makes it harder."

"Do people at NSA know about his disappearance?"

"They know everything about everything. And if *they* aren't concerned Troy was a mole, then that means Troy wasn't a mole."

Or it meant that they were more concerned with their image, Leo thought. They didn't want the newspapers or TV talking heads to know there was an Internet-age Alger Hiss out there. Would an ass-covering intelligence agency conceal the fact that one of its top men turned out to be a spy? The answer depended on how much of a cynic you were.

"He's probably going to wind up in a police station soon enough," Sentrick said, "for acting erratically."

"Like pulling a gun on a total stranger."

Silence on the line, then Sentrick said, "Wait, you mean—"

"He pulled a gun on me that time I spoke to him. He sounded unhinged. I'm convinced he was about to shoot me, only he decided last-minute not to. So I'm afraid I disagree when you say he hasn't done anything illegal."

"You didn't tell my men this."

"It wasn't a very honest conversation all around, was it?"

"Okay, you have me in an awkward spot. The truth is, Enhanced Awareness is on the verge of closing some major deals. I am concerned that Troy is trying to jeopardize them. One of my colleagues actually spotted him a few days ago not far from where we'd been meeting with a client. Said he stomped off, talking to himself."

"Why would he want to jeopardize your deals?"

"Because he's angry at the world. I think he quit the NSA because he was done with this kind of work, thought it was dirty somehow. When we offered him the job, I think he took it with the hope he could somehow redeem himself, or sabotage what we do. Or both."

"You said your partners were happy with the work he did."

"They were. He's a genius. But he hates himself."

"Because of what happened to his wife's uncle?"

"Maybe," Sentrick said, betraying no surprise that Leo knew about that. "I have it on good authority that the episode with the uncle had nothing to do with Troy or what he did at NSA, but hey, shit happens and you blame yourself. If you're of a certain inclination."

"Not that you are."

"In this line of work, are you kidding? Christ only knows how someone like Troy survived at NSA so long. Look, he was always a little weird. The uncle thing, the wife and kid dying, it broke him. Who wouldn't break after that? If you have any idea where he is or how I can find him, I'd appreciate your sharing that information before he does something to permanently fuck up my business."

"And what does Enhanced Awareness do, exactly? Or is that all proprietary?"

"Systems management." He seemed proud of how vaguely and benignly he could describe it. "We help people filter information. Anyone can tap a phone, track an e-mail, but who can keep up with all that information? How do you differentiate the important shit from the unimportant shit without having ten thousand bored-to-tears analysts combing through meaningless babble, half ready to shoot themselves? When Orwell invented Big Brother, he must have imagined the guy was an amazingly fast reader with infinite patience. But he's not. We invent the tools to filter things out, make it all intelligible, actionable."

"You don't do this for the U.S., though, because that's who you learned it from."

"We have numerous clients."

"And they're all democracies?"

A pause. "We could only grow so large if we restricted our customer base to certain forms of governance."

Leo shook his head. He was looking for shadows again, but it was dark and the three-street intersection had too many corners, the perfect place to hide and watch. He couldn't have picked a worse area to stand. Across the street was the National Archives, bursting with important papers and records and rules that people around here ignored.

"I think I should hang up," Leo said, "before I say something judgmental."

"I hardly see how you'd be in a position to judge. I'm told your current assignment involves spying on war protesters?"

"It's more complicated than that. And I'm doing it for the U.S. government, not some Third World dictatorship." He realized how weak that sounded even as he said it.

"Oh, well, that's fine then. For the record, Mr. Hastings, Enhanced

Awareness is an ethical company. We have three ex-congressmen on our board, men from the Carlyle Group and Boeing, and—"

"I didn't mean to imply otherwise. If I do see Mr. Jones again, I'll let you know. But I'll also call the police."

A Metro train hummed beneath him as Leo hung up, wondering who else had been listening.

PART FOUR

HUMAN-ASSET PROTECTION

28.

People were no doubt talking about her. Leaving work early yesterday—first to go to Walter Reed and then disappearing with Troy—and showing up late to work today, having needed the extra time to put herself together after she realized who Troy really was. Not to mention all the recent nights when she'd run off to some activist meeting or to have coffee with T.J. and pass on Leo's fake documents. So on this day she hurried to her desk and tried to immerse herself in work, willing herself not to think about Troy. She skipped lunch and kept going, placing calls, drafting memos, tracking lost documents. As if everything would work out if only she focused on this job that was supposed to give meaning to her life.

She stayed past nine, deciding it was time to leave when she realized her elbows and wrists were aching from all the typing. Despite the late start, she'd managed to bill ten hours, the bare minimum at this place. Tomorrow she'd put in a longer day.

So who *was* Troy? she allowed herself to wonder as she left. If he really didn't work for Leo, if Leo had been honest about not knowing him, then why was Troy following Tasha? Why were so many people so damn interested in her? Was it the GTK leak, or her involvement in the activist community, or her frequent and insistent calls to Marshall's fellow soldiers? What exactly had she done to land on someone's list, and why was it such a goddamn special list that it merited sending a spy like Troy to feed her lies and *seduce* her?

The Metro was nearly empty by the time the train pulled into the Potomac Avenue stop. The escalators were out of order, as they almost always were because some genius had decreed that the Metro entrances should not have roofs, and thus the mechanical conveyances were continually damaged by the rain and snow. Tasha walked slowly in her high heels, as she'd never been one to surrender style by wearing running shoes during her commute.

A few loiterers south of the station waited for the bus, silhouetted against the neon pizza sign across the street. Some Metro employees were standing just north of the station beside a white Metro van whose back doors were ajar; one of the men, in a blue jumpsuit, peered with a flashlight into a large circuit box.

"Oh, walk this way, miss," someone said, directing her to the narrow strip of sidewalk between the rear of the van and the cement wall that ran around the perimeter of the station. The street itself was blocked off by traffic cones, though there didn't appear to be any reason for it. She obeyed, not really thinking, or thinking about Marshall and Troy and the madness of these past weeks, and just as she was passing the van someone grabbed her around the waist. Two someones, because the shocked breath had barely left her body when she was lifted like she weighed nothing, like she *was* nothing, and suddenly she was in the back of the van. Invisible hands propelled her forward and she landed on a seat that had been installed facing backward. She looked up at the rear doors just in time to see the man who'd been crouching outside with the flashlight enter the van. The engine was already on, and the van started moving before he even shut the doors.

She didn't realize she was screaming until she heard people telling her to stop.

"Calm down, Miss Wilson. There's nowhere you can go, so let's have our conversation and get this over with."

Behind her was another seat on which one of the two men who'd thrown her was now sitting. Before her, two others sat on small benches that were welded to the sides of the van. Two interrogators, with a guard in the rear. Because she was facing backward and there were no windows, every time the van made a turn she felt a sickeningly vertiginous effect. Her stomach tightened, and she pressed her feet to the floor.

"What's going on?" she managed to say without sounding too, too panicked.

"We'd like to hear about your relationship with Troy Jones." That was said by the man to her left, who was bald and had a neck that suggested there was plenty of muscle hiding beneath the shapeless blue Metro jumpsuit. The partner flanking him was Asian with graying hair at his temples. Neither of them held anything, no paper or recorder or weapon. But she did notice there was a large duffel bag at the feet of the Asian guy.

"Who the hell are you?" she asked.

"Someone who just asked you a question you should start answering."

"I'm an attorney. I know my rights. This is kidnapping."

They were illuminated only by a dim light that, she hoped, would not fade off in a few seconds now that the doors were shut.

"You are an anti-government activist, driven to rash decisions by your brother's recent tragedy, allying yourself with radical domestic elements and doing everything possible to impugn the reputation of our armed services. And now you're hanging out with a former intelligence officer who recently disappeared with information valuable to the U.S. government. This isn't kidnapping, Miss Wilson; it's an example of the unfortunately extreme measures we need to take to protect our country when it's threatened by its own citizens."

"Anything you'd like to ask me, you can do with a lawyer present."

He smiled. "But you are a lawyer, as you so pompously pointed out. You're present and accounted for. So, by all means, let's do some Q and A."

She wondered what would happen if she screamed *Rape!* But the doors were no doubt thick enough to keep her from being heard. And she wasn't going to entertain them by lunging for a door handle. The van made a sharp turn, and she crammed her right hand into the seat to keep from leaning over too far.

"I don't think you fully appreciate how friendly we're being," he said. "We picked you up like this, Miss Wilson, to show you how easy it is. We can do this again, at any time. If you think your law firm connections impress us, they don't. And you won't have those connections much longer if you don't play ball."

"Why not, because you'll accuse me of leaking a certain story? Sorry, but that threat's already been made."

"It doesn't make the threat less real. We could indeed nail you for GTK, but that's just a start."

"What else do you have?" Another turn, not even a sharp one, but the lack of windows was getting to her. She told herself to breathe slowly, not think about vomiting.

"How about your connections with fringe writers who are about to launch an online story slandering a vital American contractor?"

"Which you people blackmailed me into!"

He looked offended. "Which people? All I know is, you've been accessing files from your firm, doctoring them to make them more salacious, and then passing them on to your old squeeze T.J. so he and his hacker nuts can defame the company and cast aspersions on the United States military."

"This is complete..." But she shook her head and let the words die.

"Are you trying to say I don't know the whole story? If that's the case, then please enlighten us."

"So, what, you're Leo's muscle? Someone sent you in because they didn't think he was being tough enough?"

"What makes you think we work with a Leo?" The Asian guy finally spoke.

"What you saw in that briefcase made you pretty angry, didn't it?" the bald one said.

"To realize that there are assholes who make it their business to butt into private citizens' lives? Yes, that made me pretty angry."

The van wasn't turning anymore, but it was driving awfully fast.

Like Leo, the men hadn't flashed any badges, hadn't identified themselves or their employer. But they knew about her and Troy, and the fact that she'd looked inside his briefcase.

"When everything is working properly, Miss Wilson, things like this don't have to happen."

"So when that utopia comes, people like you will be out of work, huh? That must mess with your motivations."

The van apparently tried to change lanes, and someone honked, and the van veered back to where it had been. Tasha was reminded of the fact that she had no seat belt here. The two men wore such blank expression she imagined they'd been in far more hazardous situations than this.

The bald one said, "Start telling us about Troy Jones."

"You seem to know him better than I do. You said he's a former intelligence officer?"

They didn't answer that, but their expressions—regret on the talkative bald guy's face, annoyance on the quiet Asian guy's—suggested they both wished the bald guy hadn't let that slip.

I'm not a part of that, she remembered Troy saying. *I'm not proud at all.* The look in his eyes, and the crushed tone of his voice. It hadn't made sense at the time; it was as if he were reading the script for the wrong play. But the meaning of the lines was becoming clearer to her.

"It sounds like you guys need to get your own house in order," she said, "and stop trying to make it other people's problem."

"I'm afraid this *is* your problem," the bald one said, reaching into his pocket for a cell phone. "Start talking, or I'm calling your firm, *now.*"

She took a breath and stared at the smug look on his face, and it was as if all those hallmarks of fear—her quickened heart rate and the sweat along her back and the tension in her stomach—were transformed into unmitigated rage. She had been so angry for so long, and when Leo had presented her with a target for this rage, she had mistakenly tried to contain that anger and use it toward other ends. She had been trying to walk a tightrope between Leo and T.J., and suddenly all the stress and dizziness of that performance vanished, and the thought of simply stepping off the tightrope and falling was too intoxicating to deny.

"No, actually," she said. "You know what? Fuck you both, and fuck your invisible driver. Tell him to pull over and let me out, now."

"I'm not bluffing, Miss Wilson."

"I'm not calling your bluff. I'm just saying *I don't fucking care.* Call my boss. Tell him. I'm cutting the cord." T.J. had won, and the credit cards and fifteen-dollar drinks and 401(k)s had lost. She had the feeling she was doing something headstrong and regrettable, but the surprised looks on the men's faces only made her push harder. "You have nothing on me anymore. Leo told me that the choice was mine, that I could choose either my ideals or my job and money. Well, I'm choosing my ideals. Assholes like you never have to make that kind of choice, do you, because your only ideal *is* power and money. So don't sit there judging me, just call my boss and get it over with."

They had said her law firm connections didn't impress them, and maybe that was true. But she didn't think they wanted someone to go public with their domestic surveillance activities. If they were the types to make more violent threats, then they would have done that already. She hoped.

"Very well," the bald one said, looking at his phone's keypad.

She recited the phone number for him, and he made the call.

The three of them and the silent one behind her (who hopefully was not about to put a black bag over her head—Jesus, was she actually thinking this?) sat without speaking for a few seconds. The Asian guy looked at his partner as if unsure what he would do now, as if they hadn't considered the possibility of such recalcitrance.

The bald guy listened, then typed someone's extension into his keypad, and then his eyes went to Tasha again—he seemed to think she was on the verge of reconsidering, of pleading for clemency. Silence again, and they waited as the call went to voice mail. The thug seemed to wait even longer than necessary, all but begging Tasha to beg him to stop, but she wouldn't. He finally said, "Hello, Mr.

Coyle." He was leaving the message for Tasha's least favorite partner at the firm. "I'm calling to inform you that one of your firm's associates, Tasha Wilson, is the person responsible for leaking the information about GTK Industries' delayed shipments to the press last month. You'll receive documentation proving this in a few days. I sincerely hope that you and your partners use that information to take appropriate steps for the good of your firm and your country."

She would not grant them the satisfaction of looking angry. "Congratulations. You now have no leverage over me, so pull over."

"Not so fast," he said, making another call that required the press of only two buttons. The steeliness in his eyes suddenly seemed more threatening. The van had slowed down and now it spun a bit, getting on an exit ramp, and she had to put a hand on the windowless wall. They wouldn't bother to get her fired first if they were going to do something rougher to her afterward, would they?

"It's me," he said into the phone, his voice quieter than before. "She's refused." A pause. "Yes, that's been done." His eyes on her as he waited. She told herself that these were the bored eyes of a bureaucrat calling his manager to see if an applicant's paperwork had been processed yet, and not the cold eyes of an assassin. "In my opinion, yes." Another pause. He glanced at the duffel bag. "For now, okay."

He put the phone back in his pocket. The conversation must have been piped into the front seat, because without a word from anyone, the van slowed down again, then made a turn. After a very tense minute, the van came to a stop, and the Asian guy opened the back door and got out. She saw a parking lot, and in the distance a Laundromat.

And as beautiful a sight as the parking lot was, she nonetheless hadn't liked that "For now."

She stepped out of the van. The bald one even offered his hand so she wouldn't slip. They were silent, though—they seemed to have decided she was no longer worth speaking to. The Asian guy got back in, put his gloved hand on the door to close it, and the sense of freedom flooding Tasha's limbs (so taken for granted before, and so cherished now!) hit her brain as well and made her ask something before fully considering it.

"What did you do to his wife and kid?"

The Asian guy scowled. "Nothing. They died in an accident, and then he snapped."

"Troy is not a well man," the bald guy said. "He harbors a lot of ill will against our government. Some of which is due to some misguided political opinions his wife passed on to him, and some of which is just his mind deteriorating from...what happened."

"Or so we're told," the Asian guy said. They were awfully forthcoming now, as if they thought they could elicit information from her this way. "We're not shrinks. We're just trying to find him before he causes some real harm."

Harm to whom? she thought, but this she knew enough not to ask. She just walked away, holding her breath, a larger part of her than she wanted to admit wondering if she was about to hear a gunshot. But no, the sound that came was quieter: a door closing, the van driving away.

She was in the lot of a derelict strip mall that she either had never seen before or had driven past many times without noticing it. The Laundromat, a Chinese restaurant, a dollar store, two shuttered storefronts. Northern Virginia, she guessed, which meant they'd taken her on 395 and then exited after the river.

No one was around, and few cars were in the lot. She walked to a bus stop and sank onto the bench. Suddenly her nervous system collapsed, as if it had used up all its reserves trying to remain calm and now was giving up. Her legs were shaking, as were her hands, so she hugged herself and tried to wait it out. It wasn't even cold enough to see her breath, yet her teeth clattered as if she'd been dunked in an icy pool.

When her fingers finally stopped their spasms and she regained control of her jaw, she used her phone's GPS to figure out where she was, then called a cab.

* * *

Tasha had always prided herself on her intelligence, her good judgment. Yet time and again these past few weeks, she found herself confused, her perceptions skewed, the world's signals not making sense. She didn't know if this was what it was to be in mourning, if her brainpower was being diverted from basic tasks because she was so consumed by thoughts of her brother; or if she was paying the price for getting involved in matters best avoided; or if she was indeed a tiny victim of forces so large they were beyond any one person's ability to comprehend. Why was this happening to her?

She wondered this as she paid her cab fare, looked up and down her reassuringly van-free neighborhood, and turned the key in the door of her ransacked house.

Pillaged house, destroyed house, trashed house. Inside-out house. Un-house.

The twelve-hundred-dollar sofa she'd bought from a boutique in Old Town had been gashed and disemboweled. Her shelves were bare, and her books lay on top of one another on the floor, open and upside down like victims of genocide spreading their arms to protect their children from the firing squad. Her refrigerator had been moved several inches away from the wall, her dishes thrown on the unforgiving tile floor. A couple spots in the dining room and living room where floorboards had been worn down and replaced by a previous owner were now torn out entirely; the vandals had apparently suspected those were trick doors. They had torn her fucking floor open.

She made it to the bathroom in time for the toilet to catch her vomit.

After she stopped, when she made it back into the totaled dining room—the table upside down, the upholstery of the chairs spewing out—she felt a burning on her cheeks. Like she was being watched. How long had they been in here? How many of them? It was like they were still here, would always be here, no matter how she cleaned and replaced and scrubbed. She would always feel their eyes on her, feel their arms around her waist lifting her away.

Then she realized that the jarring whiteness of her walls meant that all the decorations had been removed from them. That black rectangle on the floor, sitting in a bed of shattered glass, was Marshall's army photo, turned backward and broken open. She rushed over to it, picked it up. The print was torn in half, Marshall decapitated.

She didn't even want to see the second floor. The torn-out carpeting on the steps told her it would only be more of the same.

It was worse. Her desk drawers were pulled out and thrown down, attacked by poltergeists; erasers and pens and Post-its spread across the floor. Her computer was gone. Please, not the computer. And where were her notebooks? She looked under the mattress, which was far from its usual spot. She nearly threw out her back moving her bureau into place, hoping the notebooks and files would be revealed, but no. They'd stolen her computer and her disks and her CD-ROMs and her backup hard drive and all of her notebooks and files. In their search for whatever deep, dark secret they feared Troy had left behind, they'd taken every record she had of Marshall. All those e-mails she had painstakingly gathered, and the printouts and scans she'd made of his blog posts. The names and numbers and addresses of the men and women with whom he'd served. She tried to breathe, tried to remember if she had the information anywhere else. Some of it was online, but most of it wasn't. Marshall was gone, again.

29.

Leo had made it back to his house, not noticing any more shadows but assuming they were there. Inside his apartment, all seemed as he had left it, and the knob turned with the key the way it always did. He realized how paranoid he was becoming, to question every little thing like this.

He tried to stop running through the various bits of information he'd learned in the last twenty-four hours and focus instead on what he needed to do next. He would get an ID for Sari—he'd already placed a call to start that process and would meet with his source in less than two hours. He had researched Amtrak schedules, printing one out from the Georgetown library, just in case his home Internet usage was being monitored, and had stopped at the bank on the way back from his surreptitious visit to Sari and withdrawn thousands of his own hard-earned dollars. He'd handled that much cash before— more, in fact—but never had it been his own money. It made him feel even more vulnerable.

He was microwaving some leftover Indian takeout and brewing coffee when his phone buzzed with an unfamiliar D.C. number.

"Leo Hastings?" A man's voice. Possibly a few years younger than Leo.

"Speaking. Who's this?"

"My name is Special Agent Hale Michaels with the FBI. My partner and I would very much like to speak to you about Enhanced Awareness."

"They're a popular conversational topic lately."

"They've been popular with me for quite a while."

"Look, if this is some turf argument, we can just have it over the phone, because I—"

"We're calling because we can help you, Mr. Hastings. You've been talking to some people I've been watching very carefully, and they're the type of people you want to steer clear of."

"When do you want to meet?"

"How about in five minutes, at your place?" Michaels didn't even pause to let Leo process this. "We're just outside."

Leo said, "Sure," like he wasn't bothered by the fact that the FBI was watching his apartment. Then he speedily ate his leftovers, trying to predict what they were going to tell him. Less than five minutes later, the doorman buzzed him.

"Some guests, Mr. Hastings. They say you're expecting them?"

At least they hadn't flashed their badges. Leo okayed them, straightening his tiny living room, organizing magazines on the coffee table as if about to entertain in-laws or something. Why was he nervous? He checked himself in the mirror, wondered how obvious it was that he'd barely slept the night before and had been strung out all day.

They knocked, and Leo opened the door to the two special agents, the second of whom was introduced as Kent Islington. Leo wasn't sure if he should be relieved or alarmed to see that these were not the men who'd been tailing him earlier that day.

Michaels looked even younger than he'd sounded. He was handsome, with brown hair that seemed just shaggy enough to earn comments from his bosses; the red tie of his otherwise standard FBI dark suit was slanted, the top button of his shirt undone, as if he were getting ready for an *Esquire* photo shoot. He did the talking; Islington, who was in his late forties at least and had thinning gray hair and a slouch, seemed resigned to the fact that he was being displaced by a younger, cooler generation. He nodded a hello but remained silent. Michaels flashed his credentials; his mild embarrassment at the formality showed that he knew Leo was former Agency and wouldn't be wowed by a federal badge. Islington kept his hands in his pockets.

"Smells good," Michaels said, presumably meaning the coffee. "Planning a late night?"

"Just a caffeine junkie."

"Well, as addictions go, that one's not so bad."

Leo offered them some but they declined. He invited them to sit on his couch, and he took the one chair, sitting opposite them. Neither was carrying a briefcase, and they both glanced around the room and down the hall, as if wondering whether Leo had any other guests. He told them he didn't.

"I'm going to start things off as agreeably as possible," Michaels said. "You're ex-Agency, which means we're supposed to hate you and you're supposed to hate us and all that. But I'm one of the rare feds who hasn't yet been screwed by the Agency and therefore holds no grudge against you guys—"

"Though it'll probably happen eventually," Islington interrupted in a flat tone.

"—and as far as I know, I've never pissed off anyone at Langley. So hopefully you can hear us out without any premature judgments."

"Like I tried to say before, I couldn't care less about that sort of thing."

"Excellent." Michaels seemed legitimately thrilled to hear this. "We came here so quickly because we've been following the good people of Enhanced Awareness for quite some time." Though, judging from his unlined face, how long could that have been? "And we've been listening to Terry Sentrick's calls, so we heard your conversation with him this afternoon."

"That *was* quick."

"Which should show you how seriously we take this. As you probably noticed, Sentrick and his friends are desperately trying to find Troy Jones, and they were hoping you'd do that for them. Sounds like they met with you earlier and tried to con you into thinking they were with the Agency, and that you should tell them if Jones approached you?"

Leo tried to remember what he'd told Sentrick and figured that yes, a savvy listener would have been able to divine that much. He didn't nod, but he didn't contradict them either.

"Well, I was glad to hear you tell Sentrick that you'd call the *police* if you saw Jones. Which is exactly what you should do. Specifically, us." On cue, Islington reached forward and handed Leo two cards, the FBI crest emblazoned on each. "We believe that Jones, though erratic and possibly crazy, as Sentrick suggested, is indeed trying to sabotage their company, and that he ran off with information that could prove rather painful to them. Information that would help us nail down our case. I don't know why he doesn't come directly to us—we've tried to reach him ever since he went AWOL from the company, and we even approached him beforehand, thinking he might play ball—but, again, the man is erratic."

"Tell me about your case."

There was a two-second pause, during which the feds exchanged a glance. Michaels said, "We've been working on this for a very long time. The political mood has not always been conducive to our pursuing this company. As Sentrick mentioned to you, he has powerful connections. But I think Jones has evidence that's too large for anyone to overlook."

Leo hated how vague they were being. "Why do you think Jones will approach me?"

"Honestly, I have no idea what the man will do. But we're covering our bases, and we wanted to make sure we spoke to you right away, just in case. I could tell from your tone in that call that you don't like Sentrick, that you think maybe he's involved in something dirty. I wanted to let you know that your hunch is correct."

"You told Sentrick that Jones pulled a gun on you," Islington said. "Tell us about it."

Leo did, omitting a few details but giving away most of it. Despite the animosity that Agency people had for the Bureau, he believed the two feds. He didn't like the fact that they wouldn't tell him everything, but he understood their perspective, and frankly he was flattered that they'd come by to tell him this much.

"What do you know about this Korean diplomat?" Leo asked them. "I was near his house when Jones approached me and told me to keep away from them."

"We don't know much," Michaels said, "but I imagine the government of South Korea is one of Enhanced Awareness's clients, or potential clients. Why Jones warned you away, again, I don't know."

"You know about Jones's family?"

"We do. Honestly, that's why we thought we could turn him. Figured he was getting disgruntled with the work, would be happy to pass us some information. But he was with NSA for years, so maybe it's an honor thing—they don't like us any more than the CIA does."

Leo wanted to ask them much more, for details on Troy's family, to fill the holes in Gail's story. Who had Mrs. Jones's uncle really been, and had he indeed been rendered, and was he rotting in some Egyptian prison somewhere? Had the uncle—or even Jones's wife—been in any way connected to some Islamist extremist group, justifying his placement on those lists? Justifying all that would come later? And did the feds know something about Hyun Ki Shim that they weren't saying? Did they know he was in the hospital right now? And what about Sari? Had her residence in that house gotten her involved in something that would trail her for the rest of her life?

But he didn't want to insult his own intelligence by asking questions he knew they'd ignore. So he told them what they wanted to hear. "I honestly hope I never see Troy Jones again. But if I do, I will let you know immediately."

Handshakes all around, and the two feds left. Leo poured himself some coffee and tried to imagine what it would feel like to be Troy Jones.

30.

I t did not take long for Sari to conclude that being trapped alone in a motel room was only a minor improvement over being trapped in a maniacal household with screaming infants.

Leo's sudden visit that afternoon, to deliver food, take her photograph, and tell her his plan, was the only time she had spoken in hours. After he'd brought her there the previous night, she'd spent a long time trying to sleep before finally turning on the light, plugging in the television, and staring uncomprehendingly at grainy police dramas before sleep rescued her from their nonsense. She awoke to smiling newscasters telling her important snippets about the previous night and the upcoming day, which again she could not understand but which apparently had a lot to do with fatal shootings, a fire, predawn traffic congestion, and the possibility of rain.

She turned the TV off as well as the lights (it was still dark out) and tried to fall back to sleep, but all she could see was Sang Hee, her mouth agape with rage—those tiny yellow teeth and the undulating tongue—and her knife raised. She remembered again the sound of Sang Hee stabbing her husband, just a quiet *ppp, ppp,* like a fist against a pillow. Knives are muted. It had been so horrifying when she'd understood what was happening, so confusing and wrong, as if the knife didn't realize it was supposed to be *loud,* was supposed to announce itself. She closed her eyes and suffered through waking dreams of silent violence before making herself get up and shower.

For so many days she hadn't been afforded any time to put on makeup, and now she had plenty of time but no cosmetics to work with. The motel didn't even have a bar of soap, just a dispenser of pink slime that she had to pump many times before some spooged through the clump that had agglutinated around the spout. She re-donned the track clothes Leo had bought her and which she'd slept in, and had no choice but to put on yesterday's underwear.

She made herself watch more television because it was better than staring at the ceiling and thinking about the *ppp, ppp.* More morning news, then talk shows: chipper women with their legs crossed so tightly and their lips pursed so emphatically that they appeared perpetually on the verge of exploding. Whatever they were talking about seemed extremely interesting to them. She turned the TV off.

What was she doing here? Were people really looking for her? Would the Shims blame her for what had happened? Would American police cart her off to jail? In which case, would that be any worse than working for the Shims? Would she serve time here, or in Korea, or back in Indonesia? How had her life reached the point where she was sitting in a strange motel room pondering the existence of extradition treaties? Was Leo really trying to help her, walking the halls of American justice, pleading her case with unknown magistrates?

He had tried to kiss her last night. There had been a time she would have liked that, but no longer. While she'd been trapped in that house, the illusion of romance was something to hold fast to, the possibility of it, the escape. Now she craved a more tangible escape.

She turned the TV back on. It was an American soap opera, weirdly similar to the Korean ones Sang Hee watched. Different races, different language, same obvious problems of sleeping with the wrong people. Did Leo only want to sleep with her? Was he only playing the hero to get her to spread her legs?

No, she wasn't thinking straight. He had been cold as a machine the previous night, giving her quick, sharp orders and guiding her by her forearm, but he'd steered her to safety. Or to whatever this motel was. Clearly he had done things like this before; he didn't seem nearly as overwhelmed by the situation as she was, those three punches against his steering wheel notwithstanding.

But that didn't make sitting in this motel room any easier.

One of the soap operas seamlessly blended into another—she didn't even realize she was watching a new show until the opening credits scrolled by following a shocking revelation that left a pert blond woman speechless, her mouth wide open. Then there was a knock on Sari's door.

It wasn't Leo's coded knock. Just two knocks, hard.

She slowly stood up from the bed. Considered turning the TV off, but decided against it. Any change in volume would reveal her presence. The two knocks, again. She was holding her breath. The curtains were drawn—she'd checked many times to make sure there were no cracks through which prying eyes might discover her.

The knob wiggled. It was locked, so it didn't wiggle much, but the existence of a hand on the other side was inescapable.

She backed up silently, thinking, *The bathroom.* She remembered that there was a narrow window there, shoulder-high, opaque, and set in the wall opposite the showerhead. Did she have something to shatter it with? Where did it lead? Her room was on the second floor—how far down could she safely jump?

While bracing herself for the imminent appearance of some large body tearing the door from its hinges, she heard a gentler sound. Footsteps, scuffling a bit at the dirty floor of the outer hallway. The person was walking away.

Then she heard two more knocks, on a different door.

She crept forward this time, making her way to the curtained window. After a few more seconds, she heard the knocks on the other door again. She pulled the curtain just the tiniest fraction of a centimeter so she could peer outside. There was a man in the hallway, standing outside the next room. He was tall and white, with dark hair and sunglasses. He was wearing a suit; would men in suits come to a place like this? Maybe they would. Maybe he was not looking for her.

She stepped back, waiting. Television voices giggled with postcoital bliss.

Thirty more minutes passed as she stood there, then sat on her bed, not even watching the television anymore but afraid to turn it off.

This is insane, she thought. If people really were looking for her, she was not safe here. So there was no reason not to take a walk.

She'd been in such a fugue the night before, and he'd taken her on such a deliberately circuitous route, that she had no idea which way to go. She set off walking to the right, in what seemed to be the direction the sun was setting, based on the relative brightness of the overcast sky, but she soon reached a highway that lacked a pedestrian bridge. So she doubled back, hoping she wasn't surrounded by such roads, wasn't completely marooned here.

No one was watching her, because no one was out. This wasn't an area for wanderers. She walked in the shadows of overpasses, skirting stretches that lacked sidewalks, walking on the road itself, stepping around a few puddles and hoping drivers would pay her enough heed. The wind was picking up and she was cold in her thin track jacket, but at least she was out of her latest prison. If there was another one waiting for her, so be it, but she wasn't going to sit around waiting for it to show up.

Finally she reached a commercial district. To her left were towering buildings that, based on the familiar logos, she knew to be hotels. She imagined the top floors offered fabulous views of Washington, of the famous monuments and the government buildings decked out in their formal whites. The city looked very different from her plebeian perspective. At least no car had splashed her with a puddle of rainwater.

To her right were some shops, and she gazed into the windows with a sort of longing, not for the goods themselves but for the normalcy of a life that included idle shopping. She had done things like that, once. She'd had very little money when she worked in Korea, but she had survived. She'd cared about how she looked, she'd bargain-hunted and managed to dress well, or well enough. She'd bought CDs from street vendors and seen movies, she'd been a practicing member of the real world.

She dared to enter a bookstore, an odd choice given that she couldn't read the language. But it seemed the kind of store least likely to have pushy salesclerks chatting her up. She picked up some books, pressed her nose between the pages, and inhaled. She watched the other shoppers, some alone and others on dates, holding hands, killing time before dinner or a movie.

Farther on she passed health-food stores, a bank, what she guessed might be a Mexican restaurant, and a shop selling kitchen knick-knacks. Young professionals passed by clutching glossy bags, talking on their phones, laughing. Just another night in the capital of the free world.

This was the amazing thing about Americans: they had no idea how easy it would be for this entire facade to be torn down, for madness to take hold. She wondered whether, if she stayed here long enough, if she herself became *American,* she would forget what she knew about society's frailty, about the things that lurked beneath the facade. She wondered if she would become so blissfully free of worry, or if she would always retain that fear, that awful knowledge, and if it would keep her from becoming one of these carefree strivers, running to and fro on the sidewalk, off to this business opportunity or that party, always perfectly confident that the conference room or the full bar would be waiting for them as scheduled.

She wished for the millionth time that she spoke even a little English. She'd been very young when she left Indonesia, but even before then she'd run across kids her age who knew English well. Private-school kids, children of the wealthy, who happened to be in her neighborhood for some random reason, stopping in the store to buy candy or a soda. She'd hear them talking to one another, joking and teasing with words she didn't know. Even the poorer kids sometimes picked up a word or two from a TV show or a pirated movie they'd seen. Sari had not been hip to that trend, however, and then the riots had hit, and whether you knew English words or Bahasa ones didn't matter, words themselves didn't matter, only bricks and rocks and fire did.

So, on to Korea, another new language to master. It had taken a while—she'd lived with other Indonesians and worked with them as circumstances allowed, making her ignorance of the country's native tongue less of a hindrance—but eventually she learned enough Korean to get by. After a few years she found herself speaking in Korean more than in Bahasa. She was a foreigner there, sure, but she was trying to learn the rules. She wasn't exactly blending in—they didn't quite want that in Korea—but she wasn't making herself a target either. The riots back home had taught her that you could never predict where the next danger would come from, a surging sea or a blackening sky or your own customers or friends. She was wary. People commented on this, in the rare instances that they got to know her well enough. *You hold back,* they would say. *You're very suspicious.* Usually these were Indonesians who'd managed to leave before the riots, or native Koreans. People who didn't know what it was like to see a crowd of people running toward you. All of them looking at *you. Collaborator! Patsy! Stooge!* The rioters had known she worked for the Mings, that her family's rent and food had been paid for by their labor for the hated Chinese, which, in the eyes of the maddened, bloodthirsty rioters, made her family no better than the Chinese themselves. It made them *worse. Traitor! Backstabber!* She and one of her older sisters, Lastri, had been chased for blocks; they'd finally turned into an alley whose brick-walled dead end, they knew from more innocent childhood games, had a small tunnel at the bottom that emerged on the other side of the wall. They crawled through the narrow tunnel—not before some rocks or cans of food struck Sari in the back—their breath bouncing off the walls, tears streaking their vision. Some of the rioters probably had been thin and short enough to follow them through, but no one had pursued the girls into the tunnel. It was a crowd, acting as a crowd does. Together it was all-powerful, but none had dared be the first to crawl after them. None had wanted to separate themselves like that, to become individualized. The spell would have been broken. The sisters had crawled through, emerging in an alley on the other side of the brick wall, hugging themselves. The rioters threw more rocks and cans over the wall, so the girls pressed their backs to it, where the trajectories of the thrown objects couldn't quite reach them. Until some enterprising or drunk (or both) rioters started throwing glass bottles, which exploded when they landed, sending shards in every direction, biting at the girls like wasps. No, not like wasps—like *shattered glass bottles*. There was no greater metaphor than the thing itself. There was nothing worse than a mob of insane, violent, hateful human beings— that's what Sari learned that day.

She and Lastri held each other's hands, deciding through their tears that a sprint past the gauntlet of popping glass was a better risk than standing there and being sliced to death over time. They ran, thankful for the thick-soled shoes their mother had insisted on buying them instead of the more fashionable sneakers they'd pleaded for. They ran, the bottles blasting at their ankles and backs but not, fortunately, landing on their heads. Then they were out of the alley, turning right, because they knew the neighborhood better, and they still hadn't learned (but were in the process of learning) that just because you know a place doesn't make it safe.

Later they would hear about the rapes all over the city, what happened to the women and girls that the mob caught.

So, they were lucky. The rioters decided that since the girls had escaped, they would turn their attention to the store itself. They torched it, burning Sari's mother alive.

She had heard stories afterward, that their mother had stood outside the store calling names at the crowd, throwing the store's canned goods at the rioters, doing whatever she could to deflect their attention and rage away from her children. Those stories hadn't made much sense to her, and then she'd blocked them out for a while. Later, she'd thought about them again, imagined her mother like that, hurling cans of water chestnuts and waving a broom before being chased into the building, where maybe she thought she was safe, until she saw them coming with torches and gasoline.

Later in life, when people in Korea commented on Sari's deeply suspicious nature, when confused friends and frustrated beaux told her she didn't quite seem *all there,* she told herself she needed to find a way to let go of all of that. To stop expecting the tsunamis to rise up. To let herself trust life a little, and not assume everyone who looked at her was plotting ways to take advantage. When Hyun Ki Shim interviewed her for the nanny position, and she'd been a bit put off by his wife's brusque manner, she told herself to turn off her internal alarms, to take this chance.

And here she was wandering the streets of America (*Virginia,* Leo had called it) with an arm still sore from her employer's blade.

She walked into a convenience store and wandered the few aisles. The cashier was darker-skinned than she, maybe Pakistani, and he watched her every move. The immigrant knew his kind, knew she was unmoored and confused and in possession of little cash. So she dropped the pretense and walked up to him, mimed a telephone call. He said something to her that she didn't understand. Then he held up a box containing a new cell phone, which she imagined cost more than the twenty dollars she'd stolen from Leo, so she shook her head. He put the phone away and instead produced a phone card.

She handed him the bill and he frowned. He put the card back and gave her one of a different color, along with nine dollars and some coins for change. She started to ask another question, unsure how to ask it, but he read her mind. He pointed down the street, held up two fingers, and motioned to the right. She nodded thanks.

Following his directions, she found a pay phone. It was just outside a parking garage and across the street from a grocery store; the noise made it a bad place to call from, but she didn't know where else to go. She had no idea how to use the card, let alone an American pay phone. But she knew Lastri's number, as well as the international code for Korea, so she tried a few times before getting it right. Finally she heard an unfamiliar ringing sound, the pulse different from the American one she'd heard when calling Leo.

It would be morning in Seoul; Lastri would already be on her way to work, unless she was running late, or was sick or fired. Sari prayed that one of these minor misfortunes had befallen her sister.

"Hello?" It was her sister's voice, in their adopted language of Korean.

"It's me, it's Sari," she said, speaking in Bahasa again.

"Sari! The world traveler finally calls!"

She hadn't called either of her sisters since leaving—the Shims wouldn't allow it, and Sang Hee said she'd check the phone records and would know.

"How are you?" Sari asked.

"Fine. You know. How about you? America's too exciting for you to check in with your sisters until now?"

"No, I'm...I've been having a hard time here," Sari started, and whatever she tried to say next got caught in the tightness of her throat.

"What did you say?"

The connection was bad and there were weird delays, making them speak over each other or wait at the wrong times, but still—it was her sister, it was someone other than Leo speaking her language for the first time in months.

She tried to tell her sister what had happened, at least vaguely. That her job was a bad one, her employers cruel. Had Lastri received any money in the mail?

"What are you talking about?"

"They said they would send some of my pay to you."

"No, nothing." There was another voice in the background, one of her roommates maybe, or perhaps Lastri was out in the city chatting on a sidewalk. "Wait, hold on a second."

Lastri didn't seem to notice how choked up her younger sister was, due to either the pauses and fuzz of international telephony or her own distractedness. Sari had been on the verge of sobbing, but she held it in. She wasn't sure if her sister was boarding a bus or kicking a boyfriend out of bed while Sari stood here gripping a receiver that didn't seem to realize how important this call was.

Leo had told her she wouldn't be able to call her family any more once she was settled in the new place, at least not for a very long time.

"Sorry, I'm back. I have to go to work, though. Can you call later?"

She and Lastri hadn't been very close their last year in Korea. There had been a boy, a mutual crush; neither had won him and each had blamed the other. Besides, Lastri was always spending her free time with her older friends, and the kid sister was not welcome. They'd spoken less and less. A ticket to a job in America had seemed a welcome diversion from Sari's stunted life in Seoul.

"Sure."

"You're okay, though? Your exciting American life isn't too hard?"

Sari sucked in her breath. "I'm fine. And Kade?"

"Oh, she's the usual. New boy, new job. I'll tell you about it later."

She said good-bye and the line went quiet. To Sari, it felt like shucking off an old jacket that didn't fit right anymore. Leaving her standing there cold, and alone.

A smartly dressed white couple passed on the sidewalk. Their arms were linked, but they were both having conversations on their cells, as if they were talking to each other on the phones. The woman was beautiful and blond, and looked concerned as she made eye contact with the crying foreigner. Sari could hear them talking as they passed, their two conversations like awkward dance partners, until they turned a corner, disappearing.

After wiping her eyes so she'd look presentable, or at least not noticeable (she hoped), she walked back to the main road. What should she do now?

Stop pouting. I didn't raise pouters.

It wasn't like her mother to come to her while Sari was awake. For a moment it made her question herself, wonder if she was sleeping after all, if this was just a long and involved dream. What a wonderful thought.

I'm not pouting, Mother.

Don't expect your sisters to come in and save you. They're busy enough fending for themselves, you know that.

Yes, Mother.

You're doing pretty well for yourself, all things considered.

Alone in a city I don't know, with people trying to hunt me down?

What did I say about the pouting? I meant that all those things have gone wrong, yes, but you're still all right. You're alive, you have food in your belly.

You always had low standards, Mother.

I shouldn't have mentioned bellies. You're hungry, aren't you? That American isn't doing such a great job taking care of you. Maybe you need to do more for yourself. Here, turn right. Walk another block.

Where are you taking me?

You're hungry, right? Now turn left. From here, you're on your own. And stop thinking about the riots. It happened. I'm glad it was me instead of you. Okay? So don't even think about feeling guilty. It defeats the purpose, doesn't it, if I saved you only to have you mope forever about the fact that I'm gone and you're alone? That's why I'm sick of the pouting. Now look, down the street.

At the end of the block she saw a neon sign in two languages, one of which was Korean. She walked closer—it was a restaurant. And though she was sick to death of that cuisine, she at least would be able to read the menu.

A gawky, thin Korean girl who couldn't have been older than sixteen met her at the door and said something in English. Sari asked, in Korean, if she could have a table for one. The girl looked surprised that this clearly non-Korean person spoke her language, but she simply nodded and took her to a table in the middle of the small, dimly lit place.

Sari could indeed read the menu, and when the girl returned with a blessedly warm cup of tea (would she ever not be cold in this country?), Sari ordered some *bibimbap* she could barely afford. The girl eyed her for a moment. Her hair was long and she wasn't pretty, and she seemed to know this and wore a loud shade of blue eyeliner and lots of jangly necklaces and bracelets as if to distinguish herself in other ways. Her black blouse had ridiculous, poofy billows at the end of the sleeves. She must be the owner's daughter, Sari thought, sneaking in her rebellion where she can.

"How come you speak Korean?" the girl asked.

"I used to live in Seoul."

"Huh. I was born there. We moved when I was seven."

She seemed to be the only waitress, and when a white couple came in, she walked over to seat them. Sari tried not to think about her sisters or the Shims or Leo, tried to just take in the smells and the slightly familiar decorations, reveling in the feeling of being out with a little money to spend. She listened for her mother's voice, but she seemed to have returned to Sari's dream world.

Minutes later, as Sari was eating, the girl stopped by again. She said something in English before remembering that Sari didn't speak the language, then translated, asking how the food was.

"It's great, thank you."

"You don't speak English but you know Korean. Where are you from?"

"Indonesia. I've moved around a lot."

"Yeah, everyone here has."

"Here America, or here Washington?"

The girl shrugged. "I don't know. Kids in my high school, in Springfield, are from all over. I've been here almost ten years, which makes me really, really American compared to most of *them*."

Sari wanted to ask the girl if she liked it here, but she realized what a strange question that was. Instead, she asked, "So, you work here but you go to school too?"

"Of course. It's not like I'm going to be a waitress all my life." She didn't seem to think her comments would insult a slightly older person who worked even more menial jobs than hers.

"What are you studying to be?"

"I don't know. I always thought I'd be a doctor. But then this year we dissected little pigs and it was really, really gross. The insides and stuff." Then she looked at Sari's half-finished plate. "Oh, sorry. Bad to talk about. So now I'm thinking lawyer."

More customers walked in and the girl smiled before leaving Sari to her dinner.

Sari had already noticed, on the bottom of the mirror behind the small, unmanned bar, a hand-lettered sign advertising in Korean the need for a dishwasher. She'd had such jobs in restaurants before, not that experience would be necessary. Even in this vast foreign city there were tiny islands she could navigate. She wondered how much danger she was really in, wondered if Leo was exaggerating, if he just wanted to get rid of her. She wondered if that goofy young waitress really would be an American lawyer in a few years.

31.

Troy Jones pounded on Leo's door just as Leo was putting on his jacket to go out and obtain Sari's papers.

Leo didn't know who it was at first. He walked to his bedroom closet, and beneath the hanging oxfords he found the metal case where he stored the gun that he, as a resident of the District of Columbia, was not legally allowed to own. He turned off the safety, fed a round into the chamber, and walked to the door.

He put his eye to the peephole and saw Troy Jones through the thick glass.

"What do you want?" Leo asked.

"There are things I need to tell you." Jones seemed out of breath, as if he'd run up the stairs.

"Just you, or you and your gun?"

Jones didn't answer at first. "I'm sorry if I frightened you before."

The man sounded genuinely apologetic. Leo was leaning with his right hand pressed against the dead-bolted metal door, his gun pointed at the ceiling.

"How'd you get past the doorman?"

"I have identification. It isn't real, but he fell for it."

"Whatever you need to tell me, you can tell me through the door."

"All right. All right. There's something that needs to be stopped. Needs to be done, I mean. But I can't do it. I'm going to tell you, and hopefully it's something you can do."

"Why would I do something for you?"

"I'm going to give you some information. You're free to do something with it or not. There's nothing I can force anyone to do, do you understand? I'm just supposed to protect things. But I think I've been protecting the wrong things." He shook his head as if arguing with himself. The distorted picture Leo could see through the wall-eyed glass made Jones look even more disheveled and confused than he sounded. His hands were at his sides, and by his feet was a black briefcase. His jacket was unzipped. Nothing in the world would convince Leo to open that door. "I know I'm not making much sense."

"No, you're not, Troy."

"You know my cover. Interesting. But you don't understand. Listen. There's an organization, a network. It's called Enhanced Awareness. It develops systems, ways to track a population. Intelligence software, filtering methods. Ways to watch people. They sell their services to different countries, both allies and foes. They're in the process of closing deals with North Korea and Syria, among other hostile nations. The diplomat you've been watching is a go-between for North Korean intelligence. You said you were following his wife, but I have no information on her. Nothing in my databases. Enhanced Awareness will make the deal through *him,* and then these dictatorships will have access to information and methodologies that will allow them to more closely monitor their people—and people in other countries. It will strengthen their belligerent regimes, and something . . . very bad will happen as a result."

Leo tried to fit this into what he already knew. Hyun Ki was a diplomat with family connections in the telecom business, which made him uniquely positioned to close deals between high-tech surveillance firms and government entities. But why work for North Korea, his own country's bitter rival? He'd even married a woman who, if the stories were true, had lost everything to that Orwellian state. Still, Leo knew that people made stupid or staggeringly selfish decisions; perhaps the money was too good for Shim to refuse, or perhaps he was a North Korean spy who'd married Sang Hee only for cover.

"Why are you telling me this?" Leo asked.

"Maybe because I wanted to put your life in danger." And with that, Jones smiled, his lips skewed and almost leering through the glass. "The last person to know about this was a journalist, Karthik Chaudhry, who'd been tracking Enhanced Awareness and other intelligence contractors. He'd received certain...anonymous tips on the company's business strategies. You know of Mr. Chaudhry?"

Anonymous tips from whom, Leo wondered, *Jones himself? How else could he know this?* "I've read the news stories."

"Your news stories will never have the full information. Your news stories only know that he disappeared. He disappeared on his way to meet a source who didn't show up, and instead he was met by certain employees of Enhanced Awareness. He will never be heard from again. I was sent here because this is the best opportunity to disrupt the events. Due to some...security breaches, the company almost gets stopped before it can do real damage. But the company also employs some men with experience from *your* former employer, Mr. Hastings, men who know how to eliminate problems. They eliminated Chaudhry, and later tonight they're going to eliminate a few more people, including an activist named T.J. Trenton."

Leo's head buzzed with the not altogether pleasant sensation of disparate dendrites connecting from wrong sides of his brain. *T.J.?* "What exactly are they going to do?"

"Mr. Trenton and his associates were using a rundown house in Northeast Washington as a home base. The men from Enhanced Awareness showed up, shot them, and distributed enough drug paraphernalia to make it look like a drug buy gone bad. It helps that most of Mr. Trenton's friends indulge in a lot of marijuana. The D.C. police never thought to question it."

"Wait, this happened already?"

"Y—no, not yet." Jones shook his head. "In a few hours. I'm using the wrong tense, sorry. It's a little difficult for me to explain."

Leo took a breath, tried to make sense of this. "If this is legit, why aren't you doing anything about it?"

"I am doing something about it." His voice was raised and he glared into the peephole. "I'm telling you."

"But why *me?* You don't know anything about me."

"I know a lot about you, Leonard Hastings. You're in my files. Your future is not bright. This information might change that."

Jesus, this man was strange. He was talking like an android, someone phonetically producing lines in a language he'd never spoken before.

"But why are you telling *me* instead of someone who has authority over this?"

Jones laughed. It sounded unnatural coming from him, and he seemed to do it without smiling. "What authority are you referring to, Mr. Hastings? Someone or something that has authority over Enhanced Awareness? There is no authority like that, not how you mean. Your governments allowed businesses to take control of every task, and eventually that included military, defense, police work, and intelligence. There is no authority over stateless groups like this. Or maybe there is—I'm still having trouble with this. Either there is no authority anywhere, or there's authority everywhere, vested in everyone."

"What do you expect me to do?"

"I don't really have expectations. When you've known what was going to happen in advance for so long, life just starts to seem..." He shook his head. "I could talk to your door for the rest of my life and not explain myself right. I just... want to make something good come of this."

With that he placed his briefcase by the door. Then he backed up until he was leaning, almost slumping, against the wall. Leo was afraid the guy was going to faint, or fall asleep, and then he'd have to go the rest of the night knowing there was an armed madman just outside his door.

"Are you all right?"

"This time is very tiring. You people are under such stresses. And the unpredictability, the not knowing. You can't comprehend what I've just done. Leaving a trace like this. Maybe it won't matter, maybe you'll go to bed and ignore everything I've said. Maybe there *is* such a thing as fate, and I can't avoid it. There's this little girl I saw a few days ago, this cute little girl, black, in a pink sweater. I just wanted..." He laughed again and shook his head. "You wouldn't understand. But, please, do something with the information I just gave you. There's plenty more in the briefcase."

"You need to get help, Troy. More help than me, I mean."

Jones laughed again. "Troy Jones is dead."

"Not according to some files I looked at recently."

"Oh, that's right. He disappeared after he burned his house down and is listed in your records only as missing. His body isn't found for a few more days."

Listening to the matter-of-fact way in which this man seemed to predict his own suicide sent a chill up Leo's spine. He was glancing at the goose bumps on his arm when the doorman's buzzer rang.

"Hang on, Troy," Leo said, then dared to take his eyes from the door so he could lean against the opposite wall and press the intercom's button. "Yes?"

"Everything all right up there, Mr. Hastings?" The doorman was a reticent but cheerful older man from Southeast. They'd spoken about the Wizards and Skins from time to time, but that was it.

"Everything's fine, Gus. The guy you sent up is an old friend, that's all."

"Well, uh... You didn't hear me say this, but I just sent up two more of your *friends*."

Leo asked Gus for descriptions of the two men. Maybe they were the FBI agents, Michaels and Islington, coming up to gather Jones's mysterious evidence.

"One was bald and one had short dark hair with a little gray," the doorman said. "Big as linebackers."

Not the FBI. *Shit.* Leo caught his breath, then returned to the door. Jones was still standing against the opposite wall.

"I'm being watched, Troy. I think they've been waiting for *you,* and they're following you up now."

Jones's right hand smoothly slid into his open jacket. It emerged with a gun. "You're in danger, Mr. Hastings. They're faster than I thought."

Leo still didn't know what to believe. Jones's experience at NSA and then Enhanced Awareness meant that yes, it was possible he knew all those things. What he'd told Leo about the company's unethical and flat-out illegal dealings with Syria and North Korea did not surprise him, given his own impressions of Sentrick and based on what the FBI had elliptically mentioned. If Jones had any actual evidence, that would make the information very dangerous indeed.

"You need to act quickly," Jones said.

"No, they're coming up here for *you*. You stole their trade secrets and they want them back."

"In which case, they should call the police, not come in themselves."

"How do I know it isn't the police coming now?"

"It's the men from Enhanced Awareness. They're on their way to eliminate Mr. Trenton and are taking a detour to do the same thing to both of us, because our meeting like this only confirms their suspicion that you know too much. You have less than a minute to decide. I can protect myself from them. Can you?"

Leo was sweating, his palm slick against the door. "Put the gun away, *now*."

Jones placed the gun in his jacket pocket and presented his palms. "You need to learn to trust me."

Hoping he was not making the latest in a long line of mistakes, Leo opened the door.

"We can get out from the roof," Leo said. He quickly walked to the end of the hallway and opened the door to the stairs. He listened a moment, but no one was coming. Then he hurried up, popping the battery out of his phone so he couldn't be traced.

One of the many things Leo liked about this building was its relatively easy escape route. The real estate agent had found his questions odd, but Leo didn't care. A back stairwell led up two more flights to the roof deck, which was accessed by a door whose key code each of the residents knew. Leo punched it in, and he and Jones emerged onto the roof deck, which surrounded a small, empty pool. The breeze was strong from atop the six-story building, and a few drops of rain hit Leo's face.

Inside an unlocked custodian's closet was an extension ladder. He carried it out to the edge of the building, Jones watching him impassively. The neighboring building, identical except for the lack of a pool on its roof deck, was separated by an unusually narrow alley, fewer than ten feet wide. In the middle was a six-story drop.

Leo and Jones quickly unfolded the ladder, its metal springs and gears clicking as it grew in length. Jones figured out the plan without needing to be told, and together they stood the ladder up just in front of the four-foot-high wall that lined the perimeter of the building. Carefully they lowered it. They tried to go slowly, but the last few degrees came at a rush, and the ladder clanged loudly as it slammed into the edge of the other building.

"You've done this before?" Jones asked.

"I measured it, but I never actually got out there, no."

He was distracted by the sound of a siren, then a quick flash of red as an ambulance speeding down 16th was visible for the briefest of instants at the edge of the alley. The rain wasn't intensifying, fortunately, but still the metal ladder was getting wet. Another gust of wind came and Leo began to realize how risky this plan was. The fire escape was in the rear of the building, but he figured someone would be watching there.

Jones held the ladder in place, then Leo got on his knees and started crawling. He told himself that's all it was, just crawling. At first he tried to look forward, not down, but he missed once with a knee and realized he actually did need to look down to see where he was putting his hands and legs. He was thankful it was dark out; he almost couldn't see the ground.

At the end, he rolled off onto the other building's roof, then stood and held the ladder for Jones, who tossed his briefcase over to Leo before slowly making his way across.

They tried to lift the ladder up so they could stash it on their side, but they couldn't get enough leverage to lift it, and when they pulled it from its perch on the original building, it slipped down and nearly smashed the window of one of the top-floor units. Leo and Jones held on, struggling, regained control of it, then slowly walked backward and pulled it onto the roof deck. Leo slid it up against the wall, where it wouldn't be visible to anyone on the other side.

As they ran down the stairs, Leo tried to recap what Jones had told him. "You used to work for them, but you ran off with their *proprietary* info, and you've been tailing some of them while they try to close deals with North Korea and God knows who else. So they want to shut you up."

"That's the story."

Leo stopped at a landing between floors. "What do you mean, the *story?*"

"No, it's just . . . It's the truth. If you want to think I'm Troy Jones, then, yes, that's the truth."

"What the hell are you talking about? I *know* you're Troy Jones. I know about your wife and your daughter, and the NSA and her uncle. I know all about you."

Jones's face grew harder. "It's reassuring to know you've done your homework."

"But why did you say it was a *story?*"

Jones sighed, glancing up and down the stairs in search of pursuers. "Let me put it another way. Imagine we're in the future, maybe ten years down the line, maybe more. Countries like North Korea and Syria and Iran—as well as the dozens of other dictatorships you're so used to tolerating—control their populations more thoroughly than ever, using technology they bought from companies made up of former intelligence agents from America, Britain, Israel. These are autocratic regimes that your country claims to oppose, but you're strengthening them with these tools, however unintentionally. Time passes, such autocracies proliferate, and even democracies begin to take on those characteristics. Governments everywhere strengthen as the chasm between the watchers and the watched grows. To the people on top, this is the very essence of stability. Control, even peace. But what would happen, Leo Hastings, if, in a world like this, some rebel group actually managed to set off a few well-placed bombs? Or if the worst of the regimes, feeling more secure than ever, decided to take the next step and attack one of its enemies using nuclear weapons?"

Leo couldn't tell how serious the guy was. He certainly *looked* serious. But he was talking about this as if it had already happened.

"You honestly think that by stopping this company from doing business, you can stop a war from breaking out?"

"And now try to imagine that it was your job to ensure that everything I just explained did indeed occur. That anyone who tried to prevent it, no matter how well intentioned, needed to be stopped. That would be . . . very difficult to take, wouldn't it?"

Leo had heard about paranoid schizophrenics who were convinced that only they could avert a coming apocalypse but had never before spoken to one.

"I'm really not sure what I'm running from right now. I think you and your ex-colleagues are having a spat, and I never should have gotten in the middle of it. I think I should let you all settle your differences however you see fit."

"And Karthik Chaudhry, the dead reporter? I just invented him?"

"Anything could have happened to him."

"I can show you e-mails that Troy Jones sent him before his colleagues at Enhanced Awareness discovered that he was the leak. And what about the poisoning of Randolph McAlester, another former colleague at Enhanced Awareness who learned too much about their newest plans?"

Leo knew who McAlester was and had read the obit in the *Post*. "What's in your briefcase?"

"All the evidence you could possibly need."

Leo wasn't convinced, but he was getting there. He just wished that his one source for this story weren't so goddamned strange. If any of this was true, the FBI could build a case. But first Leo needed to read it and make sense of it. And there was still Sari to deal with.

"Why are they going after T.J.?"

"Because his network of underground journalists managed to uncover some files belonging to Chaudhry, files that Enhanced Awareness failed to track down and delete after they eliminated him last week. So now they need to stop Mr. Trenton and his friends from posting about the company's alarming business practices."

"Then you should know that *I'm* working for a company that's trying to nail T.J. too."

"Yes, but you didn't realize that they were trying to kill him."

Leo waited. "*My* company isn't trying to—"

"Your mystery client is Enhanced Awareness. They've led your boss, Mr. Bale, to believe that the plan is merely to entrap Mr. Trenton, but now that you've succeeded in proving that he is the mastermind behind that Web site, they're not going to settle for entrapment."

Leo hated having to stand there and be watched as he took a moment to absorb the information, but he had no choice. He couldn't move.

"I don't . . . I don't believe—"

"You don't *want* to believe it." Jones looked at him almost pityingly. "But you believe it."

They resumed their race down the stairs, exiting at the second floor. He took Jones down a hallway to a different staircase that led to an exit on the south side, out of view of Leo's building. Then they walked west, eventually intersecting with Columbia and merging with those who were getting a head start on the nightlife in Adams Morgan. Twentysomethings pivoting from work to pleasure, teens standing on corners with baggy jackets and too much free time, buses impatiently exhaling as they sat in traffic. Leo checked for a tail but didn't find one. His pursuers would likely be canvassing the area within minutes if they weren't doing so already.

"I still don't understand why you don't take your evidence to the FBI or someone who could officially investigate," Leo said.

"They would of course ask who I am and what else I've done. I don't feel comfortable divulging that."

"Because even you don't know who the hell you are?"

Jones stopped and eyed him.

"There are three reasons I chose you. One is that I knew you were working to entrap Mr. Trenton but that you had no idea how...malevolent your role actually was; I figured that once you learned that, you wouldn't like how you'd been used. Two is that I knew that because of your former work, you had a certain skill set that would help you deal with this. And three is that I knew you'd once come into possession of evidence that damned a powerful organization you worked for, and you knew what to do with it: you leaked it."

Leo shook his head. "Christ, you too?"

"You were the leak to the newspapers about the CIA's black sites— one of the leaks, actually. There were three. You probably didn't know that. You called the *Washington Post,* and the others called—"

"That is *bullshit.*" Leo's hands were fists.

"First you reported your misgivings internally, following protocol. But when nothing was done about it, you leaked the story to the press. I saw all this in my files when I researched you."

"If there were any files, I would be in *jail* now, and—"

"A decision was made from very high up, Mr. Hastings, that such a prosecution would be detrimental to the Agency and to America's sense of its national security. So they chose to weed you out based on some other misdeed and let the black-sites story play itself out in the media. Which it did. I assure you, though, they know you were the leak. And of course *you* do, so why are you lying to yourself about it?"

Leo looked away. *Breathe, Leo. Breathe, and take what he's saying.*

"Why are you so angry about this?" Jones asked. "As best as I can determine the morals in this beat, it was the right thing to do. They were torturing people without evidence of their wrongdoing. Based on shoddy investigative work, even guesswork. Sometimes they had the right people, sometimes they didn't. They were operating in what they considered a lawless realm and decided they could play God. It's a familiar paradigm from what I've seen. As I said, it's one of the reasons I chose you."

Leo and Jones were motionless on the sidewalk as others passed them.

Leo said, "I only wanted to weed out the people who—"

"You don't need to explain yourself to me. What you need to do is take this." Jones held the briefcase out to Leo.

"There a tracking device in it?"

"If there were, do you think I'd still be alive?"

Leo took it from him, hoping he would not deeply regret this.

"Where are you going next?" Leo asked. "They'll be here soon." He started walking again, Jones alongside step by step.

"I don't know. Up to this point, I've always known what was going to happen next. And suddenly I don't."

They were standing in front of a fried-chicken joint that probably wouldn't be there a year from now, with the winds of gentrification blowing eastward. The city was changing around them.

"I'll look into this, and if it says what you claim it does, I'll get it to the right people."

"Quickly," Jones said. "Mr. Trenton and his friends will be dead in less than two hours."

Leo ran down a list of possible explanations for Jones's behavior: that Jones had been a spy for another country while working at NSA and now was trying to take down a valuable intelligence contractor in order to weaken America's defenses; that this was all an elaborate test, perhaps by the Agency itself, to see if Leo truly was the whistle-blowing type; that Jones was just a disgruntled ex-employee of Enhanced Awareness who wanted to ruin the company out of spite; that Jones was insane. Of all of them, only the last seemed free of contradiction.

"First, tell me about your wife's uncle."

"That's not relevant to this."

Leo stepped closer and lowered his voice. "I say it is. Tell me about him. What he was into. What your wife was into. What you did about it."

Jones did not break eye contact as Leo stood too close. For a moment something passed over Jones's face, and Leo feared that the man was going to throw a punch.

The flash of anger passed, and Jones spoke in his detached, third-person manner. "Troy Jones knew almost nothing about the uncle. She had a very large family, uncles and aunts living all over the globe. He could never keep their names straight. Some of her relatives were politically active, but they'd all been vetted, otherwise Jones never would have received such clearance at NSA."

"But that vetting would have occurred before 9/11."

"So maybe the uncle was involved in the wrong things, perhaps he did have unsavory contacts. Perhaps even *he* was unsavory. But Jones didn't know."

"And so one day the Agency took the uncle," Leo said, "in Europe somewhere, rounding him up based on intel from tools *you'd* helped develop. And that was hard for you to live with."

"Like it was hard for you to live with knowing you'd delivered innocent men and women to be tortured by your Agency. Only harder, because none of those people were related to your wife." Jones held the stare for an uncomfortable amount of time. "But, as I said, Jones's family is not relevant to the events you need to be dealing with here."

Again he was hiding behind his coded language and mannerisms. The real Troy Jones was deeply buried.

After Jones caught a cab headed west on Columbia, Leo ordered a sandwich and a Coke at the fried-chicken joint, then carefully balanced the tray in his free hand as he walked to a table in the back. He wished he didn't have to be here right now, but this was when his contact for Sari's ID said he'd meet him.

He sat staring at the wall for a while. How the hell did Jones know that Leo had leaked the black-sites story? Leo had covered his tracks, left no trace. He knew they *suspected* him, sure—everyone did. He hadn't reckoned on the fact that their suspicion alone would ostracize him. He'd been removed from his post immediately after the hotel bombing. First they'd stuck him in a Bangkok office with no responsibility pending an investigation into his motives for the prisoner release. Then they'd fired him—because of the bombing, he had assumed, and not the leaked story. Perhaps he'd been wrong. Maybe that's why Gail had looked sorry for him that night, for being the only person who thought he'd gotten away with it.

Maybe even Bale knew Leo had leaked the story. Hell, it was probably why Bale hired him. Use a leaker to catch a leaker. This had been so obvious all along, and Leo hadn't figured it out until now.

Leo ignored the food and slowly swallowed his anger. Then he opened the briefcase and started reading through Jones's files. He'd been wearing his leather gloves outside, and he kept them on so as not to leave any prints. If some of the customers up front were suspicious about the white dude in back reading paperwork with gloved hands, they were good enough not to say so out loud.

There was a laptop and some flash drives in the briefcase, and there was no order whatsoever to the papers—certain spreadsheets had been stapled to unrelated memos, and later Leo would find the rest of the spreadsheet paper-clipped to a different letter. This was clearly the work of a disheveled mind. Jones was just one of those madmen who babbled at street corners, talking to God and transcribing the conversations into tiny notebooks in invented languages. Why had Leo believed him?

But as Leo read on, certain dots became connected. Cause and effect were established. He reorganized the papers as he went. The files from Hyun Ki Shim had demonstrated that he, or someone Shim represented, was a prospective client of Enhanced Awareness; in most instances they identified Shim by a code name, but the real one popped up often enough. Some of the internal Enhanced Awareness memos in Jones's briefcase seemed to imply that the company knew that Shim represented government buyers in North Korea and China. Leo did find one e-mail exchange between aghast employees ("I just can't believe we're thinking of selling to NK regardless of how we paper it over"), but these were countered with a number of memos championing the sales coup this would be ("Prosp client represents key foothold into new market, one that has demonstrated strong loyalty and is forecast to have signif growth").

There was much discussion about Chaudhry's investigative reporting into the company's business practices, and, as Jones had said, e-mails sent to the reporter from a clearly pseudonymous e-mail account at EA (hello@enhancedawe.net, likely Jones's own doing) spilled some juicy secrets. Leo also found a few e-mails between EA principals debating what they should do about Mr. McAlester, a former board member who was threatening to go public with the company's plan to pursue "clients that the public might construe as undesirable."

Buried in the briefcase was information about T.J., Tasha, and several of T.J.'s coconspirators. Some of the memos Leo himself had written and handed to Bale. Others contained details Leo hadn't been privy to, such as the location of a safe house T.J.'s group was using in Northeast D.C. There was nothing here stating that anyone planned on killing T.J., but, in light of what Jones had said, the level of detail about the activists' comings and goings became very ominous indeed. Leo felt sick to his stomach at knowing that his own work was being used this way. It was a familiar feeling.

So while Leo had been monitoring T.J. and his crowd for a client who turned out to be Enhanced Awareness, Leo had also—completely by accident—bumped into the servant of a diplomat with whom EA was negotiating a key transaction. Bale himself must not have known the connection between EA and Shim, otherwise he never would have allowed Leo to recruit Sari. Only after Leo had told the EA men in the SUV that he'd met Jones outside a Korean diplomat's house did they make the connection—and then they'd had Bale tell him to back off. This just reminded Leo how damned messy it was to do intelligence work in this city, where all the spots were taken and you never knew which extraneous plotlines you might stumble into.

There was more in the briefcase than Leo could possibly absorb in even a full day of reading, and Lord only knew what was on the laptop and in the flash drives—he wasn't going to boot up here. A group of teenagers burst out laughing and Leo felt anew the absurdity of reading such material in a fast-food joint, grease in the air and bad hip-hop thumping on the house speakers.

Leo should be calling the FBI *now,* not sitting here waiting on a guy who could get an ID for Sari. Maybe he could call T.J. himself, to warn him? No, he didn't know T.J.'s number, but surely there were other ways to get the message to him.

Afraid of being tracked via his phone, he walked back to the counter and asked the thirteen-year-old Latina in the unflattering yellow uniform if he could use their phone for a local call. She gave him a look like he'd asked her where to score drugs.

"Please, it's a local call and my phone is dead. Just a one-minute call."

She finally shrugged, reached into her pocket, and handed him her cell. Even better.

He dialed Tasha's number, thankful for his good memory (and training) in this age where people never remembered numbers anymore. Her voice mail picked up immediately, which he didn't like. He hoped it meant only that she was on another call.

"Tasha, it's me." He turned away from the girl. "You need to tell your friend that his place in Northeast is not safe. He needs to leave, immediately. Trust me and tell him to get out of there the moment you get this."

He handed the phone back to the girl just as Edwin walked in the door, a full thirty minutes late.

Leo had met Edwin while doing a bit of opposition research for TES, his first assignment for the company. The firm had been asked by a prominent Raleigh businessman to research David Franklin, three-term Republican congressman from the state of North Carolina who was expected to announce his Senate candidacy the following year (and whom the businessman despised). Before the Knoweverything project began ramping up, Leo spent countless hours studying Congressman Franklin's votes, financial disclosure statements, driving history, real estate transactions, vehicle ownership records, academic transcripts, and public comments, looking for dirt. Finally, he drove to Franklin's house one day and noticed that Mrs. Franklin had hired some contractors to redo their one-and-a-half-million-dollar Palisades colonial. Leo cased the house for a week; all of the workers were Central American. Franklin was a strict opponent of illegal immigration. Leo wondered how diligently the congressman's wife checked the legal status of her contractors.

Not very, it turned out. One day Leo approached the head contractor, a mestizo-looking man from Honduras or maybe El Salvador, sweaty and wearing a tourist T-shirt, his broad chest emblazoned with a U.S. flag, yellow fireworks, and the word ANTIETAM. Leo pretended to be in the market for a new kitchen and bathroom, chatting the guy up about fixtures and grout while trying to get a sense of what kind of help the man used. Leo eventually had the contractor over to his house to give an estimate, and while the contractor was in the bathroom, Leo asked one of the other workers if the guy could do some painting for him on the side. The worker nodded and quietly slipped Leo his own card.

Leo never followed through with the contractor, but he did call the other guy, Edwin, for an estimate on painting a couple of rooms. He befriended Edwin during the next week, handing him a beer and watching ESPN with him after each workday, paint fumes thick in the air. He learned that Edwin, a pretty cool guy with not quite as good a grasp of English as Leo had of Spanish, was an illegal from Nicaragua who was sending remittances home for his wife and two kids and hoping the Marxists wouldn't take over and the gangs wouldn't get too out of control before he found a way to get his family up here.

Just before TES handed its client evidence that the fervently anti-illegal-immigrants congressman was in fact benefiting from the cheap labor they provided to renovate his Washington mansion, Leo called Edwin to warn him. Leo told him that Edwin's boss, the contractor, was soon going to get in a lot of trouble and that Edwin might want to dissociate himself from the guy immediately if he planned to stay in the country.

They shook hands now and Leo took him to the back, where Edwin glanced oddly at Leo's tray of cold, untouched food.

"No hungry?"

"My stomach's not doing too well." Leo pushed the tray of food away and reached into his pocket for the memory card from the digital camera he'd used to take Sari's photo. He handed it to Edwin.

The painter/handyman—who had been a bank teller in Managua before he was framed for a bank heist committed by a group of former Sandinistas who'd needed funds to bankroll an election; Edwin had fled before the police could arrest him, he'd told Leo—watched the former spy for a moment.

"Tell me again why you need this."

"I have a friend who's in trouble. She needs an ID and a Social Security number, and I need it in a few hours."

Edwin raised his eyebrows at the time constraint, which Leo hadn't mentioned during their brief call.

"Guy I know, he can do this, but I don't know about that fast."

Leo figured the guy operated in this very neighborhood; there had been a few police busts for identity theft and the selling of fake passports and SSNs at some of the local restaurants and ethnic shops.

"I can pay more if he wants."

Edwin mulled this over. "Why a guy like you need this?"

"My friend needs it."

Edwin looked at the photo again. "This is for love?"

"She needs help. I don't know where else to turn."

"How I know this ain't a trap?"

"If I hadn't called to warn you that time, you'd be back in Managua. In jail."

Edwin thought about this. "Yeah. But you're the one set those guys up. How I know you didn't just warn me that one time so you could set me up again later, use me to bust more guys?"

"I didn't bust anyone. I just gathered information for someone who . . ." Leo's voice trailed off as he realized that his rationalizations meant nothing.

"I don't really know you, Leo."

Who did? "Look, you can take my money right now and just run off with it. If you do, sure, you screw me, but nothing's really going to happen to me—*I'll* be fine. But a very good woman will get deported, or worse. I'd like to stop that from happening to her, just like I stopped it from happening to you."

It was borderline humiliating that Leo, whose former employer could have provided him with false identification papers in mere hours, was reduced to groveling before a Nicaraguan immigrant in a fast-food joint. He tried not to focus on this latest evidence of how far he had fallen.

"She really your girl?"

He shook his head. "I'm not good enough for her."

Edwin grinned. "Okay, you wait. I check with my man."

Leo sat with his cold food and hot briefcase as Edwin disappeared to consult with his source, who Leo now knew for certain was in the area. Leo took the time to pore over Jones's files and connect more dots.

Ten minutes later, Edwin was back.

"Okay," he said. "Pay now. He says he leave it for you in envelope at mailbox for house at 1009 Kenyon Street Northwest. Is vacant. Someone'll put it there in two hours."

Leo opened his wallet below the table, fished out the cash plus extra for the rush charge. Then he slid it into an envelope and passed it to Edwin.

Leo left the fried-chicken place and walked three blocks—checking for surveillance the whole way—to the only pay phone left in this neighborhood. He found Special Agent Michaels's card and dropped some coins into the slot.

"Yes?"

"We spoke at my place earlier tonight."

If Michaels was annoyed or confused by Leo's cryptic greeting, he didn't show it. "Yes, of course."

"I have something you're going to want to look at."

"Already? This time I'm the one who's impressed with how fast *you* are."

"He came by, not long after you did. And he led me to believe that time is of the essence here. What do you know about a reporter named Chaudhry?"

There was a brief pause. "A good amount."

"I'm told someone is going to meet a similar fate very soon, at 702 R Street Northeast. How quickly can you meet me?"

32.

It was rather too fitting that Tasha again found herself in the back of a van. At least this one had windows, and no one had thrown her into it. She'd opened the door herself, boarded of her own free will. Or had she? How free had she been, in any of this?

After sifting through the wreckage that was her home for longer than she could stand, she'd washed her face so she wouldn't look like she'd been crying, then walked over to the house of one of her friendlier neighbors, a fortysomething gay man who liked to brag about being the first person to gentrify this neighborhood. He always brought up the time he'd seen a man chase his girlfriend/lover/prostitute down the street while wielding a bloody steak knife, a week after he'd moved into the house. Tasha was never sure how she was supposed to take these stories of the neighborhood's wayward past, and she noticed at parties and sidewalk chats how her race threw complications into the cozy narrative of white gentrifiers saving a bad neighborhood. But the neighbor was friendly, and he had a phone. (She didn't trust hers anymore, and had turned it off.) She'd lied to him that her phones were out, and she called T.J. and said there was something she needed to tell him in person. He told her to meet her at a certain street corner east of Shaw, his words unusually terse.

She'd called for a cab, not wanting to walk anywhere near the Metro station from which she'd been abducted; she was already too freaked out by whatever was happening. Who was following her, and why? She assumed that whoever had trashed her house worked for the same people as the men who'd driven her around in the van; perhaps the interrogation itself was less important than the fact that it kept her out of her house so someone could search it.

And the more she thought about it, the more she wondered about Troy. He'd tried to say something to her about "not being a part of this," whatever that meant, and he'd looked legitimately ashamed of what she found in his briefcase. She'd thought it was just more of his act. But maybe he'd been telling the truth? Had Troy's relationship with her been less of a con than she'd assumed? Had it been genuine, and had he been trying to figure out his new role in this maddening world just as she was?

The cab dropped her off at the intersection where T.J. said he'd meet her, but there was no T.J. There was no anyone, and this didn't feel like a good place to be killing time. It was cold and windy that night; acorns popped off parked car roofs like tiny firecrackers. She was still in her heels and business suit, and she felt she must look like a big wallet to someone.

A blue van pulled up. Jesus, another van. The window rolled down and she recognized the driver, a white kid with bad skin and worse facial hair, from one of T.J.'s meetings.

"T.J. says sorry for the subterfuge. Hop in back."

She hesitated, but he looked too unthreatening for this to be a dangerous proposition. She got in the back, and he asked her to keep her head low so she wouldn't be spotted. He apologized again in a hipster monotone, as if telling a housemate he was sorry for smoking all her weed. T.J., he explained, was a bit "wigged" due to a few "developments," and they were taking precautions.

"I don't remember your name," she said.

"Yeah, that's cool, actually. Probably better not to."

His radio was playing whatever fuzzy style of rock had supplanted grunge in the white kids' world. The singer was screaming, *"I won't waste it / I won't waste it / I won't waste my love on a nation!"*

Even with her head low (why exactly did she need to hide?) she could look up and see the tops of buildings. He drove them a few blocks north of Rhode Island Avenue, a part of town unreached by the

Metro lines and therefore on the dark side of the moon as far as young professionals and college kids were concerned. She'd had a friend who lived around here once, maybe in second or third grade, but Tasha hadn't been in the neighborhood since.

"It's a good spot," he said, as if hearing her thoughts. "You know, off the beaten path but close enough to New York Ave. and the B-W Parkway to be useful for getaways."

A minute later, he pulled up in front of a row house whose lights weren't on. "He's on the porch."

Even when she sat up, she couldn't see what he was pointing to, but she got out anyway. Only after he'd pulled away did she see a form sitting in a chair on the porch. She climbed the steps slowly, and then the form stood.

"Hey, Tasha," T.J. said, his voice quieter and calmer than usual. He was wearing a slim brown leather jacket, blue jeans, and running shoes whose intense whiteness was not as conducive to hiding at night. She had no idea if he'd come from inside the house or if this was a vacant place he'd chosen as a random rendezvous spot.

She made a point of looking around at the quiet, empty block. "What's going on?"

"You first," he said. "What is it you needed to tell me this late, in person?"

Her thoughts had been so muddled that she hadn't even planned this part out yet. "I need to apologize." Looking into his green eyes, though it was so dark out they could have been any color. "I got myself caught in a bind. The information that I've been giving you, about Consolidated Forces... It's not true."

He watched her for a moment. "How so?"

"I leaked the GTK story. I...I wanted to do it, I knew it was right. But someone found out about it, and they threatened to tell my firm. I would have been disbarred, gone bankrupt. So—"

"So the girl who's made compromises all her life decided to make one more."

She had busted her ass for years so she wouldn't wind up in a

397

neighborhood just like this one, yet to the raised-in-Berkeley rebel standing before her, it was all "compromise."

"I was *stalling* them, T.J. Someone tried to play me, so I played them right back. I was never going to let you run with those stories; I just needed to string them along until I could get something out of them about Marshall."

"So if you were to write a column about this in that arts weekly of yours, the hypothetical letter would say, 'Dear Tasha, I'm being blackmailed into betraying a friend who's dedicated his life to tearing down the walls of power, and I feel kind of bad about this.' And your advice to yourself would be 'The hell with him, girl, do whatever you need to keep that corporate lawyer gig.'"

She wasn't sure if he hadn't heard her explanation or if it had just sounded like so much equivocal bullshit.

"That corporate-law gig is effectively over. And I'm probably going to be disbarred, so don't ask me to defend you next time you're arrested for trespassing. But I'm sure I'll still seem oh-so-bourgeois to you and the true believers."

A familiar bass line vibrated up her feet as someone's car's subwoofer inched closer. She and T.J. both turned their heads as a black SUV cruised down the street, slowly. She realized she'd been holding her breath when it reached the end of the block and proceeded north. The beats faded and she exhaled.

He looked across the street at a row of houses identical to the ones on his side; it was as if a mirror had been lowered into the center of the asphalt, reflecting everything but themselves.

"You know, I'm not as against the mainstream media as you think I am," he said. "I do know some good folks who are reporters. But I know one fewer than I used to. This buddy of mine, Karthik. He worked for Reuters. Was real interested in all these private intelligence contractors running around D.C., acting like they're the CIA only they don't have to report to anyone. He wrote some eye-opening stories, and he was working on a new one that was going to shine a light on a couple of companies in particular, on work they were doing for other countries, and how some people in U.S. intelligence even helped out so long as they got paid their share. So they killed him."

She'd seen a file about the reporter in Troy's briefcase. She thought about voicing this but didn't see the point. She was still trying to figure out *T.J.'s* point.

"The files you were giving me, Tasha, they were interesting. But I guess whoever was giving them to you thought we were dumber than we are, that we wouldn't double-check anything. Some of the names in there are real—just enough to get us in trouble for libel—but plenty of them aren't. And the companies too—some of the ones in those memos are real, others aren't. I don't know who it was that gave them to you, but he didn't cover his tracks as well as he thought."

"So...you've known all along?"

"Not all along, no. I believed you at first. Believed you really were taking a chance on me, taking a chance on yourself, to do some good."

"Is that why we're talking on some strange porch in a dead part of town?"

"I've been followed the last few days, and so have some other folks. I don't think it's the same people that have been trying to frame us, but it could be. Doesn't matter. I've never lacked for enemies—if I ever do, it'll mean I'm not doing a very good job. So me and my folks are leaving town. Some of the other projects we've been working on will have to fall through, but that's okay. The Knoweverything story is more important, and we can do that from anywhere."

"But...the stories are fake."

"That *is* the story. We aren't going online with 'Consolidated Forces' Internal Documents Show That' blah blah blah, we're going with 'Privatized Intelligence Industry Spreading Disinformation, Tailing Activists, Killing Reporters.' Those fake docs you gave me, those are part of the story, definitely. But not in the way your black-mailers thought."

She tried to straighten this out. "So *I'm* in the story?"

"We won't use your name. But we will have to say 'an unnamed attorney at a Washington law firm who leaked the GTK story and was blackmailed for it,' et cetera, et cetera. Kind of an important point."

The way he said that, she could tell he'd already known she was the leak even before her admission tonight. He must have read the e-mails she'd sent to the *Times* reporter after all. "Jesus, might as well use my name then!"

"Are *you* expecting *me* to apologize?"

"T.J., I was going to tell you in time. I was."

He gave her a patronizing look. "I'm sure that's what you told yourself."

Leave it to T.J. to make her regret the fact that she'd warned him, or even apologized to him. She folded her arms. "If thinking that people like me are part of the problem makes it easier for you to fight your battles," she said, "then fine, go ahead and demonize me too. See how many people you wind up with on your side."

Then she realized she was almost overlooking the most disturbing thing he'd said. "The reporter you mentioned," she asked. "You're really sure that he—"

"Was killed? Yeah. By people who worked for one of the companies he was reporting on? Yeah. If you thought these were just well-intentioned government employees who don't really do anything wrong beyond trying to frame people at progressive Web sites and spying on activists, then, Jesus, open your eyes. You know how many billions of dollars the government throws at these companies? Companies that can just hide behind the flag and do whatever the hell they want? Those GTK executives who pissed you off so much, they let a bunch of soldiers die just to save a few mil on shipping costs. Tell me, if your private spook firm stood to lose millions because some journalist was going to write a story about the sketchy shit your firm was up to, what would *you* be willing to do about it?"

"I just . . ." She was shaking her head. "I find it hard to believe—"

"You've been suspending your disbelief a little too long, girl."

She thought of Leo and then Troy insinuating themselves into her life. The men in the white van. The destruction of her house. This would have been a good time to tell him about her van interrogation, and about Troy Jones, but she didn't want any of that making its way into his online diatribe. Not all of her life experiences would become fodder for a political battle. She was alarmed by what he'd told her, but she wasn't going to cross over to T.J.'s radical worldview every time one game in the grand geopolitical contest happened to go down differently than she wished it had.

"Look at what's happening in the world today," he said, "in this *country* today. They want to rewrite the rules for what a government can and can't do—no, forget rewriting, they just want to do whatever they can and make up the rules later. Hell, half the people responsible for Watergate got back in positions of power a few terms later; same with Iran-contra, and it'll be the same with Abu Ghraib and Guantánamo. Someone gets nailed for whatever scandal, and he just disappears for eight or twelve years and then comes back again, rewriting the history books every time. People never learn, or they just don't care."

We're all predisposed toward certain stories and plots, Tasha thought, as T.J. went on for another minute or two about his group's role in the vital struggle for the nation's soul. Some people are more inclined to believe that the government or amoral corporations are out to get them, that nefarious watchers are everywhere, and that they are mere pawns in games they'll never understand. Others think that's a fool's explanation for the world's entirely understandable and blameless discrepancies in power. Some believe they can do anything, that they have power vested in them by something divine or by writ of law, that even the smallest individual can change history. Others would call that a delusion of grandeur. Everyone wanted to believe he'd discovered the truth, that it had been covered up by some top-secret agency or bought and sold by a backdoor agreement between politicos and billionaires. Whatever the story, there's always evidence somewhere, there's an adherent to the cause shouting at you, directing you to certain Web sites, to books produced by small publishers; they're out there if you look in the right place, there are statistics, facts that *they don't want you to know*. Open your eyes. Believe the story, the truth. *My* truth, not the other guy's. The other guy's a tool of the system, or a kook, or an oppressor, or a loser in search of something to blame.

How cynical was she prepared to be? How idealistic? How much effort did she want to put into understanding the plot twists and intersecting story lines? What's more believable, unreliable narrators or noble heroes? Maybe T.J. was right and Tasha's credit cards and e-mails and ideas were being tracked by men who would crush her for the fun of it. But she'd met such men, just a few hours ago, and they hadn't crushed her. They'd trashed her place, yes, they'd scared and enraged her, but she was still here. Maybe that counted for something. Or maybe if it had happened to T.J., they would have beaten him to nothingness and left him on an off-ramp.

"So what's next?" she asked.

"We're getting out of town, but first we need to finish uploading a few things. And checking a couple more facts. You can help us if you want, or if you want to just come in and warm up and call for a cab, that's cool too." He walked toward the front door. It was so dark inside, she was amazed there was anyone in there. They must be huddled in back rooms behind light-blocking shades.

"And then? What happens to you?"

He would no doubt toss his cell phone. He had no credit cards, maybe not even a driver's license. He would disappear. "I'll be in a safe place, and we'll tell our story."

Z.

The worst part is the guilt. That and knowing I've been deceived, that I was on the wrong side all along.

That, of course, was what my wife was saying to me during those final days. The scorn in her voice, the hatred in her eyes; she had discovered that her loving husband's work for our government had put her father's life in danger. It was impossible for her to view it in any other terms. Maybe her emotions would have cooled over time. Or maybe not—maybe more time would have calcified her anger, hardened it like a new backbone that would never bend to the forces she saw conspiring against her.

Had her father really been guilty? Had he in fact been behind the Revisions plot; was he a forerunner of the hags, gathering information about history so they could go back and disrupt it? I had no choice but to accept the intel. What else could I have done? Believe that my life's work was being used against my own family?

What have I wasted my life on?

I wish I could talk to her about this. There are so many conversations we can't have. I think of all the silent evenings, the times we had more important things to do. The wasted time.

I'm sorry, Cemby. I'm sorry if I was on the wrong side. Please believe that it wasn't my fault. Please believe that I wasn't responsible for what happened to your father, or to you. Believe instead that I was tricked, that I was a dupe, that I was a just another misguided idealist, that I had enough love in my heart that I dared to imagine a better world, something closer to perfect. At the very least, believe that I did the wrong things for the right reasons.

What now?

What does a Protector do when he's decided not to protect the Events anymore? When he's decided that the disasters are best averted, not facilitated? If there really are any hags out here, if they aren't all figments of my damaged cerebral cortex or parts of some fantastical plot put in place by Wills or other enemies, I'm going to let them be. They are free to remake the world in their image. I can only hope it turns out better than the one I've decided to let rot, or disappear, or whatever it is that happens when choices are not made. Things that are left to others' imaginations.

I want to see Tasha again—it seems a bad idea, since all I've ever done is put her in danger. And as I sit in the cab thinking, I realize that I'm letting myself off too easy. All I've actually done is refuse to protect the final Event, and I've assumed that it was enough. But maybe it isn't—the Great Conflagration could still happen, the Events could still find a way of falling into place, give or take an hour or two, the transposition of some people and locations. There's a certain entropic force that might hold sway. I haven't done enough.

The cabbie drops me off near where I parked my car, and I get in and check my internal GPS. I'd slipped a Tracker on Leo, just in case, and I'm glad I did. He's moving north, and I head that way too. Ten minutes later I park outside a car-rental service where Leo is signing some papers; before long he's driving out of their back lot in a gray sedan.

With everything he's gone through tonight, he's likely checking for a tail, so I give him a five-minute head start, content to let the Tracker and GPS guide me. He drives into northeast D.C., first along the main avenues and then the side streets. Remembering my last experience tailing someone in the city, I mind the street signs and traffic lights so I won't have another awkward conversation with D.C.'s finest.

I'm driving through a maze of row houses when the Tracker tells me that Leo has pulled over one block away, where the residential neighborhood abruptly ends at the edge of a vast train yard north of Union Station.

Was I wrong to trust Leo? Was I crazy when I thought that I saw in him so many aspects of myself? We are, after all, only a block or two away from the safe house where T.J. is furiously uploading information into his computers before fleeing D.C. Is this mere coincidence? Has Leo come here to meet someone who will only facilitate the start of the Conflagration?

I park two blocks south of him. I quietly close my door and walk, trying without success to avoid the fallen leaves and acorn caps. I did some tracking in the woods of Poland, but not in autumn, and everywhere my foot falls, there's noise. So I walk on the road itself, and I'm almost there when I hear another vehicle approaching. I hurry off the road and crouch behind parked cars. A white van emblazoned with the Metro's logo passes, though there isn't a Metro station anywhere near here.

This is very familiar. They aren't using the parking lot by the airport this time; they must fear that the authorities have pieced together that much of the Chaudhry disappearance. This location—within the city yet remote, devoid of witnesses but booming with background noise from passing trains—is even better for their purposes. A journalist would have been too suspicious or scared to meet somewhere like this, but Leo, a former intelligence officer himself, no doubt appreciates the clandestine gesture. They're appealing to his ego, and he's falling for it.

I take the gun from my pocket and walk as quickly as I can without giving myself away. I round the corner and see, thirty yards away, Leo standing with his back against a fence, facing the neighborhood. Behind the fence is a twenty-foot-tall mound of compacted dirt and then at least a dozen tracks and dormant trains. There are some streetlights but they're all aimed at the train yard; the effect is to darken the area where Leo now stands.

The van has parked in front of Leo. A thin, younger man gets out of the driver's side—he's the one Leo described to his doorman, I now see. Then the familiar two men emerge from the back and stand flanking their prey.

Either the hags don't know about this little meeting because it is something of my own creation and not in their files, or they simply have better things to do right now. Or possibly there never were any hags, and I'm alone.

"Thanks, Leo," the younger one says as he takes the briefcase. I can only hear him because of my internal mike—I'm still too far away, and a passenger train is rolling north on one of the tracks. "I can't tell you how much this helps."

The van blocks me from their view now; I cross the street in a crouch. Leo had backed up a half step when the two big guys approached, as if he sensed what was coming but had too much pride, didn't want to risk looking scared if there was no reason. But there is a reason.

Because now the younger one is brandishing a gun, and one of the big men steps behind Leo and pins his arms back. The other one slugs him in the stomach, doubling him over. The gunman opens the van's back door so his partners can cram Leo inside.

"Stop," I say. "Drop the gun."

Four faces in various states of distress look my way. The gunman's hand, which had been held low, instinctively rises a few inches. I yell, "Drop it, now!"

"Holy shit," the gunman says. Trying to seem calm and in control, but his face looks even whiter than the contemps' faces usually do. "It's you."

I step closer, slowly, so as not to goad him into firing. A few feet behind and just to his left the others stand in a cluster. Leo's arms are still pinned back. I'm aiming at the head of the only person I can see holding a gun.

"Hands up, all of you," I say.

"Walk away now," the gunman says, "and feel fortunate you made it this far."

One of the bigger men disagrees. "We're not letting him go, Hale."

Three targets, one of them holding. I'll take him first, then the other two. I need to be careful not to hit Leo. I can probably do this. I don't make eye contact with Leo—I'm afraid to take my eyes off the gunman, Hale—but a certain relaxation of Leo's shoulders tells me his arms aren't being held so tightly now.

Because I knew what was coming in advance for so long, I felt that I was moving forward through events that were moving backward, like I was walking in place. Always hurrying but never getting any farther ahead. This is the first time since I've been with the Department that I feel completely unmoored, unsure of what will happen next. It scares me, but not as much as I would have thought.

No better ideas have come to me yet, so I keep the gun aimed at Hale's face and then pull the trigger.

I turn to the others next, but they scatter. One of them dives behind the back of the van, leaving Leo standing in the open, and another runs in the opposite direction, toward the fence that blocks off the rail yard, pulling a gun from his jacket and firing. I move my arm to follow him and pull the trigger again and again while the world flares and everything around me seems to explode. Including the van's headlight—someone else's bullet hits it, and shards of plastic and glass spray into my face. My eyes clamp shut and I duck behind the van. I put a hand to my face and feel for a wound, then pull it back and try to open my eyes. The right one refuses, and everything's blurry and wet through the left.

Still, I lean out from behind the van and fire blindly. Then, afraid of hitting Leo, I pull back and stop. I hear someone else shooting, then the clatter of a gun on pavement and the heavy fall of a body, the scrape of limp shoes.

I hear another shot from the back of the van, and then I feel motion to my left. I somehow must have missed Hale with that first shot, because there he is, coming toward me from across the street, arm extended. I turn and fire just as he pulls his own trigger. I step back frantically, my heel hits the rise of sidewalk, and down I go.

I land hard on my shoulder and the back of my head. I roll so the van shields me from him, though I don't know where anyone else is. My gun is gone. I hear three more shots, then nothing. No footsteps even. Smoke mixes with the dryness of the air, leaves descend in slow motion.

My head aches from the fall. The asphalt is surprisingly cold even through my shirt and jacket.

It's amazing how many stars they can see here, even with all the light from the city bleaching the night.

"Are you all right?" Leo asks. He's standing a few feet away, holding a gun. His eyes look wrong. He bends down and picks up my gun, looks at it like it's the solution to a puzzle that's been bothering him. The answer buckles his knees, and he lands hard on his backside and leans against the van.

It's a miracle he could stand at all. His jacket is torn by bullets in at least two places. He's breathing loudly, and now he tilts his head up as if he too wants to stare at the stars, and I see blood at the base of his neck, the stain growing as blood pumps out from behind the shredded collar of his jacket.

"Oh, Jesus," Leo says.

My right eye burns when I try to open it, so I stop trying. I hesitantly stand up. The other three men are sprawled in various poses of hasty exit from this world. The men who abducted Chaudhry and poisoned McAlester. The men who, less than one hour from now, were supposed to kill T.J. Trenton and his friends—and Tasha—in the final Event that I was sent here to protect.

I go dizzy for a moment as I take this in. I have officially blown my mission, betrayed the Department, and destroyed—if it ever really existed—the Perfect Present. Whatever happens next can't be foretold by any Archivist or planned around by the Engineers and their theories. I feel a weird chill start at the base of my neck and radiate out; my fingertips tingle with the sensation of newness and discovery.

Which is an altogether different sensation than what Leo is feeling. I stand before him now and stare down into his eyes. They're wide with questions, wider still at the answers. That horrible, horrible look on his face is a result of my own actions, not some preordained script.

"They weren't . . . FBI," he manages to say.

"No. They weren't."

His hands are on his thighs, palms facing the sky, and held limply in each hand is a gun, mine and his own. He looks at mine for a moment, then he extends his arm and points toward the train yard, pulls the trigger. We hear a click.

"What . . . the hell . . . is this?"

It's the best approximation of a contemp nine-millimeter automatic that our Engineers could come up with, that's what. But I don't feel like telling him that. Also, it seems to have run out of bullets.

"A fake gun? You shot at them . . . with a fake gun?"

The answer would take longer than he has, so instead I say, "I'm sorry, Leo."

"Oh, Jesus."

His eyes look like they'd be crying if his fluids hadn't been draining out everywhere else. It hits me now, looking at those wide, dry eyes, that I never should have involved him, that I was still a slave to the Department's mind-set, unwilling to take the necessary steps myself. My indecision killed him. My half measures killed him. *I* killed him.

"How did you . . . know about this?"

"They did it this way to Chaudhry. Different location, same idea. You described one of them to your doorman. I didn't realize it at the time, only later. They work for Enhanced Awareness. They were sent to clean up Troy Jones's messes once and for all."

I'm not sure if he's trying to find one last way to arrange the angles and make up for our many mistakes or if he's about to go under.

"You're hit?" he asks.

"No, just some glass."

His eyes convey the strongest possible envy.

"Can you drive?" he asks.

With the one eye nonfunctional, I don't see things as clearly or three dimensionally as I'd like to. But since I've already lost the advantage of a fourth dimension—knowing what will happen next—the flatness I see before me seems somehow fitting. "I think so."

"Take the briefcase...to the FBI field office downtown. *Now.* Report the gunfight too. Tell them...you were with me. We were...going to give it to them...thought they were FBI. They'd come to me...earlier today. Flashed badges...Jesus. I'm an idiot. And throw your fucking fake gun somewhere...it'll only confuse them."

I take it from him, noticing that his blood is all over the handle. I'll need to wipe it down before I toss it.

"Oh, Jesus," he says again.

I wish that I were a superstitious contemp, wish I could believe that Leo is bound for some charmed afterlife. But if there were an afterlife, I would have found it by now. I've been a wanderer through so many lives, so many afters and befores, and all I've found is myself. My flaws, my mistakes, the ramifications of all that I've done.

"There's something else...you need to do," he tells me, his voice higher pitched now. Desperate to get this out in time. "There's a girl."

34.

He watched Troy Jones walk away with the briefcase that had damned Leo despite the fact that he had possession of it for less than an hour. He heard sirens in the distance but, this being D.C., they might have been headed to some other misadventure. He hoped that Troy Jones could be just sane enough to explain everything to the FBI. He hoped that the wheels of justice would turn despite all the institutional inertia that kept them more comfortably in park, or in reverse, or just aimed at conveniently crushable objects.

He wasn't sure if Troy would explain it right, if he'd say Leo had been helping him or that he'd been helping Leo, or maybe that Leo was a partner of these three other corpses. Perhaps in the final story—if one was ever written and the story wasn't instead swept under carpets, flushed down toilets, and any other overused metaphor signifying *erasure* and *irrelevance*—Leo would be portrayed as a villain, as just another crooked green-tag who'd lost sight of his moral compass, of wrong and right, of cause and effect.

There would be no etched star in the halls of Langley for Leo Hastings.

He tried not to think about his parents.

He thought about Sari.

He realized anew that there was no one else to think about.

He was in the far too familiar position of being amazed by his own stupidity. A litany of grave errors. Literally *grave*. First some men from Enhanced Awareness had conned him into thinking they were from the Agency, and he'd believed them until he learned about their

411

company from Gail. So he'd called Sentrick, who'd sweet-talked Leo but realized it wasn't working. So Sentrick had immediately launched a second level of deception, sending more men to Leo and telling him they were FBI agents who desperately wanted to nail Enhanced Awareness, knowing that was exactly what Leo wanted to hear. Appealing to his sense of honor and decency—that he could help fellow patriots take down a crooked company bent on disseminating intelligence secrets to his country's foes—and to his desire to still be a part of the system, to play with the big boys. He'd fallen for every one of their ploys.

There was only one way to ensure that he did not fuck up any more, and they'd taken care of that too.

His last target in Jakarta had been a kid named Gunawan. The name meant "meaningful," which was hilarious, because what exactly did it mean? Only that it had some meaning, but whatever it was forever eluded Leo. Leo liked him. He liked a lot of his targets. He often reminded himself that madmen and megalomaniacs and soldiers of unjust causes could be likable, that likability need not connote innocence. It was human and normal to feel guilty after sending one of these likable young men on to the next link in the Agency's chain. Leo was allowed to feel guilty, but he wasn't allowed to let guilt cloud his decisions.

Every time he passed a name on to them, he'd have an extra drink that night, privately dedicated to the kid in question. A likable person who had been swayed by the wrong forces, the wrong reasoning, the wrong story line. Bottoms up, kid. Here's to you.

The moment he passed Gunawan on, he was convinced he'd made a mistake. *Convinced.* He couldn't bring himself to pour a drink in Gunawan's name. So he'd done everything he could to bring the kid back: wrote memo after memo, sent coded signals, pleaded with middlemen. Made himself look terrible in his superiors' eyes. Caused everyone to question his judgment.

How many ways are there to tell people you made a mistake and you're sorry and you want to undo it, but you need their help for that to happen?

If the FBI didn't believe Troy, if they arrested him for the murders of Leo and these other three green-tags, then what would happen to Sari? How many days would she wait in that motel before giving up and heading out on her own? Where would she go? Would someone else find her?

Had someone already found her?

Leo's plan had been so simple, he'd told himself that its simplicity was a sign of its genius. It felt very much the opposite now. Why was he thinking about her? With what clarity of thought? Most of his body was numb. Why was the car he was leaning against so cold? Christ, there were a lot of stars out tonight.

He would have driven her south, to the Amtrak station in Richmond. Union Station in D.C. would likely be watched; from Richmond, she could get a train that would eventually take her to Chicago.

During the two-hour drive to Richmond in a rented car, Leo would have handed her the new ID and a pretty staggering amount of cash. He would have imparted instructions on how to buy a ticket to LA once she'd made Chicago. After coasting past the apartment towers of the increasingly outer Virginia burbs and then beneath the brontosaural overpasses of the Beltway, the road would have flattened out, the tall trees of the South standing sentry at either side. He would have stopped at one of those trucker gas stations in the blank space past Quantico and bought her some more sweat clothes and some cheesy NASCAR T-shirts and toiletries and junk food. Maybe a tiny American flag.

(He'd given the cash to Troy and told him where to find the ID, advised him to hide the money and papers somewhere before stepping into FBI headquarters. Hoped he'd remember to do that.)

Leo would have asked her one last time if she'd ever overheard Hyun Ki Shim say anything about some business deal, make some weird comments about phone lines or the Internet, but she would have said no. He hoped she'd never witnessed anything important and hoped that no one from Enhanced Awareness (if Troy was unsuccessful in nailing them) or from anywhere else would try to track her down just in case.

He would have apologized that the fake license and Social Security card were all that "his friends in Immigration" had been able to do for her.

He would have said that he'd wanted to help her all along but that he'd initially thought maybe he could help her and accomplish some other goals at the same time. Those other goals had only seemed to get in the way of his helping, she might have said. He would have told her, *Yes, you're right. That paradox has always stymied me, yet I thought I could find a way around it. Either I just wasn't smart enough, or I was too stubborn to admit the way the world worked.*

It was so cold out he was surprised he couldn't see his breath. It made him wonder if he was breathing.

The Agency had pulled him out of Indonesia the day after the bombing.

In the early days, after it sank in, he'd wanted to go back, desperately. Felt it was required. He should see the shell of a building, the blackened walls, the insides blown out. He should go to a funeral, should walk down neighborhoods where he'd hear the suffering grieve. The Agency had deprived him of that penance. Just whisked him away, like the country didn't exist anymore. Like the whole damn thing had blown up.

He would have given her a pad of paper and a pen and told her to practice signing her new name while he drove. He would have told her where to put the cash, how to distribute it across her wardrobe and her few possessions.

He would have apologized for the fact that he hadn't always been honest with her. But he was honest at the end. She might have given him a look then, as if that was a strange thing to say. Which it was. Because did it even matter what note you ended on when every note up until that moment had been so discordant? The end might have worked out, sure, but the means had been hell, and that was what she would remember him for.

He would have coached her on how to buy a ticket herself, then he would have hovered behind her in line so he could overhear her doing it, practice for later.

He would have stood at the tracks with her, waiting for the train. He would not have angled for a kiss but he would have taken one if she'd offered it.

Two hours of dark highway driving back up north would have gone by quickly and then 395 would have curved round the Pentagon, and there D.C. would be, spread out before him, flat and white as if melted there by a light that had lingered too close too long. The vista would have given Leo the same jolt it always did when making that drive at night. He would see the Washington Monument in the center with its red warning beacon, would see the Capitol dome glowing to the right. Straight ahead would be the office buildings that respectfully hunched their shoulders and looked down at their feet so as not to be taller than the grand symbols of democracy to the east. Then 395 would make another sharp turn, and he'd be on a bridge, the river unseen beneath him as he glimpsed Jefferson caged in his rotunda, and then another turn, and into the tunnel that had always seemed too brightly lit when cabbies drove him, drunk, from Adams Morgan or one of the clubs on U to his old apartment on Capitol Hill. He had missed that when he was in Asia, missed those nocturnal cab rides. Sitting in the backseat while he drunkenly looked at the city scrolling past, a cab driver listening to the world's horrors on BBC radio, some immigrant who lived in outer Maryland and drove fares for a living even though he'd no doubt been an engineer or a physician back in Nigeria or Pakistan or the former Yugoslavia. And Leo sitting in the backseat wasted after a night at the 9:30 Club, having felt he deserved to blow off steam after hours or weeks of intensive training at the Agency, was entitled to a few hours of shambolic garage rock and stiff bourbon and gingers before reentering the muddled world, and the cabbie, after heading south through the city, would whisk him into the otherwise empty highway tunnel that had been carved into the earth beneath bland government buildings. Buildings staffed by clerks and associates and spies and people who maybe were going to be fired the next morning for some indiscretion they or someone else had committed; or by people putting in their time before checking into better-paying private work; or by those dedicated to remaining a part of the bureaucracy until their pensions kicked in; or by the ones who still really Believed in It and that's why they were in the office at two while everyone else was asleep or trashed. And the cabbie would be shaking his head at the BBC's stories of floods or ethnic strife back home, or maybe he would call someone on his cell phone, speaking in a language Leo never knew. Sweet-talking a girl, or telling his kids he loved them but go to bed already, he'll see them in the morning. Sometimes Leo would chat the guy up, express his genuine interest in this person's extraordinary life, but sometimes he wouldn't bother because he couldn't stand looking like that stereotypical privileged white guy slumming it with the real folks. Couldn't stand the way it made him wonder who he really was, what he was doing, why he was here.

Then he'd tip the cabbie well and climb up to his safe row house less than a mile from the U.S. Capitol building, and try to let all this slip away as he fell asleep.

She was so beautiful.

Standing there surrounded by overpriced canned goods, hits from the early nineties faintly playing around her. The sounds of his high-school days, The Cure and the Lightning Seeds, reincarnated as a shopping sound track, and he wanted to dance with her. Only she looked so confused. And scared. His eyes drawn to hers, and to that crescent moon darkening her face. Leo thinking, *There is something I can do. I can't let her walk away. I need to tell her something.* Pushing his grocery cart toward her, thinking up a line.

Then she dropped that can, and he managed to say something, and she looked at him for the first time, and he didn't feel so cold anymore.

35.

Tasha didn't sit on her stoop as much as she should, she realized. The autumn sun was beaming down on her, just enough light to warm her on this breezy morning. Above her the oak tree's last holdouts were descending in the wind, and she could faintly hear a high-school marching band practicing for the weekend's big game. Sitting on a stoop was such a stereotype of poor black folk that she'd felt compelled away from her own stoop, not a consciously political act so much as a stylistic one, as if stoop-sitting were the same as Afros or bell-bottoms, something any wise Gen Xer would avoid. But it felt so good to sit here, the bricks cold and solid beneath her, the street quiet but for the occasional cars winding their secret routes to avoid the congested avenues.

Another gust of wind and some of her papers almost blew away, but she grabbed them in time. There was a loose brick in the top step, so she picked it up and placed it on the pages to keep them there. Still their edges fluttered, humming at her like the wings of a bird.

She had spent the previous two nights at her parents' house, too afraid to return to her own looted home. After walking into T.J.'s safe house and nodding to the assorted rebels who were busily typing and uploading and looking very engrossed indeed in their various screens, she'd borrowed a phone and called for a cab to Maryland. It was late by the time she got to the block where she and her family had moved many years ago, abandoning the city and its crime and cocaine and horrid schools, hoping these suburbs would turn out to be better. Fleeing history and hoping that the future would eventually catch up. Capitol Heights had been a good place to live, but her parents had seemed pleased when Tasha, after finishing law school, had decided to get a job in D.C. *and* buy a place in the city, as if her home purchase were not only a wise financial investment but also a reclamation of family history, a righting of past wrongs. The better future was indeed here, or close enough.

The lights were out and it was too late to ring the doorbell, but she had a key. She let herself in, walked through the hallway, and heard her mother, Lynn, ask who was there. Lynn was sitting at the kitchen table, the scent of chamomile in the air.

Tasha told her only that she hadn't wanted to sleep at her place that night. Her mother looked in her eyes and, misunderstanding, told her that it was all right. They hugged and Tasha felt herself crying. She didn't want to tell her mother why she was really crying and what had happened that night. But the longer they stood there together, the more she wondered why she was crying, whether the reasons were more complicated than even she could understand.

So, two mugs of tea then. "Neither of us has been sleeping well lately," Lynn said. "But I have trouble falling asleep, whereas your father falls asleep just fine but then wakes in the middle of the night and is up for hours. So we have incompatible insomnias."

"There are worse things."

"I know it."

Lynn and Reginald Wilson had been married thirty-two years, and, though Tasha had witnessed plenty of debates and loaded moments, they'd never had any major troubles she was aware of. Tasha was almost alone among her friends in having such strong matrimonial role models. She wasn't sure if that was because their relationship had been forged in the cauldron of civil rights activism, if they really were a perfect couple, or if they were just lucky. But she'd recently seen some frightening numbers about the prevalence of divorce in couples who lost a child. Marshall wasn't really a child, of course, but he was still their child. Funny that English didn't have another word for it; if you were someone's child once, you always were. You never grew out of it and into another word.

They finished their mugs of tea and were on to second helpings of a carrot cake a neighbor had brought over, and which Tasha tore into, realizing she'd never had dinner, when Lynn asked, "Are you still calling the men in Marshall's company? Trying to find out what we weren't told?"

She'd spoken calmly and matter-of-factly, as was her way, which always made it annoyingly difficult for Tasha to detect any opinion. Tasha knew her father was opposed to her research, but Lynn hadn't commented on it.

"I might be giving that up." She told her mother, very briefly, about her experience with Velasquez, the mutual and immolating guilt of their conversation. "I felt terrible. So, I don't know, I've been thinking maybe I need to let it go."

Lynn nodded. "How do you feel about that?"

"I don't know. Not good. But it seems like the lesser of two evils. Better to...let it go and hope, I don't know, that it fades. The anger, I mean. The anger about not knowing." She looked at her hands, then at her mother. "What do you think?"

"I've felt the same as your father on this. I think...you needed more time. It's a generational thing, sweetie. You all have your phones and your computers and you seem to need to know everything, immediately. Honestly, you've always been like that"—and she smiled—"but all these changes, the technology, they bring it out in you more." She shrugged. "Your father and I, maybe we're just old. I'm more comfortable not knowing some things, at least not right away. I hope they were telling us the truth when they say he went quickly. I hope they were being honest when they said he was trying to save his men and that it wasn't friendly fire. I hope all those stories are true. I'm just not anxious to disprove them."

Tasha slept there in her old house, in her old room, one door down from Marshall's. The next morning she was startled to see their framed version of Marshall's army photo, the same one that had been destroyed in her house the night before. She could always photocopy theirs, she told herself.

She called the office, said she was ill. She wondered how quickly the partner was moving after receiving that anonymous tip about Tasha and GTK; she didn't check her work messages or voice mail, didn't even turn on her phone. She stayed in with her mother, ran some errands with her, pretending this was regular life again. Trying to make it so. It almost felt like being home from college on break, and that evening they rented some ridiculous comedy about characters driven by situations that had nothing to do with the terrors and confusions of real life. Her parents didn't ask how long she was staying or if she was hiding from anything.

The second morning, she'd taken the train back to her place, holding her breath when she walked by the stretch where the Metro van had abducted her two nights earlier. Checked behind her back several times to see if she was being followed. Wore old clothes salvaged from her former closet and felt exhausted, physically and mentally.

She would hire a lawyer, she decided, but would put herself at the firm's mercy—she knew she would be fired and would never get even a mediocre reference to justify her two horrible years toiling there, but she crossed her fingers that they'd let her off with that and would not recommend disbarment. Hopefully they would realize the cost to the firm of public disclosure and the benefits of keeping this in-house. She started wondering what it would be like to be a public defender; and even if she did lose her license, there were plenty of infinitely more fulfilling jobs that she'd too quickly assumed were impossible for her to take given her school debts. So she'd need twenty years to pay them off rather than seven; so she'd need to sell her row house and downsize. She felt a shiver of fear at the vastness of the changes before her, but also a kind of clarity, an almost puzzling lack of puzzlement. Maybe she could do anything.

As she approached her house, she saw something that didn't belong. Given the last day and a half, she would not have been completely surprised to find the entire structure had vanished, to see nothing but a blank space between the neighboring row houses, the result of some celestial erasure. What she saw was reassuringly minor in comparison: the house was still there, and none of the windows were shattered, and nothing was burned, and there were no strange men waiting for her with windowless vans or guns or television cameras or handcuffs. But nestled in the grating of her metal security door was a large UPS envelope.

The sender was Troy Jones. Or at least someone claiming to be Troy Jones. She wondered if it could be a lethal mistake to open it. Perhaps one of her important, mysterious, powerful enemies had sent her a little something explosive or poisonous as a final farewell. But the way the men in the van had talked about Troy was softening her on him again. Maybe he wasn't what she had feared he was in that white-hot moment when he came down the stairs; or maybe she was still blinded by her earlier feelings for him, maybe her heartache was tricking her into a sympathy he didn't deserve.

She opened it anyway.

Tiny bits of cardboard and stuffing blew in the wind, and she puzzled through the barely legible handwriting of the cover letter.

Tasha—

I know these will interest you. I'd have provided them sooner, but cracking into this system took longer than I expected. I hope this relieves you of some of the weight of uncertainty about your brother's final moments. I didn't fully understand how you felt, as I myself tend not to be uncertain about how events will unfold. I think, however, that I'm understanding it better now.

I'm sorry again that I deceived you. Please believe I had the best of intentions. Or at least I thought that I did. It's so hard, isn't it, when the ends and the means feel so very different? We trick ourselves sometimes; we justify things we shouldn't.

I won't bother you again, and I'm glad I met you, that we were able to share a moment I'll take with me. If anything, what your brother experienced here only echoes that.

She was more confused than ever, unsure what motivation Troy had to dig up files on Marshall after she'd blown his cover. Was he trying to win her favor? Show off how powerful and connected he was? Or was he really apologizing and trying to help?

After the cover letter were thirty pages of e-mails. They had been printed, she saw, from a cached version of e-mails Marshall had saved in his drafts folder. The account was dead, but Troy had found its ghost in cyberspace. These were messages Marshall had written but not finished, things he'd wanted to send at a later time that never came, or things he had preferred to hide in a place no one could see.

She thought about what her mother had said last night. Still: How could Tasha *not* read them?

A couple of letters were intended for Tasha, and as she read she recognized them—Marshall had ultimately sent them to her. But then she'd catch a few subtle differences, discover omitted sections. These were longer, unedited versions of those e-mails. It wasn't just misspellings and silly anecdotes he'd cut. There was something larger: Marshall Wilson had fallen in love.

He'd tried to say this in a few of his e-mails to Tasha, mentioning a certain someone, Sunny (not her real name?), in those original e-mails but always editing her out before sending it. Why would he do this—simple embarrassment, some macho thing? He didn't want to tell his sister about his new girl, didn't want to misrepresent his stint in the desert as a romantic adventure? Was he ashamed to have violated the army's anti-fraternization policy?

She could see that he had tried to tell her (and her parents, and some of his friends) many times—she found no fewer than seven drafts of attempted "Hey, sis, I met a girl" e-mails, each of them trying a different angle. Flippant, casual, serious, guilty. For a moment she even wondered if Sunny was in fact a man, as that might have explained the secrecy, but no, there were too many references to her appearance; she was clearly a woman. Yet Marshall had never been able to tell his family or friends about her.

Tasha read everything twice, the morning commuters walking

past her on the sidewalk, and finally she took out her phone. She turned it on for the first time in two days; there were three new messages from the firm and one from Leo a couple nights earlier, all of which she deleted without listening to.

Velasquez answered on the second ring and, to her immense relief, seemed happy to hear from her.

"I had this fear that I ruined your day when I visited," Tasha said.

"Ma'am, my day is ruined ten times before eight a.m. Goes with the territory. But I put it back together every time."

"There was one more thing I wanted to ask you about Marshall."

"Fire away."

Tasha tried not to sound too much like the cross-examining attorney when she asked, "Could you tell me about Sunny?"

She could hear him suck in his breath. "What do you want to know about her?"

"I'm just wondering why Marshall kept her a secret from my family. I mean, had he just not gotten around to telling us, or—"

"Telling you what?" He was trying too hard to sound confused.

"That he was in love with her. I found some of his old e-mails, okay? I've seen it in his own words."

"I'm really not sure what—"

Exasperated, she read from one of his e-mails. A couple of sentences about a walk Marshall had taken with the mystery woman, the way he felt in her presence.

"Why didn't anyone tell me?" she asked. "Everyone I've talked to in the platoon, they dodged me or played dumb. Why?"

He didn't answer for a few seconds. "Not many people knew about the two of them, just me and some others. And we didn't... We didn't feel there was any reason to hurt his name like that. He was a great soldier, so we kept our mouths shut."

During Tasha's many conversations with other soldiers, and with other families, she'd been told about how commanding officers and fellow soldiers continued to protect the deceased. If they found letters to a lover on the person of a fallen—and married—warrior, they burned the letters. Ditto anything that looked like a suicide note. This wasn't censorship, everyone told Tasha, it wasn't revisionism—it was respect. You respect the dead and what they've suffered for. You erase the secrets, destroying anything that might tarnish the family's memory. You let the reputation live, the honor and duty that the soldier stood for. But she hadn't thought that could apply in Marshall's case; she'd been unable to imagine his doing anything that required a cover-up. And what was the big deal about falling in love?

"Was she in his platoon?"

"No, no. That would've been real bad. I mean, it's against general orders for *any* officers and enlisted soldiers to, you know, get together. But especially if one serves under the other. And, honestly, I don't know if the two of them ever actually—*you know*. But I could tell they were a thing. Becoming a thing ain't easy out there, believe me, but it happens."

Tasha thought about that modern way in which people become "things."

"Why didn't you just tell me this from the beginning? You all made me think there was some grand conspiracy against him or something."

He exhaled loudly. "She was one of the hostages I told you about." He paused. "They'd been missing a couple of hours, then someone in our platoon got a tip on where they might be, and Lieutenant Wilson ordered us in. Even though she wasn't in our platoon and wasn't technically his responsibility."

She remembered then how Velasquez's eyes had looked at Walter Reed when she'd asked him if the hostages had lived and what their names had been. He'd been lying then, gently steering her away from Marshall's indiscretions.

New dramas were slowly unfolding in Tasha's mind. Velasquez seemed crushed by guilt that some perceived failure of his had resulted in Marshall's death. Yet surely he must see that the same could be said in reverse, that Velasquez would still have both legs—and

Marshall and the two other men who'd died that day might still be alive—if only Marshall hadn't been blinded by his emotions.

"So some people think Marshall...made a mistake."

"It's not like that." His voice quieter now. "We loved Marshall. What happened, it happened." He drew in a long breath. "I mean, ultimately...how can you blame someone for falling in love?"

Of all the hard questions she'd faced of late, that might have been the hardest. It lingered while she scanned some of her brother's lines, trying to better understand what had happened.

"I still don't see why he stopped contacting people back home for a week or why he took down his blog."

Again there was a pause as Velasquez weighed his response. "I can't swear to it, ma'am, but it seemed to me they'd broken things off around then. I kind of...overheard them arguing one day. I don't know if he was breaking it off with her, if she was dumping him, or if one or the other of them finally decided it was too risky. But I'm pretty sure they ended it about a week before he died. And afterward he was...different. A little shorter with people. However it happened, I guess his head was in a bad place and he needed to shut down, you know?"

"Yeah." That sounded exactly like Marshall; he'd always been one to close himself off when he was down. "This Sunny—you said she's still alive?"

"Yes, ma'am. Her tour ends in a month or two, I think. But she's still out there."

"Sunny's not her real name, is it?"

"No, ma'am."

"What *is* her real name?"

"I'm sorry, but I'm not saying."

"Why not?"

"Because Marshall wouldn't want me to, ma'am." He paused. "I'm sure someone as bright and determined as you could track her down eventually, but I'm telling you, you shouldn't. Out of respect for your brother, let it go."

There were few tasks that Tasha was less constitutionally suited to than refraining to acquire some item of information. If it was out there, she needed to have it. To make her smarter, to strengthen her, to gain an advantage in this infuriating world. The existence of this latest piece of unknown knowledge seemed to hover in front of her, a tangible thing, and all she needed to do was reach far enough and she'd grasp it. What Velasquez was proposing was nearly impossible.

A gust of wind blew and the pages fluttered in her hand as if pleading for release. Tasha stuffed them back in the envelope. She thanked Velasquez and hung up.

Marshall had died for love. At least she could say that. No matter how she felt about the wars or the politics of her age or the feuds in Washington and the wider world, her brother had found something good to hold on to, and had sacrificed himself for her.

Maybe if Marshall had never met her, he'd still be alive. Or maybe not. Maybe you could drive yourself crazy trying to chart backward all the causes and effects, all the ends and means, tracing everything to some original sin that may or may not have actually occurred but that people accepted as true, or true enough. Maybe staring into the eyes of all that history was a dangerous thing to do, as her mother had calmly warned her. Maybe you were supposed to move forward armed with just enough history to help you figure out the present without obsessing over the past. But how much was enough? Where was the gray area between ignorance and obsession?

Tasha stared at her tiny front plot. The tall oak was no doubt decades older than the 1912 row house, which had been a blue-collar family's home for years, then a crack house during the eighties when this block was among the nation's most neglected, and then an abandoned building for a full decade before the previous owner had started fixing it up. Tasha was doing the rest: she'd put in a new bathroom, removing the matching all-black toilet and sink and bathtub (all the better for finding your spilled cocaine, apparently), and she'd patiently re-topsoiled the front plot, removing pieces of broken bottles and the occasional razor blade, and planted new bushes and perennials. She'd spent an entire weekend the previous spring gardening and, the very next Monday morning, had been stunned to find that two of her new bushes—each a fifty-dollar sarcococca—were gone, in their place nothing but two gaping holes. What the hell? Had she bought migrating bushes? She'd stood there, confused and enraged, as her neighbor, the friendly gay man and proud survivor of worse times on that block, informed her that such crimes occurred now and again. Botanical thieves would dig up expensive-looking shrubs and hock them at yard sales. Tasha was floored. *Shrubbery theft?*

So the next weekend, early on a Saturday morning in March, she'd driven around the Hill in search of yard sales. She hadn't found many, but there was an enormous market set up in the vast parking lot of RFK Stadium. Stalls of pirated CDs, incense, secondhand clothing, baked goods, and folk art were perched there on the banks of the Anacostia, as if people were selling all the belongings they couldn't carry with them as gentrification pushed them farther southeast. It had taken Tasha only ten minutes to find the lady with the bushes.

Two of the sarcococca had looked familiar, though she couldn't be certain. She knew of no way to DNA-test bushes. But her rage, and her righteousness, had burned hot enough.

"Where do you get your bushes?" she asked the heavyset woman who sat on a wheeled office chair that was as out of place here as everything else was.

"Oh, my grandsons grow 'em." She wore a thick blue sweater and had a blanket across her knees even on that glorious spring morning. Her voice was pure country by way of two or three generations in D.C., from the state of North Carolina to North Carolina Avenue Southeast. "Which ones you innerested in?"

Tasha looked around but didn't see anyone grandsonish in the vicinity.

"I'm looking for the kinds of bushes that don't up and walk away."

The lady laughed, genuinely mirthful. "Girl, I ain't never seen that happen!" She slapped a knee and managed to recover. "Though, in *this* town? Wouldn't be the craziest thing I ever seen."

The satisfaction wouldn't be there, Tasha realized. So she reached into her pocket and allowed her two fifty-dollar shrubs to be price-cut down to twenty-dollar shrubs.

She'd just started wondering how exactly she was going to get the two bushes into her car when the old lady whistled.

"Ay, Darnell! Delivery, boy!"

The kid wandered over from one of the CD stalls. Wearing a black Heat jersey over a black tee whose sleeves reached past his gawky elbows. High school, if he still went. He loaded the two shrubs onto a flat hand truck and asked Tasha which way her car was, never making eye contact. She didn't recognize him from the neighborhood but wondered if she'd start noticing him around now. If he recognized her, he didn't show it.

She walked alongside him, his crooked red Phillies cap facing her even though he did not. He had long, skinny fingers, and she imagined them tearing into the earth. He slowly weaved his hand truck through the stalls, and the sun off the asphalt was warmer than it had been in months.

She popped open the back of her hatchback. He didn't bother to protect the young boughs as he muscled the plants inside.

"You know, my little brother used to steal stuff too."

He looked at her. "Huh?"

"My little brother. Though I doubt he ever boosted a bush."

He adopted the blank look with which she'd once been annoyingly familiar. "I ain't know what you talking about, lady."

"I've never had to plant something a second time before. But I guess there's nothing wrong with needing a second chance, so long as you use it right."

His blank stare vacuumed her own gaze for a moment, then he turned without a word, the now-empty hand truck squeaking on its wheels. Tasha shook her head. She would have to tell Marshall about this, she thought. He'd get a kick out of it. He was out in the desert again, doing God knows what and hopefully being safe, and she'd just bumped into his past on the ever-changing streets of D.C.

* * *

She read through a few of the e-mails again, then looked up at her reclaimed bushes—which weren't doing so well due to the dry fall and her complete failure to water them since August—when she saw Troy Jones, a bandage covering his right eye and two more on his left cheek, same damn clothes as before, walking her way.

Z.

She's sitting on her front stoop surrounded by text. I wondered if she might back away at the sight of me, but she watches calmly as I walk down the sidewalk and up the short path. I stop at the base of her steps. Bits of the padded envelope stuffing are sprinkled on the steps like gray snow.

"Surprised to see you," she says, voice decidedly neutral. Which is an improvement over how she sounded the last time. "I assumed you'd just vanish into wherever it is you people hide before popping up again to follow someone else."

"That's what I'm supposed to do, actually. But I'm not doing it anymore."

She watches me for a moment, judging. The wind blows; leaves scrape their fingers against the brick sidewalks.

"Thanks for sending this to me," she says.

"I'm sorry I didn't get it to you sooner. I wasn't sure how to show you without…"

"Without letting on the type of work you do?"

"Used to do."

"You're very past tense today."

"I'm feeling the opposite. That night, at the restaurant. When I told you some of us can imagine a better future? I'm putting that theory to the test."

She doesn't dare smile or lighten her voice, yet her eyes are round, more vulnerable than she wants them to be.

"Your brother. I'm sorry I read his messages, but I needed to, to find what you were looking for."

"Wow, an apology. Aren't you used to reading other people's things?"

"I'm apologizing anyway."

"It's okay."

She watches me for another moment, then pats the stoop beside her. "Pull up a brick."

I sit there, our knees almost touching, the angle of the autumn light so sharp I have to squint.

"There's a lot that I need to explain," I say. "Once I figure out how."

"You're in the obfuscation business. Truth doesn't come so easily, huh?"

I don't answer that one.

"What happened to your face?"

"I spent the last thirty-six hours with the FBI, and—"

"The FBI did that to you?" Eyes wider now, ready again for the world to confirm her worst opinions of it.

"No, no. They patched me up. And I needed their help with something else."

I was at the Washington field office of the FBI for more than a full day. I explained my story to at least three underlings and sat for hours in a windowless holding room before they finally sent someone with any kind of authority over or familiarity with what I was talking about. Special Agent Westerberg, he introduced himself, and we spoke for hours. He asked me to tell my story, then asked for it again, then asked every conceivable question that might trip up a liar. But I had the facts down, my internal databases there to guide me, my own experience and memory as well, though those are decidedly less reliable.

"You're technically a missing person, as I understand it," Westerberg said at one point.

"I've been found."

I showed him some of the files in my briefcase, explained their relevance to what was happening, what had already happened, and what might still happen if he and the Bureau didn't step forward and impose some order on this chaos.

I told him about the gunfight, and Leo. While we sat there he dispatched other agents to the scene, which, one hopes, was already being investigated by local police by then. At some point a medic came in to clean my wounds and look at my eye. He told me I should see a specialist immediately because I risked permanent damage to my vision. But I'd already lost so many things, this latest loss seemed fitting. First the GeneScan, then the ability to foresee what would happen next, and now basic three-dimensionality. All these extra layers were being peeled away from my world, or from my perception of it. And is there any difference? Everything before me now seemed flat, stark, a blank canvas.

By the time I left, they'd dispatched teams to keep watch around Mr. Sentrick and Enhanced Awareness's other senior staff and were also monitoring Hyun Ki Shim, who was due to meet with Sentrick to close a deal that afternoon. Westerberg shook my hand before I went, telling me to stay in touch and assuring me that they'd be calling for me shortly.

"Are you in trouble?" Tasha asks.

"Not anymore. And neither are you. I wasn't following you before, I was . . . trying to protect you. The people I was protecting you from, you won't need to worry about them anymore."

I'm staring ahead, at the tree that dominates her tiny plot, this massive motionless thing that will be so rare one day soon. Or maybe not. Maybe everything that I take for granted about my Perfect Present has been uprooted; maybe I would never recognize the new world to come. The world I've helped remake.

Her head seems the slightest bit closer, her voice quieter. "Do you want to tell me about your family? Your job? What you *used to* do?"

"I do. But later." I try not to wonder about the Department and whether they have the ability to send more Protectors back, whether they'll try to undo what I've done. Maybe I'll have to spend the rest of my life fending off their attempts to resteer history in their favored direction. And maybe that's exactly what it's like to simply live through the present like everyone else does, something I've nearly forgotten how to do.

I realize that she's been looking at me with sympathy. It took a while to recognize because I'm not used to it.

Her voice is a whisper. "What did they do to you, Troy?"

"Nothing. I did it to myself."

She puts her hand on my face, trying to trace the outline of something she can't fathom. I hold it there and we watch each other.

And I know this is bad timing, but my sense of timing is perhaps permanently off, so I say, "I need a favor. I made a promise that I don't think I can keep on my own."

"Which is?"

I ask her again what kind of law she practices.

Leo told me there was a coded knock, but I can't remember what it is. Too much has happened since then.

"Open, please," I tell whoever's behind the door after I knock. If she's really there. "We're with Leo." I say his name again, in case it's the only word of English she knows.

Tasha says the same thing, hoping a feminine voice might make us less threatening.

The door opens, slowly, and by only a few inches. Sari is young, and scared. I try to look kind and accommodating—not one of my skills. She waits a moment, then backs up and lets us in.

Her room has been invaded by crumpled food wrappers and empty juice bottles. Her expression and stance are tense, like she's trying to choose the best time to bolt past us, out the door. Her sleeves are rolled up and she has a large bandage on one of her forearms. Behind her, the made-up faces on the morning talk show are mute in horror.

"What the hell did he do to her?" Tasha says, quietly.

I close the door behind us. I've already tried to make sense of what

Leo told me that night, and what he'd told me a few nights earlier when I surprised him in his car. Still, this woman doesn't look like someone who belongs on a cross-country train, with or without a fake ID and lots of cash.

Tasha asks her if she speaks English; Sari's eyes betray nothing but fear. Then Tasha takes her phone out of her purse—just the act of opening that purse makes Sari flinch, as if she's expecting a gun—and opens the Internet. I see a tiny map of the world.

Tasha uses her fingers to show her how it works.

"Where?" Tasha asks, as if keeping it to one word makes it comprehensible.

Sari hesitantly touches two fingers to the tiny screen, opening and closing them, dragging her fingertips until she's found her country of origin. I see mostly blue water and some islands.

"Indonesia," Tasha says to me, then switches to another Web site. "These translator sites aren't very good, but they're better than nothing."

She types a question, the site renders it into another language, and Sari can't resist the tiniest smile of recognition. This black American woman's phone "talking" to her in Indonesian. Then Sari demonstrates that she is no stranger to cell phones or texting. Her fingers madly dance over the keypad.

She and Tasha trade questions and answers, writing her story in slow motion. During this exchange, Tasha looks up at me. "It's not my specialty, but I know some international affairs people, and they owe me a favor. Could take a while, though."

Sari offers her the phone again, another secret conveyed. Tasha reads it, thinks for a moment, starts typing. I hear cars on the highways that surround us, anxiously careening headlong toward their next appointments and trysts, betrayals and rescues.

I assure her that we have plenty of time.

ACKNOWLEDGMENTS

The song that the nameless activist listens to on page 396 is "Weapon of Choice" by The Black Rebel Motorcycle Club.

Thanks to Col. George Reynolds (Ret.), USA, for military guidance; Laurel Hatt for cultural pointers; and Dave Ricksecker Esq. for legal advice not followed.

My unofficial D.C. and Atlanta writers groups allowed for needed venting and idea vetting: Louis Bayard, Keith Donohue, Susan Coll, Charles McNair, Marc Fitten, and Jon Fasman.

My agent, Susan Golomb, remains indispensible. My editor, John Schoenfelder, poured fuel on the dying spark of a crazy idea.

All past, present, and future accomplishments are due to my wife, Jenny, and my family.

You've turned the last page.

But it doesn't have to end there...

If you're looking for more first-class, action-packed, nail-biting suspense, visit www.mulhollandbooks.co.uk for news about our authors, competitions, reviews and guest articles. You can also meet fellow thrill-seekers, add your own content and join in the debates on our blog.

For regular updates about our books as well as what's going on in the world of crime and thrillers, follow us on Twitter @MulhollandUK.

There are many more twists to come.